Justine Lewis writes uplift... contemporary romances. S[he lives]... with her hero husband, two [teenagers and an] outgoing puppy. When she isn't writing she loves to walk her dog in the bush near her house, attempt to keep her garden alive, and search for the perfect frock. She loves hearing from readers and you can visit her at justinelewis.com.

Karin Baine lives in Northern Ireland with her husband, two sons and her out-of-control notebook collection. Her mother and her grandmother's vast collection of books inspired her love of reading and her dream of becoming a Mills & Boon author. Now she can tell people she has a *proper* job! You can follow Karin on X, @karinbaine1, or visit her website for the latest news—karinbaine.com.

Also by Justine Lewis

Swipe Right for Mr Perfect

If the Fairy Tale Fits… miniseries

Beauty and the Playboy Prince

Invitation from Bali miniseries

Breaking the Best Friend Rule
The Billionaire's Plus-One Deal

Also by Karin Baine

Mills & Boon True Love

Cinderella's Festive Fake Date

Mills & Boon Medical

Nurse's New Year with the Billionaire
Tempted by Her Off-Limits Boss

Christmas North and South miniseries

Festive Fling with the Surgeon

Discover more at millsandboon.co.uk.

HOW TO WIN BACK A ROYAL

JUSTINE LEWIS

TEMPTATION IN A TIARA

KARIN BAINE

MILLS & BOON

All rights reserved including the right of reproduction in whole or in part in any form. This edition is published by arrangement with Harlequin Enterprises ULC.

This is a work of fiction. Names, characters, places, locations and incidents are purely fictional and bear no relationship to any real life individuals, living or dead, or to any actual places, business establishments, locations, events or incidents. Any resemblance is entirely coincidental.

This book is sold subject to the condition that it shall not, by way of trade or otherwise, be lent, resold, hired out or otherwise circulated without the prior consent of the publisher in any form of binding or cover other than that in which it is published and without a similar condition including this condition being imposed on the subsequent purchaser.

® and TM are trademarks owned and used by the trademark owner and/or its licensee. Trademarks marked with ® are registered with the United Kingdom Patent Office and/or the Office for Harmonisation in the Internal Market and in other countries.

First published in Great Britain 2025
by Mills & Boon, an imprint of HarperCollins*Publishers* Ltd,
1 London Bridge Street, London, SE1 9GF

www.harpercollins.co.uk

HarperCollins*Publishers*, Macken House, 39/40 Mayor Street Upper, Dublin 1, D01 C9W8, Ireland

How to Win Back a Royal © 2025 Justine Lewis

Temptation in a Tiara © 2025 Karin Baine

ISBN: 978-0-263-39676-8

04/25

This book contains FSC™ certified paper and other controlled sources to ensure responsible forest management.

For more information visit www.harpercollins.co.uk/green.

Printed and Bound in the UK using 100% Renewable Electricity at CPI Group (UK) Ltd, Croydon, CR0 4YY

HOW TO WIN BACK A ROYAL

JUSTINE LEWIS

MILLS & BOON

For Peter.

Again.

Because he makes me laugh
more than anyone else in the world.

CHAPTER ONE

'WHAT'S NEXT ON the schedule?' Isabella di Marzano, Princess of Monterossa, kicked off her red designer Italian pumps and lifted her bare feet onto the plush sofa. She leant her head back and groaned. Her feet hurt, her head ached and now she was alone with just her twin sister Francesca for company, she could no longer ignore the tightness in her chest that had been with her on and off for the past few weeks. Worry. An ever-present, persistent worry, lurking at the back of her mind like an intruder ready to pounce.

The last year had been Isabella's own *annus horribilis*: first the abrupt end of her engagement and now her father's illness. A skin cancer diagnosis that had shocked everyone. King Leonardo was in his early sixties and they'd thought he was fit, but a routine examination had discovered not one, but two melanomas that had already spread to his lymph nodes.

Isabella desperately hoped her sister's answer would be 'Nothing,' and that she could run a hot steamy bath and submerge herself in bubbles and fragrant oils, but that was rarely the case these days. Ever since their father had become ill, she and Francesca had increased their already busy schedule of public engagements and private duties to ease the pressure on her parents.

'Mother's coming to talk to us about London,' Francesca said.

Isabella sat up straight at that. *This* was a public engagement she'd been looking forward to, despite everything going on. She had a plan. And it wasn't the plan her mother was about to talk to them about.

In a few days she and Francesca would travel to London for the coronation of the new British King. With their father still in hospital and their mother wanting to stay with him, Francesca and Isabella, the twin princesses of Monterossa, would attend and represent their parents. It would be one of the largest events either princess had ever attended, with many reigning monarchs and heads of state from across the world attending.

Isabella knew some of the guests going, was distantly related to several, but many she knew only by sight. From the magazines and newspapers, just like anybody else. An event like this would be a dress rehearsal for the real thing. The life that awaited her older sister.

Born on the same day, at the same hour, yet five crucial minutes apart, the Princesses were destined for different lives. Despite this, or maybe because of it, their parents had insisted the girls be brought up and educated together. Isabella had essentially been trained for a job she'd never have. Her parents explained that Isabella's role was to support her sister. They insisted that being her sister's best friend and closest adviser was a valid job description, though Isabella wasn't so sure. So far, for the first twenty-nine years of their lives it hadn't mattered too much. They came as a pair of princesses. Two for the price of one.

But all that might soon be about to change.

Two months ago her father had undergone surgery to remove the cancers, but his recovery had been slow, with more complications than anticipated. After commencing immunotherapy he had developed an infection, necessitating return to hospital, where he remained to continue his treatment. At first Isabella had tried to tell herself it was a precaution—he was the King after all and everyone was being particularly cautious—but as the weeks and a further surgery went by, she no longer knew whether to believe the doctors' assurances. Isabella had been reading everything she could about skin cancer, its causes and treatments. She could hardly believe that, living in a sun-soaked Mediterranean country as they were, they had all been so nonchalant about the risks. Isabella was beginning to wonder if this new state of affairs, with her sister carrying out the bulk of the royal duties, would soon become permanent.

She usually discussed everything with Francesca, but this was different. This wasn't just their father's health—which was worrying enough—it was the one thing that would change their close bond as nothing else would.

There could only ever be one queen, and that would be Francesca.

Francesca stood up straight, flicking efficiently through something on her phone. Isabella had no doubt Francesca would make a wonderful monarch—that was not what worried her. What worried her was how Francesca becoming queen would change their relationship, because surely it would.

Francesca was everything a monarch should be: dedicated, poised, intelligent. In comparison, Isabella often felt like the support act or a trusty sidekick. She tried not to be the comedic relief in the story that was Francesca's life, but it was hard when the press expected her to take on the role of 'the irresponsible spare' or 'the playgirl princess'. Isabella was neither of those things. She was as serious about representing her country as her sister.

A quick knock at the door announced the Queen's arrival. She swept into the room and studied them both briefly, taking in Isabella's bare feet on the sofa, Francesca's flawless appearance.

She didn't say anything, but she didn't have to. Every expression on their mother's face told an entire story. She was, by training, an actress. A qualification that had been particularly useful to a queen over the years. Being able to feign delight or surprise and smile on demand was particularly useful now when her daughters both knew that what she really wanted to do was crumble with stress.

'Thank you both again for going to London on our behalf,' Queen Gloria said.

'Of course, you know we'll do anything to help you,' Francesca said.

'I know, but I want you both to know that we do appreciate it very much. It's going to be an exhausting visit.'

'How so?' Isabella imagined she'd be sitting down in the abbey for much of the time. Attend a few parties, but these sorts of parties were never debaucherous all-nighters. She'd be expected to sit on the one glass of champagne all night and be home in bed by midnight.

The Queen talked them through their schedule for the day of the coronation: wake at five a.m. Five a.m.! Breakfast, hair and make-up before they were picked up from their hotel at seven. A car would take them to one of the gathering points where they would get on a coach with the other dignitaries.

There would be no pulling up outside the abbey in their own car or carriage for them, or for most of the guests— royalty, politicians, and celebrities. Most guests would be shipped to and from the abbey in large buses. They would arrive several hours before the ceremony to ensure everyone and everything was in place and afterwards they would be collected the same way.

'I'd watch how much you drink. You'll be sitting in the abbey for close to six hours with no bathroom breaks.'

Francesca looked at Isabella and said, 'And they think being a princess is glamorous.'

They both laughed. Being a princess was often very much

the opposite of glamorous. Eating fermented Baltic sea herring on an official trip to Sweden, standing in high heels for hours at a time, often in the sun. Having your private life spoken about and analysed by the rest of the world.

Their mother shook her head with an exasperated sigh. Representing your country was an honour and a privilege that outweighed the downsides was what she would've told them, if she hadn't already told them that weekly for their entire lives.

Isabella *knew* it was an honour and she loved supporting her sister and her parents, but glamour, she thought, was not all it was advertised to be.

After six hours in Westminster Abbey, with no food or toilet breaks, they would attend a late lunch stand-up reception at the palace with the new King and other important guests.

'At least the food is good at the palace,' Francesca said, and they both nodded, remembering a particularly nice dinner they had all once enjoyed hosted by the former King. 'Do you remember the chocolate and praline ice cream?' The sisters groaned with delight at the memory of that dessert.

Their mother shook her head again. 'After that, you'll have time to get dressed for the official function that evening. The King isn't hosting anything, there are too many dignitaries in town for an official state dinner, but the new Duke of Oxford will host a private party at the Ashton. A private club in Mayfair, not far from the palace.

'We understand the King and Queen may attend the event at the Ashton, though won't be the official hosts. And who can blame them? They'll have had an exhausting day. Barbier will come tomorrow to arrange your outfits for the coronation and the party afterwards.'

Isabella tried to hide her grimace. Christian Barbier was her mother's favourite stylist, but his recommendations tended to make both princesses look older than how Isabella preferred to dress. She preferred younger designers, more contemporary styles, outfits she had put together herself, but this was not a fight she wanted to have with her mother right now.

Not this week.

And maybe not this year.

'And I've sent you both something. A special file. That I'd like you to keep confidential.'

The sisters exchanged a look. As princesses and one and two in line to the throne they were sometimes trusted with classified information, but it was shown to them by their father or the government. Not their mother.

'What is it?' Francesca asked.

'I've put together a list.'

'Yes?'

'Of some of the guests attending the coronation and the party.'

Isabella closed her eyes. She had a horrible feeling what her mother was going to say next.

While neither the King nor the Queen would ever dictate who their daughters should marry, they did have firm ideas on the *sort* of man who would make a suitable life partner for both their daughters. Someone who was prepared to put Monterossa first. Someone who understood a princess's role and duties. Someone who wasn't easily spooked by public attention. All specific criteria added after the abrupt end of Isabella's engagement last summer.

'There are some photos and biographies.'

'Of men?' Francesca guessed.

'Single men. Eligible single men.'

Francesca turned to Isabella and they shared a look of sympathy and commiseration. Francesca had her own failed engagement in her past as well. Benigno, a duke, had called off his engagement to Francesca, but, unlike Isabella's reaction to her broken engagement, Francesca seemed more relieved by this than anything. Isabella was too, if she was honest. While her parents thought Benigno was perfect for Francesca, Isabella knew they didn't love one another.

Unlike her and Rowan.

'It's not that I don't trust you, it's just that, as we've said, we know it will be easier if you find a man who's from our world, or who at least has an understanding of it. Its responsibilities.' The Queen turned to Isabella. 'And its pitfalls and hazards.'

Isabella looked down, unable to meet anyone's eye.

'I'm not trying to tell you who to choose, but I don't want to see either of you hurt again. The men in this file are men with similar backgrounds, like-minded values, but also with compatible expectations.'

'Mother, is this really the time for either of us to be dating?' Francesca said.

Isabella knew exactly what her mother was trying to do—steer them in the direction of men from their own class, so that neither of them faced the Rowan situation again. Isabella also knew that, in her own way, her sister was trying to defend her and even Rowan. The man who had broken off their engagement three days before their wedding last summer.

She didn't hate him, which was a pity. It might be easier if she hated him, but she couldn't even despise him for his timing. It wasn't until a week before the wedding date that the truly vile headlines had come out, calling him a social climber, a gold-digger...neither of which were even true. Rowan had a larger fortune than Isabella would inherit, several times over. One he had made on his own.

Instead of hate, what was left was simply grief. And the knowledge that there never would be a man she could ever trust again with her heart. She was a princess, she had to avoid gossip and scandal of any kind. The last two men who had become engaged to Monterossa's princesses had broken off those engagements, leaving a mountain of headlines and gossip in their wake. So Isabella was hardly about to race to the altar with anyone at the moment—whether he was on her mother's list or not.

'I'm simply suggesting you consider who you might speak to at the celebrations, that's all. I'm asking you—imploring you—to keep the file secret. It's information only, nothing more,' the Queen said.

Francesca rolled her eyes in Isabella's direction, but so their mother couldn't see.

A timely idea and a passion had helped Rowan James, a working-class boy from South East London, make his first billion. His brilliant business skills had helped him make the next five. Barely into his twenties he had launched the first of what was to be a whole suite of apps supporting mental health, with guided meditations, breathing and mindfulness exercises, and plenty more besides. He had designed one specifically for eating disorders, another for addiction and, as Isabella had recently read, he would soon be launching one for teenagers. He was in demand for so many reasons and his business was growing stronger each year. He had had no problem relocating to New York after their failed relationship. She couldn't even blame him for leaving her, not when the press had been so cruel. She wouldn't wish that sort of attention on anyone she cared for.

Her family had never disapproved of Rowan. Like Isabella, they had also thought that he was her perfect match, but it turned out they had all been living in their own bubble and hadn't anticipated the interest the world's media would take in them or the ferocity of that interest. The press had hounded Rowan, and when that had yielded no attention-grabbing headlines, they had gone after his family. His brother, but most of all Rowan's father.

Right now, particularly with her father's illness, Isabella

had no plans to date anyone, let alone get married. Maybe she never would, and that was fine. All she wanted to do in the immediate future was let her hair down a little. Have some fun and for a few precious moments forget everything that was happening with her father. And Rowan.

So she didn't open the file with her mother's list. Instead, she flicked over the pages of the itinerary. It was called 'A celebration' but it certainly wasn't going to be a relaxing party. It was a strictly choreographed event. Each minute accounted for, down to the one allocated toilet break. It was an appearance. Good practice for the next coronation they had to attend. One at which one of them might be a participant, not just a guest.

No. Isabella refused to even think about that. It would be years away.

Not if Father abdicates.

It was a matter she'd thought she'd overheard her parents discussing before she'd entered his hospital room last week. She'd caught her mother saying, 'You can't do anything without discussing it with Francesca.'

'And Isabella?' the King had said.

'No. Not yet.'

Isabella's heart had sunk when she'd heard those words. The first fracturing. A recognition that she and her sister were not equals, were not destined to follow the same path.

Isabella had slipped away, gone to the bathroom to press a cold towel to her burning face, before returning to the hospital room, this time announcing her arrival with a loud knock. There had been no mention of abdication or anything like it since then, and Isabella hadn't mentioned what she had heard to Francesca.

'No one in this room is getting any younger,' the Queen added. 'You're both approaching thirty.' She said this often, as though it were some kind of cut-off date, but that didn't stop irritation rising in Isabella's chest.

You weren't raised a royal! Isabella wanted to retort. Her mother, who had been born and raised in the United States and been a successful actress, didn't know the first thing about being a queen when she met Leonardo. Though she had been accustomed to being in the public eye, which probably had helped, as had the fact that she had married before the advent of the Internet and social media.

Looking from one daughter to the other and their stricken expressions, Gloria softened her expression and said, 'Love never comes on time.'

'Is that a song lyric? Are you quoting pop music at us?'

'And what if I am? My point is that love comes around when it does, never at the perfect time.' The Queen picked up her things. 'Anyway, I'm going back to the hospital.'

'Send Dad our love,' Francesca and Isabella replied.

When their mother had left, Isabella fell back onto the couch.

'Argh! Isn't there enough pressure on us going to this thing? Now she wants us to bring an eligible man back.' She groaned.

'She just wants us to be happy,' Francesca said.

'I know.'

'You especially.'

Isabella ground her teeth together. Realised what she was doing and rubbed her jaw. The break-up with Rowan had crushed her, as her sister was well aware. Isabella didn't want to dwell on those dark weeks and months; she needed to look forward.

'I have an idea about London. And it doesn't involve Mother's list.'

Francesca raised one of her perfect dark eyebrows.

'I think we should sneak out of the party and go and do something on our own.'

Francesca laughed. 'We can't do that.'

'Why not?'

'It's an official engagement—we're representing not only our parents but also the country. Besides, it's at an exclusive club. Where else in London would be better than that?'

Just about anywhere, Isabella wanted to mutter.

'Leanne is having a party.' Leanne was a singer and friend of Isabella's.

Francesca laughed. 'We really can't go there. Too many people we know would see us.'

It was a good point. 'Okay then, just to a normal bar, where regular people are.'

'There will be eligible men at the Duke's party,' Francesca said.

'Name one.'

They both opened up their mother's list. It wasn't long. There were some aristocrats, some other royals they already knew. The pool of young royals and aristocrats in Europe was hardly deep and they both knew it.

'We've met most of these guys before.'

'The Earl of Hereford?'

'Gay.'

'The Count of Westphalia?'

'The one who grabbed my arse at our father's jubilee?'

Francesca groaned.

At least she's thinking about it though. She hasn't dismissed the idea of sneaking away outright.

'I can't date an ordinary person,' Francesca said.

'Ordinary? I'm not suggesting you date an ordinary person. I'm suggesting you find an *extraordinary* one who doesn't happen to be titled and at the stuffy Duke's stuffy ball.'

'Someone who is already in the public eye, someone who understands our world would be a better match. Like Mother was.'

The romance between their father, a prince, and their

mother, the beautiful actress, had been called a fairy-tale romance. For the twins, their parents' marriage was the gold standard of relationships. Their parents still adored one another deeply and passionately after over thirty years. Their father's ill health had hit their mother hard.

Francesca and the Queen did have a point; someone who understood the pressures was less likely to freak out at the circus that came with dating a princess. As Rowan had.

But Isabella's intention wasn't for either of them to meet someone in London. Isabella wasn't about to make the same mistake she had with Rowan, rushing into a serious relationship before either of them were ready, and definitely not pushing someone into it, as she had with Rowan. All she wanted was a few moments of freedom. Of being out, alone with her sister, pretending they were regular people. Forgetting their responsibilities, the weight of other current stressors for a few hours. It was a whirlwind trip away from Monterossa, just forty-eight hours. She wanted them both to make the most of it.

'Could we do both? We need to go to the Duke's party for a while at least,' Francesca asked.

Isabella knew she was wavering. Now to reel her in with her plan.

'Sure, we put in an appearance at the Duke's party and then slip out to the real world.'

'Mother will know if we leave early.'

'No, she won't. We'll sneak out the back. No one will know. Don't you ever want to do something *you* want to do? Be spontaneous? Step outside your comfort zone?'

Francesca looked down.

'I don't have the luxury of being spontaneous. I don't wish for things I can't have. It's counterproductive.'

Isabella felt a moment of pity. It was just as well she was

the spare, not the heir. She chafed against her royal status in a way her dutiful older sister didn't.

'You don't have to be sensible all the time, you know.'

'Yes, I do.'

'Okay, maybe most of the time, but can't this be the one per cent of the time when you aren't?'

She nearly had her.

'You're probably going to be married soon,' Isabella said, trying her winning argument.

'I'm no closer to getting married than you are.'

'Yes, you are. You just need to find the right person. And believe me, he's not on Mother's list.'

Francesca rolled her eyes.

'We may not be about to be married but things might be about to change,' Isabella whispered, even though no one could hear except the palace walls. It didn't do to say things like 'Father might be about to die and you'll be the Queen,' too loudly.

'You don't know that.'

'No, but we both know they will one day. It might be sooner than we thought. This could be your last chance to go somewhere we're not recognised.'

'They still recognise us in London.'

Isabella looked at her beautiful sister and had to agree; no disguise in the world could hide her gorgeousness. Francesca had inherited her mother's sultry movie star good looks. She had long dark hair that flowed in thick, shiny tresses and flawless skin.

The twins were fraternal and while Isabella knew she was attractive, she also knew she wasn't quite in her sister's league, and that was perfectly fine.

'Yes, but not as much as here. Besides, there'll be millions of people in London this weekend. Hundreds of other royals, celebrities. No one's going to notice a couple of princesses from a rock in the Mediterranean.'

Isabella received another glare. While the palace they lived in was technically on a large rocky island—the Gibraltar of the East, it was sometimes called—the kingdom of Monterossa was comprised of a group of islands and a chunk of mainland Italy's heel as well.

Francesca hated it when she called Monterossa a rock. Which was why Isabella did it.

'What if something happens?'

'What's going to happen? The streets will be teeming with police and security.'

'What if we get separated?'

Isabella took her sister's hand and squeezed. 'Not us. Never.'

CHAPTER TWO

ROWAN JAMES HAD lived in London most of his thirty-five years, but he'd never seen it look as it did today. The rain that had threatened to overshadow the coronation early that morning had cleared, leaving only occasional puddles that reflected the lights and added to the sparkle of the city.

The city where Isabella di Marzano was currently walking and breathing. Though, not this part of the city. The other part. The part on the other side of the river with the royals and the coronation guests.

Rowan was in his part of London. On the other side of the Thames. Though, granted, he was in a pretty nice bar, called Twilight, with some of his oldest friends. Celebrating what should have been a momentous night for his brother, Will, but it was only bringing back memories of Rowan's own pre-wedding celebration. An evening that had not ended well.

Rowan rubbed his chin, still not used to the beard he was currently wearing. He'd grown it through the itchy stage and it was now reasonably thick. He only hoped it would do a good enough job of making him slightly unrecognisable. His plan—or, perhaps, hope—was to slip into the country for a bit without anyone but his family and friends realising.

Will noticed. 'What's with the beard?'

'They're fashionable.'

Will raised his eyebrow. 'When have you ever cared what's fashionable?'

'Okay, laziness.'

'Again, that's not you at all. The man who came up with the idea of MindER when he was just eighteen and turned that idea into a multimillion-dollar business? Single-minded? Yes. Stubborn. Definitely. Lazy? Not a bit.'

Rowan let his brother's gentle ribbing wash over him. He didn't want Will to know the real reason for the beard, the real cowardly reason. It was better that way.

Better for whom?

For Rowan, for starters. He was only on this side of the Atlantic for a week. Will's wedding was next weekend. Tonight was an informal night out for friends who had travelled to London for the wedding. It was definitely *not* a stag night; they were all being careful not to call it that after the disaster that had been Rowan's.

Last year, Will had thrown Rowan a pre-wedding party over a weekend in Paris but it had been crashed by a group of women. Women who had turned out to be hired by a tabloid. Rowan had been oblivious to the women's presence, talking to a friend, when a woman had come up next to him. Rowan had tried to leave, but it had been the image of him trying to push past her that had looked like an embrace that had been published. Rowan had been able to see she was wearing a skimpy top that was the colour of her skin but the subsequent photos had made her look topless. Will and his friends had been similarly caught. Nothing untoward had happened but the photos had made it look as if it were about to. The palace of Monterossa had come down hard on the paper, also feeling guilty they hadn't thought to send a palace official with Rowan, but that hardly mattered. Rowan was a fool for not having anticipated something like that himself.

His friends had suffered unacceptable stress and heartache. Relationships had almost been destroyed. Everyone's trust had been shaken. That, on top of the number the media had done on his family, exposing their lives and secrets, had been too much. He'd had to step away. He had loved Isabella deeply, but he couldn't put his family and friends through what the sharks of the tabloids had been doing to them.

Now, Rowan was about to launch his newest app, one designed specifically to help teenagers manage their mental health. For some businesses media attention was a good thing. Not in Rowan's case. He'd designed and built a suite of applications to support mental health, so photos of him with scantily clad women the week before his wedding, however innocent, did not help business. He couldn't be seen as a playboy. The untrue allegations that he, his friends and colleagues had partied excessively and engaged prostitutes had damaged their brand. Not to mention their personal relationships.

Apart from visiting his family, seeing a few close and trusted friends, and tonight, Rowan intended to spend the week in his hotel suite working on the launch of MindER. Immediately after the wedding he would travel back to New York. The beard, as pathetic as it was, would hopefully help him slip under the radar a little.

Rowan had no intention of upstaging Will and Lucy on their big day. And if his photo was taken in London he almost certainly would.

Rowan had lived in New York for less than a year, but he loved the way he felt anonymous. It wasn't so much that no one knew who he was, it was just that, with so many people even more famous than he was for far more scandalous things, no one really cared that he was Rowan James, Princess Dumper. They also forgot that he was a school dropout and an alleged gold-digging social climber.

The press attention given to Monterossa was nowhere near as febrile as that reserved for the British royal family, but it was greater than he'd first believed. Monterossa was a small but glamorous kingdom that had attracted worldwide notice thirty years ago when its handsome prince had married Hollywood royalty, the current Queen Gloria. The then prince and princess had produced beautiful twin daughters, Francesca and Isabella, and the world had been similarly captivated.

Isabella had been born into a fairy tale and he had grossly underestimated the attention that would bring to him. He'd been foolish enough to believe that the attention would be a good thing. Good for his business, for raising awareness of mental health. He couldn't believe how naive the Rowan James of two years ago had been.

Following their engagement, the tabloids had made his childhood sound positively Dickensian, implying his parents had been neglectful and that he'd practically been raised on the streets. They twisted stories about both his parents, reporting that his mother was a cocktail waitress when in truth she was the manager of a local pub. Worse than that, they had lapped up his father's past. Rowan's father had done time in his early twenties for dealing a small quantity of heroin. The dealing had been to support his own habit, a habit he'd kicked successfully while in prison. Rowan's father had gone on to have a long and well-regarded career as a social worker, helping people who suffered the same problems that he had, and Rowan had had a secure and comfortable childhood. Far from being the pauper described by the papers, he had been better off than many people he knew.

But of course, the headlines never told you about life's complexities. You couldn't explain things like this in two hundred and eighty characters.

One thing that was undeniably true, though, was that his childhood had not been like Isabella's.

A beautiful princess, she'd walked straight out of a fairy-tale kingdom and into the bar where he'd been sitting at a global mental health summit he'd attended in Geneva two summers ago. He'd been relaxing after giving a successful talk about the development of MindER.

Rowan had never been a good student. While he'd liked the social aspect of school, he often had difficulties concentrating and sitting still. The only thing that could make him concentrate for long periods of time was computer gaming, a hobby that both his parents discouraged and which led to an endless cycle of arguments. They insisted he was intelligent, but the further Rowan fell behind at school, the less he believed this. He left school early when his English teacher suggested that there was little point in him continuing and picked up casual work in the pub in which his mother ran. He was lost, a failure, and made to feel bad about the one thing in the world he really enjoyed. Gaming.

When Rowan was a teenager, smart phones were beginning to become commonplace. With his knowledge of gaming and coding, he began to think of ways in which apps could be used and developed a few basic games. At the same time, his father, a life-long smoker, had been trying to quit and Rowan decided to see if he could develop a game to help him. With some basic coding knowledge, he developed an app to distract smokers with games and track days without cigarettes.

His father used it and recommended it to some friends and Rowan began to spend more and more time working on the game, which was how, to begin with, he thought of it. He roped in some friends who knew more about coding than he did and came up with a plan. It became, over time, MindER, which now had a suite of applications to support various aspects of mental health, guided meditation, mindfulness, sleep, exercises, movement and even dance. In two weeks they were launching their newest product, an app especially designed for young teenagers.

It had been a steep learning curve; he'd had to learn about coding, psychology and most of all how to run a multimillion-dollar business. But he'd been lucky. Lucky to have the right idea at the right time. Lucky to secure an investor. Lucky enough not to make any bad deals. Lucky to expand the business at just the right rate, not so quickly that he overstretched. Not so slow that he didn't capitalise on the need for the services his app delivered. Lucky that this was something that a school dropout could manage to do.

He'd been lucky.

And catching Isabella's eye in the bar of that Geneva hotel had been similarly lucky. She had wandered in with her sister, two discreet bodyguards in tow, and he'd happened to look up at exactly the right moment.

She was beautiful.

Heart-in-your-throat-type beautiful. See-her-face-behind-your-closed-eyelids-overnight-type beautiful.

Plus she was confident. And he liked that. It was sexy as hell. It made him confident too. She wasn't afraid of sitting down next to him at the bar and asking what had brought him to Geneva. Despite his success, Rowan generally kept a low profile, which was difficult when you had a business to promote, but he preferred to let the product speak for itself. MindER was the brand, not him. They hadn't talked about their backgrounds, but about their passions, their dreams, things so utterly unconnected to real-life problems that it wasn't until several hours into the conversation—when he was already half in love with her—that she told him she was a princess. By then it was too late.

Buoyed by the success of the talk he'd given at the summit, he'd been brave that evening too. Brave enough to ask her for another drink, brave enough to ask for her number. Brave enough to keep messaging her.

She saw him. She understood him. Despite their different

upbringings, they understood one another. And that made him brave and her confident.

But then the bubble had burst, and she hadn't in fact been confident enough for both of them. And he had not been brave enough at all.

You made the right decision.

He knew that. He absolutely knew that.

Isabella knew it too.

In fact, the whole world knew a dropout like him didn't belong with a princess. The only one who hadn't caught up with the news was his stupid heart.

It was probably knowing she was in London tonight that brought thoughts of Isabella back to mind. Who was he kidding? She was never very far from his thoughts. Despite doing his best to erase her from his consciousness by working fourteen-hour days, making endless visits to the gym, swimming countless laps of the pool, it was all futile. It still didn't allow him to sleep at night and not lie awake thinking of her.

Sleep brought its own problems though. When his thoughts were untethered from consciousness he would dream about her. Dream she was in his arms. In his bed. Dream she was standing two metres away from him in a bar in London.

Rowan stepped back, into the shadow of the group of men standing next to him. He took several deep, even breaths. He was delirious. Losing what remained of his sanity. Isabella di Marzano, Princess of Monterossa was not in this South London bar.

He leant forward just a fraction.

Except, yes…yes, she really was.

Isabella stood alone off to the side of the bar, glancing occasionally at her phone, trying not to look as though she'd been abandoned by her sister.

She leant against the barrier at the edge of the leafy rooftop bar, Twilight, which afforded her a view over the edge of the building and the city. The sun had just set and the lights across London sparkled. The crowd circled around her. Behind the expansive bar, hundreds of brightly coloured bottles were stacked and under the lights glowed like gems. The music was fast, with an invigorating beat. After another drink or so she might be able to convince Francesca to find a dance floor.

Isabella had slipped off her jacket and draped it over her arm. She wore a fitted red dress that stopped just above her ankles. The scooped neckline and thin straps allowed her bare skin to luxuriate in the warm evening air. With the jacket she looked elegant and formal enough for the official party, without the jacket she looked classy, but not overdressed for this upmarket bar.

Francesca was chatting to a man she'd spied at the bar. She was laughing and the man looked captivated, as well he might. It was good to be around people but with no one looking at her for a change. No one watching her every move, judging every innocent remark. The lack of scrutiny and pressure made Isabella feel lighter. Almost untethered. She hadn't yet decided whether that was a good thing or not. All her life she felt the tension between staying calm, keeping every emotion inside her contained and letting them all go. The two forces fighting against one another, tonight she was struggling to keep her feet on the ground.

This is the plan, remember? A night out as ordinary people before whatever happens is going to happen. She wanted Francesca to have fun. One last hurrah. Heck, *she* wanted to have some fun. That was the point of sneaking out of the Duke's party and going to a random bar in South London. The plan had also been to leave their bodyguards behind as well, except somehow Gallo had caught wind of their plan and made them agree to him coming along. He was, however, a discreet distance away, glaring at everyone in the bar in that way he had.

Despite standing here alone looking like a wallflower she didn't have the slightest regret. Her sister looked happy as she flirted with the stranger. Isabella looked around the room at the groups of friends enjoying a night out, breathed in the warm air of the summer evening and the mood of optimism that had settled over the city.

She turned her gaze to the other side of the bar. There was a group of men, all tall, broad shouldered. They were dressed casually, as though they'd come from a football match. They were acting like friends who had not seen one another in some time. She tried to listen in without wanting to be too conspicuous. Then one of the men stood and turned to one side, revealing another man. And he was frowning.

It was a face she knew well. One that was tattooed on her heart.

She recognised the frown, the narrowing of his light brown eyes and the sudden tenseness in his shoulders. But there were differences as well. The beard for starters. Auburn, like the rest of his hair, thick and well established. It was clipped neatly and well groomed. Not the result of neglect, but purposeful.

He *wanted* to look different.

She didn't blame him one bit. She'd often toyed with the idea of dying her own light brown hair to see if she'd be able to go unrecognised.

Beard or no beard, she'd recognise this man anywhere.

Why here? Why now? Why him? This was her 'get out there and forget Rowan James' weekend. This was *not* meant to be her 'run into your ex unexpectedly' weekend.

They were separated by two metres but an ocean of grief and pain. She stepped towards him, half wondering if he would simply turn and flee. She wouldn't blame him if he did. Her instincts told her to do the same.

But he moved in her direction as well, always the gentlemen, ever polite. He wouldn't have changed fundamentally in the eleven months since they had last seen one other.

'Rowan,' she said, her voice lilting embarrassingly upwards.

'Your Highness.'

She flinched at the title, one he had never ever called her by previously. He was wearing a fitted blue collared shirt that set off his beautiful eyes, and dark trousers. She hugged her own jacket tighter.

Should they kiss on the cheek? Shake hands? Or just continue to shift awkwardly from foot to foot as she was doing now?

Rowan was less hesitant than she and bent down the half-foot in height necessary to kiss her lightly. As his rough cheek brushed against hers she caught his familiar cologne, high notes of citrus, heart notes of desire and bass notes of heartbreak.

Her olfactory memories jolted everything to the front of her mind. Their first serendipitous meeting in Geneva, short and chaste, followed by several giddy weeks talking on the phone all hours of the day and night, and then their first days back in the same city with one another.

London.

Where they didn't leave her suite at The Ritz. Where they consummated their passion and cemented their devotion to one another. Before reality intruded and everything went wrong.

'What are you doing here?' she asked.

'What am I…? What are you doing here? Were you looking for me?'

Her cheeks burnt. *You dumped me three days before our*

wedding. Why on earth would I come looking for you? 'No, of course not. I had no idea you'd be here.'

'Oh.'

He had a point though. This was his stomping ground, his favourite pub and club. A fact that she had known when she'd suggested to Francesca that she knew somewhere fun and normal. But then *he* wasn't meant to be here. He was meant to be five thousand kilometres away on the other side of the Atlantic. Isabella suddenly had an inkling of how Elizabeth Bennet must have felt being caught visiting Pemberley.

'I thought you lived in New York.'

'I do. I'm here for a wedding. Will and Lucy's.' Rowan tipped his red head in the direction of one of the men he was with. She recognised his brother, Will. Rowan was nearly as close to Will as she was to Francesca. Will nodded and smiled, but after acknowledging her, Will looked back at Rowan and raised an eyebrow.

Heaven knew what Rowan's friends thought of her. Or his family. The press had labelled him the bad guy, but it hadn't been like that at all and Rowan's loved ones would know this. They would know the real reason why the royal wedding was cancelled with not even enough time for the caterer to cancel their order of scampi.

'It's next weekend. I flew in this morning. We're having a catch-up.'

'Like a stag night?'

'We're not calling it that.'

'Of course not.' If Isabella's cheeks had been hot before they were as obvious as a flare now.

Rowan's own stag night had marked the beginning of the end. That incident, on top of the stories about his family, his father in particular, had been the final straw. Rowan had come to her to let her know that he couldn't do it. He couldn't, as much as he might want to, marry a princess and put himself, his friends or his family under that sort of scrutiny. It wasn't fair and it wasn't right.

She'd had to keep her emotions in check and play it cool to avoid even further drama so she'd told him she understood, that she didn't blame him. They had both thought he'd be able to handle it, but neither of them had counted on the fact the media would go after his family. They had rushed too quickly into their engagement. And she'd wondered, deep down and in the early hours of the morning, if it had all been her fault anyway. She'd been so infatuated she'd pushed him into it before he'd been ready.

'I assumed you were in the States and I had such a good time when you brought me here. I wanted to bring Francesca out for the night. Have some fun. Pretend…' *Pretend everything is normal, pretend my father isn't sick, pretend you still love me.* She didn't have to finish her sentence but he nodded. He knew. He'd always understood her.

'I'm sorry to hear your father's unwell. How's he doing?'

The kindness in his voice rippled through her body and nearly broke her. She felt tears rising behind her eyes and sniffed. Rowan reached up and pressed his open palm to her bare elbow. Simultaneously comforting and supporting her. Her legs swayed and her body wanted to fall into him and let him catch her in every imaginable way. But she locked her knees firmly in place and swallowed the tears back.

'He's not out of the woods yet.'

Out of the corner of her eye she saw a few of the other patrons were looking surreptitiously in their direction. Standing alone, she wouldn't attract much attention, but with Francesca people always recognised her. Now—standing with Rowan—she was equally identifiable.

'People are looking,' she whispered. He should leave. She should leave. This whole thing must end. She searched the bar hopelessly for Francesca. 'I should go.'

'No, not like this. You're upset. Come with me.'

'Where?'

With his hand on her elbow, his fingertips burning a brand on her skin and sending her pulse skyrocketing, he steered her into an alcove just off the bar.

'What the...?' was all she could say before he'd opened the closest door and looked inside. It was small and dark except for some ambient light coming in via a small high window. He nudged her inside. She expected him to leave but he stepped in as well and closed the door with an ominous click.

Out of the frying pan, so to speak.

'Are we allowed in here?'

'Your Highness, I'm sure no one will mind.' He smiled at her properly for the first time that evening. It was the same smile that used to make her insides somersault but now it made her blood cool.

'Please don't call me that.'

'Why not?'

'Because it's not my name.'

'Under the circumstances...'

'Under the circumstances I think you should call me by my name. We're not strangers and calling me by my title won't change that.'

Rowan lowered his head and he spoke to the floor. 'Your Highness... I'm doing it for me, as much as you.'

She shouldn't have come here. Should have chosen somewhere else. Or not sneaked out of the coronation party to begin with. Stayed and looked for one of the men on her mother's 'approved' list.

Prior to their engagement, her father's office had coordinated and released information about Rowan, his childhood and business successes. Her parents had adored Rowan, Francesca had too. Mostly because they could see how much Rowan and Isabella loved one another. It was more than simple attraction—though that was undeniable—they clicked. They shared views and values and a sense of humour. If her family had any reservations about their relationship they had kept them to themselves.

Isabella had not seen any issues; she didn't think she could've imagined a better life partner. Rowan was everything she was looking for: kind and intelligent. Interesting and interested. And he made her laugh.

They planned to divide their time between Monterossa and London. He would continue his work; she would continue to represent the royal family. They believed they could make it work. They became engaged six months after meeting, and set to wed six months after that. In hindsight it was too quick, but no one was going to tell the Isabella and Rowan of eighteen months ago that.

She should have paid more attention to the cracks that began to appear when their engagement was announced. More attention to what was being said about Rowan beyond the official messages being circulated by the palace.

Isabella didn't pay much attention to social media. She never had. It was one of the strategies she used to manage her mental health. She trusted the palace staff to tell her what she wanted to know and didn't let the background noise of the twenty-four-hour news cycle intrude into her thoughts.

Rowan did notice though. He knew what was being said about his family. How reporters were trying to contact his friends, waiting outside their homes, their workplaces. How they were even so desperate as to contact schoolteachers he hadn't spoken to in a decade and a half.

She advised him to ignore it, not to go on social media. As if that would make the problem go away. He tried to, for a while, but he couldn't ignore the reports from his friends and family about what was happening to them.

It all came to a head in the weeks before the wedding as

press scrutiny intensified. The stories about his father, his mother. His brother. Rowan's childhood. With a family who had been innocently minding their own business until their son became engaged to a princess. They didn't deserve the headlines.

'We pay for the royal family! We have a right to know!' screamed the pundits.

And maybe they were right.

But no one paid Rowan, or his family and friends, and the world did not have a right to their business. Or their lives.

It had been a calm break-up. No screaming, no fighting. Just soft tears of resignation. He'd taken her for a walk in the palace grounds—not to her favourite place, along the walls near the sea, as though he'd known that the conversation they were going to have would ruin that place for her for ever, but to a secluded garden she didn't often visit. And he'd sat her down on a bench under a magnolia tree and told her that he was sorry but that he couldn't do it. He couldn't do it to his family and friends. That even though he cared for her, it wasn't going to work.

He'd helped her family undo all the arrangements, offered to pay whatever needed to be paid, an offer that had been refused by her parents, and then he'd left. Left her to cry the hard, angry tears alone. In private.

So when he said calling her 'Your Highness' was self-preservation, she reluctantly understood.

They could never go back to how things were.

'What would you like me to call you?'

Rowan stepped back, but the room they were in was really just a large cupboard, and he bumped into the door.

'What do you mean?'

'Would you like me to call you Mr James?'

'Are you joking?'

'No. But I can tell you want to maintain distance between us.'

'Yes, but...you are a princess, Your Highness.'

'I'm not different from you.'

He sighed long and deep. 'Rowan, call me Rowan, Isabella.'

As soon as he said her name she realised her mistake. The syllables rippled through her, like a wave. Pleasure laced with the sharpest of pains.

She stepped back, instantly bumping something hard with the small of her back. Now her eyes had adjusted to the dim light she saw that they were indeed in some sort of cupboard. The boxes were labelled with liquor names, spirits and wines.

She laughed. 'Want a drink?'

'Heck, yes,' he said and they both laughed.

'I'm sorry I came here,' she said.

'Don't be. I know you liked it. I always wanted to bring you back.'

'And here we are.'

'Did you say Francesca is here as well?'

'Yes, out there somewhere. We were at the Duke of Oxford's party.'

'And you left that to come here?'

'Yes.'

A crease appeared between his eyes.

'Things have been hard at home. I wanted a little break. I wanted Francesca to have a break.'

The crease deepened. 'Isn't that risky?'

'It's just for a few hours. A chance to escape...'

'I'm so sorry things have been hard for you. And I'm sorry about your father.'

At the mention of her father, of everything that had passed between her and Rowan, she swallowed back the lump.

This was silly! She'd been strong, she was okay! Being

back with Rowan for a few moments, suddenly the defences she'd built around herself began to crumble. She shook herself. She just needed to get out of here, find Francesca and a Rowan-free bar instead.

'I'm sorry I haven't been able to be there for you, through all this.'

She had to get out quickly!

'I do understand, you know. I don't blame you.' More lies. But what choice did she have? There was already enough drama in her family. She had to stay calm.

Rowan's Adam's apple bobbed with a deep swallow. 'Thank you. The last thing I wanted to do was hurt you.'

But he had hurt her. And being in this cupboard with her, he continued to do so.

'It just wasn't meant to be.'

'I'm sorry I wasn't strong enough,' he added.

'What? No. Don't say that.'

She'd thought it. Wished he had been able to set aside his reservations for her, but every time she had thought that she'd realised that that would have made him care less about his family and friends and *that* would have made her love him less. It was easier to lie, to tell the world she understood. That she was fine.

'I'm sorry as well.'

'What for?'

'Not giving it all up.'

'What on earth are you talking about?'

It was one of the many possibilities she'd thought through in the horrible days after the wedding that wasn't. Leaving Monterossa and running away with him, somewhere different. Somewhere anonymous. The end of the world.

'I had this thought that we could run away to New Zealand.'

'New Zealand?'

'It's the most remote place I could think of. It's meant to be pretty. They have good wine, rugby…it sounds great.'

He shook his head. 'I think they still have newspapers and photographers in New Zealand.'

'I think they do too, and I don't think being a princess is something you can ever actually give up. If anything, people become more interested in you if you try to walk away.'

'Yes, I think you're right. But, Isabella…' Rowan leant forward and it didn't take much before he was close enough to her that she could feel the warmth from his tall, strong body surrounding hers, seeping into every one of her pores. 'I would never have asked you to do that.'

In the dim light of the room she could only just make out the angle of his jaw and the hard lines of his shoulders. She could feel him though. They weren't touching, but every cell in her body knew he was close and thrummed and vibrated accordingly. Stupid cells, stupid body.

'I know. I wanted to let you know…that I thought of it. I thought of everything.'

'I thought of everything as well. I thought of every way we could possibly make it work. Believe me. I did.'

She nodded and looked down because if she looked into his amber eyes the emotion she'd been pushing down would probably flood over.

He slid two fingers into her hair and twirled them around a lock, but he might as well have taken her heart into his hands by the way in which her insides twisted. She closed her eyes and breathed him in again for the last time. If she didn't pull herself away now she didn't think she'd be able to.

'I'll get Francesca and we'll leave. I should've thought this through better. I'm sorry for coming.'

'Don't be. It was nice to see you.'

'Really?' Isabella laughed, at the same time as she was still biting back tears.

'You'll always be special to me.'

Special. That was all she was. Like a friend.

Not a soul mate. Not a one and only.

It was goodbye. A bow tied around the goodbye they had shared last year. But this time it was final. This time they both understood why it had to be and had made their peace with it.

'We should go,' she said, the weight of everything pressing against her chest, the air in the room suddenly non-existent.

CHAPTER THREE

Taking Isabella out of the way of prying eyes had seemed like a good plan, until he'd unintentionally directed her into a cupboard the size of a toilet cubicle.

It was difficult enough dismissing thoughts of Isabella when she was a continent away. He'd barely managed to control his heart rate when she was standing across the bar from him, but now, with her perfume swirling around his head like a dense fog, he felt control slipping from his grasp.

It had just taken every ounce of his self-control not to pull Isabella to him and tell her he'd made a horrible mistake. Thankfully, she saved him from himself when she said they should go. Isabella would leave as soon as she located her sister and this would truly be the last time he saw her.

They emerged from the cupboard, blinking in the comparative brightness. A man stood between them and the rest of the room. He was holding up a camera. The man wasn't just using his phone, but had a camera, with a professional-looking flash, and he was pointing it in their direction.

Rowan groaned. Hadn't he learnt anything? Of course some grubby pap would be waiting for them to come out of the small room together.

'Princess! Rowan! Are you back together?' yelled the photographer. A flash illuminated Isabella's perfect face and she squeaked with fright. Rowan turned his back to the camera, wrapping his arm around Isabella to shield her as the flashes flickered around them both, the camera capturing everything.

Was there nothing these bastards wouldn't do?

'We have to get out of here. Is there a back door?' she asked.

Something in Rowan snapped. This was his bar, *his* place. Everyone in here had a right to privacy. He wasn't going to go through this again. He wasn't going to wake up tomorrow morning to a headline that they were back together when that would be nothing more than a heartbreaking lie.

He drew a deep breath and turned to the man. 'Give me your camera.'

The photographer laughed, but not before he took one last photo of Rowan staring him down, with Isabella next to him, her hand on his arm. Her cheeks still flushed from their encounter.

No. They were not going to get this photo. This headline. This *lie*.

'You heard him—give us the camera,' Isabella said.

A crowd had gathered behind the photographer, mostly interested strangers, but Rowan noticed Will and their friend Rob, an ex-rugby player. They stepped up, blocking the man's path.

The photographer turned his body and tried to weave his way through the crowd. Isabella yelled, 'Stop him!' across the bar.

Will and the others moved to encircle the man but with a quick turn he slipped past. With blood rushing in his head and Isabella's words echoing in his ears, Rowan moved after the man, chasing him to the stairwell. The other patrons slowed the photographer's path long enough for Rowan to catch him and grab his sleeve.

'Stop. Give us your damn camera. At least delete the photos.'

The man looked down at Rowan's hand on his own arm then glared at Rowan with a challenge. *Are you seriously going to make this physical?*

Knowing that would instantly take the situation from salvageable to sensational, Rowan let go of the man's arm. The photographer bolted. A chuckle floated behind him as he bounded down the last steps and out of the front door. 'Give it up, mate,' he yelled.

But Rowan would not give it up.

And he was not his *mate*.

They were not getting one more falsehood about him out into the world. Rowan bounded down the steps two at a time and followed the man out into the night.

The photographer set off on foot down a nearby street. He was moving at a brisk pace but Rowan smiled to himself. His Vespa was parked just around the corner and he ran to it now. The man would not get away.

Rowan mounted his bike but as he was about to accelerate fingers curled around his arm.

'Wait for me,' Isabella pleaded.

'No, stay here. With Francesca.'

'I can't find her,' she said as she hooked a leg over the seat and climbed up behind him. 'Go!' she said.

Realising with a sigh it would be far quicker to take her with him than argue with anyone as determined as Princess Isabella, he accelerated. Rowan instantly felt her grip around him tighten as she held on, but he tried to ignore the way her palms were currently pressed against his stomach, thinking instead of the fact that neither of them were wearing helmets, and another, even more worrying headline popped into his head.

Rounding the corner, he spotted the man further down the street. While the footpaths were busy with pedestrians, the roads were reasonably clear. They followed him around a few corners, with each turn away from the Thames and the crowds. When the man stepped into the stairwell leading to a pedestrian underpass Rowan braked.

'No,' Isabella groaned.

He knew where the underpass headed. 'Get off,' he ordered.

'No, we can still catch him.'

'I know, just get off.'

Eyes wide, but thankfully not arguing, she climbed off. He opened the storage hold and took out the helmet, handing it to her. 'You'll need this.'

The smile that broadened across her face made his heart swell. But he ignored that sensation, just as he ignored the way his heart hitched as she ran her hand up his arm and climbed back on the bike.

'Hold on,' he said, this time bracing himself for the sensation of Isabella's soft curves pressing against his back. It helped. A little.

The underpass had two exits and he had to choose which was more likely. The one that led back to the Thames and the City or the other.

He chose the second. As they rounded the corner and the exit came into view he smiled—the man was walking quickly along the end of the road. Rowan accelerated. Isabella held on even tighter and his limbs tingled with the sparks zipping up and down them even faster than the bike was travelling.

They caught up to the man just as he stopped outside an apartment building. Rowan pulled up and cut the engine as Isabella slid off the bike. She ran, with helmet still on, to the door but reached it just as it clicked shut. Rowan stayed behind, realising the futility of her mission. She pushed and tugged on the door handle and of course it didn't give.

The building was modern, sleek and had about a dozen door buzzers. Few enough that they could try them all, though Rowan knew this man would be the one who didn't answer. Isabella pulled the helmet off and ran her hands through her soft, shiny hair, fluffing it out and up. The vision did nothing to calm his already elevated heart rate.

They stood in the streetlight, facing one another. She had her hands on her hips, he put his face in his.

'It was worth a try,' he said.

'Of course it was worth a try.'

'Come on, I'll take you back to Francesca.'

'It's still worth trying. You're not giving up this easily, are you?'

Giving up. Easily.

The words tore at his deepest fears. His deepest regrets.

He was a school dropout. A princess dumper. That was his thing—he gave up.

'You want us to press each buzzer? He won't answer.'

'No, but if we can just get into the building.'

As though her words had summoned it, a couple emerged from the elevator and headed in their direction.

Without speaking, Rowan turned to the Vespa and secured it. Isabella walked to the door as the couple were departing, catching the handle just before the door shut. The couple didn't look back and Isabella and Rowan slipped into the building as though they were meant to be there. She marched up to the lift and pressed the call button. It opened immediately and they stepped inside, but Rowan instantly saw the problem.

As he expected, the elevator required a code before it would take them to the upper levels.

She stomped a red stiletto-clad foot and he grinned.

'Damn. I thought we had him,' she said.

'He's not just going to hand the photo over.'

'But if we offer him money, more than he can sell it for?'

'He's probably posted it already.'

Rowan looked around the building they were in; it was a reasonably upmarket place. This man wasn't just an opportunist, most likely he did this for a living. Rowan couldn't even begin to guess what he'd been doing in Twilight. For all Rowan knew, he'd followed the Princesses from the party. If the man was trying to find a buyer for the photo they might have more time, though not much. It was only that thought and the glimmer of hope it provided that stopped him saying, 'Let's go.'

Instead he sighed.

Isabella shook her head, backed against the wall and sank to the floor. Rowan copied her action.

'We can't stay here all night,' she said.

'I don't want him to sell or post that photo any more than you do.'

He knew why he didn't want this photo to get out. He'd spent the last year trying to get the world to forget him. This would enliven all the attention on him and his family once again.

But Isabella? Scrutiny was part of her life. What was one more photo?

She's ashamed of you. You always knew you were never good enough for a beautiful princess. You might be rich now, but everyone knows where you came from. Everyone knows you're a dropout. A failure.

'It won't be the first time we've been photographed together.' He tried to keep the hurt out of his tone and wasn't sure if he'd succeeded.

'Of course not, but I do know this is the exact sort of thing you've been trying to avoid.'

That stumped him for a moment. 'Exactly. It's my problem. You should go.'

Isabella turned to him, placed her hand on his. 'It's my

problem as well. We may not be together but I hope we're still friends.'

His throat tightened. Friends was an optimistic hope. He couldn't imagine a time when he was 'just friends' with Isabella. That would imply that a part of him no longer longed for something more. From where he sat now, that seemed as far away as it had one year ago.

He gently slid his arm out from under her hand.

'We are friends, and I'm sorry I got you into this situation. You should go. I'll stay and do what I can.'

'What on earth are you talking about?'

'I'm sorry you were photographed with me. I should've been more careful.'

'You keep saying "I". We used to be "we",' she said softly.

Yes, but that was before...

'And you sound like you think I'm ashamed of being caught with you,' she added.

'Aren't you?'

I dumped you and now I've got you into this mess.

She looked into her lap. 'I've never been ashamed. Not of what happened. And certainly never of you.' She looked him straight in the eye and it was as though she'd pressed a knife against his gut. He was bound to the spot.

'My worries about the photo don't have anything to do with you being in it.'

'They don't?'

'Is that what you think?'

He didn't say anything, just sat there. Of course she was ashamed of being with him. He would be! Once again he'd shown how naive he could be about royalty and their relationship with the press, once again he'd let himself be photographed in an apparently compromising position.

'I wasn't meant to be at Twilight. I'm meant to be at the Ashton, in Mayfair, with two thousand other people, representing my country at a party being hosted by the Duke of Oxford. I don't want it getting out that I left the party. I don't want my parents knowing I let them down and encouraged Francesca to do the same.'

It wasn't about him. She didn't hate him. It was something worse, something important. It wasn't simply embarrassment. It was a fear of upsetting her already worried parents.

'I'm not embarrassed about being seen with *you*. I'm worried about embarrassing my parents. And my sister.'

She crossed her arms and lowered her head. Conversation over.

Rowan stood, wandered around the foyer. Counted the number of door buzzers, stared at the generic print on the wall. Wondered how he'd ended up here.

Two years ago his life had been on its upward trajectory. Busy, but relatively uncomplicated. The relationships he'd had in the past had been pleasant and satisfying, but they hadn't upended his life.

And then he'd walked in a hotel bar in Geneva and everything had changed. While he didn't regret breaking off his engagement with Isabella, if he had to go back to a moment in time, it would be to that night. Where it all began. To when life was straightforward and he hadn't been forced to choose between the two things he loved the most. It had been an excruciating decision to make, but he'd known that it would be easier in the end for Isabella. She would find someone else who could handle the attention and he would have his business and his family. It had been painful, but it had all worked out.

Isabella was better off without him, and it showed. Seeing her here tonight, so strong, so confident, so completely over him, he knew he'd made the right decision. He'd always felt more for her than she did for him. His heart had been a wild beating mess, hers had continued to beat calmly and serenely.

'Is that why you really left?'

Her voice was soft and he wasn't sure he'd heard her or imagined her. He turned back to her. She was looking up at him, eyes wide and her gorgeous face open and vulnerable. His heart cracked.

'What do you mean?'

'Did you leave because you thought you weren't good enough?'

He scoffed.

'Of course not. I mean, there's no denying we're from very different backgrounds.'

'In some ways. But not in all ways. We both care about things. We both work hard, we both want to make a difference. That sounds pretty similar to me.'

Those were the same things he'd told himself for the first year: that their backgrounds didn't matter because they had their future in common. But it wasn't true. He'd been so ridiculously optimistic. Dazzled by his feelings for Isabella.

'I didn't leave because I didn't think I was good enough. I left because I hadn't realised how much pressure there would be on me, my family and my friends. I shouldn't have been so naive. I will always be sorry for that.'

She nodded and Rowan sat back down next to her. He wasn't sure why. He knew they should leave, get back to Twilight or go home.

'You could let your parents know first? About the photo.'

'No. At least, not tonight. Not yet.'

'Then shouldn't you let Francesca know where you are?'

'No to that as well. She'll be fine. She looked like she was having a good time. She probably hasn't realised I've left yet. I want to sort this out before I go back.'

Isabella took out her phone, switched it off and slipped it back into her small bag.

He raised an eyebrow in question.

'I don't want her calling me.'

'Can't she track you?' He remembered that both sisters' and their parents' phones had the geolocators switched on so they could see where the others were.

'We switched that off before we came out. Didn't want Mum and Dad knowing.'

He tried not to let the shock on his face show.

She really had broken palace protocol this evening. She'd be in a lot of trouble if they found out what she'd done.

'It's not like they can ground us, I mean, we're grown women but…'

He nodded. You never stopped being your parents' children. You still worried about your parents and they worried about you. He understood completely. That was why he was waiting here on this pointless mission as well: so as not to upset his family further.

'How has she been? Francesca?' he asked.

'Good, but it's been a difficult past few months for both of us.'

While news about the Monterossan royal family was rarely something he sought out, he had occasionally looked for updates about the King's health. Leonardo was a good man, and always welcoming and generous to Rowan. He had also been understanding when Rowan had called off the engagement.

'Better to do it now than after the wedding. I appreciate this would have taken a great deal of bravery,' the King had said to him.

As well as being concerned about their father's health, the sisters would have been working extra hard as well. Royals didn't get time off to grieve—if anything they had to work harder in times of illness and death. No wonder Isabella and Francesca had wanted to slip away for an evening and forget all their worries and responsibilities.

'How have *you* been doing? Really?'

Isabella gave him a shy shrug. 'I'm okay. It's been hard since Dad was diagnosed, but weirdly all the extra work has been distracting. And that's been good. Is that silly?'

'Not at all. I often find distraction and solace in work. Sometimes it's the one thing that's easiest to control.'

He'd never spoken truer words; his job, his business, had been his one solace in the past year.

'How's New York?' she asked.

He told her how he'd come to love the pace, the people. How he felt he'd settled in and how good it had been for him professionally. He didn't mention his personal life, not that there was anything to say about that. Since Isabella, he'd steered well clear of any entanglements, casual or otherwise.

The conversation meandered easily into all sorts of other topics: movies, music, books. They had so much catching up to do. He remembered all the many things he'd wanted to tell her over the past year and she did as well. Little, big, funny, sad. He didn't know how much time had passed and was barely aware of the elevator bell dinging, signalling someone entering the foyer.

It was him.

The photographer. The man froze at first, wide eyed and shocked. Rowan and Isabella scrambled up, just as the photographer was putting two and two together. He looked back, as if to go back to the elevator, but Isabella, who was closest, blocked his path. Rowan then stepped to the front door. Goodness knew what they both thought they would do to stop the man if he really wanted to run, but he didn't. He stood in the middle of the foyer and laughed.

'You cannot be serious. You chased me here?'

'Please don't publish the photograph. It was nothing, really, we aren't back together,' Isabella blurted.

The man looked from Isabella to Rowan and back again

and smirked. Rowan's chest burnt. He didn't appreciate the man's judgement.

'Seriously, publishing the photos will just cause further hurt to our families. How much do you want? We will beat it,' Rowan said.

The man narrowed his eyes, continued to look between the pair. Laughed again.

'Royals hunting down paparazzi? That's a new one.' He laughed again. Rowan was beginning to get very sick of the sound of the man's cackle.

'Tell us what you want; we'll pay it,' Isabella said.

'It's too late.'

'You posted it?' she asked.

Rowan's heart fell.

'Sold it. If I knew you were both so keen, we could've had an auction. They're great photos.'

'There's more than one?' she asked.

'Of course. There's a couple of you both before you disappeared into the cupboard. Of him comforting you. They're quite sweet. But of course the ones where you come out of the cupboard looking red-faced are great too. The one of him putting his arm around you. Really, they tell a whole story.'

He wanted to strangle this man. No. He wanted him ruined.

'Nothing happened!' she cried and the man laughed.

'Sure, sure.'

'Who to? Who did you sell it to?' Rowan asked.

'Ah, now, I can't tell you that.'

'Why not?'

'Professional ethics.'

Rowan laughed and Isabella shouted, 'Ethics? You expect us to believe that a slime ball like you has ethics?'

The man looked taken aback. 'Yes, journalistic ethics.'

'You're not a journalist,' she muttered.

Rowan agreed with her but felt the conversation slipping away from them.

'I think the public deserve to know that a princess who is meant to be at an official coronation party was in fact hiding in a cupboard in a bar on the other side the city with her ex-fiancé, don't you?'

'No, because we weren't together and it's no one else's business.'

'Isn't it? Isn't it your job, your responsibility, to be at the official function? Isn't your country paying for you to be here to represent them?'

Isabella's shoulders sagged.

Rowan clenched his fists. 'Her father is sick. Have some compassion.'

'I know her father is sick. All the more reason for her not to be gallivanting around the city—'

'You…' Rowan felt the blood rise up in him and everything went white. He stepped towards the man, unsure what on earth he was going to do. He knew what he wanted to do, but that was out of the question. He felt a warm hand on his arm.

'What my friend is trying to say is that it's been a tough few months for me, a tough year for both of us. Publishing that photo won't help. It'd be kicking two people who are already down. Please, please just tell us who you sold it to.'

'It would be against the terms of the contract. It wouldn't be honourable.'

Honour? Rowan bit back the words. He knew this man was scum. He was just protecting his money, nothing else.

'Can you give us a hint, then?' Isabella asked.

'What do you mean?'

They looked helplessly to one another then back to the man.

'Twenty questions. You just say yes or no. You won't say the name. It'll be fun.'

'If that's your idea of fun, you need to get out more. No, wait, that's what got us here in the first place.'

'Did you sell it to a newspaper publisher?' asked Isabella.

He was slow to answer but eventually said, 'Yes.'

'London based?' asked Rowan.

The man nodded.

'Broadsheet?' Rowan asked, hoping the answer would be yes, rather than the other choice, tabloid.

The man shook his head.

'Does it start with T?' Isabella asked.

The man nodded and grinned.

'They all start with T, because they all start with *The…*' Rowan whispered to her.

'Oh, yes. Does the second word start with T?' Isabella asked.

The man nodded again and said, 'You're right, this has been fun. But if you'll excuse me…' He slipped past them both, out of the door and into the night.

'The Truth?' she guessed. It was an ironically named paper, known for printing anything but.

'It has to be.'

'Well, that's the end of it. The photos will be all over the place tomorrow. We should go,' said Rowan.

'No.' Isabella shook her head and looked out of the door. 'We're going to talk to them. Ask them not to print it.'

'The paper? The editor?'

'No. The owner.'

'How? Do you know him?'

'Never met him.'

'Then how?' Rowan had always admired her energy and optimism, but now feared her positivity was bordering on delusion.

'Because I know where he's going to be tonight and,

what's more, I have an invitation.' There was a glimmer in her eyes that made his heart lift.

'The party at the Ashton?'

'Yes.'

'Who is he?'

'Sir Liam Goldsworthy. He owns a publishing company, magazines, books, but also *The Truth*.'

'Why did he get an invite to the party if he publishes a tabloid like *The Truth*?'

'Ah, because of his wife. She's been friends with the new Queen for ever. Besides, with the usual hypocrisy tabloids are famous for, *The Truth* likes to focus on Hollywood celebs and European royalty. Tends to leave the Brits alone.'

'Got it. But you've never met him?'

'Never!' she said, as though this were a good thing.

Rowan glanced at his watch. It was close to ten p.m. He thought her chances were next to zero, but said, 'I guess it's worth a shot.'

'Absolutely it is. Come on.'

'You want me to come?'

'You've got the bike. I don't fancy my chances of hailing a cab on a night like tonight.'

'Do you want me to drive you there?'

'Yes, absolutely. We're in this together.'

'And I'll just wait outside the front door for you?'

'Don't be silly. We'll sneak in the back. The same way I sneaked out.'

'You said you had an invitation.'

'I do, but I can hardly just walk in the front door.'

It was late and Rowan was still on New York time but according to his body clock he'd just missed a night's sleep.

'I'm not following.'

'And you're meant to be the smart one.'

His cheeks warmed at the compliment.

'I don't want to make an entrance. Besides, the party started hours ago. How would it look if I arrive three hours late, especially when everyone thought I was already there? No, you have to help me sneak in the back. Once I'm in, no one can say anything because I'm meant to be there so they can't kick me out.'

He shook his head. It seemed unnecessary, but he was prepared to drive her to the Ashton. Even if it meant more time with her arms wrapped around his waist, her soft chest pressing against his back, and her thighs tightly gripping his.

Steel. You are made of steel.

'How about this? We try the back door and if that doesn't work, we go in the front,' she said.

Her continued use of the word 'we' troubled him, but he chose to believe it was an oversight rather than intentional.

'Lead on,' he said, heart sinking.

CHAPTER FOUR

IT WASN'T EXACTLY *Roman Holiday*.

Audrey Hepburn had looked so free and delighted on the back of that Vespa, whereas Isabella gripped Rowan as if her life depended on it, and indeed it did. She could barely open her eyes, let alone enjoy the wind in her hair. Much of the traffic—endless lanes of cabs—was largely at a standstill. But a Vespa? A Vespa could weave in and out of the slow-moving traffic at a great pace. And Rowan did. They had made their way over London Bridge and were now hurtling along the embankment towards the West End.

Rowan was right: for all her bravado she thought there was a very slim chance she'd be let back into the hotel via the back door. And even if she was, then what? How would she find Sir Liam? What if he'd left the party already? What would she say to him? What if he said no?

Even though these were the problems she should have been solving as they ducked in and out of traffic, all she could think about was how thin Rowan's cotton shirt was. How she could feel the warmth of his back against her chest. How she didn't want to hold his torso too tight because when she did she could feel his stomach, his washboard abs. How snuggly her thighs were wrapped around his. How the whole thing was making desire fizz up inside her, through her legs, and into her core.

When he was an ocean away her longing for him was

painful, but theoretical. Now she was wrapped around him. Literally. And she wanted to explode.

Keeping her desire in check was one thing. She could probably manage that.

But keeping in her emotions? Holding her shattered heart together? This wasn't just a man she was attracted to. This was *Rowan*. The love of her life. Her tragically star-crossed love. The man she could never be with.

The man who didn't love her enough to be with her.

She understood the practicalities. The reasons. After all, she understood the pressure of being in the public eye. She felt its weight with every step she took.

Hold your head up. Smile. Be polite. Don't offend.

She knew that her behaviour reflected not just on her, but on her family. On Monterossa. She'd been told, before she could even talk herself, that she had to watch what she did and said in front of anyone. More than that, she knew what it was like to have your slightest failings magnified and analysed, to have lies spoken about you.

And she wouldn't wish the scrutiny she had endured on anyone she cared for.

Yet...

A small part of her—the smallest part, the part that woke her at two a.m.—asked, 'Why didn't he love me enough?'

When the sun came up each morning, reason returned. She wasn't enough because no one would be. No one sensible would want to marry her and have their life dragged through the muckraking of the press. And she didn't want to be with someone who wasn't sensible.

But that was a problem for later. She had to figure out what to do *now*. They zipped along Piccadilly and Regent Street, Union Jacks and red, white and blue bunting hung across the road, the streets still swelled with people. They were only a few blocks from the Ashton.

Then what?

You don't need to know how to fix it. You just need to do the next right thing.

But she had no idea what the next right thing was.

This had all been her stupid idea—*Go out on the town! Leave your security! Live like a normal person!*—and now here she was, on the back of a Vespa, hurtling through London on the way to sneak back into the party she'd just sneaked out of.

But with her ex.

There had been bad photos of her taken before. The time she'd had too many cosmopolitans on her eighteenth birthday and brought most of them back up into a nearby fountain. The time she'd accidentally tucked her skirt into her pants during a break in the middle of her father's birthday concert. But this, while she was fully clothed and sober, was bad. Her parents and her country would know she had neglected her duties and convinced her sister to as well.

And with her father's health so precarious. Nausea rose in her stomach. And it was not the fact that she was wearing the single helmet, or that Rowan had only narrowly missed a cab in his hurry to get them to the Ashton. No. It was the fear of her father finding out what she'd done and the look she'd see on her mother's face.

You'll figure out a way. You always do.

That voice again.

Her sister's voice.

Isabella looked around almost expecting to see her, as she had always been, every day of Isabella's life. But she wasn't there.

And soon that could become a permanent state of affairs.

Isabella pushed that thought aside as well.

They approached a set of lights that had just turned amber and she expected Rowan to stop, but instead he accelerated and went through the junction as the lights changed to red. Isabella did what she'd been trying not to do and clutched Rowan tighter. She tried not to think about how good she felt with her chest pressed against his back, her breasts pushing against him. Her poor nipples standing to attention.

He braked suddenly and she was pushed against him again, causing more friction and pleasure. When would this ride be over?

She wasn't even a teenager when she first realised that the world expected her to be rebel. She was the second and therefore the naughty one. But Isabella had no desire to be a rebel, she didn't want to upset her family, she just wanted to do some good in the world. Only she didn't know what that looked like for her. Raising money for charity? Visiting hospitals? All worthy, but none felt right for her. Isabella had plenty of second-born princesses to look to as role models, but the one she identified with most was the fictional Princess Anna. This—a pointless chase through London on the back of a Vespa—was a very Princess Anna thing to do.

She laughed and Rowan turned his head with a confused look.

'Watch where you're going!' she yelped.

The world wanted her to be a rebel, because that was the stereotype. They looked for misbehaviour, watched for her to step out of line. And she wouldn't give them the satisfaction. She was going to track down Sir Liam and get him to stop publication of the photo.

If only she knew how.

The public were fascinated by Isabella to a degree they weren't with other second-borns. Royal twins were rare, but royal twins directly in line to the throne were practically unheard of. People always wanted to know if she was upset she'd missed out on the crown by five minutes. What no one appreciated was that everything about royal succession was arbitrary and accidental. It made little difference to be five minutes behind in the line of succession or five years.

Except that, being the same age, she and Francesca were brought up together. They did everything together. When she'd been fifteen and decided she would much rather stay at the local school she was at than go to the boarding school in Milan her parents had in mind, she'd had an argument with her father.

'I don't see why I have to do the same training as Francesca.'

'To support her.'

'But I won't ever be queen.' Isabella had always been happy about this. Relieved almost. She saw what her father did and it didn't look like fun to her.

'Besides, you'll be qualified for many jobs. Diplomat. Queen consort,' her father had said and Isabella had bristled.

'I thought we didn't do that any longer.'

'What?'

'Trade off spare princesses in diplomatic deals.'

'You're second in line to this throne,' her father said.

'So? I may as well be fiftieth! When Francesca has kids I may as well be commoner.'

'That's not true. Supporting your sister is a very important role. Being a monarch is a lonely, lonely job. It's important to have someone with you who understands you and the job.'

'But when she marries...'

And her father didn't have an answer for that.

At the moment her sister wasn't close to marrying. Since her break-up with Benigno, Francesca's love life had been as uneventful as Isabella's had been lately. But one day Francesca would find someone who would sweep her off her feet and then where would that leave Isabella? Third wheel? No longer the spare, just someone who used to be famous. Isabella wasn't sure how she felt about that. Either way.

Francesca's accession to the throne had always seemed like a far-off event, but even though no one came right out and said anything things were changing. Isabella felt it.

Rowan drove past the front of the hotel. Outside the grand entrance were several people milling about in their party clothes. The hotel was still brightly lit, from inside and out. The party was still in full swing.

He drove around the corner and into a laneway. Once the bike stopped Isabella was even more conscious of their closeness, his warmth. The beat of her heart, which had been drowned out by the motor, was now thumping in her ears so loudly she wondered if Rowan could actually hear it. She unhooked her arms from around his torso and they began the process of disentangling themselves from one another and getting off the bike.

Rowan looked as though he was also catching his breath. His face slightly red, his hair wild from the ride. He ran his hands through it and looked around. 'Are we being ridiculous?'

'No more ridiculous than this whole situation.'

He was as unsure as she was. One of them had to be the brave one. And at this moment that looked as if it would have to be her.

'How do you propose we sneak in?'

'Relax, it's not as if it's Buckingham Palace.'

Bravado was not the same as bravery and she hoped he didn't notice the tremor in her voice.

'Won't there be heaps of security? Think of all the dignitaries who are here.'

She waved his question away. 'The US president isn't here. It's mostly minor royals, aristocracy. For instance, like the Earl of Hereford. The Count of Westphalia,' she said, remembering her mother's list.

'That seems like a very precise list.'

Her cheeks flushed. She led the way around to the exit she, Francesca and their bodyguard, Giovanni Gallo, had come out of several hours earlier. Isabella had always just thought that security was there to protect her. It was never something she had to figure out a way around.

Except tonight.

'Should I distract them? Point to the sky and yell, "Look!" so you can sneak in?' he asked.

'Please tell me you're not serious?'

'At this point I don't know what I am.'

She shook her head. Nor did she.

'No, here's what we'll do. I'll just tell them who I am. We need to get you in as well.'

'Me? I can't come.'

'Why not?'

'I'm not invited. It'll attract more attention. You don't need me.'

He would've kept reeling off excuses if she hadn't reached over and placed her hand on his forearm. 'I do need you. I don't know what I'm going to say.'

Rowan shook his head. 'I don't know either.'

'Between us we can come up with something. Please, can we just try?'

When he'd come to her, three days before the wedding, and told her they needed to talk, she hadn't begged. He'd set out his case so clearly and rationally.

'The press intrusion is more than I thought it would be. My parents and friends are being placed under unreasonable pressure. I can't marry you.'

She hadn't argued or begged. She'd wanted him to marry her willingly and happily. Not under pressure. She hadn't even cried. Not until much, much later.

But now she needed him. Just this one thing. And then

they would say goodbye for ever and she'd never set foot in a country again without first ascertaining his whereabouts.

'I won't ask you anything else. Ever. Please. Come in with me.'

He looked at the dark sky and she squeezed his forearm. It was just as strong and firm as it had always been. Her insides melted. She wanted to press her face against his chest and sob.

'I'm not going to sneak and I'm not going to fight,' he said.

She smiled and pulled him by the hand. 'Of course not.'

They approached the two security guards standing outside a nondescript door. Isabella knew it was the back entrance to the Ashton, because she and Francesca had let themselves out of it several hours earlier. She made a mental note to remember to reassure Francesca that she was okay in a way that didn't prompt questions. She wanted to have this whole thing fixed before she dragged the heir to the throne into it.

Isabella recognised the guards, a tall woman and a shorter man. A man carrying two large rubbish bags exited the door and the security guards stepped out of his way.

'Come on,' Isabella whispered and grabbed Rowan's hand. His hand in hers was no less tempting than her thighs wrapped around his, but it did make her feel better. Besides, she didn't want to risk him chickening out and doing a runner.

The guards straightened their backs as Isabella and Rowan approached. 'Hello! You remember us, don't you?' Isabella said.

The guards exchanged a look.

'I'm Princess Isabella of Monterossa and this is Rowan James, my plus one. We were at the party earlier and now we need to go back in.'

'This isn't a concert. You can't come and go.'

'Of course not, but since you saw us both leave earlier,

and since I don't want to have to embarrass anyone by going back in the front entrance, I thought you could help us be discreet by letting us back in.'

The woman shook her head. 'We don't do that.'

As she finished speaking, the man with the rubbish bags returned empty-handed and the man opened the door for him.

'He didn't have an invitation,' Rowan said.

'He works here,' said the woman.

'And we're guests. You saw us. Me and my sister.' Isabella directed that remark to the man who had definitely seen her, Francesca and Gallo. He'd even said, 'Have fun, ladies,' as they'd left.

The man studied Rowan. 'Is he the man you left with?'

'Of course he is. Don't you remember? You're a security guard!'

Her heart was thumping in her throat as she waited to see if her bluff worked. She hoped that in the darkness he wouldn't have noticed the fact that their bodyguard, Giovanni Gallo, had classic Mediterranean looks while Rowan's red-headed ancestors hailed from Scotland.

The woman rolled her eyes and turned away. The man then reached behind and opened the door to them.

A rush of relief and adrenaline ran through her.

They were in!

The hotel looked different from this angle. She hadn't paid much attention to the layout as they were leaving. To her right she could hear the unmistakable sounds of a large kitchen and her stomach rumbled. When had she eaten last? As soon as she'd spoken to Sir Liam they would definitely find something.

'This way,' she said, and directed Rowan away from the kitchens. They walked along a quiet corridor and then up half a flight of stairs she recognised from when she'd walked down them earlier.

At the top of the stairs they could hear the music and laughter coming from the main ballroom and it was clear where the party was.

'Wait,' he said and pulled her to one side, just as she heard people approaching from around the corner. Rowan opened the nearest door and tugged her inside. The room was dark and they both fumbled around for a light switch, Rowan eventually locating and tugging on a string that turned on a flickering yellowish light above them.

It was a small room, lined with boxes on one side and shelves on the other. It was bigger than the cupboard they were in at the Twilight Bar, but not by much.

'Our tour of the storerooms of London continues,' he muttered. 'I sure do know how to show a princess a good time.'

'Nonsense, these are the places you can't see on the cheap tour.'

He smiled, but his heart wasn't in it.

'I don't know what I'm doing here,' he confessed.

'Moral support.'

'Immoral, more like it.'

Then she laughed. This was why she'd wanted him by her side—because life was just better when he was.

She shoved that unhelpful thought to one side.

'We may as well put out our own press release saying we were caught in a cupboard in Twilight. I think being caught at this party could just make things worse.'

'Yes. We don't want to get caught in two confined spaces in the one night. We have to do something.'

'But what?'

You don't need to know how it ends...you just need to do the next thing.

Isabella looked around where they were now. A different sort of storeroom. Bigger. It was lined with shelves of clothing. Uniforms to be precise.

'Ah, Rowan.'

'I'm not going to like what you're about to suggest, am I?'

'That depends on whether you brought your adventurous spirt.'

She pulled out a cropped black jacket from a nearby shelf and shook it out. It had gold buttons and the Ashton Hotel crest. She held it up against his blue shirt.

'No.'

'What have we got to lose?'

'Our dignity?'

She laughed. 'Seriously, we lost that when we chased a photographer across south London.'

'Our privacy?'

'That's why you're wearing this uniform. They won't know it's you.'

'Someone will recognise me.'

'Do you look at wait staff?'

'I do, as it happens.'

Yes, Rowan was just that kind of person. Isabella tried to be, but knew she often fell short. She also knew that most people, whether they admitted it or not, did not.

'You do, but most people don't, and you know that. Besides, you have a beard now. You're utterly unrecognisable.'

'You recognised me,' he muttered.

I'd know you anywhere, she thought, looking into his whisky eyes and feeling herself falling into them.

In a year many things had changed—his demeanour was more serious, the beard, many of his expressions—but his eyes were the same. *I'd know you in another life. I'd know you in heaven.* She felt herself falling forward, shook herself and straightened.

No. Rowan was in her past and he had to stay there.

She turned to the shelves and the stash of uniforms stored there. Rummaging around, she found a white shirt, a starched white bib and finally a tie. She held the shirt up against him again. It looked about the right size. Now for some trousers.

'What choice do we have?' she said.

'You could go out there by yourself.'

She felt her insides crumple, but held her back straight, glad she was facing away from him.

She didn't do things alone. She was always part of a pair. A double act. It wasn't that she couldn't. At least, she didn't think so. She wanted him with her.

'We got in this together, we'll get out of it together.'

'Isn't it riskier?'

She located the trousers and searched for a pair that looked big enough for his tall frame. Her heart was racing as she neared the bottom of the pile without locating any, but at the bottom was finally a pair that looked large enough. She handed them to him.

'I don't know what I'm going to say to him. How I'm even going to find him,' she said.

'I can't talk to him for you. You have to do it yourself.'

'I know. But you can be close.'

Rowan lowered his brow and when he looked at her, her skin prickled. She'd said too much.

'And you can help me find him,' she added.

'I don't even know what he looks like,' Rowan pleaded.

'Old. White. Rich.'

'Like everyone in there.'

'I'll google him while you get changed.'

He still hesitated, looking at the clothes but not reaching for them.

You owe me this, she almost said. *You left me once. Don't leave me now.*

He will always leave. He doesn't love you enough to stay.

He shook his head. 'I don't think it's a good idea.'

'Of course it's not. I thought we were in this together. But I guess…'

You're not in this together. You haven't been a team since he left you three days before your wedding.

Rowan closed his eyes and breathed in through his nose. Then he sighed and said, 'Fine. You're right. It's my problem too. We are in this together.'

Her heart flipped a happy beat. 'Give me your phone and I'll show you what he looks like.'

Rowan handed her his phone and she searched for Liam Goldsworthy.

Sir Liam was exactly as she'd flippantly described to Rowan: old and white. On the other side of seventy, with short clipped grey hair and blue eyes that shined out from the photo she was looking at, bright and friendly.

Hopefully that friendliness was genuine and not a mirage.

Sir Liam owns a tabloid rag. Do you honestly think he's going to be co-operative?

What other choice did she have?

The sound of a belt unbuckling made her look up. Rowan had taken off his shoes and was now taking off his trousers. He was facing away from her, thankfully. She looked down, to his bare legs, his usual tight black shorts. His thigh muscles flexing as he pushed down his trousers and bent his legs.

She looked at the other wall, her heart fluttering against her ribs.

Was one little photo worth this? Standing in a too small and suddenly too warm room while her gorgeous ex stripped off?

'Um, when you're ready, I've found his photo,' she said to the wall.

'Just a sec,' he replied.

Knowing it was a bad idea, but not being able to help herself, she turned her head for a second. Seeing he was still facing the other way, she felt safer to fix her gaze on him. The trousers she'd found fitted him perfectly, but he did have one of those physiques. Tight across the seat and well fitted around his thighs. Her throat went dry as she admired him. He unbuttoned his blue shirt and she watched as he took his arms out and his muscles rippled beneath the surface of his taut, smooth skin. A swimmer's shoulders, even broader and firmer than in her memories. Her fingertips tingled as they recalled the smoothness of his skin under them. How she could trace patterns and words into his body for hours with her fingers, and her lips. Her mouth salivated with the memory of his taste.

What if the photos got out there? Sure, she'd upset everyone she loved most in the world, but she wouldn't have to be *here*. Watching this. Watching everything she'd lost, so close she could almost taste it. Taste him.

Luckily Rowan didn't turn as he reached for the white shirt, his muscles stretching, flexing and rippling again as he slid his long arms into it. Crisp white cotton slid over warm, pale skin. Sprinkled with just a few freckles. Smooth and entirely lickable.

He turned and showed her the shirt, holding out his arms and then, for good measure, doing another spin.

'You look good.' Her mouth was dry. Both understatements.

'Thanks, I think.' He folded his own trousers and shirt neatly, laying one on top of the other, and slid them onto a nearby shelf.

Isabella picked up a loose white tie and he stepped towards her. Instead of simply handing it to him, her hand looped it around his neck. She lifted his collar and slipped the fabric under. His Adam's apple bobbed with a deep gulp.

She adjusted the fabric and rested her palms against his shoulders, sliding them down to rest on his collarbone. She knew she should lift them away, she'd lingered too long, but his chest felt so good, so nice. His muscles tensed under her touch and, finally, she took her hands reluctantly away.

'I actually have no idea what I'm doing. I can't tie a half Windsor let alone one of these things,' she confessed and stepped back, head down.

''S okay,' he said, his voice rough. 'But there isn't a mirror. Could you please hold up the camera of my phone?'

'Good idea,' she said. Glad to be useful and glad to have an excuse to watch him weave and bend the fabric over and under itself in deft, practised moves as the fabric became a perfect bow tie.

Tie tied, he picked up the black jacket and shrugged it on. 'How do I look?'

'Honestly?'

Honestly, you always look hot. You couldn't not look hot. I want to rip those clothes right off you again and make love to you on this dusty floor.

But she didn't say that. She reminded herself that this was the very same man who had destroyed her trust in all men and happy endings, and turned away. The man who had changed his mind about her and their life together as soon as things began to get a little difficult. Isabella didn't care about Rowan's father's past and didn't see that Rowan should take it all so personally either. She wasn't even angry about the photos from Rowan's stag night; everyone knew the press loved to manufacture compromising situations for celebrities to get caught in. Isabella believed Rowan was blameless and only trying to extract himself from the situation.

She had trusted him, forgiven him and for what? He'd left at the first complication. And if Rowan, the man she'd loved more than any other, had done that, how could she possibly trust anyone again?

A box on a nearby shelf caught her eye. She pulled a disposable face mask out of a box and handed it to him. 'Maybe put this on. Just in case.'

'I thought you said I was unrecognisable in the beard?'

'I was joking! Wear the mask.'

Confusion creased his face but he took it.

'Okay, show me what this guy looks like.'

She reopened to the photo of Sir Liam and handed him back his phone. 'The next one is with his wife.'

'So, he looks like every other middle-aged man who is here tonight.'

'Yep.'

While Rowan gathered his wallet and pulled on the borrowed jacket, Isabella contemplated sending a message to her sister.

She had no intention of telling Francesca everything, particularly not about all these 'getting stuck in confined spaces with her ex' shenanigans, but that didn't matter. Her sister would be worried.

Though Francesca would want answers to questions Isabella couldn't answer.

'Let's do this, then.' Rowan gently touched her shoulder, turning her then nudging her to the door. But Isabella stopped short of it, her hand in mid-air, not yet touching the doorknob.

'We need to go separately.'

'Definitely.'

'So I'll go, you'll follow.'

'I'm right behind you. I promise.'

Still she paused.

'I don't know what I'm going to say.'

'Ask him not to print it.'

'Just lead with that?'

'Well, butter him up a bit at least. Ask him how he enjoyed the coronation.'

'Lame.'

'I've got nothing else.'

'You're the clever one. What would you say to him if you were me?'

Rowan grasped her shoulders and turned her back to face him. 'You, Isabella di Marzano, Princess of Monterossa, are the smartest and most charming woman I've ever known. And the most self-assured.'

Maybe. But that was before I met you. Before everything changed. Before I began to doubt everything, including myself.

CHAPTER FIVE

ISABELLA STILL DIDN'T BUDGE. Rowan looked at his watch. It was after ten p.m. They had to get out there now and find the newspaper owner. He had no idea how long a coronation party would last. Maybe until after midnight? But how long would a newspaper owner party on? They couldn't take their chances.

'We need to get out there.'

'I know. But I still don't know what to say to him!'

What happened to the bright confident woman he'd known?

You did this.

He pushed the thought down. No. That wasn't so. Isabella was far better off without someone one like him. She'd been absolutely fine when he'd ended their engagement, calm, serene. She hadn't argued. She certainly hadn't cried. He didn't doubt that she cared for him, but the way she'd reacted so well to the break-up convinced him she would get over him soon.

The woman before him now was not the same woman. She was as beautiful and compelling, perhaps more so than a year ago. But something was missing.

'You can do this,' he said again. 'Just use your famous charm.'

'My *famous* charm?' She smiled and dipped her head, lifted her gaze.

His insides flipped. '*That* charm.'

'I wasn't trying to be charming.' She still looked up at him through fluttering lashes.

'Regardless, it comes naturally to you.'

'And now?' She lifted a manicured hand and removed some non-existent fluff from his lapel. When she removed her hand the slide of one finger brushed ever so gently under his chin and his throat closed over. He was never entering a small room alone with her again.

'Now you know you're being charming.' His throat closed over.

'Flirting. It's not exactly the same thing.'

'I think for this evening's purposes we shouldn't quibble with semantics. Do what needs to be done.'

'I can't flirt with Sir Liam! He's married.' As she spoke, she placed her hand on Rowan's shoulder.

'I wasn't saying you should flirt, I said you should be charming.'

'Where's the line between being charming and flirting?'

'I think it's like obscenity or art—you know it when you see it.' He was pretty sure he was looking at that line right now. They were standing closer than ever, but he wasn't sure if she'd stepped forward or if he had. They seemed to have exhausted all the air in the room and his head spun. Common sense must have been as scarce as the oxygen and he said, 'You're looking so beautiful tonight, I'm sure if you just walk up to him he'd do anything you ask.' His voice was rough but he was powerless to change it. He couldn't get enough air into his lungs.

'Now who's flirting with who?' Her voice was as ragged as his.

Isabella's dress was fitted to her curves, the neckline was low and, not for the first time that night, he forced himself to look into her soft hazel eyes and away from her supple cleavage, shown to perfection by the cut of the dress. Their bodies moved even closer and by instinct he lifted his hand to her waist, the beading of her dress a little rough against the silk. He might have been holding her body, but he was also holding her at a safe distance from himself. A safe distance.

You think this distance is safe?

The voice in the back of his head squawked with laughter. Nothing about this moment was safe.

'Just go out there, introduce yourself. People love meeting a princess, you know that.'

'Even in a room full of other princesses and duchesses?'

He couldn't believe how insecure she sounded.

You did this.

No. Isabella was fine without him.

She let out a deep sigh that he felt in his gut.

'There's a lot riding on it. For both of us. I want this to work.'

'I know. Ask him how his night has been. And then ask him not to print the photographs. I for one would…'

He closed his eyes. It was too much. This room, this moment, Isabella standing so close to him, smelling like Monterossa, long nights and languid, lazy mornings.

'You for one would?'

'Do anything you asked.' He exhaled and pulled her closer.

'Anything?' Her voice was as whisper thin as his resolve.

'Anything.'

A glimpse of her tongue touching her top lip was all it took to send him back twelve months, back to before the wedding, before everything about his family came out. Back to the time he could tighten his arms around her, pull her close and press his mouth against hers whenever he wanted.

As he did now. He heard her take in a breath of air sharply as his body collapsed into her, his mouth opened, his arms pulled her against him. He tasted her, trembled as her tongue slid against his, erasing a year of self-control in an instant.

His body tightened, his head exploded. The inevitable conclusion to this situation. He was powerless in her arms, lost, adrift. He devoured her like a starving man.

And then she was gone. Air where her body had been.

'Not everything,' she panted.

No. Because while it was easy to give her this, he couldn't give her a future.

The guilt crashed over him again, hot and bitter, with no cure.

'I'm so sorry, I shouldn't have—'

'I guess we've established at least I can still get your attention.' She looked at the ground and drew a circle on the floor with one of her red shoes.

'Isabella, I'm sorry. I shouldn't have…'

She shook her head. 'It takes two, but I guess we've established where the line between charming and flirting is. I won't try that with Sir Liam.'

'Isabella…' He tried to speak again but couldn't find the words. His brain kept freezing as soon as he said her name.

'I know you're sorry. I know you wish things could be different. I know you think you can't change things,' she said.

Her choice of words snagged in his muddled brain. 'Of course I wish things were different.'

I know you think you can't change things.

Of course he couldn't change things! No one could change the fact she was a princess and he was a school dropout who couldn't even manage to keep himself and his family out of the papers. The whole world could see he wasn't good enough for her.

'I wish things were different, but I can't change the world. We are who we are.'

'Of course,' she said. But it was clear she wasn't buying it. If she wanted someone to change the world then she was definitely stuck in a small room with the wrong man. 'Rowan, we can't talk about this now. We need to get out there.'

'So go,' he said. The clock was ticking. For all they knew, Sir Liam might have left the party already.

She nodded, but still looked unsure.

You did this.

He nudged her chin up with his index finger and took her gaze in his. His insides tumbled and twisted like the most daring of acrobats. How did she not realise how amazing she was?

'Walking away from you was the hardest thing I've ever done in my life and I seriously doubt any man, particularly one who has probably enjoyed quite a few post-coronation champagnes, could seriously say no to you.'

She smiled but it seemed as though she was trembling.

Isabella turned and this time she couldn't grab the doorknob fast enough.

'You should wait a few minutes. The ballroom is that way,' she said and waved her hand, but neither of them were in a state to be paying attention to directions at this point. He could hardly have sworn which way was up and which was down, his head still spinning from the kiss.

'Good luck,' he said as she slipped out of the door, closing it behind her.

Rowan took the moment to compose himself.

You kissed her? What were you thinking?

He had been thinking of the palace in Monterossa, of The Ritz, of all the times they had been alone together. Of all the moments they had shared. He had *not* been thinking of self-preservation.

If Isabella was uncertain about their mission, then Rowan was positively pessimistic. Not only was this mission most likely futile, but it was also downright risky. He knew hotels like this were meant to have a 'no photography' policy but hundreds of people might see them. And it only took one to tattle.

Rowan James sneaks into Duke's coronation party to woo royal ex!

The potential headline made him shiver and the bow tie tightened like a noose around his neck. He slipped the face mask she had given him over his mouth and nose.

If only he'd put that on five minutes earlier.

That he shouldn't have kissed Isabella was a no-brainer. It had shaken him and clearly surprised her, further muddying all the waters between them.

He'd never denied that he still had feelings for her, he'd just realised that those feelings were not strong enough to make way for everything else.

It's just the fact that you were close together, reassuring her that she can do this. It was a blip, a natural mistake. Forgive yourself.

It didn't mean anything.

They were not getting back together. Another reason it was imperative he got out into this party and helped her track down Sir Liam.

Rowan opened the door slowly and looked out into a warren of narrow hallways leading in all directions. Left, he decided, though wished he had something to stick on the door so he'd be able to find his clothes again. Or better yet, a pocketful of breadcrumbs to make a trail back.

The hotel was like many Mayfair buildings, several hundred years old and, even though it had been recently remodelled, it had been renovated to look as though Queen Victoria were still the monarch. The narrow back corridors were for the servants, which should have made him feel more comfortable but when one of the staff rushed past him, he gave Rowan a filthy look.

If you're dressed like the staff you need to act like it!

Rowan nodded and hurried away. He needed a tray of glasses to carry as soon as possible.

Luckily, he'd always identified more closely with the staff at these events than he had with any of the guests. Aristocrats. Royalty. Old money. Rowan might be just as rich as many of the people here, even more so, but he was not of this world. He was from a flat across the river, which his family could only afford with the help of the housing benefit.

At the end of the corridor was half a flight of stairs and at the top of the stairs the noise of the party was loudest. He walked up the stairs, pushed open the door at the top and found himself in a large room.

He'd been to a few charity galas in his time and this was a lot like one of those. The room was crowded with almost identical-looking people: the men wore dark suits, the women dressed conservatively in blacks and dark blues. The most daring wore silver, or perhaps a deep purple. He could easily spot Isabella in her red ensemble as soon as he entered the room. Like a beacon.

Or perhaps that was simply because he could spot her in any crowd. Even if the face mask had been covering his eyes he'd still have had a way of knowing Isabella was nearby. The air would feel different. His bones would know.

Worse than that, other people always noticed her. Even if they hadn't shared a history, he would have seen her. A stand-out beauty.

As Rowan stood at the door, frozen, another woman, one dressed in the same black and white get-up as him, stared at him. Not with the annoyed look of the other man but with a 'Who the hell are you?' look.

He nodded at the woman. 'Busy night, hey?' he said, and she walked away shaking her own head. Hopefully she wasn't heading off to find someone with the authority to kick him out.

He might have been better off just coming to the party as himself.

Don't be silly. Everyone knows that Rowan James doesn't belong at a party like this.

He was a waiter. He needed to act like one.

With his heart rate increasing, he decided that as the newest member of staff he should collect empty glasses. He didn't need to know where to take them, as long as it looked as though he was moving around the room.

He weaved his way through the crowd, trying simultaneously to search for empty glasses and Sir Liam, while also keeping his gaze down.

A challenge at the best of times.

As he approached the doorway across from the one he'd come in, his stomach fell. There was a whole other room, a much larger one, where people were dancing.

Damn.

He spotted a bar. The two men behind it were too busy preparing drinks to notice him slip in behind them and pick up an empty black tray. Good, he felt better. If anything he could use it to cover his face. Rowan had a flashback to the time before his business has taken off, working in his mother's pub. His mother always said it was fortunate he came up with the idea for the app because his ability to carry a tray of drinks left something to be desired.

'What are you doing just standing there? Those glasses need clearing.'

The man looked Rowan up and down.

'Yes, sir,' Rowan said before ducking away to search for some empty glasses to put on his empty tray.

The situation encapsulated his relationship with Isabella in a nutshell. She was swirling around with royalty and aristocracy, looking elegant and jaw-droopingly gorgeous. Charming everyone in her path.

And he was in a waiter's uniform. Collecting empty glasses. Pretending to be someone he was not.

Rowan kept his head down and picked up empty glasses. How would he know when Isabella had been successful? They should have been coming up with a better plan instead of kissing, he thought as he made his way around the edge of the room.

He balanced a final champagne flute on the tray and turned to head back to the bar. A man walked past him quickly and gesticulating, requiring Rowan to step back suddenly, causing him to tip the precariously balanced tray to one side.

The noise of shattering glass made everyone around him jump.

This was bad. Very bad. His face was burning under the mask and sweat began to gather on his forehead.

'What on earth?'

It was the man who had viewed him suspiciously in the corridor earlier.

'I'll clean it up.' He almost added, 'And of course I'll pay.' An instinct that thankfully he kept to himself.

'You bet you will.'

Rowan bent down and stacked the tray with the chunks of glass, thankful most were in large pieces, not shattered into sharp shards. Another man crouched down next to him and began helping. He was wearing a suit, but of a far finer fabric than the rough jackets given to the staff. Rowan looked at the man's face. Grey hair, blue eyes. It was Sir Liam.

Worse still, the man looked into Rowan's face and his eyes widened with recognition.

Damn!

You were never good enough, but you really messed things up with her. Royally.

He couldn't even laugh at his own joke.

'I can manage, thank you, sir,' Rowan said, but Sir Liam kept stacking glass onto the tray. Rowan kept his eyes down until the tray was finally full and no pieces remained. He nodded to Sir Liam without making eye contact and turned away.

Now, while he was carrying a tray of broken glass, he had to find Isabella, and point her in the direction of the commotion he'd just caused.

The last time he'd spotted Isabella's red dress she'd been in the first room. He had to get to her, direct her to the larger room with the dancing.

Rowan was headed in that direction when he was stopped by a hand on his shoulder, heavy, insistent.

'May I have a word?' said the deep voice belonging to it.

Isabella made her way through the party, head spinning. She could hardly focus on the faces around her. Her lips were still sensitive from the kiss Rowan had given her in the storeroom. It had been like a summer shower—unexpected, heavy and very brief. And it had left the air around her steamy afterwards.

He'd apologised, but she had goaded him into it, with all her talk of flirting. For a moment, locked away from the rest of the world, it was almost as though she'd forgotten they had broken up. Like one of those dreams she kept on having in which they were still together, only to wake up and be cruelly reminded all over again that she was alone.

Abandoned.

She'd pushed him into it, just as she'd pushed him into the engagement. Thinking only of herself, her own desires. She had to compartmentalise.

It was a strategy she'd practised many times over the past year to get herself through engagements, or even dinner with her parents, when all she really wanted to do was curl up in bed, cover her face with a duvet and cry.

Compartmentalise. Smile serenely. Push it down.

The kiss, and analysing its implications, or even reliving its magnificence, had to wait until she'd found Sir Liam.

The crowd at the party had thinned since she'd been here three hours earlier, but the average age of the guests hadn't decreased at all. She was still likely to be one of the only people under thirty. Heaven knew how her mother thought she'd find someone suitable to marry here.

These are your type of people. People who understand your family and way of life.

But walking through the crowd, she didn't feel as though she belonged at all. She felt as if she were floating to one side of them all. They didn't understand what it was like to be her. Very few people in the world really understood. Even the two people in the world she was closest to didn't understand at all. One had abandoned her. And the other would move on to a new life shortly.

The fact that neither of them intended to hurt her didn't lessen her pain one little bit. Rowan had chosen to protect his family and friends. Francesca would only do that which was her destiny.

But they were still leaving her.

Isabella couldn't see Sir Liam anywhere. Or Rowan for that matter. Certain Sir Liam was not in the first room, she picked up her pace and moved to the next. She had to stop the photograph being published.

Her family hadn't been rocked by the kind of scandals other royal families had faced but her parents had made her and her sister well aware of them.

'It's always best to learn from the mistakes of others than to make them yourself,' her father often said.

This potential scandal was hardly on the scale of some scandals but she would disappoint her parents, on what was meant to be her sister's chance to show them that she was ready to represent Monterossa. With her father still in hospital, it would embarrass her family when they needed it least.

She sighed.

Compartmentalise. Smile.

This next room was a lounge, filled with small tables and chairs. She surveyed the room, looking for Sir Liam. But also for Rowan.

She had no luck with either and moved on to the next. The ballroom was three times the size of the two rooms she'd already come through, but with ten times as many people. She began her circuit of the room, smiling and nodding at those who she recognised, or at those who recognised her.

The band was still playing, a mixture of swing and jazz, the sort of thing she always heard at these sorts of parties and never anywhere else. They paused at the end of a song and she heard it. Shattering glass. She, like everyone in the room, turned to the sound of the commotion.

Damn.

There was Sir Liam, but worse than that. He was crouched on the floor next to a man picking up the glass. A man she'd recognise anywhere.

And they were speaking to one another! What if he recognised Rowan? He was supposed to stay inconspicuous, yet here he was dropping glasses and speaking to their target.

Though, she supposed, the chances of Rowan staying inconspicuous anywhere were always low, even before he'd been engaged to a princess and the world knew his face. His face had always been handsome, his figure always striking.

He's dressed as a waiter, bearded and wearing a mask. No one will recognise him.

She no longer believed the pep talk she'd given him. This was a ridiculous plan. She needed to separate Sir Liam from Rowan, talk to him and get both her and Rowan out of the party as soon as possible.

By the time Isabella had reached that side of the room, Rowan had disappeared. Her heart beat faster with each step.

'Even if you aren't confident, you need to give the impression that you are.'

Words her mother had said to her and Francesca over and over again.

'Pretend you're in a movie, and the world is your stage.'

Something that was easier for a trained actress to espouse.

Start with the wife.

She wasn't sure why or even where the thought came from, but it seemed like a natural way to ease herself into their conversation. She stood to one side of Lady Goldsworthy, a friendly looking woman who was clutching a glass of red wine and laughing animatedly with the woman next to her. This was good. Older women were more practical, less spooked by royalty. She caught Lady Goldsworthy's eye and smiled. The woman smiled back. The other woman, curious about what had captured her companion's attention, also turned and, noticing Isabella, also smiled. 'Your Highness.'

'Hello,' Isabella began, because there was no better way to begin a conversation. 'Are you having a nice evening?'

'Oh, yes, it's been lovely.'

They chatted about the party and the coronation earlier that day. Lady Goldsworthy poured Isabella a glass of their wine and Isabella almost forgot her mission.

The sound of the women's laughter attracted Sir Liam's attention and Isabella met his eye.

'Your Highness,' he said as he joined them.

At least he knew who she was. That was a start.

'The Princess was just telling us what the Prime Minister was overheard saying at the coronation.'

'You've had a good day, then, Your Highness?' Sir Liam smiled at her knowingly. He *had* recognised Rowan! This was very bad.

Next time she would listen to Francesca when she told her a plan was risky.

'Yes,' she said, not trusting her voice to stay even.

'And your sister?'

'She's around here somewhere.' Isabella waved her hand in the air and pretended to search the dance floor for her sister.

'She's probably out there dancing,' said Lady Goldsworthy. 'You young things should be on the dance floor, not talking to the old folks.'

'I agree. But I don't think for a second that any of you are old. You should join me.'

Lady Goldsworthy laughed. 'Oh, not me.'

'Sir Liam?' Isabella asked. 'Would you do me the honour?'

His wife chuckled and Sir Liam hesitated for a moment before his wife said, 'Go on!'

And that was how Liam Goldsworthy, owner of *The Truth*, happened to take Isabella's hand and lead her onto the dance floor at the Ashton.

She hoped Rowan was somewhere in the room watching. They'd done it!

Well, not quite yet. She'd found him and got him alone but still had to ask him not to print the photograph.

You're looking so beautiful tonight I'm sure if you just walk up to him he'd do anything you ask.

'Are you having a good night?' he asked.

'I'm having an interesting night,' she replied truthfully.

He chuckled. 'The very best kind.'

'Yes, well, I'm glad you agree. I think yours might be about to become even more interesting.'

He narrowed his eyes and studied her. It felt strangely like dancing with her grandfather.

'Have you ever had a relationship go wrong? End in heartbreak?' she asked.

'Why do you ask?'

'Have you?'

He nodded.

'And it isn't nice, is it?'

He shook his head.

'Well, it's a hundred times worse when the entire world knows and is speculating about it and making assumptions and judging you. And you can't even get out of bed.'

'I'll have to take your word for it.' He cleared his throat. 'So…'

Just ask him!

'Has this got anything to do with the fact that your ex-fiancé is here tonight?'

'What?' she spluttered.

'You didn't know? For some reason he's here as a waiter, but not doing a very good job of it. I think he might be about to be fired.'

'You recognised him?'

'Was I not meant to?'

Isabella grimaced.

'Are you back together?'

'No,' she said but knew her face was turning red.

It was just a kiss, a mistake, it didn't mean anything. He didn't want to marry a princess. They were definitely *not* back together.

'Yet, he's here tonight.'

'About that.'

'Yes?'

'We ran into one another, earlier. At another place. But accidentally, it wasn't planned. We haven't seen one another since…'

'Since he broke it off?' Sir Liam prompted.

He seemed very kind and understanding. He would hear her out and agree to her request.

'Yes, and we were talking and trying not to be seen because, well…'

'You wanted privacy.'

'Exactly. But we were seen and photographed. But we're not back together.'

'You said that. Where are you going with this?'

'The photograph was of us coming out of a storeroom together. Nothing happened, but we were in a cupboard together. And he had his arm around me. And the photographer, a pap, sold the pictures to one of your papers.'

'Ah. And you don't want them printed.'

'Yes, that's it! Could you, please, as a favour, please not print them?'

'I don't make editorial decisions.'

'Not usually, but you can in special circumstances.'

'That's true. But what was really so bad about this photo? What's the big deal?' Liam Goldsworthy seemed like a decent man, and he had a very nice wife, so she decided honesty was the best policy.

'Rowan left me because of the press intrusion in his life, but mostly his family and friends'. As much as that broke my heart, I do understand it and I want to respect his wishes.'

'He's a grown man, and a successful one at that. I'm sure he can handle publicity.'

'But his family shouldn't have to. At least, not the kind of negative and hurtful attention they were subjected to. People telling their secrets, interfering with their lives.'

Sir Liam sighed. 'It's the price of public life.'

This man owns newspapers! What were you thinking asking him not to print a picture that will surely sell more papers? She needed to try a different angle.

'But it isn't just that. I don't want my father to see the photos.'

'He's been unwell?'

'Yes, very. That's why Francesca and I are here in the first place. I wouldn't want to upset him. Or my mother. That's really why I don't want the photos being published. It will embarrass my family and I want to avoid any more heartache for them.'

'I see.' He nodded and for the first time in hours Isabella felt lighter. He would agree not to publish! It would all be okay!

'I will ask my editor not to publish the photographs of you and Rowan James.'

'Oh, thank you, thank you!'

'Provided...'

Provided you pay me. Provide you have lunch with my wife... Provided...

'Provided you call my editor before seven a.m. and agree to do an exclusive interview with the paper instead.'

'Me? An exclusive interview?' She could do that. She would have much more control of the narrative this way. It would still be okay.

'You *and* him.'

'Rowan?'

'Yes. Both of you. Together. With all topics on the table. I'm not just going to tell my editors to give up photos like that, without something in return. Think of it as a way to put your side of the story out there. Some of the things you just told me. Though you won't have to mention what you were doing at that bar.'

'I... I'd have to talk to Rowan.'

'Of course. I don't require an answer now. My editor's name is Karl Brown. Call the paper before seven.'

He released his hold on her, leaving her unsteady as the other dancers whirled around her.

'Thank you, I appreciate it,' she said.

Liam made his way back to his wife, clearly recognising their transaction was over.

She had to find Rowan. And quickly.

Isabella spied a clock on the wall. It was nearly eleven. She had eight hours to convince him to tell his story to the press. She already knew that she wanted to accept Sir Liam's offer, but would Rowan, who guarded his privacy so closely, see that it was the best choice? She wasn't sure.

The last time she'd seen him he'd been carrying a tray full of broken glass to the back of the ballroom, so she went in that general direction now.

They'd have to leave out the back. The front door was still not an option, not with Rowan and he was her ride, not to mention still her only chance of stopping publication of the photo.

An interview.

Together.

She shivered.

This night just kept getting worse.

CHAPTER SIX

It was all over.

Even if the photo of him and Isabella sneaking out of a cupboard wasn't published, a headline saying that he'd dressed as a waiter to sneak into the Duke's party probably would be.

What would be the consequences? Would he be charged with trespass? Fined? He wanted to throw up. Whatever the legal consequences were they paled into comparison with the ones that would follow if news of this got out. So much for keeping a low profile.

He needed an excuse, and fast.

'Come with me this way,' said the voice again.

Good. Hopefully they would go somewhere private. Rowan hated bribery and corruption but what would it take to get this man to stay silent?

'How about I just leave and we—?'

'Leave? The broken glass has to go out to the utility room. I don't know where you think you're taking it.'

'I... Ah...' Rowan added and looked properly at the owner of the voice for the first time.

'Have I seen you before?' the man asked.

'No, this is my first night here. You needed extra staff. I've come from...' *Think! Think!* 'The Duke's own household.'

'Of course, sorry, you don't know your way around.'

'I have no idea where I'm going,' Rowan said truthfully.

'And I would be very grateful if you could point me towards a broom.'

The man led him out of a different door and into more back passages and to a room with rubbish bins and cleaning products.

'Thank you, I think I'm all right from here,' Rowan said to the man.

'Good.' The man turned and Rowan exhaled.

But then the man turned back and studied him. Rowan's face turned hot under the mask. 'Most of us are going out for a drink after this is all over, if you want to join us?'

'A drink would be great. It's been quite a night.'

'Indeed.'

Finally the man turned and left.

Rowan rested his head against the wall and took some, deep steadying breaths. His limbs tingled from the adrenaline coursing through them. They needed to leave!

When his heart rate had returned to close to normal levels he disposed of the glass and searched for something with which to clean up the rest of the mess. As much as he wanted to slip out of the nearest door, he had to get back out there, find Isabella and point her to Sir Liam. His disguise was not going to work for much longer. For starters, the face mask was beginning to stick to his face with all the sweating that last encounter had caused. He spied another box of face masks, took another two and pocketed them.

At least with a broom he looked as though he had a purpose. With a deep breath he ventured back out to the ballroom.

Sir Liam was no longer anywhere to be seen. Great.

A waiter walked past him with a tray of full champagne flutes and he had to stop himself from grabbing one.

Once you find Isabella you can go to the nearest pub and order several Scotches neat.

The thought spurred him on. He went back to the place he thought he had dropped the glass and swept it up slowly. If he stayed in one spot, she might find him.

He took as long as he thought he possibly could sweeping the section of the floor but still Isabella did not return. Just when he was about to leave a flash of red caught his eye. Without making eye contact with her, he walked in her direction. Eventually she stepped into a corridor leading away from the ballroom. He followed.

'We have to get out of here,' she whispered.

He nodded. 'I just need to get my clothes.'

'No time. Sir Liam knows you're here.'

'Damn. I was worried about that.'

'So we have to leave *now*.'

'What did he say?'

'Later. Come.'

She tugged his arm and pulled him down the corridor. It was narrow and led off to another maze of hallways.

'I need to get back to my clothes.'

'Were you very attached to them?'

'I'd like to keep them. Besides, I can't keep walking around dressed like the staff. They keep getting angry at me. I'm a terrible waiter, as it happens.'

'I'll buy you some new ones. We have to go. No. Wait.'

Isabella spun him towards her, grabbed the lapels of his jacket and tugged it over his shoulders and off his arms. She balled it up and tossed it behind a large pot plant nearby.

'There, now you just look like a badly dressed guest. Let's go.'

But before they could take another step the sound of laughter floated down the hallway, behind them.

They could not be seen together like this! He grabbed her hand and was momentarily stilled by the firmness of her grip, the easy fit of her hand in his and the sensations distractingly skittering up his arm. A laugh down the corridor brought him back to the present and he pulled Isabella away from the voices. This part of the hotel was no less of a maze than the rest but around two more corners they saw a sign for a fire exit. He looked at her. 'Out here?'

'It's as good a door as any.'

He pushed on the heavy door it and it gave.

Unfortunately at the same time his ears began to sting with the sound of a large, urgent alarm.

'Ahh, there's a fire!' she said.

At least that was what he thought she said over the noise. No.

There wasn't a fire. Just an alarm. One he had just set off.

'Damn.'

He pulled the door closed quickly but the noise continued.

'What are you doing?' she asked.

'I set off the alarm.'

'Yes, so now we really have to go.'

He pushed the door all the way open and seconds later they were out into the fresh night air. The problem was that within moments other people were emerging out into the street as well. They had exited onto a side street that was busier than the laneway where he'd left his bike, which wasn't ideal, but, even worse, they couldn't get back to his bike without passing all the people that were now streaming out of another nearby door.

They looked at one another. Without speaking, they both inclined their heads towards another laneway, nodded and then walked as quickly as they could away from the Ashton, Sir Liam, Rowan's clothes and his Vespa.

They walked in since down the deserted passageway. Next to him he felt Isabella trembling. Was she frightened, crying? He wanted to turn and check on her but it was more important that they got well out of the way of the other people.

When he was satisfied they were at least two blocks away and the crowds had thinned, he ducked into a doorway and pulled her in with him. She was trembling.

With laughter.

'Oh, my God. You set the alarm off. Each time I think this night can't get worse, it does.'

Tears streamed down her face and she was trying hard not to throw her head back and laugh as loudly as she could.

'It's not funny. It's stressful.'

Not to mention the stress of the fact that I kissed you back there. That I'm still holding your hand in mine.

Rowan untangled his fingers from hers and let her hand drop.

'It's funny because it's awful. I can still hear that alarm. We've ruined that party.'

'Please tell me you spoke to him?'

'I did. Thanks to you and your tray-dropping trick.'

'It wasn't a trick, it was an accident. What did he say?'

'He agreed not to publish the photos.'

'Great!' Rowan wrapped his arms around her waist, picked her up and twirled her around.

'Put me down.' She slapped his arm. 'It's not that simple.'

'I guess it was too much to hope for.'

'But it's okay. He won't publish the photos if we agree to an interview with the paper.'

'You?'

'Both of us.'

'Oh.'

'Together. And we have to let his editor know by seven a.m. I think we should do it. We can choose what we say, and we'll have much more control over this whole situation. And then no one will find out about the cupboard. Or Twilight.'

Rowan shook his head. 'They'll ask all about my family.'

'And it's your chance to set the record straight. Better that you answer the questions than that they go through your parents' rubbish.'

She had a point, but his gut still said no. Doing an interview together would prompt questions about their relationship. How and why it ended. How he *felt* about it. It would be a lose-lose situation. He couldn't refuse to answer the questions, but how could he answer every question with absolute truth? Do you miss her? Do you still have feelings for her? Why did you really break up with her? No. A photo would be preferable. It wasn't even that bad. So what if they were together? In a small space? Nothing had happened.

'No. The photo isn't great, but it's far better than a tell-all interview!'

'We don't actually tell them everything. We decide how we answer the questions. The interview is a far better option.'

'No, letting the photo out is the best thing to do.'

For you.

For Isabella it would not be. It would upset her parents, embarrass her family.

'We should go somewhere and talk properly.'

'I agree, but where?'

They turned back to the Ashton but knew the streets around it would still be teeming with the people who had had to evacuate the party. It was too risky to go back for his bike.

'We walk somewhere.'

'Where? We can't go to my hotel. If you come in with me, Francesca could find out.'

'No, but we can go to mine.'

'You're staying in a hotel?'

'Yes. I sold my town house.'

'What? But you loved it.'

He had loved it. He could have afforded to keep it when he'd relocated to the States but he'd preferred to let it go. As he had with so many things that reminded him of Isabella.

It was simply easier that way.

'I'm staying at a hotel,' he repeated, avoiding answering her question.

'Near here?' she said hopefully.

'It's a walk.'

'Does that mean a long one or a short one?'

He looked down at her feet. He could manage but stilettos were not designed for a cross-city hike.

'I think it's too risky to get a cab,' he said.

'I don't think we could even if we wanted to.'

The street where they were was quiet. If they went towards the main streets and the traffic they would run into the crowds.

'I can manage. Just come over here for a moment.' She opened her small bag and pulled out something. He watched, amazed, as she unfolded a pair of what looked like ballet slippers.

'What?'

'Spare shoes. For just this sort of thing.' She handed him her bag and the spare shoes and he watched while she braced herself against a nearby wall and tugged off her stilettos.

'You can walk in these?'

'I mean, I probably wouldn't do the Camino de Santiago trail in them, but they'll do for a walk across London.' When she was done changing her shoes she gave a little bounce and took back her bag and high heels, which she hooked under a finger. 'Let's go.'

'You always have those?'

'Not always, but Francesca broke a heel once so we've tried to carry some ever since. Just in case. She has the hairbrush.'

'Pardon?'

'She has the hairbrush in her bag. And the tampons. We each have our own lipstick.'

'I don't understand.'

'As long as we're together, we're covered. And we don't both need to carry heaps of stuff around.'

'You've always done this?' How did he not know?

'Pretty much. When you're always together, it's easier.'

Like a married couple, he thought, but fortunately stopped himself from saying it aloud.

Another reason why breaking off their engagement was a good thing. He'd only get in the way of what she had with her sister.

'I hope she doesn't need the emergency shoes,' Isabella mused.

'Where do you think she is?'

'Hopefully having fun and not worried about me.'

'She will be though. Shouldn't you call her?'

'Not until I've fixed this. I can't even begin to explain to her where I am until I've sorted this. She'll be fine.'

He wasn't sure if Isabella was trying to convince him or herself.

'Lead on.'

'I'm back across the river. Maybe thirty minutes away?'

'Easy.'

'Oh, and here, I got us these,' he said, handing her one of the two face masks he'd taken from the Ashton.

'Great, at least something has gone right,' she said.

He shook his head. Nothing about this evening had gone right as far as he was concerned.

The back streets of Whitehall were much quieter than Mayfair and St James's, which had hundreds of revellers still pouring down the Mall and around St James's Park. She let Rowan lead the way as he was far more familiar with the area than she was and he knew the right streets to detour down.

'I'm sorry, I'm not taking the direct route.'

'I understand, we're avoiding people. I appreciate it, thank you.'

It wasn't until Westminster Abbey appeared in front of her that she realised where she was. It was all lit up with gold and white lights. Its gothic facade looked almost magical.

'Is it always this pretty? I don't remember it being like this,' she said.

'They have special lights for the coronation. It's quite something, isn't it?'

Less than twenty-four hours ago she'd walked through the great arch of the west door, Francesca by her side. The world's media looking on.

Francesca had stopped at the door, Isabella remembered, and she had looked up at all the stone figures carved around them. Isabella had followed suit, but couldn't see what Francesca was looking at.

'What must it feel like? To be one of the handful of men and women who have walked through those doors in the last thousand years, to be crowned? I wonder what the crown feels like when they place it on your head,' Francesca had said softly.

Isabella had noticed the line of guests stall behind them. This had not been the moment for Francesca's existential crisis, so Isabella had said, 'Heavy, I imagine,' and tugged her sister gently down the main aisle of the abbey, which had been buzzing with the voices of several thousand people.

She'd forgotten that moment, distracted by all the people and the spectacle of the coronation. But she remembered it now. She'd been focusing on what her sister's ascension would mean for her and her life, but hadn't let herself wonder what Francesca could be going through with their father's ill health hanging over them.

'I need to call Francesca.'

'Good idea.'

Isabella plonked herself down on a nearby bench. She put down her shoes, took out her phone and turned it on. There were several missed calls and at least a dozen messages from Francesca, each getting more frantic than the last.

Where are you?

Seriously?

I'm not your mother but I need to know you're okay.

Call me!!!

Isabella groaned. It was too much to hope that Francesca wouldn't be worried about her and would just go on enjoying her night. This was even one more mistake to add to the increasingly long list she was compiling this evening. She had only wanted to fix this mess before she called Francesca, she should have got in touch much earlier. Shouldn't have been so distracted by Rowan. And hugging him on the Vespa. Or watching him get changed.

She dialled Francesca, but she didn't pick up.

When the voicemail kicked in Isabella said, 'I'm so sorry, so so sorry. But I'm okay. I'll be back soon.'

Back soon? Really, Isabella, it's nearly midnight and you're on your way to Rowan's hotel room!

Yes.

Back soon.

They'd have something to eat and drink, she'd convince him to do the interview and then she'd call a car to come and get her.

Back to her hotel in plenty of time for her midday flight.

'Was it amazing? The coronation?' Rowan asked.

Even though it was only earlier that day, it felt like weeks ago. 'Yes, but it was also tiring. Don't laugh. You have to sit properly for six hours in case a camera pans over you.'

And they were always on the lookout for that sort of thing. An eye roll, a scratch of your nose or a badly timed laugh. Anything to find fault in. Any reason to mention that it was a good thing she was the spare princess.

'Let's get going, then.' He held out a hand to help her up and she looked at it. How she wanted to take it and hold it and pull herself into him for one big hug. Just an embrace of comfort, nothing more. Her emotions had been through the wringer over the past few hours.

But if she let herself take a comforting hug, she'd want more. It would be a very slippery slope that she would be powerless to stop herself sliding down. She stood and nodded.

You can do this on your own.

'It would probably be quicker to go across Westminster Bridge but that can be quite busy. Especially with all the tourists along the South Bank. I suggest we go along the Embankment and across Waterloo.'

She followed him until they reached the Thames and the city opened up in front of them. Isabella let herself exhale. It was getting close to midnight, but the lights of the city had been left on and the skyline glowed with many colours.

Even if they were coming the long way, it was something to walk along the Thames at night. The London Eye was to their right and also appeared to be lit up especially for the coronation. They soon approached the bend in the river and the rest of the skyline revealed itself to them.

Isabella walked to the ledge overlooking the river and leant on it, resting her elbows on the stone and looking around. From this vantage point you could see upstream to Westminster Bridge. Downstream were the other bridges and the shiny new buildings on the South Bank.

Only when she stopped did she realise they had set off in such a hurry she hadn't picked up her shoes.

'Damn. I left my shoes behind at the abbey.'

'Oh, no. You don't want to go back, do you?'

'No way. Your clothes, my shoes. I hope someone with the right size foot finds them and likes them.'

He laughed.

The shoes were lovely, but replaceable. Their reputations were not.

They still hadn't talked properly about Sir Liam's offer, and she sensed they were not going to agree.

'No one can hear us now. What exactly did he say?' Rowan asked.

'He wants something in return. Which we should have guessed.'

It had been a brief exchange, and she hadn't got anything in writing, but what choice did she have? She hardly had the best negotiating position.

'I think an interview is preferable. We have more control, we don't need to answer questions we don't want to. And most important of all, no one will know that Francesca and I left the Duke's party or that you are in London for Will's wedding.'

'I've thought that through. Either way I'm going to leave London as soon as I can. It's too risky to go to the wedding.'

'Rowan, no. That's not right either. They want you there.'

'No, the only important people at that wedding are Will and Lucy. I've caused them both enough grief; I'm not going to ruin their big day as well. That wouldn't be fair.'

When the photos from Rowan's stag night had been published, Will had been one of the most affected. Social media had been splashed with photos of Will standing very close to two scantily clad women, everyone looking intoxicated.

Nothing had happened, but it had looked bad and Lucy had been understandably very upset. Isabella didn't know all the details as she'd been weathering her own personal crisis at the time, but she understood that for a few days it had seemed as though Will and Lucy's relationship might not survive.

It had though, and hopefully they were stronger for it, but what they had gone through had hurt them. And it wasn't their fault.

But it wasn't Rowan's either.

'You can't stop living your life because of an inconvenience.'

He rounded on her. 'It's more than an inconvenience—it's harassment. I can handle it, but those around me shouldn't have to.'

It took all of Isabella's restraint not to say, 'Easy for you to say. I don't get a choice.'

As usual, she swallowed her true feelings down and instead she said as calmly as she could, 'But you're not handling it.'

'What?'

'Running away isn't handling it.'

'Yes, it is. I'm *managing* it. I'm saving my family and friends from it.'

'Well, that's all very well and good for you, but what about the rest of us, the ones who can't run away? If you're so great at handling it, what are your tips for me?'

She stared at him, slightly exhilarated by her outburst. It was as if something had been unlocked, a room full of fury she hadn't known existed.

'Isabella, I didn't mean…'

'No, you didn't mean anything because you didn't think. You did what was best for you, and didn't worry about anyone else.'

'That's not fair. I was thinking of my family, my friends.

And yes, I chose them over you. But not because I wanted to. I never wanted to have to make such a decision.'

Yet he had. And with an ease and surgical swiftness that he couldn't have done if he'd really cared for her.

'Your concern about your family sounds noble, but, honestly, I wonder if it's just an excuse.'

'What are you talking about?'

'Your family are really the reason you left?' she asked, knowing the real reason he'd left was because he didn't love her. Because if he had he would have stayed.

Rowan scoffed and stepped back. 'I didn't use them as an excuse. You saw what happened to them.'

She nodded. She knew what Rowan's family had gone through, but she also knew what sort of intrusions she'd had to endure over the years. She put up with them, others did as well. Why couldn't Rowan?

Because he doesn't love you enough.

These were the fears that usually taunted her in the middle of the night and they were even doing so in London with Rowan standing next to her.

Besides, this wasn't the argument they were meant to be having. There was no way of fixing her broken heart, but they could deal with the problem at hand.

Compartmentalise.

She swallowed down the emotion that was ready to flow over and said, 'I think we do the interview.'

'I think we let the photos be published.'

'I'm hungry.'

'What has that got to do with anything?'

'Nothing, I suppose. Only that maybe it will be easier to decide if we have something to eat. If we can sit somewhere in private.'

She looked around again. London was big. She knew this,

logically, but while she could walk across the main city of Monterossa in an hour, London was something else entirely.

'Whose idea was it to go to your hotel?'

'Um, yours?'

'Whose idea was it to walk?'

'Yours again?'

'Yeah, well. I was wrong.'

So wrong. But she hadn't stopped making the wrong decisions all night. This should hardly be a surprise.

A boat with music and a loud party chugged slowly past them.

Tonight was meant to be fun. A celebration! A mood of optimism was in the air in a way it hadn't been for years. But her feet hurt and her stomach growled.

She wondered what Francesca was doing. Hopefully she was already in bed.

Isabella groaned.

No. Francesca wouldn't be asleep. She'd be worried.

Even more reason to get on with this and decide about what to do next.

CHAPTER SEVEN

It was now well after midnight, but with the extended opening hours of the bars and pubs, people still wandered the streets. The route he'd navigated for them hadn't been too crowded and he felt as though the face masks had provided some cover, but he was still relieved to see his hotel come into view. Thankfully the area surrounding the steel and glass reception area was mostly deserted. The sight of him dressed as a waiter from the Aston stumbling into the hotel at one a.m. with a princess was not one they wanted anyone to see.

'Here?'

He was staying in an exclusive boutique hotel, in a high rise overlooking the city. So discreet no one would know at a glance what this unassuming lobby led to. Thankfully, the hotel was so exclusive and used to high-profile guests with odd whims that they didn't even blink when he entered in his waiter's uniform, but simply said, 'Mr James.'

'You're not staying. I've just come to get changed and then we can figure out what we're going to do and get you back to your hotel,' he said to Isabella.

'Of course,' she replied, the same strain he was feeling evident in her tone.

Neither of them wanted her to go back to her hotel tonight, even though they both knew she had to.

He steered her to the elevators, grateful he'd kept his phone and all his cards on him when he'd changed into the uniform at the Ashton. He swiped his card and the elevator took them to the fiftieth floor.

'My ears just popped. Did yours?' she said with a smile.

He'd missed her so much. It was easy to forget the happiness and delight she found in simple things when she wasn't around, but now she was here? Her happiness was infectious.

As they entered his room she gasped.

'Wow. Just wow. This beats a stuffy hundred-year-old place in Mayfair any day. Are we higher than the London Eye?'

You should see it in the daytime, he wanted to say, but didn't.

Because then he really wouldn't get her out of here and back to her hotel by morning.

The view from his room was the best in the hotel, northwest over the city. They could see the London Eye, the Houses of Parliament, the river. Everything. Even the dome of St Paul's could be made out from the bedroom window. Though he didn't tell her that, in case she went to look.

Food. Discussion. Send her home. That would be all.

His suite had several rooms, including a large living space with several comfortable sofas, all arranged to take advantage of the view. There was a kitchen and dining room too, along with a large bedroom and more bathrooms than either of them could use.

Isabella flopped onto one of the sofas and tugged off her shoes, which, while better than the stilettos, seemed flimsy.

She groaned with pleasure as she rubbed her feet. 'Oh, that feels amazing,' she said.

He had to turn away and compose himself at the sound of her satisfaction.

'I'm absolutely famished,' she said, looking up at him with pleading eyes.

He was hungry as well, the snack he'd had before going out now just a distant memory. 'Of course. What do you want?'

He dialled down to Room Service for cheeseburgers and fries for both of them. Chocolate cake for dessert and a bottle of red. She raised an eyebrow when he specified the Californian pinot, but said nothing further.

Isabella shuffled her body around in her dress, the dress, or more likely her undergarments evidently giving her grief. 'My bra is killing me. I wish I could get changed.'

If Isabella was relaxed and comfortable, she'd be more likely to think rationally about the photos. They hadn't decided what they were going to do about Sir Liam's offer. They'd reached an impasse and he found he was wound tighter than Isabella's underwear.

'The concierge can probably get you some other clothes if you don't want to go home in your dress.'

'Now?'

'They're pretty good.'

'Do you know this from the last time you brought a woman up here?'

He coughed. 'No, I... I once spilt coffee on a shirt I needed for a meeting and they got a new one for me at seven a.m.'

'Oh.'

The question hung out there, though, unasked. Unanswered.

Have you been with anyone since me?

The answer was short and simple: no one.

He didn't want her to ask the question, not because he didn't want to answer it but because he didn't want to feel compelled to ask the complementary question back. Had she found someone else? He didn't want to hear the answer.

He wanted her to be happy, he needed her to move on, yet the answer would break him, nonetheless.

He handed her the phone. 'A man named Dennis is looking after me tonight. Dial one and ask him for a change of clothes. You'll be more comfortable. Even have a bath if you want.'

'What?'

A warm bath had always been Isabella's stress relief of choice, and he'd suggested it without thinking.

'You always used to, that is. When you were stressed. I'm not sure if you still do.'

Why hadn't he just offered her a stiff drink, as he was planning on having? The idea that Isabella might be naked, wet and slippery two rooms away was psychological torture. Not to mention dangerous.

'I might just get changed, if that's okay.'

'Good idea,' Rowan said.

Yes, a far better idea than suggesting she have a bath.

Rowan looked down at himself and realised he was still wearing the wait-staff outfit from the Ashton. He went into the bedroom and took it off. It felt good to get out of it finally and slip on some of his own clothes. A pair of old, soft jeans and a black T-shirt.

While he waited for Isabella and the food he scanned social media for mentions of them. There were several photos of her and Francesca at the coronation. They both looked beautiful, Francesca in a white dress and coat, but it was the photos of Isabella in her sky-blue dress that made his heart clench. The general consensus was that they were two of the best-dressed guests. Apart from that, there were no other mentions.

Thank goodness.

How could she think he was using his family as an excuse? *Why* would she think that? Of course protecting his family was his main concern, that was why he was currently in this hotel room, hidden away from the world.

And now only one room away from Isabella who was probably taking her clothes off at this very moment...

He had to get her home as soon as possible.

The wine was delivered and he poured them both glasses, starting on his own. Shortly afterwards, the bathroom door opened, and Isabella emerged, wrapped in a giant white bathrobe. She'd washed her face and pulled her hair back into a loose bun.

Unintentionally or not, she looked as though she was settling in.

'Ah,' he managed. 'The change of clothes isn't here yet.'

'No problem, this is just fine.'

He passed her a glass of wine but didn't make eye contact.

This was all just a little too cosy for comfort. His body was starting to relax with the wine. It was nearly two a.m. and nothing good ever happened after two a.m. Everyone knew that.

She found a spot on the sofa, tucked her ankles up under her bottom and sipped her wine. 'This is just what I needed. Thanks.'

Even as he remembered all the reasons why their breakup had been the right decision, the steady, persistent thrum in his chest was still thumping to the tune of *You idiot...you made a mistake*.

No. Breaking up had been exactly the right thing to do. Didn't tonight prove that? If they had stayed together their life would have been spent dodging paparazzi and managing the media. That wasn't what he wanted.

Her words from earlier popped back into his thoughts.

'That's all very well and good for you, but what about the rest of us, the ones who can't run away? If you're so great at handling it, what are your tips for me?'

It was different for her. The machinery of the palace protected her. He seemed to be a lightning rod for attention and she was better off without him. This wasn't the time to reminisce, or even look backwards, they had to figure out what they were going to do next.

He joined her on the sofa. 'What did you specifically say to Sir Liam?'

'Ah, you know.' She waved her hand around in the air.

'No, I don't, that's why I'm asking.'

She gazed out of the window to the horizon and the edge of the city. 'You can see the planes taking off from Heathrow from up here.'

'And I can see procrastination.'

'I asked him if he could see his way clear to not publishing the photos.'

'You just came right out and said that?'

'Not exactly. I think I asked him if he'd ever had his heart broken.'

'Oh.' The guilt hit him afresh.

'And I asked how he'd feel if the world was publishing stories about him being left at the altar when he was struggling to even get out of bed.'

'Isabella, is that true?'

She gave her head a quick shake. 'I figured the dumped princess card was the best one to play so I had to tell him that, didn't I?'

Rowan's chest constricted.

'Could you really not get out of bed?' His voice cracked on the words. He hated that he'd hurt her. He should never have spoken to her in the bar in Geneva. Never got them both into this mess.

'Well, I wasn't back doing official engagements the next day.'

'But not getting out of bed?'

'I don't remember, honestly. It's probably an exaggeration. I'm fine.'

But was she? Or was she holding something back? No, that couldn't be. She'd always been honest with him and she had no reason not to be now.

But she was different, as he'd noticed earlier in the night. More cautious, not as confident. Whereas a year ago her smiles were instantaneous, now they wavered.

You did this.

'I'm sorry.'

'I know you are. Please stop saying that. I'm fine.'

'No, I'm sorry for ever going over to speak to you in Geneva.'

'Don't say that either.'

'Why not? It's true. You'd have been far better off if I'd stayed away. You'd probably be engaged to a duke, or a Hollywood actor. Someone who's far more comfortable with a public life than I am.'

That was the problem all along; Rowan might have made his fortune, he might have a public profile, but at heart he was still just a kid who'd dropped out of school, who couldn't even balance a tray of glasses. Who didn't know what to do at a duke's ball. Or how to cope with media attention.

'I don't regret knowing you and I never have. I'm sorry you're now stuck doing an interview with me.'

He sat, dumbstruck, ignoring the fact that she was clearly set on them doing the interview.

He had hurt her. Despite all her assurances to the contrary, she'd told Sir Liam that she hadn't been able to get out of bed, that she'd been heartbroken.

From the moment he'd come to her to end the relationship, even to earlier in the evening, she'd insisted she understood and that she was fine. But then, when they'd been looking over the Thames, she'd challenged him. Told him he was using his loyalty to his family as an excuse.

Ultimately, though, it didn't matter if she was over him

or not, because not only was he not good enough to marry someone like Isabella, he'd also already been the architect of the biggest royal scandal in recent Monterossan memory—a stag night gone wrong and a cancelled wedding. There was no coming back from something like that, no matter who he was.

A knock at the door saved him. Saved *both* of them. Their food had arrived, not just allowing a very needed change of subject but also a well-needed blood-sugar hit. They ate their burgers in silence except for Isabella's gentle moans at the taste of the burger. They were mopping the sauce from their plates with the fries when she said, 'Oh, my goodness, I think that was one of the best burgers I've had in my life.' She took a large sip of wine and fell back in her chair.

He had to agree. Apart from being extremely satisfying, it had successfully shifted the mood between them. But they still needed a solution to their problem.

'Cake?' she asked, spying the desserts still on the tray. Two large pieces of next-level-looking chocolate cake. The thick slices appeared to be moist, covered in a glistening icing, the plates decorated with other chocolates, and a custard cream sat to one side. He could tell before he even tasted a bite that it would be one of the best slices of cake he'd ever tried.

'Not until we decide what to do.'

'You're holding the cake ransom?'

'No, I think I'm holding us ransom. No cake until we are agreed.'

'You know chocolate cake is my favourite food in the world.'

'I do. That's why I ordered it.'

He met her gaze and held it. It was a mistake because she did as well, rising to the challenge. Calling his bluff.

'To hold it over me?' she asked.

'Honestly, I thought I'd convince you just to agree to let

the photos go out. I didn't plan on dragging this innocent cake into our negotiations. It's not to blame.'

She gave him a wry smile. 'You thought you'd be able to convince me to let the photos be published?'

'Yes, but not because I think I'm a master negotiator. I just thought you'd be able to see that a photo or two of us together is far preferable to a tell-all interview.'

If the interview had been with him alone, or even them separately, he might have considered it. But together? With him having to watch her give her answers and repeat the lie that she was fine. That she understood why he left. With him sitting there, wondering how much was the truth and how much was the lie.

You want her to be okay, don't you?

The belief that Isabella was not crushed when he ended their relationship had comforted him over the past year. It had been the one thing stopping him getting on a plane and flying across the Atlantic to beg her forgiveness. He had convinced himself that she also knew he wouldn't have made a very good husband for her. But if he'd been wrong, if she'd been hiding her hurt for all this time, then where did that leave them?

Exactly where they were one year ago. The reasons might have changed, but the facts remained: she deserved better than him.

He couldn't bear the thought of either of them being questioned closely on the end of their relationship. The way things stood between them now was for the best; with her in Monterossa getting happily along with her life, and with him in New York, keeping a low profile. It was best for everyone.

'For starters, they'll plan their questions, they'll ask the most private, most probing things possible,' he said.

'And we will have prepared answers.'

He sighed.

'They'll twist our words, misrepresent them.'

'That's always a possibility, but when you don't say anything at all, they just make up things to fill the void,' she said.

'All they can claim is that the pictures show two single people who used to be engaged talking to one another. It's hardly scandalous.'

'Neither of us want anyone to know we were there, and you can't go back to the States and skip your brother's wedding! If we do the interview, you can still go.'

But Rowan had already resigned himself to the fact that he would miss his brother's wedding. Coming back to London had been a mistake. One he wouldn't make again. They were all better off—his mother, father, brother and especially Isabella—if he stayed away.

'That's not going to be possible.'

'Oh, Rowan, don't be like that! Your family want you there.'

'So they can read defamatory stories about themselves the next day?'

'It won't be like that.'

He looked at her and let himself study her properly for the first time since she'd come out of the bathroom. She was sitting back in the dining chair, twirling the stem of her glass. Her brown hair that had been so perfectly groomed into shiny waves early in the night was now tied back loosely. Her face was clear of make-up, revealing the real Isabella behind the perfect princess mask.

His Isabella. Because this was how he remembered her when he let himself think of her. Dewy, gorgeous. Real.

He looked away quickly when he realised her robe was falling undone, giving him a glimpse of too much reality.

The sooner they made a decision, ate the cake and got her home, the better.

'How can you still trust them to be half decent?' he asked.

'The press? The public?'

'Yes, after all that's happened?'

She shrugged. 'I guess I think very few people are truly bad. Most people are just doing the best they can.'

He turned away. She always had been able to see the best in people, but, like the privilege of her birth, it was something he'd never be able to share with her.

And where did it leave them? Precisely nowhere and disagreeing on what they should do next.

She reached for the cake.

'Woah, woah. What are you doing?'

'Eating the cake.'

'So we're letting the photo out?'

'No.'

'Then we can't have the cake.'

'I thought you were joking.'

'I never joke about chocolate cake,' he said.

She sat and stared at the cake.

He stared at her.

'Tonight has been an unmitigated disaster,' he said.

Isabella opened her mouth to agree but stopped. His comment felt harsh. Yes, things hadn't gone to plan, but was seeing her, spending time with her, an 'unmitigated disaster'?

According to Rowan, yes. According to Rowan, he couldn't get to the other side of world fast enough. To be away from her and done with her for ever.

He doesn't love you. He probably never did.

'It's been unexpected, unusual, but it's also been an adventure.' She tried to hide the hurt from her voice.

Has it been that horrible to see me?

It had been stressful, at times frighteningly so, but there had been moments. Like in the storeroom at the Ashton. Watching Rowan get changed and then...

He kissed you.

He had kissed *her*. Not the other way around. Urgent, but tender. Her pulse spiked at the memory.

Why had he kissed her if he didn't care for her? None of it made any sense.

'Some of it was fun,' she continued.

'Oh, come on. We were trapped in small rooms. We set off a fire alarm. We got caught in several compromising situations.'

'Yeah, those were the most fun,' she muttered, her face warming, knowing he probably wouldn't appreciate the joke.

She looked up and saw him twisting his mouth. Trying not to smile.

Ah.

He *had* enjoyed the kiss.

A sensuous, passionate kiss that had sucked the air from her body and left her still reeling.

'It was stressful and awkward and all those things. But it was just what I wanted tonight to be.'

'You wanted to get papped and walk halfway across London?'

'No. I wanted to have an adventure. Yes, I wanted to have it with Francesca, but I wanted to do something out of the ordinary, something unplanned.'

'This was definitely unplanned.'

'I got to ride on a Vespa. I walked along the Thames at night. I danced with Sir Liam Goldsworthy.'

'That was a highlight?'

'Yes. Not because he's a good dancer but because I was brave.'

'Come on, you speak to heaps of people every day. You were trained to speak to strangers.'

'Yes, I was trained to make polite small talk. Tonight I had to negotiate. I had to go off script and ask for something.'

'And that's unusual?'

'You know it is. When we go to events, they're planned to the last detail. People plan what they're going to say to us, and we know what we have to say back. This was...not like that.'

'So a career as a negotiator awaits you?' He grinned, but he'd touched on something sensitive.

She pulled the robe tighter. 'No, not that. But something else.'

'What do you mean?'

'Things are changing. I need to figure out what I'm going to do with my life.'

'What are you talking about?'

Would he understand that when Francesca's role changed hers had to as well? No one said so, and there were no rules about this sort of thing, but it was just something she felt. She couldn't stay still and keep doing what she was doing while her sister took on an even bigger role.

'My father isn't well.'

'I know. Do you want to call him? Check on him?'

'From your hotel room? No, thanks, I don't want him to have a relapse. No, I mean...'

She took a sip of her wine, but it only contained the last drop. Rowan wordlessly filled her glass and his and waited for her to speak.

'I overheard my parents speaking a few weeks ago. They were alluding to something they didn't want to speak to either me or Frannie about. Mum said he shouldn't decide anything until he'd spoken to Francesca. And then said they shouldn't mention anything to me at all.'

'What do you think they were talking about?'

'Abdication, of course.'

'Why?' He pulled his 'you must be mistaken' face.

'Because that's the one thing that affects her and not me. You know how Francesca and I do everything together, how we always have. We went to school together, we work together. We're the twin princesses. But when she's queen...'

'I thought you didn't want to be queen.'

'I don't. That isn't what this is about. But when she's queen, I'll lose her.'

'You—'

She held up her hand. 'I know I won't lose my sister. But I will no longer be a twin princess. I can't be a twin princess on my own.'

'You're going to have to pretend I don't know what you're saying.'

'I know I'll still have a job, I'll still be Princess of Monterossa, but she'll have an entirely different role. She'll sign all the papers. She'll sit at the head of every table. She'll open parliament every year. She will be the one getting crowned.'

'Ah. Is that what you were thinking when we stood outside the abbey?'

Isabella nodded. Then. All day. And most of the time when she hadn't been distracted on this escapade with Rowan.

'We've always done everything together and now everything is about to change. And I...' She stumbled over her words. 'I feel like I'm being left behind.'

There it was. Raw and true. Her deepest fears. She was, after all, the second princess, the spare. It was probably, subconsciously, why she'd pressured Rowan into marriage as well. So she wouldn't be left behind.

'You don't know that's what they were talking about. It could have been anything.'

'Sure, you guess what they were saying. You need to talk to Francesca about what we will have for dinner. But don't talk to Isabella. You need to talk to Frannie about our summer holiday, but there's no need to talk to Isabella.'

'You need to speak to Francesca about her taste in men. But there's no need to talk to Isabella.'

She let her lips twitch into a grin. 'Okay, point taken. But you know how sometimes you just *know* something? And not because you're being paranoid, but because you just *know*.'

He nodded.

She'd *known* he was going to tell her their relationship was over as soon as he'd walked into her room that day.

She'd *known* that something was wrong when her mother had sat both her and Francesca down to tell them about their father.

'Dad has been really sick.'

'I know, but you said he's on the mend.'

'Yes, but he's weaker and this has shaken them both. The cancer spread to his lymph nodes. There's no guarantee of recovery, particularly as he's had so many complications. He might live another five years, even another ten.'

'None of us know how long we have left.'

'No. But my parents have more reason to doubt than others. I think they may want to make the most of the time he has left. And if it were up to me, honestly, I think he should abdicate. I think he should relax. Not work so hard. I want him to stay with us for as long as possible.'

Her eyes filled at the realisation. Something she hadn't been able to articulate before this point. She actually *wanted* her father to abdicate. She wanted him to look after his health!

Even if that meant Francesca would become Queen.

Even if it meant her own life would change.

'I don't know what this means for me. Where it leaves me. I don't know what my job is anymore.'

She wasn't prepared for the emotion that rose up in her as she said those words aloud for the first time. Seeing her wipe her eyes, Rowan moved to the chair next to her. He picked up her hands and squeezed them.

'Hey, it is all going to be all right.'

She sniffed, tried to fight back the tears, but then Rowan was next to her, comforting her. And when he put his arm around her shoulder what was she supposed to do but snuggle in and let the tears fall? He was warm and smelt of clean clothes and happy memories.

Her father would be okay, but Francesca would be queen. And she would be...alone.

A solitary princess, a single woman.

And that would be okay, because everyone around her would be happy. Her sister would be happy, her parents would be happy. Rowan would be happy because he was protecting the people he loved.

Yes, she would be alone, and that would be okay because that was how it was all meant to be. She took some deep steadying breaths with her eyes closed. She was finding her centre, reaching contentment.

She was brave. And it would all be okay.

She opened her eyes but two amber eyes, brimming with concern and mere inches away, looked back at her.

He held her shoulders and what choice did she have but to keep looking at him? To hold his gaze, to give in to the way her body swung towards him?

After everything they'd done tonight this felt the riskiest. But also the most difficult to stop. It wasn't even as if this would be the first kiss they'd shared this evening, but the second. If you were counting. Which she was.

They weren't getting back together—she was silly but not *that* silly—but he was here, and she was here, and it would be a shame not to enjoy the moment. Life was precious and you only lived once. You had to enjoy every moment you were given, suck every drop of joy you could out of it. Tonight, she wanted to be touched. She wanted to feel alive. So she closed her eyes. She wasn't sure who moved the last inch, him or her, but once their lips were touching it didn't matter. Everything stilled.

She wasn't sure who moved their lips first, but once his were slipping against hers her mind went blank. She wasn't sure who opened their mouth first, but it also didn't matter once her tongue was sliding next to his, his fingers sliding through her hair, her fingers reaching for the fabric of his shirt and clutching it in her greedy fists.

Unlike the earlier kiss, this one was less of a surprise. She had time to take everything in, the things that were the same: his taste, the softness of his lips. The things that were different: his aftershave was new…and of course the beard. It was softer than she'd thought it would be, and it heightened all the sensations in her face and around her lips. But his mouth, his tongue felt the same. And most of all his hands were as they always had been, strong and sure and slipping up her neck, into her hair and sending her body and mind reeling.

Her robe fell further undone and she did nothing to stop it. His hand spread over her shoulder and his fingertips scorched her skin like a flame.

She'd missed this. All of this. Everything about it. She'd missed him…

The sweet sound he made when he kissed her, half whimper, half groan. She'd missed the feeling rising up in her belly now, tight, full, urgent. She moved closer to him, needing to feel his hard body against hers. Needing to act on the want building and whirling inside her.

Her robe fell easily undone like a poorly wrapped present. Realising her bare breasts were tumbling out of it, nipples erect and eager, Rowan jumped away from her, as though he'd been scalded.

'Oh, come on, you've seen them before,' she said, trying to hide the disappointment in her voice. She pulled the robe back around her. It was all too good to be true and she should have known that he would pull away eventually.

'That's the problem. I know exactly what I'm missing.'

That remark filled her with more warmth than his last kiss. He wanted her as much as she wanted him. It wasn't just one-sided. He looked pained, his gorgeous face creased with hesitation.

'You don't have to, you know. Miss it.'

'Izzy, seriously.'

'Seriously. In a few hours the world's going to think we made out in a cupboard. What harm can it do?'

'As compelling as that logic is, it isn't right.' He stood.

She jumped off the couch and went to him.

She wanted this memory. She wanted to remember their last time. Know that it was happening and commit every caress to memory.

'We can worry about the consequences tomorrow.'

'It already is tomorrow.' He raked a hand through already mussed hair. She stepped up to him and repeated his action, running her fingers through his hair, holding his face in her hands. How she adored his thick, soft hair. The colour of golden caramel. He didn't stop her, but put his arm around her waist.

'Well, the next day,' she said.

After they figured out what to do about the photo. After she'd gone back to Monterossa.

She stroked his face, explored his new beard. Studied it closely from all angles. She hadn't thought it would suit him, but it did. It made him look older, more distinguished. Stronger.

'I like it.' She ran a fingertip along his jawline.

'You need to get back,' he croaked.

'Everyone's going to think we did it anyway. So what's the harm?'

'The harm is that it was difficult enough to walk away from you the first time.'

Nothing could possibly be as difficult as that, she thought.

'It doesn't have to mean anything,' she said. 'It could just be rebound sex.'

'Isn't that usually with another person?'

Was it? She honestly didn't know. The only thing her body was screaming right now was that it had been a year since she'd been with anyone. And that had been the man she was standing with now, her nipples straining to be kissed by him, all sense of logic and sense forgotten when she'd walked through the hotel room door.

'I don't think that's a hard and fast rule.'

She had no idea what was what any more. But it didn't matter—the only thing that mattered was the sensation swirling through her. She was with Rowan. His arms were around her waist and his body was pressed against hers, warm, strong and everything. She was burning inside, desperate.

But sex was just sex, wasn't it? She wanted it and, judging by the way his body felt pressed against her, he did too. They didn't have to deny themselves.

Just rebound sex, but with her ex.

Everyone did it.

Didn't they?

Rowan's eyelids dropped, giving her a moment to study him without being watched. Everything about him was tight, his brow creased, his jaw clenched.

She slid her hand up the nape of his smooth neck and into his hair. Her fingertips almost sparked with the tension crackling over him.

'It doesn't mean anything,' she whispered.

'Isabella.' He said her name in a groan and his lips crashed back to hers. All hesitation gone, the last taste of doubt banished.

Her knees buckled and he caught her, but his mouth didn't leave hers, even as he lifted her up high enough for her to wrap her legs around his waist, even as he carried her effortlessly to the next room and the large bed. Her insides cried with delight and relief.

She fell backwards on the bed and he tumbled on top of her. Shifting her hips, he was now properly on top of her, his hand sliding down her side, over her thighs.

His fingers slid over the softest part of her, the sensitive, secret folds between her legs, and pleasure spread from that point through the rest of her. Her blood fizzed. Realising she could climax at any moment and not wanting to miss the main event, she rolled out from underneath him and turned her efforts to him.

She slid her hands up the back of his T-shirt, desperate to feel the muscles she'd glimpsed earlier that evening. She lifted the hem of his shirt and kissed his stomach, moving higher to his nipples. At some point she was aware that he'd slipped the shirt over his head, given her uninterrupted access to his glorious chest. As she flicked her tongue over his nipples she was vaguely aware that his jeans were going the way of the T-shirt.

'Protection?' she asked. 'I'm still on the pill but maybe we should use something.'

He scrambled around for his wallet and the condom it hopefully contained.

He rolled back to her, the foil packet in his shaking hands.

'Hurry, please.' Desperate, clutching at the last of her resolve, ready to break. 'It's been ages. I haven't...' she panted. 'Not since us.'

He groaned and she felt it vibrate through her, not helping her current status in the slightest. 'Me either.'

That was the cold water they both needed. He held the unopened packet in his still quivering hand.

'It's nearly been a year.'

'I wasn't keeping track.'

'I was. Every single day. There were three hundred and forty-seven of them.'

She opened her mouth from the shock of his confession. He hadn't been with anyone else. He did miss her, truly missed her, in the same way she had missed and longed for him. He stroked her cheek with his thumb, considering, contemplating his next move but somehow his thumb slipped into her mouth, still open with surprise. She caught it, wrapped her lips around it. She could have let it go, but when she saw his irises open she clenched it tighter between her lips, slid her tongue around it and, after a gentle suck, she released it.

His mouth quickly found hers again and any thought of protection evaporated. The last twelve months also evaporated like a dream she'd just woken up from. Rowan lay back on the bed and she slid her body over his. He shifted his weight, helped her on top of him and she was home.

The muscles between her legs clenched and contracted with each stroke as every cell in her body jumped to attention. Most of all, his arms held her and his lips whispered to her, even as he covered hers with soft kisses.

She was out of practice and had been ready to lose herself ever since his lips had first brushed hers in the storeroom, but it was still surprising when the wave hit her. He held her for each shock that came after and they fell together. And they kept falling.

CHAPTER EIGHT

ROWAN SAT IN an armchair angled towards one of the many floor-to-ceiling windows in the suite. The sun had long since come up, and he had watched the light in the sky change from black to blue to pink. Now he looked at the sun bounce in bright bursts off the glass of other buildings across the city.

In the next room he heard her stir.

He hadn't slept all night—there had been more chance of him running a marathon in record time. He clutched a mug of coffee, long since gone cold, waiting for Isabella to wake.

He wished he could say he couldn't believe he had slept with Isabella, but the truth was he'd known all along he'd be powerless to stop it from the moment he'd seen her in Twilight.

You could have stopped it. You could have stepped away.

And the earth could turn away from the sun. Not a chance.

It doesn't have to mean anything.

Those were her words. In the heat of the moment he'd taken them as agreement that this was a one-off thing. But this morning, in the bright light of day, would she still think so? Did he?

A startled 'Argh' could be heard from the other room. 'It's nearly eight!'

He steeled himself.

She swept into the room, pulling the robe closed even as

she did, not before he had a further glimpse of what he'd already seen too much of last night.

'We slept in!' she cried.

'You slept in. I was awake.'

'And you didn't make the call?'

He shook his head. 'No. I called him.'

She dropped into the nearest chair. 'You did? Rowan. Thank you.'

She said his name in a rush and he felt it through his skin. 'Why?'

'You convinced me it was the best thing to do.'

That was a white lie. Giving the interview was the brave thing to do. It meant doing something active, taking his destiny back into his hands as opposed to leaving it to the pundits on social media.

And if Isabella could be brave, then he could be too. Though the thought of actually giving the interview had his intestines in knots. Guilt was also a powerful motivator, but he didn't want to tell her that. Guilt about leaving her just before the wedding. Guilt about kissing her last night. Guilt about sleeping with her. Guilt he hadn't been stronger when it had really mattered.

'I did? Really?' Her brow creased and she rubbed her eyes, still heavy with sleep.

'It's what you wanted, isn't it?'

'I never wanted this. Any of this. For either of us.'

'I know.'

'You could have let it go. Pretended you missed the deadline.'

He made a face. 'I'd never lie to you. I'd never do that. No, I think—at least, I hope—you're right. We can have more control over the story this way. It's the sensible thing to do.'

The brave *thing*, he thought.

She stared at him, a goofy smile plastered on her face,

the sun streaming in on her, still warm from bed, a crease in the side of her face. She'd never looked more beautiful. A lump rose in his throat and he coughed. 'Well, there's some breakfast in the next room. And some coffee.'

'Great.' She didn't move. 'So are we doing the interview today?'

'No. They haven't decided who they'll assign it to and they'll need time to prepare, but they think later in the week. Probably Friday.'

'I can't stay here all week. I need to get back.'

'They suggested they come to Monterossa.'

'But... How would that work? That would mean you would have to come, too.'

The thought didn't exactly appeal to him, but the thought of attracting more attention in London wasn't great either.

'I have meetings in Paris this week for the launch of the app, so it would be reasonably easy to get to you. Of course, you'd have to clear it with your parents.'

She slumped back down in the chair. 'My parents. I'm going to have to tell them, aren't I?'

Despite last night's dash across London being about protecting her parents, there didn't seem a way around it.

'I'm sure it's far better that they hear something from you than from someone else. And far better that the public doesn't know.'

Isabella chewed her lip and he winced, surpassing the urge to go to her and kissing her worry away.

'I'll figure something out. But are *you* sure?'

Now you ask. 'Yes, I'm sure.'

Go back to Monterossa? To the scene of the crime, so to speak? There was nothing he wanted less. Apart from perhaps answering questions about his relationship with Isabella with one of Britain's most notorious tabloids.

Had he been a serial killer in a previous life? How else

could he account for the luck he'd had in the past twelve hours?

Isabella leant forward. The robe she was wearing gaped open and he looked out of the window.

Definitely a serial killer.

'Thank you. Truly. Thank you. This will be fine, I promise.'

He wanted to believe her. He wished he could. But it felt as though he'd just...

'And about last night...'

His stomach dropped. 'Last night was crazy, and stressful, and fun, but we both know it was a one-off.'

Because it's clear as anything that I've blown all my chances with you.

His heart was hammering as he waited for her response.

She smiled broadly and jumped up. 'Good, I'm glad we agree.'

He watched her walk into the dining room and pour herself a cup of coffee.

It doesn't have to mean anything.

But what if it had?

Isabella dressed in the pair of blue jeans, white T-shirt and blazer she found in the bathroom. They must have been dropped off while she'd been sleeping. She couldn't believe she'd slept in and missed the deadline.

Of course you slept. Rowan just gave you the best orgasm you've had in over a year. You haven't felt so relaxed or satisfied in months. With her body as soft as jelly, it was a miracle she'd woken before midday.

Rowan hadn't been kidding; the butler could get anything. The clothes were exactly her size. There was also a pair of white trainers. When she slipped them on she thought of her poor, beautiful red shoes, left behind somewhere near Westminster Abbey. She called her security detail and requested a car to pick her up.

She had no idea what she was going to say to Francesca, but she'd worry about that when she saw her. She sent her sister a short message.

Good morning, I'm on my way back now.

Rowan was looking at his phone when she came out of the bedroom. Whether it was because he was attending to some work or avoiding her, she wasn't sure.

'Thank you for these,' she said, gesturing to her outfit.

He looked up. 'No problem.'

'And thank you, also, for agreeing to do the interview.' It wasn't what he wanted, but she hoped he'd realise it was the best thing to do.

She desperately hoped it *would* turn out to be the best thing to do.

Last night it had seemed like the best course of action, but this morning, with the reality of having to sit down with Rowan to answer questions, the thought of Rowan coming to Monterossa…all of it…small doubts were starting to creep in.

'No need to thank me.'

'There is. I know it isn't what you wanted.'

'It's the least I can do.' He spoke to the ground.

'Hang on, did you agree to the interview out of guilt or do you really think it's the right thing to do?'

'Can it be both?'

She sighed. 'You don't have to feel guilty. I know it was a lot. Being with me.'

If she repeated this line enough she might actually believe it. At the very least, everyone else would believe it and that was the most important thing. She was a princess, she had to avoid gossip and scandal of any kind. She wasn't heartbroken. She wasn't destroyed. She was *fine*.

Rowan put down his phone and walked over to her. He placed his hands on her upper arms and for one glorious moment she thought he was going to pull her into an embrace. Instead, he looked into her eyes sternly and she felt she was about to hear a lecture.

'It wasn't too much. I was just not enough.'

'Rowan. Don't say that.'

'It's true. You need to find someone who isn't such an obvious target for attention.'

'What are you talking about?'

'Me. My background. My family.'

'There's nothing wrong with your family! The press just go for any angle they can find. It isn't your fault.'

He hung his head. 'Of course it's my fault. I don't have the first clue how to stay out of the papers—as last night's adventure proved.'

She shook her head. 'None of that is because of anything you did.'

'Exactly, it's about what I didn't do. What I *can't* do.'

'Rowan, you can do anything. You're amazing.'

He sighed. 'No, I can't.'

I can't marry you, was what he was saying. And in the end did his reasons matter?

They had come full circle. Just when she was allowing herself to get her hopes up. To think they might have had a breakthrough, that maybe there was a way around this for them, it came back to this.

There would never be a way around this, there was no way he would ever decide to upend his life and his family's for her. She was in the public eye and everyone she loved would be too. And Rowan, for all his gifts, wasn't prepared to handle it. He didn't love her enough.

'I'd better go,' she said. 'I'll see you later.'

See you in Monterossa. My home. Where we shared so many lovely times. Where you proposed to me. Where I thought we were happy. And where you broke my heart.

Maybe just letting the photos out into the world would have been the better plan.

But it was too late for that.

She lifted herself onto her toes and touched her cheek to his. Her effort not to breathe in his scent was futile. It surrounded her. Coffee, mint and the bed they had shared last night.

Alone in the elevator that took her down to the street, she pressed her palms to her face. This was all her fault, this whole mess. The plan to sneak out of the party at the Ashton, the idea to go to the club Rowan was most likely to be at. The decision to speak to him! And then the decision to do the interview. She'd made mistakes at every corner she'd turned.

Everyone was right; there was a reason she'd been born second. Francesca would not have made these mistakes.

A car was waiting outside the lobby, with a very stern-looking Giovanni Gallo standing next to it. He looked exhausted; dark shadows framed his dark eyes.

'Your Highness.'

'I'm sorry for running away last night,' she said. Now she saw the look of disappointment and annoyance on his face she was even more ashamed. 'Is my sister at the hotel?'

'Yes, ma'am.'

'And...'

Is she very angry? Isabella was about to ask, but thought better of it.

She'd find out soon enough.

Too soon, in fact, she thought as the car pulled up outside her hotel in Mayfair a short while later. Francesca was wide-eyed and pacing the room when Isabella entered. It took about two seconds for her expression to change from relief to fury.

'Where have you been? Where on earth were you? Are you safe?'

'Yes, yes, I'm safe. I was…a few places.'

'Where did you spend the night?'

'At a hotel.'

'Not this one!'

Isabella shook her head.

'Who with?'

Isabella drew a deep breath.

'Please don't yell.'

'That means I'm going to.'

'I was with Rowan.'

'Rowan? *The* Rowan? Rowan James who broke your heart? Rowan James who you still cry over!' yelled Francesca.

'Shh!' Isabella said. 'You said you wouldn't yell.'

'I said nothing of the sort. I've been out of my mind. I've been looking everywhere!'

'I'm sorry.'

'Sorry! You're sorry? I found these!' Francesca reached down and lifted up a pair of red stilettos.

Isabella gasped. 'My shoes!'

'So they *are* yours? Bella, think for a moment how you'd feel if you came across a pair of my shoes, abandoned, outside Westminster Abbey. You have no idea the scenarios that went through my mind.'

'I told you I was safe.'

'Yes, in one single voicemail message hours after you disappeared.'

'I didn't mean to worry you, I wanted to fix things before I called you. And I didn't mean for you to find the shoes, I didn't mean to leave them behind.'

'I thought you'd been kidnapped.'

Isabella's knees buckled.

This was all her fault.

Second Princess Syndrome struck again.

'I'm so sorry. About everything. About making you leave the Ashton, about taking you to Twilight. About always messing up. About everything.'

And then she burst into tears.

Rowan wore jeans and an old shirt, matched with sunglasses and a battered baseball cap, for the walk back across London to his Vespa. Even though he wasn't with Isabella, he still took the back streets to avoid people as much as possible. It was broad daylight after all.

He was mildly surprised to see the Vespa exactly where he'd left it. The back of the Ashton looked different in the day, with no guards or trace of a fire alarm.

He cringed.

He studied the door they had sneaked in through and remembered Isabella talking to the guards, smiling, persuading, and his chest felt tight. She had been brave. She *was* brave.

And she was also right—last night had been fun.

For the first time since they'd broken up, he'd felt alive. Yes, it had been stressful and awful and all those things, but he'd been with her. Even though everything had gone wrong, there was no one else he'd rather have had at his side.

He placed his hand on the bike seat, where she'd sat last night, her breasts warm against his back. Then his mind flashed to later, her bare ankles hooked around his, her bare breasts warm against his pounding chest. Both of them sticky with sweat, dizzy, and spent.

She'd agreed that the love-making had been a one-off. A factor of the circumstances. Nothing to worry about. Or stress over. Just one more strange thing in a very strange night.

It doesn't have to mean anything.

He pushed the thoughts away and climbed on the bike, heading for home.

His parents still lived in the flat he'd grown up in. He'd tried to buy them a bigger place but they'd refused. They loved their home and couldn't imagine leaving it.

'Will said you left early last night,' his mother, Heather, said, sitting across the kitchen table from him.

'Yes. I was tired. After the flight.'

His father, Alistair, laughed. 'He also said you happened to run into a certain princess.'

'What else did he tell you?'

'He didn't say much, only that Isabella was there, there was a kerfuffle with a photographer and you both left in a hurry.'

'Yeah, well.'

Alistair and Heather leant forward, waiting. So he told them. How they'd chased the photographer, how they had been offered the chance to prevent the photos being published in return for the interview. He left out most of the colour and detail.

'We agreed to do the interview. I don't want the press getting wind of the fact that I'm in town and that Will and Lucy are getting married this weekend and Isabella doesn't want to embarrass her family.'

'I think you made the right decision. It will give you more control,' his father said, as though he and Isabella had shared notes. 'And it's an opportunity to promote the new app.'

'I doubt they're going to ask about that.' The media didn't care about his app. Or mental health. If they did, they wouldn't send paparazzi after princesses.

'Maybe not, but tell them anyway. *Use* them.'

Use them? In Rowan's experience he was the one to get used by the press, not the other way around.

'I'm going to do an interview,' his father said.

'You're what?' Rowan mustn't have heard properly.

'I'm going to talk to some people your communications team lined up.'

Rowan's skin broke out with hot prickles. 'They approached you?'

'No, no. I went to them.'

'I don't understand.' Understatement of the day. Why on earth would his father go looking for an interview? Rowan had spent half the night trying to get out of one.

'I want to support you. I want to help promote this new app. I know you do all right without me, but I want to help. Especially with this one.'

Rowan blinked, studied his sixty-five-year-old father. He knew his lined, weathered face so well that sometimes he didn't even really see.

'When I was a teenager I went through a hard time. You know that. I made decisions I regret, but the thing is, it would have been easier if I'd had support. This app that you've come up with, it's a game changer. A *life* saver.'

Rowan shook his head. It made him uncomfortable when people said that sort of thing to him. He came up with the tools, but it was up to the people to use them.

'Apps like this provide more than just exercises, they destigmatise mental illness, they promote discussions about mental health. It would have changed my life. I feel passionate about it.'

Heather picked up Alistair's hand and squeezed it.

'So I approached your communications team and asked how I could help.'

This was all very well and good but the thought of his father putting himself out there like this, feeling as though he had to, made Rowan agitated.

'You should have come to me first.'

'So you could say no?'

'They'll twist your words. They'll bring up your past.'

'That's the whole reason for doing the interview. I want to talk about it. I'm ready to.'

'You can't!'

'Why not?'

'Because…'

Because he wanted to protect his family. Everything he was doing was to protect them, keep them safe, and now his father went and did something like this?

Rowan put his face in his hands. He hadn't slept last night and was running on adrenaline. His father's words upset him but he couldn't think straight enough to pinpoint exactly why.

'That's what you came to tell us?' asked his mother. 'That you're doing an interview?'

'That and… I've decided it's too risky for me to go to the wedding.'

'No, Rowan! You have to come.'

He shook his head. 'I don't want to ruin their day.'

'You'll ruin their day by not being there!'

'No, they won't miss me. But they will notice a press contingent and they will notice paparazzi and speculation and goodness knows what other mayhem I might bring along with me.'

His parents looked at one another again and he knew they didn't agree with him.

'The photos may not be published but anyone could have seen me and figured out why I'm here. It's not worth it.'

'Have you told Will?'

'I'm going there next.'

'Maybe think about it a few days, wait until all this calms down.'

'No, he'll need to get another best man. Best I tell him sooner rather than later. My relationship ended because of the lies; I don't want theirs to as well.'

'Hm.' Alistair sat back in his chair.

'What?' Rowan asked, knowing he'd regret it.

'You listened to them, didn't you? You believed the headlines.'

'I don't know what you're talking about.' Maybe he would after a proper night's sleep. Maybe he would if he didn't still smell Isabella on his skin.

'I never believed the headlines. Your mother never believed the headlines and I'm sure Isabella didn't either. But you believed them. You took them to heart, didn't you?'

'The photos with the women weren't real.'

'And all the things they said about you not being good enough weren't true either.'

Rowan grunted. That was debatable. Besides, he had turned out to be an unworthy coward, just as they'd said. A dropout. A failure.

'I'll never believe anything published in the papers again after everything with Isabella.'

Alistair shrugged. 'And you should trust everyone else not to as well. We're big kids, Will is too.'

'It's not that.'

'Then what is it again? Why did you really end things with Isabella? Did you not want to marry her?' his mother said. 'If that's the case, then that's fine. But what if it isn't?'

He wanted to groan but kept it in. He'd never wanted to break up with Isabella, he simply wished he'd never got involved with her in the first place.

Which was why he'd had to end things. To protect everyone. Isabella included.

His temples throbbed.

Protect them from what?

Maybe his father was right. Maybe he did think he wasn't good enough.

Preposterous. You're clever. Kind. Successful. Strong.

He'd been strong enough to break off his engagement to protect everyone he loved. He'd been strong enough to stay away from Isabella every day for the past year. He'd ended the relationship to protect his family, to protect Isabella. They were all wrong. He'd done the right thing.

The Saint Francis hospital had carpeted floors and original artwork on the walls but it still smelt like a hospital. Her father was in the largest suite, reserved exclusively for royalty and VIPs, but it didn't matter how luxurious it was, this was still a hospital and the King was as vulnerable as anyone else to disease. Not for the first time, Isabella felt helpless, but also guilty. It was an entirely preventable disease that had brought him here.

She stood at the door and braced herself to see her parents, but her resolve crumbled as soon as she saw their smiling faces turn to her. Her heart dropped and any sentences forming in her head evaporated. They were sitting in the two armchairs next to a window overlooking the hospital gardens and holding one another's hands.

Isabella was almost thirty, yet she didn't want to disappoint them. Or hurt them in any way, particularly not now. Exhaustion was catching up with her; she'd travelled to London and back in the past forty-eight hours and had barely had eight hours sleep, on top of everything else.

Francesca hadn't let what had happened in London slip to their parents and neither, as far as she was aware, had the bodyguards. They were no doubt worried about what her escapade would mean for them, but everyone had come home safely and Francesca seemed to have smoothed it over with the security detail. For that she would be eternally grateful, though she had no idea how she'd managed it.

As discreet as everyone else had been, Isabella had decided it was best to come clean with her parents about everything. More lies on top of the current mess would only make her feel even sicker about the whole thing than she already did.

Besides, she had to let them know why she was doing an exclusive interview with *The Truth* without going through official palace channels and why Rowan would be stopping by Monterossa for a visit later in the week. That would hardly go unnoticed.

'Darling!' said her mother, 'It's so good to see you. How was London? We saw the photos.'

Isabella's heart stopped.

'Photos?'

'Of the coronation. You both looked beautiful.'

Isabella's heart began beating again, but her fingers still shook from the adrenaline shot resulting from her mother's remark. 'Thanks. How are you both?'

'Very well,' said the King, almost beating his chest. 'They're saying I may be able to go home as early as Tuesday.'

'That's great,' Isabella said but her voice was tight.

Her mother studied her through narrowed eyes and Isabella sat on the edge of the bed.

'What's up, darling?'

Before she could change her mind, Isabella let it all fall out. The crucial points anyway. The kisses and the lovemaking she kept to herself, but by the end of the rush of information they knew that she had persuaded Francesca to sneak out of the Duke's party, that she'd run into Rowan and agreed to an exclusive interview in exchange for not publishing the photos proving she had left the party.

'I'm so sorry, I didn't mean to let you down. It won't happen again.'

She expected them to say, 'Damn right it won't,' but her father asked, 'Why did you do it?'

'Why?'

'Yes, why?'

'Because...' She couldn't tell them this, could she?

Her father reached out and took her hand in his. His was pale, cold. And even though it looked like his hand, it was thinner and covered in marks it had never had before.

'Because I'm worried. I thought this might be our last chance to do something like that.'

'Why? What's happening? Is there something wrong with you? With Francesca?'

'No. But there's something wrong with you!'

Her parents exchanged a glance.

'I'm going to be fine, didn't you hear? I'm going home.'

But you're still frail and you won't live for ever and I know you're thinking of abdicating.

Isabella dropped her head. 'I'm worried about you, that's all. It was my fault. I have to take all the blame.'

Her parents exchanged another look. They had always been like this, able to communicate without words. She longed for that kind of connection and it felt like a stab in her gut to know it was unlikely she'd ever find it with anyone.

Anyone other than Rowan.

'I'm the flaky one, and this just proves it,' she said.

'Flaky? What do you mean?'

'You know, I'm the unreliable one. Francesca is the sensible one.'

'What on earth are you talking about?'

'You know exactly what I'm talking about. She's going to be queen, I'm going to be...well, I'm not sure.'

'But she's going to be queen due to an accident of birth, not because she's better than you.'

'But she is, we all know that. We all see it. She's responsible. I sneak out of parties. She's discreet, well behaved, clever. Charming.' Isabella waved her hand around. 'I make messes. I let the family down.'

Her mother stood and walked over to her, then she wrapped her into an enormous hug.

'I don't even know how to begin to unpack all of that,' the Queen said, pulling away and shaking her head.

'What's to unpack?'

'You don't honestly think of yourself as irresponsible, do you?'

'I try not to be but…'

'Exactly, you try not to be irresponsible, which means you probably aren't. So you made one mistake.'

'More than one. An entire sequence.'

'You made a misjudgement and you tried to fix it. That doesn't mean you're fundamentally irresponsible or unworthy. Everyone makes mistakes.'

It wasn't just one mistake. It was having every single transgression, however small, pointed out to her. And the world at large. The torn dress she'd worn to visit a homeless shelter—completely unintentionally, but she'd been criticised anyway. Calling the prime minister by the wrong name once—disrespectful, but also unintentional. Being dumped three days before her wedding and having to bear the cost and embarrassment of a cancelled wedding—bad enough if you weren't famous, but excruciating when you were.

The list went on and on.

She couldn't afford to make mistakes.

Isabella knew her sister better than anyone else in the world and even though Francesca could be stubborn and selfless to a fault, she didn't make mistakes. Francesca would be a perfect monarch.

'Darling, did you go to that particular bar on purpose?' her mother asked.

'What do you mean?'

'On the off chance you might run into Rowan?'

'I thought he was in New York. Of course I didn't expect to see him.' But what had made her choose *that* bar? There were thousands of others in London. 'I just went there once before and thought it might be a good place to take Francesca. But I didn't expect to see him.'

'Do you still have feelings for him?'

'Oh, no,' she said but felt her face warm as she spoke. 'I mean, I guess I still care for him.' An understatement if ever there was one. 'But I know he doesn't feel the same way. And I've accepted that.'

It wasn't too much. I was just not enough.

Her mother took her hand. 'You were ready to spend your life with him. It's okay if it still hurts. It's only been a year.'

'Yes, but it's been a whole year! I shouldn't still feel…'

'Feel what?'

Isabella shook her head. She still cared for Rowan but she couldn't still love him. She didn't trust him, for starters. Seeing him was a setback, that was all. By the end of the week he'd be gone again and life would get back to how it was before.

'Nothing, I'm fine. In fact, if this last day has shown anything it's that we could maybe be friends. Really, everything is good.'

She squeezed her mother's hand.

CHAPTER NINE

THEY PUT ROWAN in his old room.

The one immediately across from Isabella's.

It was just for one night, he told himself. His return flight was booked for straight after the interview tomorrow.

Did you really think they would put you in a room on the other side of the palace, far away from Isabella, as though you have been banished?

No, everyone at the palace, the King and Queen especially, had been understanding of his decision to break up with Isabella. No one wanted a royal divorce and everyone knew that the pressure of a very public life was not for everyone. But even so, to be given his old room again. To have to sleep in this bed, where he'd shared so many nights curled up with Isabella, planning their future together...

It wasn't too much. I was just not enough.

He hadn't meant those words. They'd been made off the cuff, without thinking straight. He'd done what he'd done to protect everyone, not because he thought he wasn't good enough. His father had been mistaken.

When the knock at the door came he felt it in his chest. He knew that knock, *her* knock. His body knew her, whether his brain liked it or not.

One more night and then they'd never see one another again.

One more night and you'll never *see her again*, his body whispered.

He opened the door and there she was. Her hair was loose, unstyled, and falling around her face in soft waves. She wore only a little make-up and a navy-blue shirt dress, cinched at her narrow waist with a belt. Chic, but relaxed. Ready for anything. Unlike him.

'Hi,' she said and took a step forward.

He stepped back into his room but still she came forward. She planted a soft, awkward kiss on his cheek, though the awkwardness was all his fault. To make up for it, he leant forward and tried to kiss her cheek, but since she'd already started to move away his lips fell on her nose. Her skin tasted sweet and his head swayed as her scent swirled around him.

He took two steps back.

Ridiculous.

She pressed her lips together, biting back a smile, and closed the door behind her.

'Nervous?' she asked.

'About what?' That awkward greeting? You being in the room across the hall from mine?

'Um, the interview?'

'Yes, I mean, no. I'm trying to stay relaxed.' Trying but failing.

She raised a disbelieving eyebrow but said, 'I expect you're more nervous about the launch next week. Or your brother's wedding.'

Rowan had spoken to Will and Lucy and told them about his decision not to attend the wedding. Will had not accepted Rowan's decision and nor had Lucy.

'I'm not getting another best man, so you'd better come,' Will had told him.

They'd agreed to discuss the matter again after the interview. Rowan knew Will would never forgive him if he didn't attend the wedding, yet would he forgive him if Rowan did go to the wedding and ruined it completely?

He should have been more nervous about the launch of the new app next week, he should have been entirely focused on that. But no. The matter that was taking up all of his grey matter was the one standing in front of him now. And annoyingly, awfully, the thing he was most nervous about was *this* moment. And any other moment where he was alone with her.

Especially like this, in his old room.

'It's just us for dinner tonight. My parents are spending a few days in Sicily, recuperating. And Francesca's making herself scarce.'

He was selfishly relived he wouldn't have to see any of her family members—those were encounters he really would rather avoid, though the flip side of that was that he had more time alone with Isabella. And that might prove to be just as difficult.

'I hope Francesca isn't doing that on my account. I'd love to see her.'

'No, you wouldn't. She's not happy with you.'

'Me? What did I do?'

'No, you're right. She's more annoyed with me for convincing her to leave an official party and then abandoning her. You just got caught in the blow back.'

'Does she know about the interview and why we're doing it?'

'Yes. I came clean with her and my parents.'

'You told them everything?'

She looked down. Was that colour high on her cheeks?

'Not everything. Just about the photos and the interview.'

It wasn't his business what she'd told them, or even what they thought. The only thing he needed to know was that they were letting them do the interview.

'I'm glad they found out from me and not the papers. They

agreed that we made the right decision by doing the interview and not causing further embarrassment to everyone by having the photo get out.'

Rowan bristled. Not for the first time that day he remembered his father's words; Alistair had also thought an interview was the best course of action. Everyone thought doing the interview was preferable to letting the photos out and perhaps they were right. But it was easy for everyone else to say that when they weren't the ones who were going to have to bluff their way through a tell-all interview and convince the world that everything was fine between the two of them.

'We had a good talk. About me. About Francesca,' she said.

'And abdication?'

She shook her head. 'No, we didn't talk about that and I didn't think it was the right time to ask. As much as it hurts me to acknowledge it, it isn't about me. It's between my father and Francesca.'

'It still affects you. It's going to change your life as well.'

'Yes, but not in the same way. Besides, it affects many people, but it is still just something between the two of them.'

He wanted to go to her then, wrap her in his arms and tell her how proud he was of her, how wise she was, but apart from the fear that he'd sound patronising, there was the fear that his gesture would be misinterpreted.

'And we talked about other things as well. They aren't angry with me for leaving the party, at least that's what they say. They say that everyone makes mistakes.'

He shook his head. 'They may be right, but we can't afford to, not when the world is watching.'

She pulled a face and he wasn't sure what she was thinking. Last weekend she'd been as keen as he was to avoid a scandal, now she was saying it was all right to make mistakes? It didn't make any sense.

'So, since it's us just us, I thought we could have dinner out on the terrace and game-plan tomorrow? I think we should think about possible questions, that sort of thing. Our PR team has given me a list of things we should think about.'

'That's a great idea.' Not the 'having dinner alone with Isabella' part but the 'preparing for tomorrow' part.

'See you around seven?'

'Yes, sounds good.'

She turned and stepped to the door and he took the moment to let his muscles relax, but then she turned back.

'And, Rowan. About London.'

'Yes?'

He held his breath. What was he hoping she'd say? That it had been wonderful? That she had no expectations but that she wouldn't mind if it happened again?

'I know it was a mistake. And it won't happen again.'

He nodded, exhaled and felt unexpectedly sad.

Thank goodness it was a lovely evening, not too hot, not too bright. She wanted to be in the open air of the terrace, not inside. And definitely not in one of their private rooms. She'd planned this evening to the last detail. What she would wear, how to do her hair and make-up. What they would eat. She needed to look effortless, nonchalant. And most of all calm. Even though she was in full duck mode—gliding serenely across the surface, but paddling like mad below.

She wasn't exactly sure how Rowan felt about the fact that they had made love in London.

No. Had sex. She had to keep referring to it like that. They had sex. One-off break-up sex.

It didn't mean anything.

And it couldn't happen again. For starters her heart couldn't take it.

The terrace was one of her favourite parts of the palace.

It was a sandstone patio overlooking the Adriatic, planted with hydrangeas, lavender and lemon trees. Watching over the whole area was a chestnut tree that was said to be older than the royal family. It was a small comfortable area, used mostly for intimate family occasions. To her it was home. Her back garden.

Rowan had seemed overawed by it the first time she'd brought him here, but she thought he'd become more comfortable over time. This evening though he stood awkwardly, waiting for her arrival.

He wore tan trousers and a white shirt, no tie, with the top button only undone, and looked as though he'd rather be anywhere else in the world.

A jug of iced water sat on the table, glistening with condensation. She poured them both a glass.

'So,' he said as she passed it to him. 'We need to get our stories straight.'

'Don't we have them straight already?' She knew why he'd left, or thought she did. She'd swallowed his excuse, accepted it at face value. The pressure was too much and he didn't want to expose his family to the spotlight.

'Yes, I mean...' He wouldn't meet her gaze and her body stiffened.

'Rowan, did you lie about why you ended our relationship?'

'No. Of course not. It was because of my family. The pressure they were under.'

She did believe him—she always had trusted him—and she'd also always known that any partner of hers would have to be willing and able to put up with the sustained pressure of public scrutiny. But why would he start this conversation with the comment he had? What story did he need to get straight?

It wasn't too much. I was just not enough.

'You're shifting from foot to foot,' she said.

'So?'

'So, Rowan, what's going on? What aren't you telling me?'

'Nothing. Nothing at all.'

'I don't believe you.' It felt good to say it, to challenge him up front, even if she didn't want to hear the answer. She was being brave.

'If you must know...' He pursed his lips together.

'I must.'

'My father said something that's upset me, I suppose. He said he thought I'd used them as an excuse.'

Nausea rose up through her, rippled through her in unsteadying waves. She'd accused him of the same thing.

'But it's not true,' Rowan said.

Isabella's hands shook. 'Then why would he say such a thing?'

'Because he thought I was scared, I guess.'

'What would you be scared about?' Her voice came out ragged.

What if he hadn't broken up with her because he'd wanted to protect his family? What if the real reason was that he simply hadn't wanted to be with her? That he'd changed his mind about her? It was the fear that woke her in the middle of the night. The one that chased her in her dreams.

He just didn't love you.

'Nothing, that's just the thing. I think he was trying to tell me that it was okay, that he didn't mind the articles about him, that he didn't mind his past being picked over and criticised.'

'And?' But if Rowan's problem had never really been about his family, but something else, about his feelings for her, then it didn't matter what his father said. She held her breath and her heart held its beat waiting for his answer.

'It doesn't change anything. They might think they are

happy to be tabloid fodder but I'm not happy for them to be so.'

'You're still hiding behind them, then?'

'What's that supposed to mean?'

Indeed. What was it supposed to mean? What did she want him to say? That he'd used his parents as an excuse because he hadn't loved her enough to marry her?

Or that he'd made a thoughtless mistake and that he wanted her back?

She shook her head.

Yes. That. There was still a part of her that wanted him to say that.

Of course, it was a perverse kind of hope, because even if he did say that she couldn't seriously say yes.

He dumped you! Humiliated you in front of the world!

She couldn't get back with him. It was a ridiculous idea.

'We're going to have linguine with clams for dinner.'

He smiled. It was his favourite.

'So, should we start going through this list from the communications team?'

'Yes.'

They sat on the sofa in the shade of the ancient chestnut tree and faced the ocean. The sun was setting behind them, out of their eyes but lighting up the sky in gorgeous pinks and oranges.

She took out the papers the communications team had given her as well as a notebook and pen so she could jot down ideas for answers. Rowan spied them.

'It's okay for you, your memory is freakish. Some of us need help,' she said.

He shook his head. 'It's not that. Are you nervous?'

She shrugged. 'Maybe a little. I don't do this sort of thing often. And it was my idea, so I'll feel responsible if it goes wrong.'

But the main reason I'm nervous is because you'll be sitting right next to me as I have to answer questions about us. About why and how our relationship ended. And questions about how I feel about it. All while holding myself together. And sounding like I'm honestly okay with it.

'It won't go wrong.' His voice was soft but it didn't reassure. It simply made her pulse spike. 'We can answer these questions. What have you got?'

'The first is, how did you meet? Easy.'

And it was. He repeated the story about how he'd been in Geneva for a Word Health Organisation mental health convention, how she'd wandered into the bar and they'd begun talking. How he hadn't known who she was to start with.

'They love that part of the story,' she said.

'They do.'

The story was always spun as Rowan hadn't known he'd fallen in love with a princess, but what no one really knew was that she hadn't known who he was either. She hadn't known about his work, or his wealth. They had just met as two people in a bar who'd struck up a conversation about the band that had been playing in the bar.

They watched the sky darken and reminisced about the early days of their relationship, their whirlwind courtship. She laughed more than she had in months. When the sun set they lit candles. The food arrived and they shared a bottle of wine. The questions were easy, straightforward. Factual. They didn't have secrets from one another so it was easy just to give an honest answer. There were questions about their childhoods, quite a few about his career. The usual predictable ones about how she felt about being the second twin. Whether she envied Francesca. She'd answered that question so many times she could recite the answer in her sleep.

Of course not. I love my sister and she will make a far better queen than I ever could.

Every word the absolute truth.

By the time they had finished eating and drained the bottle of wine she was feeling relaxed and confident. This was a good idea—she'd known it from the beginning.

'Next question.' She read it to herself and said, 'Oh.'

'What is it?'

'Tell us how he proposed.'

'Oh. But that's okay. Isn't it?'

It was. It was a story she'd told many times, only she hadn't told it since the break-up.

'I'll answer that one,' he said.

'No, if they ask me, I have to answer. Besides, it's not as though it isn't on the public record already anyway.'

Her body prickled with awareness and memory. 'Right here, at sunset. You got down on one knee and gave me the ring.'

He nodded. It was the story they had told the world and technically when the proposal had become official, but there was another, far more meaningful moment earlier than that. One that only two people in the world knew about.

He had been heading back to London after a quick visit and she had still been in bed.

'I don't want you to go,' she'd said.

'I don't want to go either,' he'd replied.

'Stay.'

'I have to get back.'

She still remembered how his words had stopped her heart. She'd thought she knew what he meant.

'Stay. Marry me.'

They had stared at one another then, in silence, wondering, waiting. His next words could be life changing.

'Are you asking me to marry you?' he'd said.

She'd nodded.

He'd looked away and the bottom had dropped out of her

world. But then he'd turned back and said, 'I suppose there are things to think about, protocols and such, but yes. If you're sure?'

She'd nodded, unable to speak, tears welling in her eyes, and he'd climbed back onto the bed and pressed his soft lips to hers.

Now, Isabella looked out at the dark sea and remembered afresh: *she* had asked him. She'd pressured him into it. That was why he'd left. Because he hadn't meant to propose to her at all. Because she'd pushed him into it too soon.

'I'm not going to tell them the truth. It's too late for that and would sound weird,' she said.

He nodded. 'Yes, it would be strange to tell them that story now.'

She stood and walked to the edge of the terrace and the low stone wall. Looked at the ocean that was now black and invisible.

'Rowan.' She spoke into the darkness. 'If I hadn't asked first, would you still have asked me to marry you?'

'Of course I would have.'

'But were you going to?'

'Yes.'

'When?'

'I don't know. I hadn't set a date.'

'So, you weren't going to.'

'I wanted to marry you. I *wanted* to spend my life with you.'

'But you didn't know when you were going to ask me.'

'No. Isabella, I don't understand what you want to hear.'

She shook her head. She already knew everything she needed to know.

He reached for her hand but she turned her body away.

'Isabella, I loved you. I wanted to marry you. It wasn't easy figuring out how to propose to a princess. But once you asked me, it was easier.'

She went back to the sofa they had sat on earlier, and where the jug of water was. She poured herself another glass for her parched mouth. The water was warm now, but it gave her something to do with her hands.

He joined her.

'I'm not sure why you're asking me about this,' he said.

He was right. There was no point. There was no need to dig up these things. No need to dredge over this history, of all things. No one was going to ask them about her proposal and it didn't matter what his answer was. It didn't change anything and, most of all, it couldn't change anything into the future either.

You were the brave one. And look where it got you.

'No point. You're right. I don't know what I'm saying. Let's get back to the list. The final question.' Her throat was still dry, her body suddenly spent. 'They say we should be prepared to answer a question along the lines of how did you feel about the break-up?'

He looked down.

She knew he felt guilty but it didn't make her feel any better about the situation. If anything, it only made her like him more. None of this was his fault. She could only blame herself.

Just one more mistake to add to the growing list.

'I'm going to say that I was heartbroken, but that I understood your decision and that ultimately it was a decision we made together.'

'That's very kind of you.'

'And I'll say we continue to be good friends.'

'That's also very kind.'

'But it's true, isn't it?' she asked.

Her gaze snagged in his and he held it there. They hadn't seen one another all year because it was for the best, but now they had been thrust together, maybe they could forge a friendship.

He picked up her hand and even as she knew it was risky, this time she was powerless to pull hers away. 'I thought you thought it was for the best if we didn't see one another. I think I thought it would be easier too,' he said.

'And maybe it was what we needed at the time. But now... I don't know.'

'Are you saying you think we can be friends?'

'Yes, no, maybe. I don't know. What do you think?'

'I think...' He continued to watch her as his words trailed away.

Her throat became tight, then the muscles in her chest clenched, the tightness gradually spreading through her body as she sat, still and immobilised under his golden eyes, until he closed them and moved his face towards hers.

She closed her own eyes and fell into the kiss as though she were stepping off a cliff without checking to see how far she had to fall. Without even caring.

She surrendered herself to his lips. And the consequences. This entire evening had been confusing but this kiss was so simple. The easiest, most natural thing in the world. The absolute only thing in the world she wanted ever again.

Luckily he caught her, kissed her back, pulled her closer. His lips told her a clearer truth; no matter what he might say to her, this was the only story she wanted to hear. The only one that mattered.

He slid his hand up her skirt. Her underwear was thin, practically a formality, and his practised fingers found her soft folds and all the sensitive parts they contained. The desire grew up inside her, the tightness rising to its ultimate climax. He continued to kiss her as his fingers rubbed and stroked and the stars spun in the sky above her like a planetarium. Thinking of the stars, she looked down at herself, at him, his hand up her skirt, her heart exposed.

What are you doing?

Isabella pushed him off her. He moved easily but it was still the heaviest weight she'd ever had to move. She couldn't do this with him. Not again. Not now. Not here.

'I think that being friends with you is risky,' she panted. 'I'm not sure if we have the same definition of friendship.'

'I… I'm sorry. I didn't mean… I got carried away.'

She straightened herself up. 'I let myself get carried away.'

'No. I…'

'What are we doing here, Rowan? What's going on? Once is a mistake, twice seems deliberate.'

'I thought you said mistakes were okay.'

'I meant *public* mistakes.'

Not the kind of mistake where I put my heart and body on the line and you stomp on them.

'I don't know what is going on. I don't know why we can't seem to keep our hands off one another,' he said.

'Could it be that we're not over one another?' It could be as simple as that. Or as complicated.

'Maybe, but, Isabella, you know as well as I do we can't go back.'

She nodded.

Of course they couldn't go back, but could they go forward? Could they start again? Would things be different this time around? No. Because he didn't love her. At least, not enough.

'And you said you understood that we just weren't meant to be,' he said.

Had she said that? She could hardly be expected to remember everything she'd ever said. Or have to hold to everything she'd said to fool herself. And fool him that everything was okay.

Because suddenly it just wasn't.

'I wouldn't quite put it like that.'

He shrugged. 'But you seem happy.'

She blinked. 'Of course I seem happy. I'm putting every ounce of energy and effort I have into seeming happy.'

'So, you're not? Happy?'

Something snapped. They were no longer rehearsing the interview. She didn't have to pretend. She didn't have to put on a brave face.

'No! I'm not happy. I'm angry and hurt and embarrassed!'

The dam was cracked and soon it was fully breached. Everything came out. 'You dumped me three days before our wedding! And that would be bad enough except that everyone in the world knew! No one calls off a royal wedding just before it's about to happen! Never! My name is never printed anywhere without being preceded by the word "jilted".'

Rowan's mouth was open, jaw flapping in the breeze. She didn't care and she couldn't have stopped herself if she'd wanted to.

'*"Jilted Princess Isabella and her sister Francesca attended the coronation." "Princess Francesca and her jilted sister, Isabella, were seen visiting their father in hospital."* Every. Single. Time. It's okay for you, your name is always preceded by "billionaire" or "tech genius" or even "entrepreneur". You are never, ever, *"Love Rat Rowan James"* or *"Princess-Dumper Rowan James"*. Yet you tell me that you're the one being treated poorly by the press.'

Rowan looked down and she caught her breath, shaking with adrenaline.

'Are you finished?'

'I'm barely started. I might be understanding, but I'm still hurting. I'm still angry. I'm still upset.'

'Oh.'

'You broke my heart. I might understand why you did, but that doesn't make my heart full and healed.' Her heart would never be complete again.

She'd been trying so hard, so, so long to stay cool. To give the impression that everything was fine. That she understood. Not to make a scene. But it wasn't fine.

She wasn't fine.

She hurt. While logically she knew why he'd done it, her heart did not.

'What more could I have done?' he asked.

'You could have fought for me. You could have tried. You could have been stronger.'

His face was nearly as red as his beard. 'Isabella, I tried. But I couldn't do it. I couldn't make it work. Maybe I wasn't good enough to fix it.'

'You keep saying that, but I don't believe you for one second. You are amazing. You were always enough. There was nothing you had to fix. The truth is you just didn't love me enough. So how about we start calling it what it was? You didn't love me.'

'Isabella.'

This was his chance to deny what she'd just said. To explain.

To say something.

It was strange that a simple flick of the eyes could break your heart, could pry your heart open and crush it. And the look he gave her just then did exactly that.

'We have to be over. I can't do this. We can't go back,' he said.

'No. We can't.'

With shaky knees she stood and walked away as quickly as she could.

CHAPTER TEN

RICHARD WEBBER, THE JOURNALIST from *The Truth*, arrived promptly at the palace, with a photographer in tow. Both men were shown into the reception area where Rowan and Isabella were waiting. The Blue Room was a large airy room with cool stone floors and a view of the ocean. Its walls were lined with artwork by the old masters. It was a room the family only used for official business, designed, he supposed, to give the family a home court advantage.

Which suited Isabella, but Rowan felt as much a guest in this room as Webber.

Rowan hadn't spoken to Isabella since she'd stormed off the terrace last night, leaving him shaken and reeling. Paralysed with guilt. He'd kissed her, begun to make love to her and then tried to tell her it was just a mistake. And she'd rightly given him a dressing-down. And not just about the kissing and making love when he had no intention of taking things further, but also for his behaviour last year.

She was right; he was a coward.

Always would be.

He'd stuffed up.

He'd gone to her room later last night, when he had judged that she might have cooled down, but she hadn't answered his knock.

And his cowardly self was glad because he didn't know what he could possibly say to her to make it up to her. All this time he'd been deceiving himself with the thought that she understood why he'd had to leave and told himself that made it all okay.

But even though she had understood, she still hurt. She was still angry. He'd been fooling himself, telling himself that she wasn't heartbroken, that she didn't love him. But that had just been a story, a way of softening the scandal. It was easier to swallow than the truth.

The air zapped between them while they waited for Richard. Isabella was wearing a white shirt and a full linen skirt that accentuated her waist and gave her a classic elegant silhouette. Her hair was tied back neatly. She looked sharp, sophisticated and utterly untouchable.

After the interview they would each have some photos taken, but not together. They had specified that in the fine print of the contract; even though they were giving a joint interview they did not want a visual image suggesting they were back together going out into the world.

Especially not after last night.

He'd hurt her. More than he'd thought.

No, you hurt her more than you let yourself believe.

She was right, he'd hidden behind some sort of moral prerogative to protect his family, but really he'd been a coward.

The truth gnawed at him, sickened him.

He watched her now. She stood at a window, looking out onto the garden and, beyond it, the sea. She had been polite this morning. But the politeness was damning and perfunctory. He was counting the minutes until the interview would be done and he could leave Monterossa.

Yes, run away, like the coward you are.

He bristled at his inner voice. But what other choice did he have but to leave? She hated him. There was nothing to stay here for.

You fool. She loves you! Still.

That was what her outburst last night was all about. If she didn't have feelings for him would she be that mad? She'd been hiding her feelings about the break-up because she thought that was the sensible thing to do. She'd been taught all her life not to make a scene. To be calm. Composed. *And that's what she did with you when you called off the wedding. But it's all been a lie.* She was hurt and wasn't at all fine. Leaving Monterossa wouldn't fix it.

What could he do to fix it?

Tell her how you really feel. Tell her you were terrified of marrying a princess.

He shook his head. That wouldn't help anyone one bit. And it wasn't true. He'd be stacking lies on half-truths. Rowan was wrestling with these thoughts when the journalist was finally shown into the room.

Isabella's demeanour changed instantly from frosty to warm. An act for Richard Webber's benefit. Rowan tried to muster up some fake warmth of his own.

Webber seemed nice, friendly. A little bumbling even. Rowan didn't feel intimidated by him one bit.

It's an act. Just like the one you and Isabella are putting on. He's trying to appear unassuming, to put you at ease so you think you are friends and so you spill your guts to him.

After they exchanged greetings and pleasantries, Richard said, 'I must say I was surprised to hear that you had agreed to do this interview together. And that you approached *The Truth*.'

'Sir Liam is a friend of mine,' Isabella said smoothly and sincerely.

'But why now?'

So the journalist didn't know about the photos in London. Or if he did, he was going to wait for one of them to say something first.

'Enough time has passed, I guess. And we wanted to set the record straight. It felt like the right time.'

'Very well.'

Richard started by turning his attention to Isabella and made the usual enquiries. Questions Isabella could answer in her sleep.

'It can't be easy being number two?'

'How was it growing up next to Francesca knowing she would one day be queen but you wouldn't?'

'The second in line to a throne is usually the naughty one. What was the worst thing you did as a child?'

'Didn't you ever want to rebel?'

She'd been answering these questions all her life. She had this.

Rowan realised he was watching her closely as she gave these answers and pulled himself back.

'Are you ever jealous of your sister?' Richard asked.

Isabella smiled but the side of her mouth hardened, in a way he hadn't noticed before. It was probably because he rarely saw her side-on. The sensitive skin at the corner of her lips looked brittle.

She was hurt. The questions were hurting her. How had he not seen that before? She might be smiling and giving well-practised answers but each time she did, she ached.

'Not at all. If anything, she's jealous of me.' Isabella smiled broadly and her eyes twinkled, but to one side, he could see the muscles in her neck tighten against her delicate skin. At that moment he wanted to reach over and strangle Webber, but he kept his own hands clenched in his lap.

'How did you feel when Rowan left you days before the wedding?'

She gave the answer she'd rehearsed the previous evening. Calmly, even smiling. 'It broke my heart, but I understand why he had to do it. It isn't easy being royal, it isn't easy being in the public eye and, honestly, how could I wish that on someone I care about? It wouldn't be fair.'

It broke his heart.

That was the answer she'd always given, and it was what she'd told him when he'd ended their engagement. But he knew now that it was a lie. It was what she felt she had to say, to keep the peace, to avoid upset. To avoid making a scene. But inside she was truly hurt—and still hurting.

It was bad enough he'd done that to her, but now she was forced to keep reliving it—while smiling!

Rowan wanted to push his face into his hands and howl but he kept a sad, contrite look on his face.

This was how she felt all the time. Smiling while her heart was breaking.

Rowan was so busy reeling from these revelations he didn't notice at first when Richard turned his attention to him, which meant he was on the back foot from the outset.

'Tell us about your childhood.'

'It was a normal, happy childhood. I lived with my parents and my brother. They worked hard, loved us both. Gave us all the opportunities they could. My parents are dedicated workers who have helped people all their lives. My brother, too. He's a nurse. I'm in awe of how they have all dedicated their lives to helping other people.'

The edges of Webber's eyes twitched. 'Doesn't your app do that too?'

'Yes, of course. I only meant it takes a very special person to care for and directly support people in need.'

'Of course, we know about your brother, Will, who was with you at your infamous stag night.'

'Those photos were taken out of context. The newspaper sent the women there.'

'Of course, of course,' said Webber. 'I just meant we know that he has had some relationship troubles since that night.'

Rowan had had to end his relationship with Isabella because of press intrusion, so to have this man question him about this now was causing every muscle in his body to knot. His jaw was hardly open as he said, 'My brother and his fiancée are very happy and I do not wish to breach their privacy any more than it already has been.'

Isabella sucked in a deep breath. Rowan turned and saw that she was smiling warmly and nodding. 'It's okay. Keep going,' her expression said.

Rowan felt as if the interview was already heading off track. He hated answering questions about his family and he sensed that he had said something wrong but wasn't sure what it was. All he knew was that he was furious; if it hadn't been for the likes of Webber and the paper he worked for, he and Isabella might still be together. If only there were a future where tabloids didn't exist, a future where social media didn't exist.

'Tell us how you came up with the idea for MindER.'

He exhaled. This was easier, he was on much safer ground. It was a story he'd told many times. About his father's smoking habit, about how he had come up with the idea at just the right time. How supporting people's mental health was his passion. He almost began to feel comfortable again.

'The app uses many of the same techniques that other apps do. We offer guided meditations, breathing exercises, but also self-guided cognitive behavioural therapy.'

'And what is that?' Webber asked.

'It is a type of therapy that involves breaking down your thoughts, feelings and beliefs and challenging negative thoughts. While we can't change what is happening to us, sometimes we can change the way we think about it.'

'You can't change the world, but you can change what you think about it,' Webber clarified.

'Yes. We're launching a new feature for teens next week

and hope people find it as easy to use and as helpful as the other applications we have. Teenage mental health is a difficult area and I'm looking forward to seeing what people think and then continuing to make these apps as good as they can be. But I do always want to stress that while our apps can help, that cannot replace the advice of a fully qualified professional and they are designed to be used in conjunction with other treatment plans.'

It seemed like only moments later that Webber turned his questions back to Isabella.

'How's your father?'

'He's doing much better. He had us worried for a while but he's out of hospital now, which is a big relief to us all.'

'We're all glad to hear that, but do you think he will remain king for much longer?'

'Hey,' Rowan said. That was none of Webber's business. As Isabella had said, that was between Francesca and her father.

'That wasn't one for you, Mr James.'

'No, but is it one for her?'

She touched his knee. Rather than having the calming effect she intended, it made his heart rate spike.

'It's okay,' she said. Turning to Webber, she continued, 'My father is making a good recovery and we have every reason to think that he will be with us for a long while yet.'

'How do you feel about the fact that your twin sister will shortly be queen? What will you do with yourself then?'

'As I said, my father is going to be with us for many years yet and I will be delighted for Francesca when she becomes our queen. She will be a wonderful monarch and I look forward to doing what I've always done: supporting my family in any way I can.'

Webber smiled. He almost seemed sincere. 'Thank you, I think we're nearly done,' he said.

Relief rose up like a giant bubble in Rowan, instantly making him feel lighter.

They had done it! There had been a few hiccoughs but, overall, it had gone well. He turned to Isabella, who was looking serenely ahead, and he couldn't help but smile. As he always thought when he saw her, she was the most beautiful woman he'd ever laid eyes on.

'I just have one more question. In the future, do you ever see yourselves getting back together?'

Unlike the other questions, this one wasn't directed to just one of them. Who should take it? They looked at one another, and at the same instant she shook her head and said, 'No,' he said, 'The future?'

Webber stifled a snigger. 'Does that mean you are back together?'

Rowan looked sideways at Isabella, hoping for assistance, but she was red-faced and wide-eyed.

'No. We're not. Definitely not. I mean, I just meant…' Rowan stumbled over his words. 'It was the way you phrased it. The future is a long time.'

'And what, exactly, does that mean?' Webber asked.

Rowan couldn't explain because he had no idea himself.

'Of course, what I meant to say…'

Two sets of eyes looked on eagerly.

'We're friends, clearly, otherwise we wouldn't be doing this interview together. And circumstances, such as they are, are not…that is… There were good reasons we broke up and those reasons remain. But we are good friends.'

Webber stood. 'Have you considered a career in politics?'

Rowan, shocked, shook his head.

'Good, because you'd have to be far better at answering questions than that.'

'Hey, I just…you're not going to put that in the article, are you?'

Webber nodded. 'I doubt my editor would publish it.'

That wasn't the reassuring answer Rowan was looking for.

'Richard, would you like a tour of the palace before you leave?' Isabella asked. Webber's eyes sparkled.

'I'd love that, thank you.'

Isabella waved Rowan back down dismissively. 'No need for you to come.'

Webber looked from him to Isabella and back again and said to the photographer Rowan had completely forgotten about, 'Why don't you take Mr James's shots now, Thommy?'

Isabella and Webber stepped out and Rowan stood to face the photographer. He tried to smile and pose as best he could but he kept wondering what on earth Isabella and Webber were talking about.

'You have to relax, mate. I'm sure she can handle herself,' Thommy said.

Rowan glared at the man. If he was ambivalent towards photographers before, now he positively loathed them.

Isabella showed Richard Webber out of the door and into the rest of the reception areas of the palace. As the Palace of Monterossa was the main residence of her family most of the year round it was not open to the public. Visitors, though, did appreciate tours of select public reception areas and Isabella led him through them now. He smiled and murmured appreciatively as she pointed out the artwork, the furnishings and the sculptures the di Marzanos had collected over the years. He would hardly notice the favour she had to ask him.

'It's funny, you know, how people get nervous in interviews.'

'Were you nervous, Your Highness?'

'No, not me. But I think Mr James was.'

'Why would he be nervous? He's a successful businessman, entrepreneur. He speaks publicly all the time.'

Indeed, thought Isabella. Why on earth would someone as successful and accomplished as Rowan ever be nervous? About interviews? Or marrying princesses? Or marrying the woman he professed to love?

No. He wasn't insecure about marrying her, he simply didn't love her enough. Even though he'd broken her heart, she had to defend him. Both their reputations depended on it.

'The scrutiny a member of a royal family receives is intense. It is hard to understand how intense until it happens to you. He might be comfortable when he's working, but giving an interview with your ex, who just happens to be a princess, is a completely different thing.'

'What are you trying to say?'

'Only that he just stumbled over that question because he thinks it will hurt me less not to deny it. He didn't mean it. We're not getting back together. He just said that to protect me.'

Because after everything that had happened, he still thought of others first.

'But would you?'

She looked around, to look anywhere but Richard Webber's face. She caught her reflection in one of the many mirrors nearby. Just as she thought. Bright red.

'Don't be ridiculous, the man practically left me at the altar. Of course we don't have a future together.'

Webber gave a non-committal shrug.

'So to print that we might would just be cruel. And untrue.'

'I understood this was to be a tell-all interview. No topics off-limits.'

Why was she bringing even more attention to what had just been an awkward stumble?

Because it wasn't nothing.

It was important to you.

When he'd said, 'The future?' the crack of hope she'd been trying to clasp tightly shut had begun to pull open again.

'Yes, you're right. I'm sorry. I was only trying to protect him.'

'We're off the record now, Your Highness. So tell me, why would you want to protect him after what he did?'

Isabella knew there was no such thing as off the record. A principle her parents had instilled in her from an early age.

'Because it's the decent thing to do.'

He raised an eyebrow.

'It seems to me that…things might be more complicated than you are saying.'

'Things are always complicated, but trust me when I say that Mr James and I will never get back together. Now, I think Mr James will be done with his photos. I imagine it's my turn.'

Richard Webber just nodded and followed her out of the room.

Isabella knew she should smile and continue the friendly banter, but her heart was in her throat, stifling her vocal cords.

Rowan had left the room when she returned to have her own photographs taken. Isabella suggested they go outside into one of the palace courtyards; she wanted to distinguish her photos from Rowan's. She did not want to do anything to make it look as though they were back together.

They were not getting back together. If that wasn't already obvious to her, he'd told her as much the night before. Their one night in London had been a blip only. A setback. It hadn't been the beginning of a new future as she'd let herself believe for a few unexpected moments last weekend. They were over. Finished. And there was no path around that. If she let herself wonder about that for even a moment she would fall down a dangerous rabbit hole of hope, fantasy and ultimately pain.

Except...

The future is a long time.

Isabella smiled, looked calm. Smiled again. She had done so many photo sessions in her time she could teach models how to do it. Push your chin forward, tilt your head. Breathe out, small smile, big smile. Repeat.

It wasn't long before she simply said to the photographer, 'I think you should have everything you need.' She didn't wait for him to object and returned directly to the Blue Room.

Rowan was standing there, suitcase at his heels.

Isabella inhaled. This was it.

Goodbye.

For ever.

Except...even as she knew she should simply turn and leave, she had to ask. '"The future is a long time?" Rowan, what was that about?'

Rowan shrugged, studied the Botticelli hanging on the wall. 'I don't know. Maybe it was the way he phrased the question.'

I managed to answer it, she thought with gritted teeth.

It wasn't just last Saturday. Last night he'd had his hand up her skirt, she'd been seconds away from ripping his shirt off.

'What did last Saturday mean to you? What did last night mean? Really. I know I said it didn't mean anything, but why did it keep happening?'

He grimaced, as well he might. 'Isabella, when it comes to you, I'm powerless. I still care for you. I've never made a secret of that. But you know we wouldn't work.'

She nodded and looked away.

'I'm not sure why you're so upset. It's not as though you would take me back,' he said.

Would you? Would you take him back?

She'd be a fool. Worse than a fool, she'd be…she'd hurt her family, her country. She'd look like a chump.

'Are you asking?'

'I…no. I was being rhetorical. I expected you to say, *Of course not*.'

Of course he wasn't asking. Which was just as well because of course her answer would be no.

A hard, definitive no.

He tilted his head.

She shook hers.

'No. We don't have a future.'

The future is a long time.

What if…what if the world changed? What then? What if *he* changed?

Rowan stepped up to her. 'Isabella,' he began, and her insides melted. Every time he touched her, Isabella's defences disintegrated. It couldn't go on. She couldn't go on like this. She needed a clean break.

This had to be over. And now.

'It's time for you to leave. But before you go, I want to make one thing very clear.' She was going to be brave. She could do this. 'We will never get back together. Not now and not at some time in some theoretical future. I need someone who will stick by me no matter what. I need someone who can be strong for me when I can't be. I need someone who can handle the circus of the palace. I deserve someone who is all those things. That person may not exist and that is fine. But I can't keep doing this. I can't keep pretending I am fine. I can't keep lying.'

A noise behind her made Isabella turn her head.

Richard Webber and the photographer were standing in the doorway.

Perfect.

Of course they were.

Of course nothing would ever go smoothly, nothing would ever go as planned.

This was life. You couldn't change everything, you couldn't fix everything, and you couldn't hide everything.

Isabella nodded to them and turned back to Rowan. She was sick of pretending, sick of being calm. And tired, so tired.

'You hurt me. You didn't just break my heart, you crushed it. You crushed *me*.'

'Isabella, we're not alone,' he hissed.

'I know. And I don't care anymore. I'm so tired of pretending.'

'Izzy...'

His nickname for her hardened her.

'No. There is no Izzy. And I need to set this straight.' She glanced over her shoulder back at the journalists to be sure they could hear.

'I need someone who can be strong. And yes, I know being with me isn't always easy, but do you know what, Rowan? No relationship ever is. Every long-lasting relationship is hard. Every relationship will have ups and downs and you are going to face something far worse in the future than an intrusion of privacy. Someone you love inevitably will get sick, people will leave you. And those are the things you have to be able to get past. Not some silly photographs.'

He looked down. As well he might. She knew she should stop, but she also knew that, like life, things were now out of her control. So she let go.

'I see now you're not the person for me. You're not strong enough, or brave enough. You can't help the person you are and I have no desire to change you. So it's over.'

He looked up and straight into her eyes, his whisky eyes light, his skin pale.

'Really over. We can't be friends. This last day proves

that. And if we ever run into one another, accidentally or otherwise, we smile, say hello and go on our way. Agreed?'

'Isabella…'

'Agreed?'

Rowan nodded, looked at the ground and she swept out of the room, as elegantly as she could on knees that had turned to water.

Rowan reached for the handle of his suitcase but his hand only caught the air. When his focus returned, he grabbed for it and tugged. He had to get out of there. Away. He couldn't get back to his apartment in New York fast enough.

The problem was a journalist and a photographer blocking his exit from the room.

How fitting.

His heart rate was practically through the extra-high ceiling of the palace room but he put his head down and pulled on his case. Webber and the photographer stepped towards one another, actively sealing off his escape.

'You know she's right, don't you?'

Yes, he did, which was why he wanted to leave. Immediately.

'Which part in particular are you talking about?' Rowan said with a sigh.

They both laughed.

Both men were older. Both had worn-looking rings on the third finger of their left hands.

'The part about some random photographs not being the most important thing in the world?'

The part about her father.

The part about her family.

The part about him being a coward.

She was right about almost everything.

'I have a family to protect as well. That's why I did this.'

'Really?' asked Webber.

Rowan shook his head. 'You can hardly think I'm going to open up to you.'

'Why not? The interview ended when we said it did. We're not going to publish anything about her outburst just now, or whatever you might say now, without your permission.'

Rowan raised an eyebrow.

'We're not the bad guys you think we are. We do adhere to a code of ethics.'

'Excuse me if I don't believe you. I had to call off my wedding because of the things your colleagues did.'

'Not all journalists ignore professional ethics. And despite what you think, we are rarely trying to destroy people's lives.'

'No, that's just a bonus,' Rowan said.

It was snarky and the men could have been offended, but they smiled.

'The public have a desire to know about public figures, an insatiable need. I agree, there are bad eggs in our profession, but people do have a right to know certain things. There are things you want to know about public figures, aren't there? Politicians, leaders, business people?' Webber said and Rowan couldn't argue.

The press were important. But did they have to care so much about him and Isabella?

'Whether you wanted to be or not, you are a public figure. You have a public platform. You're a person the world wants to know about. And when you're with a woman who is universally beloved, especially when you hurt her, the world wants to know. They want to know if you're good enough for her.'

'Which I'm clearly not.'

Rowan wasn't sure where the words came from. The two men exchanged glances.

Great. So much for controlling the narrative.

This whole interview was meant to bury the last photo they didn't want released. And now one thing had led to another. And then another. And now he was spilling his guts to the enemy.

But Richard Webber and Thommy Spencer didn't look like the enemy, they just looked like two regular guys trying to do their job. Rowan sat in the nearest chair.

'It will never end, will it?' Rowan asked.

Spencer, the photographer, shook his head. 'You're famous, you always will be. But someone else more famous always comes along.'

'But how do I live like this? How can I change it?'

'A wise person once said, you can't always change the world, but sometimes you can change what or how you think about it.'

Him. He'd said that. Not thirty minutes ago.

'You can't protect your loved ones…you can't stop bad things happening. But you can be with them if they do. I think that's what she was saying.'

Rowan clenched his teeth. He didn't need this man—this stranger—to tell him what Isabella was trying to say.

Except he did. Because he hadn't really been listening to anything Isabella had been saying lately. He'd listened to her words, but not the real meaning behind them. He hadn't seen her pain, he'd only heard what he'd wanted to hear, that she was fine, happy even, when really she was only pretending to be. For everyone's sake. Especially his.

Rowan looked at the men and didn't see a journalist or a photographer but two men he wouldn't mind going for a pint with.

'What am I going to do?' Rowan asked.

'I'd probably start with grovelling. And if that doesn't work, some sort of grand gesture. And maybe more grovelling,' Webber suggested.

Rowan didn't have time for a grand gesture. He didn't have time at all. He had a very small window before Isabella called palace security to throw him out of the place for good.

He didn't even have time to think about what he was going to say.

CHAPTER ELEVEN

JUST AS ISABELLA had known she would be, Francesca was waiting when Isabella returned to her rooms.

'So?'

'So...' Isabella flopped onto the nearest sofa and kicked off her shoes. 'I really need a bath.'

'You can have one in a minute, after you tell me how it went.'

'It went fine—'

'Great!'

'To begin with. And then it was an unmitigated disaster. I yelled at Rowan in front of the journalists, told him he'd broken my heart and made him promise never to speak to me again.'

Francesca's jaw dropped. 'Oh.'

'Oh, no, is more like it.'

'I'm sure...' Francesca began and then moved quickly around the room. 'Maybe we get the communications team to speak to them, reach some sort of understanding? Maybe you could speak to them again?'

Isabella shook her head. 'No. I'm done with this. I'm done trying to smooth this over, to hide my pain, to pretend everything is fine. I'm tired, Frannie. But most of all, I don't care if they think I'm heartbroken. I didn't say anything that wasn't the truth. I'm sick of putting on a perfect facade.' She tugged at the elastic holding her hair back and rubbed her scalp with her fingertips, fluffing out her hair. 'I don't care what they think of me anymore.'

As she spoke the words she was hit by their truth.

She didn't care. It was how she felt. And they were natural feelings. And justifiable. She didn't have to pretend. She had loved Rowan and he'd hurt her, let her down, and she wasn't afraid to say it.

'I'm sorry if that makes things difficult for you, and Mum and Dad, but I'm sick of being perfect.'

Francesca studied her sister. 'What brought this on?'

'Thirty years in the spotlight?'

Francesca smiled. 'I mean, you're different.'

Isabella opened her mouth to contradict her sister. She was the same person she'd always been except…she did feel different. She wasn't falling apart, she wasn't on the verge of tears, even though she'd just messed up the interview she'd been focusing on for the past week.

No. She felt together.

She felt strong for the first time in months. Even though she'd ruined the interview and she knew there would be fallout, she'd told Rowan how she really felt.

She'd been brave.

'You have a choice you know.'

'What do you mean?'

'You can choose your destiny.'

Isabella shook her head. 'I'll always be a princess.'

'I'm not saying you can choose who you are, because you're right, you can't, but you can change what you do and how you live. You don't have to stay here, you know, in Monterossa.'

'Are you trying to get rid of me?' Isabella joked, but her sister's words made sense.

'Not at all. I'm only saying that you have the skills and the qualifications to do so many things. And now you've told

Rowan how you really feel, maybe you're ready, for not just a change, but also a challenge.'

She had wanted a change, for a while, but a change would mean leaving Francesca. Leaving Monterossa.

'I don't know if I could leave.'

'Not for ever, or anything like that. Maybe we've been selfish wanting to keep you here.'

'You haven't been keeping me here. I've been keeping myself here.'

Francesca nodded. She understood. The ties that bound Isabella to Monterossa were loyalty and love only.

'You love Paris. And London. They aren't very far away.'

'I do feel ready for a change.' She'd once thought that marrying Rowan would be that change, but since that wasn't going to happen, it was up to her. 'I… I really could go anywhere. Do anything!'

You know what you want to do. You've known since your father got sick.

Francesca's face lit up, mirroring the joy that Isabella suddenly felt.

She wasn't stuck. She was free.

'I won't be gone for ever. I'm not abandoning you.'

'I know you're not. But soon it might be time for me to start the next part of my life, and it's time for you to as well. I might want you by my side always, but it would be selfish of me to insist on it. You need to build a life that doesn't revolve around me.'

'But I love you.'

'And I love you. And I will still love you, no matter where in the world you are.'

Isabella wondered if there was something else her sister wasn't telling her. Something she wasn't yet ready to. But either way, it didn't matter.

'Are you sure?'

Francesca laughed. 'I'd miss you, but of course I'm sure. I've never expected you to shadow me for my entire life. I could not have asked for a more dedicated sister.'

'No.'

'It's not as though we'll never see one another. We'll talk every day. But you have a whole new adventure to have and you have to go and have it.'

So many possibilities suddenly presented themselves. She knew she wanted to learn more about skin cancer, but also to make sure others knew what she did.

'I love Monterossa.'

Francesca laughed. 'I know you do, but the world, literally, is your oyster.'

'Oysters? Yuck. Why can't it be my chocolate cake?'

'It can be whatever you want. The world can be whatever you want.'

Isabella went to her bathroom and turned on the bath. She had so many things to think about. She only had an idea, but now she realised she had time. And freedom. And she couldn't wait to get to work. The room quickly filled with steam and the noise of the running water and the thought of submerging herself in the tub already began to soothe her. She unbuttoned her skirt as she walked back into her bedroom. The door to her living area clicked and she called to her sister. 'Frannie? What's up?'

'I had to talk to you,' said a voice that was most definitely not her sister's.

'What are you doing here?' Isabella pulled her skirt around her and tried to button it back up. A task that was made harder with trembling hands. 'I said I didn't ever want to see you again.'

'I haven't left yet.'

'Clearly.'

Couldn't he get the message? She couldn't have made it clearer. We. Can't. See. One. Another. Ever. Again.

'I just had to tell you that you were right,' he said.

'I know I was right, which is why I told you I never wanted to see you again.' Because each time she did she felt her newfound resolve wavering. Something rose up inside her and pushed her to him.

'Yes, but that wasn't the part you were right about. I hope you'll agree you got that part very wrong. You were right that I should have been braver. Stronger. I shouldn't have hidden behind my family. I shouldn't have used them as an excuse.'

She knew it! He had been using his family and the media as an excuse all along. But for what?

'And what is the truth, Rowan?' Her voice shook and her body braced itself for fresh heartbreak.

That you don't love me enough?

'That I was scared I wasn't good enough for you.'

Oh.

She wanted to say, 'But that's ridiculous' and yet…

I'm sorry I wasn't strong enough.

She swallowed and thought back to London and the comments she'd brushed aside.

'Why would you doubt yourself?' she asked.

'Isabella, you're a princess.'

'So? That's a birthright, not an achievement.'

'I flunked out of school…'

'And then you developed a super-successful business that helps millions of people.'

'That was luck.'

'No, it wasn't. It was brilliance.'

'I listened to the haters. I'm sorry I did, and I will be sorry for ever for hurting you. You hid it so well, and I didn't question it. I wanted to believe that you were okay because it made things easier for me.'

Wow.

Isabella nodded. She understood, because she also understood that it wasn't always possible to be brave. It was often easier to push your feelings down and take the simplest path.

'Thank you for admitting that. It took courage.'

He laughed nervously. 'Hopefully next time my courage will be better timed. I don't know how to say this, and I don't have time to do anything grand because I suspect if I don't tell you this soon you'll have me thrown out of the palace. In fact, there's a good chance you'll have me thrown out anyway.'

'I don't know what you're saying.'

'I'm saying I love you. I love you and I never stopped loving you.'

She shook her head.

'It's true.'

'Why tell me this?' Why now? Nothing had changed with this revelation and the longer he stood in her bedroom, the harder he was making things.

'I had a chat with Richard and Thommy.'

'You spoke to the press?'

'Off the record.'

'Off the record! You know as well as I do that there's no such thing.'

'Maybe. But I trust them.'

As Isabella breathed in she shuddered. 'We went to all this trouble…'

'Yes, we did. And I hate to point it out, but you did go a little off script earlier as well.'

She couldn't meet his eye but could hear the smile in his voice. Her cheeks were on fire.

'You hurt me. A lot. I don't know if I can trust you again.' There, that was also the truth and hard to admit. Even though she longed for him, she couldn't just go back. She wasn't the woman she had been a year ago.

You aren't even the woman you were an hour ago.

'I thought you didn't care,' he whispered and then he was standing next to her, his feet beneath her gaze.

'I had to say that. I had to pretend it was all okay.'

'But it wasn't, was it? And I thought… I told myself that it was okay I wasn't strong enough because you didn't really mind.'

'Of course I minded! I love you and you broke my heart!'

Rowan took a step back. 'I'm sorry I didn't see it earlier.'

'You weren't meant to see it. I was pretending to be strong. I was pretending I was okay. I couldn't stand the idea of the world seeing how hurt I was.'

'I know, and I'm sorry you had to do that. I'm sorry about everything.'

She nodded, 'Thank you for saying that. But it's okay. And I meant what I said. I can't keep doing this. You need to leave.'

'Did you hear what I said earlier? The part about me loving you? And never stopping?'

She'd heard it, but it was words only. She'd never doubted his affection, only his commitment.

'But what's different? You still want to protect your family. I'm still a princess. Neither of those things will ever change.'

'No. But maybe I have. I realised something in London: bad things will happen, I can't run away from them. I can only get through them. And it's always easier to get through things with you.'

She smiled, and her chest filled with warmth and love.

'I thought the same thing. As stressful as that night was, I almost didn't mind, because I was with you.'

Without knowing who moved first, she was in his arms, her cheek pressed against the warmth of his chest, his heartbeat reverberating around her.

She looked up into his golden eyes and found him staring down at her, smiling and enveloping her in his love.

Isabella lifted her feet and brought her lips the last few inches home. Home to Rowan.

His mouth opened to welcome her, caressing, kissing, confirming with each kiss how much he loved her. She fell deeper and deeper into the kiss, letting his embrace and his love surround her.

It couldn't be this simple, could it? Isabella shook herself and took a breath.

'Rowan, this is lovely, but I meant what I said. I can't play games anymore.'

'I know that.'

'So…' *Be brave. Ask for what you want. Ask for what you need.* 'It's all or nothing, Rowan, I meant what I said before.'

He took her face gently into his strong hands. 'Isabella, I am asking for all. I love you enough to risk your parents' anger. I love you enough to stand up in front of the world and tell them I made a horrible mistake. Isabella, most of all, I even love you enough to knock on Francesca's door right now and tell her that I want you back.'

Isabella pressed her lips together, holding back a laugh.

'And that I want to marry you.'

Isabella closed her eyes and her stomach clenched. Images flashed across her mind, of her wedding dress, of Rowan's face when he told her he couldn't marry her, of the way none of the palace staff could meet her eyes for at least a month…

He stroked her cheek gently with his thumb. 'But you don't have to say anything about that now, and we don't have to make any decisions until you're ready. I need you to know that, no matter what, I'm in this for ever. If you tell me to leave, I will. But if you tell me to stay, I'll stay for ever.'

She looked at him, his eyes hopeful and full, just like her heart.

If he could be brave, she could as well.

'Stay,' she said, and he pulled her into his arms.

EPILOGUE

ISABELLA HAD OFFERED Rowan the option of an elopement, or a quiet wedding, but he'd refused. If she was comfortable then he would meet her at the end of the main aisle of the cathedral in Monterossa, just as they had planned last time.

The idea gave her family pause, but Isabella knew it was the right thing to do and this morning she'd been proven right, when she'd walked through the main arch of the cathedral just before eleven a.m.

Unlike last time, the wedding was in December, though in Southern Italy that was hardly cold. Isabella had worn a new ivory silk gown by a young, unknown designer, with several dozen tiny buttons up its back. She turned her back to Rowan now. 'I thought you might want to do me the honour of unbuttoning my dress.'

'You thought correctly. Though…' Rowan spun her back to face him. 'I would just like to look at you in this dress a little longer.'

She laughed. 'Really? I can't wait to get out of it.'

'And let me guess, into a bath?'

She smiled. 'No. Not just now.' Even though it had been a long day and the lead-up to the wedding had been intense, she didn't feel wrung out. She felt calm, centred. 'I meant I can't wait for both of us to get out of our clothes.'

Rowan's face expanded into a knowing smile. 'I see. But

there's time for that. I would just like to admire my beautiful wife in her wedding gown for a few more moments.'

Isabella felt herself melting, as she often did, under his loving gaze. It was hard to believe she'd ever doubted his feelings for her, when everything he did and said confirmed how much he loved her. Day after day.

'You always look beautiful.'

'But?'

He grinned. 'But this will be the last time I see you in a wedding dress and I want to savour it.'

'I see you in a suit all the time, so I'm happy for you to take it off.' She grinned.

The lead-up to the wedding had gone smoothly. There had been negative publicity, of course—after all, this was the second wedding they had planned—and 'Will they? Won't they?' and 'Second time lucky!' were some of the less egregious headlines that had come out. But they both saw the headlines for what they were—click bait and an attempt to sell newspapers. Only they both knew the truth, which was that they were undeniably, irrevocably in love with one another and committed to each other for ever.

After a short honeymoon in Sicily, they would return to their new home in New York. Rowan would continue to work on his business and Isabella would return to her work at the Monterossan Embassy. In addition to that work, she was also working with Rowan on a secret project. Francesca joked that their 'secret project' was baby-making, but in truth it was developing a new application to monitor skin health. They were still working on the details, but it would involve a person tracking moles and skin irregularities over time to see if there were worrying changes. The work had made Isabella feel more energised and useful than she ever had in her life.

She was also in almost constant contact with Francesca, messaging each other at all hours of the day.

And when they were in Monterossa, which they planned to visit regularly, they had a new suite of rooms, where they were now. Still in the palace, but in a different wing, separate from the others. It would be their second home, their own space whenever they visited. It had several bedrooms in case their family grew and a balcony with a view over the sea.

She opened the French doors and walked out to the balcony now. Rowan followed her and wrapped his arms around her and she leant into him.

'Did you see the papers?' she asked. Isabella hadn't picked up her phone since the night before.

'No, I'll leave that up to the communications team to deal with, but I'm sure it will be fine.'

Richard Webber and Thommy Spencer had been sent back to Monterossa to cover the event and they had given their only exclusive interview to them. They trusted them, especially after the lovely article they had first written about the pair of them. Webber had been true to his word and the piece had been honest but without any mention of the off-the-record confrontation he and Thommy had witnessed. The article had also been particularly complimentary about Rowan's new app, which had become one of the biggest selling of all time within the first week of its launch.

'I'm not going to give a single thought to the rest of the world and what they're saying about anything for at least…'

'A night? A week?'

He laughed. 'I was going to say for ever.'

They smiled as Rowan pulled Isabella into his arms and they looked together over the sea and the setting sun.

* * * * *

TEMPTATION IN A TIARA

KARIN BAINE

MILLS & BOON

For Dad x

CHAPTER ONE

PRINCESS FRANCESCA DI MARZANO couldn't breathe. Despite Twilight being a rooftop bar, she felt caged in. Trapped. The pressure that had been building since the second she'd stood outside Westminster Abbey with her sister, Isabella, now crushing her ribs and lungs.

She tried to focus on the present. On the fabulous décor of the swanky bar. The huge canopies overhead to shelter patrons from sun or rain, and the trailing purple and white fake wisteria hanging from trellises dotted around the floor, made to catch the eye. As were the huge sofas for the comfort of the clientele, and private booths where VIPs could be seen but not approached. Not to mention the pink fountain in the centre of it all, which people congregated around with cocktails in hand. Yet, despite the opulence, and attention to detail to give the illusion of a vast open-air garden, Francesca still felt as though she couldn't get enough oxygen into her body.

'Your Highness? Are you okay?' Giovanni Gallo, her royal protection officer, stopped to check on her, and Isabella disappeared into the crowd ahead.

If Francesca could've caught her breath, she would've called after her to stay close. She'd known this was a bad idea from the start, but her twin sister was the only person she felt close to in her life and it was difficult to say no to her. Even to something as hare-brained as ditching the evening celebrations the Duke of Oxford was hosting across the city in honour of the King of the United Kingdom's coronation. An event they were only attending to represent their father, who was currently recovering from his treatment for skin cancer at home in Monterossa.

Their homeland—a kingdom consisting of a group of islands and a small part of mainland Italy—couldn't be more different from the city of London. The very reason they'd wanted to explore it on their own terms.

Once they'd done their royal duty, it had been Isabella's idea to have one last night of fun, of trying to be normal, before Francesca possibly had to step into her father's role as monarch. She'd been preparing her whole life to become Queen, but now it was becoming a reality, she felt the pressure more than ever. Her father's cancer had spread into his lymph nodes, and, though they'd been removed, recovery had taken longer than expected due to infection. There was a question mark hanging over his health, and whether or not he'd be fully fit to return to his duties. That meant the notion of Francesca, as next in line, becoming Queen was a strong possibility. A prospect that was seriously daunting.

However, freaking out in public was not the way to deal with it. She and Isabella had given the press enough juicy gossip to deal with over the years. Isabella's fiancé calling off their wedding shortly after he was pictured in a compromising position with two women on his stag night, followed by Francesca's failed engagement to Benigno last year, had given them more publicity than they could ever have wanted.

If she wasn't careful, Francesca was going to hand them more on a silver platter. Except, she couldn't seem to regulate her breathing.

'I. Can't. Breathe,' she gasped, clutching a hand to her chest. The pain indescribable. Surely at twenty-nine years old she was too young to be having a heart attack?

Giovanni took her by the arm and guided her over to the side, away from everyone around them. But the thumping music reverberating through her whole body and the flashing lights were assaulting her senses. Not giving her the space she needed.

'Focus on me.' Giovanni held her by the shoulders, his deep, authoritative voice forcing her to look up at him.

He was at least a foot taller than her five-foot-four stature. An impressive figure. Staring at him wasn't a hardship either, and she did her best to focus on his big dark eyes.

'Deep breaths,' he insisted, placing her hand on his chest so she could feel the steady rise and fall as he inhaled.

She was focusing all right, but probably not on the things he was expecting her to. Francesca had harboured a crush on this particular member of the security team since he'd come on board four years ago. Although it was safe to say that, with his slicked-back black hair, stubble-lined sharp jaw, and impressive muscular build, most people who came in contact with him probably fancied the pants off him. Boxer briefs, she imagined...

Not that she had ever shared her impure thoughts about her bodyguard with anyone, not even her sister. It wouldn't be becoming of a future queen to contemplate a relationship with a member of staff. She was expected to marry someone of noble birth, even though that hadn't worked out so well for her so far. But Francesca always did the right thing when it came to her royal status. She did as she was told; did what was expected of her by her family and the country. What she wanted was never part of the equation.

Exactly why watching the British monarch's coronation had sent her into such a spin. Knowing that some day, probably soon, she was no longer going to be just Francesca, doing as she was told. From that moment on she would be Queen. With even greater expectations put upon her. Even the thought was enough for her to start gasping again and she had to focus on Giovanni, blocking out all thoughts, sights and sounds other than his handsome face.

'In…and out,' Giovanni instructed, and Francesca was compelled to follow until her breathing was gradually regulated back to normal.

'I thought I was dying,' she said eventually. Part of her wondered if that was wishful thinking. Then she wouldn't have to deal with the coronation or contemplate marriage to someone else she didn't love.

Benigno had been right when he'd called off their engagement, realising that she wasn't in it for the right reasons. But how could she ever marry for love when her country was the one thing that had her heart and her loyalty? Marriage for Francesca wasn't the romantic fantasy most grew up harbouring. From an early age she'd been told that it was her duty. She would marry because it was expected, and to someone deemed acceptable for the role of King alongside her. For no other reason.

Finding a soul mate, someone she'd be content to veg out with in front of the TV at night, wasn't a luxury she thought she could have. So she'd gone with Benigno as a viable option and tried to make it work, but apparently he had been hoping for that soul-mate connection. Now she was back at square one. In want of a husband. According to her parents, at least.

Her mother had even provided files on the eligible bachelors in attendance today, putting the emphasis on her finding a replacement for Benigno soon.

This wasn't the first time Francesca wished that those five minutes between her birth and Isabella's had been the other way around. Her twin sister at least didn't have quite the same worries as she had, and might actually be able to marry for love. She'd already come close to marrying a commoner. And yes, their father, King Leopold, had married Gloria Gold, an actress, but that had been a scandal too. Francesca didn't want her reign to start with any more black marks against her. Besides, she was running out of time on that front too.

It would be preferable for her to already have married by the time she was crowned so that her love life was not the main topic of conversation surrounding her reign. A nice marriage of convenience between her and someone suitable, arranged by royal advisors, would save a lot of time when she could spend a lifetime searching for someone able to capture a piece of her heart. Something that wasn't going to help her position any.

'A panic attack. Not surprising when you and your

sister are out in public without the usual security team. You know when you attend anything we usually put weeks of planning in first to assess any risk…' It was clear Giovanni was ticked off at her for putting them both in this situation, but at least no harm had been done. Perhaps she should take his advice before something did happen that would put them in danger. The last thing she wanted was for anyone to get hurt, or her parents to have cause for concern.

'I know. This was a stupid idea. We'll get Isabella and go back before anyone notices.' Even better, they could just go back to their hotel and forget this ever happened.

'Are you feeling better?' Giovanni didn't take his eyes off her and Francesca felt the air go from her lungs again.

She swallowed hard. 'Yes.'

Once he seemed satisfied that she wasn't going to pass out on him, he let go of her shoulders. 'Okay. We'll get Isabella and go.'

Francesca nodded, happy for him to take charge. This had all been very exciting in theory, but the reality was too much. She'd spent so much of her life being told where to go and how to act that being left to her own devices was overwhelming. Like one of those caged animals whipped into submission that, even when they were released from captivity, still paced the small path they were used to.

Francesca wouldn't even know what to do with a life of her own.

Giovanni took her by the hand and they walked towards the bar. She might've been tempted to sample the rainbow wall of brightly coloured bottles if she weren't already feeling sick. It wasn't how she'd imagined tonight going. When Isabella had first suggested it, Francesca had pictured dancing and cocktails, and not the formal dancing expected at functions. Real cutting loose on the dance floor.

Although that didn't seem to be the norm here either. Most people were just milling about, drinks in hand, probably trying to find a hook-up for the evening. Something else she wouldn't know anything about. It occurred to her that, for an almost thirty-year-old woman, there were an awful lot of life experiences she hadn't had the opportunity to explore. However, tonight was not going to be the night for that either, when at the first whiff of freedom she'd gone into a tailspin.

'Can you see her anywhere?' Giovanni was straining to see around the bar area.

Francesca looked for the siren-red outfit her sister had chosen for this evening. Although she'd deemed it a bit too eye-catching for someone who needed to stay under the radar, it should help them find her in this crowded area. Except she was nowhere to be seen. As they moved around the rooftop with increasing urgency, Francesca couldn't help but worry.

'I'll check the ladies' bathroom,' she suggested when it became clear that her sister was not in the immediate vicinity.

'I'll check first.' Giovanni prepared to swing into bodyguard mode, his hand on the door before Francesca could go in.

'I thought we were trying not to draw attention to ourselves.' Although it was protocol for him to scout out everywhere she went first, this was taking it to extremes.

Giovanni nodded and agreed with some reluctance. 'At least let me keep the door open so I can respond as quickly as possible if something happens.'

She wasn't going to argue, knowing this was seriously testing his need to control everything, and let him hold the door open with his foot whilst she checked the cubicles.

Apart from a couple of young women chatting at the washbasins there was no one else inside.

'Excuse me? You haven't seen my sister anywhere, have you?' Francesca approached, showing them the photo on her phone that she'd taken of Isabella just before they'd left the hotel.

'We passed her on our way in downstairs a few minutes ago.'

'Oh, yeah. I saw her leave with some guy on a scooter.'

The blood in Francesca's veins chilled at the thought that her sister had just taken off into the night in a strange city without even telling her.

'Was she struggling? Did she go against her will?' Giovanni pushed his way inside to interrogate the stunned women.

'Giovanni, I don't think this is the place—' Despite her urgency to find her sister, Francesca was still aware of causing a scene.

'Was she upset? Who took her?' He dismissed her concerns to continue his line of questioning.

The women blinked at him for some time before answering, probably trying to process the fact there was a handsome six-foot-plus man in here.

'She seemed okay.'

'I wasn't paying that much attention. I was more worried about getting past the bouncers. Did you see the bald one checking my ID?' The redhead giggled to her blonde friend, and it was clear they'd had other things on their minds besides the stranger they'd passed on the way in.

Francesca supposed it was good that neither she nor Isabella had been recognised at least.

'You must remember something,' Giovanni insisted.

Francesca put her hand on his arm. 'I think we should probably go.'

Her attempt to persuade him to drop this before they did draw attention seemed to work when he sighed, his shoulders dropping as he took his leave, Francesca joining him.

'So she's not here and doesn't seem to have been taken against her will. It wouldn't be beyond Isabella to decide to go off on her own. Why don't we go outside where I can hear myself think and I'll give her a call?' Hopefully she could tell her how silly she was being and persuade her to come back before any damage was done.

'What about the geolocator on her phone?'

Francesca flushed pink. 'We turned those off. We didn't want anyone to know where we were going.'

In her defence, she hadn't realised she'd lose her sister within five minutes of having their freedom.

'You girls will be the death of me,' Giovanni muttered under his breath as he led the way back out of the building.

It made Francesca smile to see the usual cool and collected bodyguard show his frustration. So, he was human after all. Sometimes she wondered, when he seemed as emotionless as she was accused of being at times.

'Well, don't plan on dying until we're all safe and sound back at the hotel.' She batted her eyelashes at him, ignoring the serious side eye he gave her.

Such was the nature of their relationship. A back and forth where she made him subtly aware it annoyed the hell out of her having a shadow everywhere she went, and he tried to get her to take her security seriously.

Though tonight she was sorry she hadn't taken his advice for once when he'd told them both in no uncertain terms, when he'd caught them sneaking out of the party at the Ashton in Mayfair, that this was a bad idea.

'The first thing we should do is try and contact her.' At least Giovanni was thinking clearly. Francesca needed him to teach her how to be so calm in a crisis. A skill she was going to need sooner rather than later. It was fine when she had everyone doing everything for her, dressing her, planning her day, advising her on what matters she'd be dealing with, but becoming Queen was going to require more independent thinking and a strength she apparently had yet to find.

Francesca pulled her small phone from her diamanté clutch bag, which didn't hold much else beyond her lipstick and her hairbrush, but she was glad to have something practical to do.

She pulled up her list of contacts and tapped on her sister's icon. She waited to connect, but the call was put straight through to voicemail.

'I'll send her a text in case she's somewhere she can't hear her phone.' Francesca waited, hoping for a response, but none came.

'Where would she go?' Giovanni had clearly moved to the next phase, which she suspected would include them scouring the city to find Isabella. Something Francesca had hoped to avoid, but it looked as though this wasn't going to be wrapped up so easily.

She could only blink at Giovanni in response. She had no idea where Isabella had gone, or why. More importantly, Isabella hadn't confided in her about what she was doing. If she'd gone of her own volition, it implied she hadn't wanted Francesca to know the answer to any of those questions. Suggesting it wasn't going to be anything she would approve of. Courting trouble they certainly didn't need.

It made her wonder if this had been her sister's plan after all. If her proposal for this evening had had nothing to do with Francesca having one night of normality, and more about giving Isabella the chance to sneak away and do whatever she wanted. The moment she knew for sure her sister was all right, Francesca was going to kill her.

'Think, Francesca. Who does she know in London?' Giovanni knew they were all in serious trouble. He'd taken his eye off the ball. Let his fondness for the Princesses override his common sense and, more importantly, protocol. Now he was solely responsible for whatever happened to Isabella and Francesca, and with one of them missing, it didn't bode well.

'She doesn't know anybody.' Francesca's big amber eyes were full of worry. It was clear she was struggling to focus on the matter at hand, concern for her sister overriding everything else.

Giovanni knew how they close they were. They did everything together, and he was sure right now it felt as though Francesca were missing a limb. However, he needed her to be her usual strong self. He'd seen her deal with some tough stuff in the years he'd been employed at the palace, her petite frame belying the strength of character within that he so admired. She was going to make a good queen when the time came. He just had to do his job as well and make sure to get both her and Isabella safely home.

'Does she talk to anyone online? Has she met anyone from the UK before? There must be someone she knows in the country.' Although it seemed as though he were putting all the responsibility on Francesca right now, he knew he was the one who'd fallen short in his duties.

As an ex-soldier, he should have known to keep his eyes, and his mind, on the targets at all times. The last time he'd been distracted, his army buddies had been hurt. He prayed his neglect wouldn't have the same outcome here. Not only for his sake, but for Isabella's, and Francesca's too. He was already carrying enough guilt over hurting people close to him, without causing the royal family more distress.

The whole reason he'd taken this position was to atone for those he'd hurt in the past. Becoming a royal protection officer, bodyguard to the Princesses, was the ultimate way to pay back to his country. His job was his life with no room for relationships outside the one he had with his employers. He'd hoped that meant no one ever getting close enough to end up hurt again. Only time would tell if he'd managed that.

Though this was a job where he couldn't afford to

make any mistakes. One slip-up could mean Francesca's safety being compromised. Not only was she the future Queen, but also someone he'd become very fond of.

Something he'd done his best to ignore, hoping that any affection he felt towards her was temporary. That it would fizzle out the longer he was in the job, getting to know the person beyond the tiara. Except it hadn't worked out that way. If anything, spending more time with Francesca had only made him admire her more.

She was devoted to her position in the royal family, and didn't take anything for granted. In his previous security work he'd dealt with other privileged people who had a tendency to be self-centred, thinking only of their own wants and needs. The opposite to how Francesca conducted herself. It took something special to be so focused and carry the weight of responsibility she did without complaint. He should know.

So it was natural he should be impressed by someone so beautiful inside and out. Her flawless olive skin, perfect plump lips, and the tumbling dark waves of hair falling to her shoulders made her look like the perfect fairy-tale princess. But she was so much more than her looks. He was attracted to her strength of spirit as much as her curvy little body.

It wasn't until she'd got engaged to Benigno that Giovanni had realised his feelings for her went beyond admiration. He'd never thought it a suitable match. Francesca needed someone as strong as she was, who was capable of supporting her once she became Queen. That wasn't Benigno and it had frustrated Giovanni no end to think of her tying herself to him for the rest of her days. Apart from anything else, there hadn't been a spark between them. Not like the one Giovanni and Francesca had. Even though he was far from suitable either. He'd been glad when the wedding was called off, sure that Francesca would get over the initial hurt in time, and he'd been right. It didn't mean she wouldn't find another partner he'd find difficult to see her going out with.

However, he was a professional too, and Francesca's safety had to be his priority over any feelings that could come to nothing.

When Francesca didn't answer his question, he had to refrain from shaking her. Royal protocol dictated that he shouldn't touch her unless it was in the line of duty, guiding her out of harm's way. Which probably wasn't a bad thing in the circumstances. He needed to keep some emotional distance. 'In that case, I'm going to have to call this in as a security alert and we're going to have to let the police deal with it.'

Something he was reluctant to do when it was sure to cause an incident large enough for the royal family to hear about. So much for the discreet night out the girls had promised before he'd agreed to this craziness…

'Please don't do that, Gio.' Francesca grabbed his arm, her full pink lips pleading with him. 'As far as we know, she went willingly with someone. We just have to find her. If we alert the security forces this whole thing is going to escalate and it's the last thing my family needs right now.'

Giovanni was torn between doing exactly what he knew he should, and the Princess calling him Gio, asking for his help. And touching him, making it personal. For once, he let his heart rule his head. 'Well, we're going to need somewhere to start. London's a big city.'

Francesca thought for a moment. Then those big eyes grew even wider with that childlike enthusiasm he saw in her every time she was on a royal engagement meeting new people.

'Oh. I think she stayed in touch with that pop star, Leanne. You know, the one with the baby-pink hair and star tattoos on her face.'

'Is she the one who sang that weird whispery song with the bells?' He wasn't up to date with the latest music, he had more important things to think about, but he remembered Isabella playing it over and over again in the car. Whispering barely heard lyrics accompanied by handbells wasn't his idea of music, but she was apparently popular.

'Yeah. She was supposed to play at Isabella's wedding.' Even the mention of the doomed wedding made Francesca flinch.

It had been a big tabloid headline when Isabella's fiancé had been photographed cavorting with other women on his stag do. Swiftly followed by another announcing the end of the relationship only days before the wedding. It had been a nightmare all around, not only for Isabella and her family, but for the palace PR department, and those who'd had to inform all of the dignitaries who were supposed to be attending the event.

'What about the ex? Are you sure she's not with him?' It wouldn't be unheard of for someone to get back with their ex, even though he personally hadn't ever done that. He took a casual approach to relationships and made sure the women he hooked up with realised that. Then no one got hurt.

Francesca shook her head. 'As far as I know Isabella hasn't spoken to Rowan since everything happened.'

'What makes you think this Leanne might be a good lead? Do you know where she is?'

'I know she's hosting her own party in the city tonight, not far from here.' Francesca shrugged.

It was as good a shout as any, he supposed. 'Okay. We'll head there and you keep trying Isabella on the way.'

Giovanni at least had a plan, somewhere to start. Usually he preferred to work with a lot more information, but this whole mess was his own fault. He just hoped he was the only one who'd suffer the consequences of his bad decision-making this time.

CHAPTER TWO

Francesca showed Giovanni the address of the club where Leanne was hosting her coronation party, praying this was a one-stop fix.

'Should we get a taxi?' Usually, she didn't have to worry about transport—someone always arranged that for her. She was aware of her privilege, but it had never really been an issue for her until now, when it became apparent she didn't really know how to function in the real world, never having to arrange anything herself. The royal family had people who did everything for them.

Thank goodness for Giovanni, one of the few people she knew who had experience of reality outside the palace walls. This might not be his country of birth either, but at least he knew how to get stuff done. A soldier who'd seen action knew how to survive a lot tougher situations than this.

The romantic fantasy of being in the city alone was a lot scarier in person when she didn't know anyone here, or how to get around. It made her wonder how on earth she and Isabella had thought they could do this themselves. Though her sister took more risks—the perks of being the second born—she had no more real-life experience than Francesca.

The thought of the two of them wandering around this bustling city without a clue made her shudder. At least she had Giovanni to hold her hand. Wait…he was literally holding her hand and leading her down the street. She yanked her hand out of his grip, refusing to let him trail her any further. Okay, so she was at his mercy, but that didn't mean he got to take liberties with her. Not with something as intimate as hand-holding.

He must've seen the fury on her face at his impertinence when he turned to see why she'd stopped. Except instead of an apology, he was smirking.

'Listen, Princess, you're going to want to hold my hand before you get lost on the underground.'

'What are you talking about?'

'The Tube. You have heard of it? It's the quickest and easiest way to get about this city, otherwise we're going to waste time sitting in traffic.'

She hated that he was right, but that wasn't the only thing bothering her. 'Of course I've heard of it, but it'll be full of…people.'

His grin grew even more smug. 'Commoners, you mean? You're going to have to get used to it, Princess. You wanted to be normal for the night. That means being herded into too hot, too cramped, germ-ridden public transport instead of your golden carriage. This is how the other half actually lives.'

Although the concept was alien to her, she couldn't afford to be snobbish about getting on a train with the British public. She was the one who'd agreed with Isabella that going incognito would be a good idea, so she couldn't expect any special treatment. If they were going to keep this whole mess from their parents, she was going to have to blend in as best she could.

'Do you think I'm going to fit in?' It was one thing coming directly to the bar from the party in a car Giovanni had insisted on arranging upon hearing of their escape plan, but an entirely different story mixing with the public and hoping she wouldn't be recognised.

Giovanni looked her up and down and clicked his tongue. 'Hmm... Now you mention it you are a tad overdressed. We don't want to draw any more attention than the average pretty woman.'

Francesca stood patiently awaiting instruction, trying not to get too hung up on the fact that he'd called her pretty. Giovanni wasn't one for dishing out compliments. If anything, she thought him immune to her charms when, no matter what occasion or outfit, she never raised as much as a smile in response. Not that his appreciation was her goal when she was getting ready...

'Well, what do you suggest?' She folded her arms in defence against the things he was making her feel.

'This, for a start.'

She was tempted to back away when he reached out to her, afraid to let him touch her again, but she remained steadfast. Her heart beating frantically as he unpinned her hair from its sleek confines, letting her tresses fall freely around her shoulders.

Then he moved so close her face was almost buried in his chest as he undid the diamond and sapphire necklace around her neck. She could feel his breath on her cheek, smell the spicy scent of his cologne, and she had to force herself not to react.

'Put that in your bag.' His voice sounded more gruff than usual and she followed his command as he backed away.

Still, he wasn't done. He bent down and grabbed the tiered hem of her long cobalt-blue, off-the-shoulder silk dress, yanking until he managed to rip away one ruffle, then another. Leaving her feeling half naked now her body was exposed from the knees down.

'What the hell are you doing, Gio?' Never mind that he'd just shredded a very expensive designer dress, but his fingers were grazing some very intimate places in the process.

'There. Now you look like you're going clubbing, and not to a formal ball.' He looked so pleased with himself as he deposited the torn remnants of her dress into the nearest bin, Francesca thought he needed taking down a peg or two before he became unbearable.

'Well, you could do with some styling yourself if you want to blend in.' Now it was her turn to make him feel uncomfortable. Francesca undid his tie and slipped it from around his neck.

'Put that in your pocket,' she demanded in a tone not dissimilar to the one he'd used with her. Then she opened a couple of his shirt buttons, along with the one on his jacket.

'You could probably lose that altogether, you know. And roll your sleeves up.' Okay, so that was just a kink of hers, but he had lovely tanned, thick forearms and it was a shame to keep them hidden.

'Are you done now?' he asked sardonically.

'I guess.' Francesca shrugged, not giving anything away about how much she'd enjoyed stripping off some of his clothes with him standing helplessly, letting her do it. The frisson of power had at least taken her mind off her sister for a little while.

Wordlessly, he took her hand again and led her towards the underground station. She followed him down the steps and into a bustling hall full of commuters coming and going all around her. Francesca clung a little closer to her protector. He waved a card at one of the small barriers and passed through, but when Francesca approached it wouldn't budge. She tried again to push through it.

Noticing her absence, Giovanni turned and sighed. 'Use your credit card. You have to pay, Princess.'

'I don't have a credit card,' she muttered through gritted teeth. Despite the family having a lot of money, they had very little to do with it in reality.

'Oh, yeah. I forgot you people don't actually carry anything with you. Just how far did you and Isabella think you were going to get on charm and looks alone?' He pulled his wallet from the jacket he was carrying and took out another credit card, scanning it on her side of the barrier so she could get through and join him.

'I guess we didn't think things through.' Francesca felt her face grow hot with shame, embarrassed that they hadn't even thought about money. They were so used to having everything done for them they never had to pay anyone directly for anything. She'd taken her life of privilege for granted, never having to think about the practicalities of everyday living like everyone else.

'I guess not, Princess. Thank goodness I caught you both when I did. You hadn't even organised any transport, for goodness sake.' He shook his head, furthering her embarrassment when he clearly thought she was nothing but an airhead, and she had yet to prove otherwise to him.

'Do you think you could stop calling me that? I thought we were trying not to draw attention.' It was the only comeback she had.

'Princess? It's not in deference to your title. It's more...'

'An insult?'

'A term of endearment.'

They spoke over one another, but Francesca suspected her explanation was the truth. He thought her nothing but a spoiled, pampered princess, in every meaning of the word. What was worse than that was the realisation that it was true.

'I can't help the world I was born into, Giovanni. Yes, it comes with privileges most people aren't lucky enough to experience, but it isn't always a bed of roses being part of the royal family.'

'I know that, Francesca. I see you. I see how dedicated you are to your role.'

'Okay, then.' She decided to let the matter drop before he paid her any more compliments, letting her see a softer side of Giovanni that she wasn't used to.

'Okay, then.' He smiled and led the way over to the downward escalator leading to the train platforms.

When she faltered at the top of the moving stairway, he took her hand and urged her on with him.

'You have to stand on the right-hand side,' he told her.

Francesca bristled, and disentangled her fingers from his. 'I think I know how to stand on a step.'

It was one thing letting him guide her in this unfamiliar world, but he wasn't the boss of her. He had to remember his place.

'Excuse me.'

'Move.'

'You're supposed to stand on the right so people can pass on the left,' he repeated.

A stream of seemingly angry commuters pushed past her, knocking her into Giovanni. Forcing him once again to come to her rescue. He grabbed her around the waist, his big hands almost completely encircling her body, and transported her effortlessly onto the step in front of him. On the right.

'It's a stupid rule,' she fumed, not even looking back to see his smirk.

When they reached the bottom of the escalator they were faced with two signs and on this occasion she was happy to let Giovanni point her in the right direction. The platform wasn't too crowded and she stood patiently waiting for the train, which, according to the board, was due imminently.

She looked down at the dusty tracks, marvelling at the great feat of engineering providing links to the whole city and beyond. It occurred to her too that the location would make a great setting for a horror movie. Long, dark tunnels, and the Victorian-style architecture, made the thought of a creature hiding in the shadows entirely possible. So when she saw a little mouse scamper along, right in front of her, she let out a shriek and jumped straight into Giovanni's strong arms.

'It's all right. He won't come anywhere near you. He's just looking for food and somewhere quiet to rest.' Giovanni's voice was soft and soothing in her ear, and for a brief moment she thought about him whispering sweet nothings instead.

This was the problem. Giovanni was paid to be her protector, and, in turn, he made her feel like a fragile princess. When she was with him it was the only time she didn't have to be strong, make decisions, and pretend she was holding it together. Giovanni was always there to look after her; to see the real Francesca behind the royal front she had to adopt for the cameras and the general public. He made her feel safe, and, well, like a woman rather than a title.

She would have been content to stay in his arms the rest of the night, except a waft of cold air, a roar in the tunnel, and the glare of headlights announced the arrival of the train.

'Hold my hand.' He didn't have to ask her twice.

As the doors opened, everyone on the platform swarmed forward, barely waiting for those on board to disembark before shoving their way onto the train. Francesca was carried on board in the wave of people, her feet barely touching the ground. Giovanni was her lifeline, holding her hand to keep her with him.

By the time the doors shut, she was pressed tightly up against him again, with no one paying them any more attention than anyone else. Strange that this uncomfortable experience was the most chilled she'd been for a while. Francesca was used to people doing things for her, and telling her what to do. But it wasn't that often she got to switch off that royal persona. Didn't have to be on guard, watching everything she said or did. The circumstances she'd found herself in tonight weren't ideal, and she hoped Isabella was okay, but she was enjoying this little piece of freedom. As long as Giovanni was here to guide her through it.

The train jolted as it pulled away from the platform and she struggled to find her balance, grabbing Giovanni's shirt in her hand so she didn't fall.

'You might need to hold onto something else,' he growled, taking her hand and moving it from his chest to the bright yellow pole she was standing next to.

'Sorry.' She took a step back, embarrassed by her own neediness tonight.

'You're like an alien, you know.' At least he was smiling at her now, instead of that scowl he'd worn only moments ago. Even if he was insulting her.

'Pardon me?'

'It's like you've just been beamed down onto another planet from the mother ship. Everything's so new and bewildering to you.'

'Sorry I'm so annoying.' It seemed as though she was apologising a lot simply for being her tonight.

'No. Not at all. It's endearing when I'm so cynical about everything these days.' Giovanni didn't expand on his reasons for that, and Francesca had to wait until they were off the train and through the exit barriers before she could quiz him.

Walking out into the city again was another assault on the senses. There were so many people. Usually there was a barrier between her and the rest of the world, so it was no wonder she had some anxiety. Giovanni was right about everything being new and bewildering to her, but it was also terrifying.

She'd been wrapped in a bubble her whole life. One that she'd mostly resented but had no choice but to accept. It was her life to be a princess and then a queen some day, so of course she wasn't going to live like everyone else. She wondered how Isabella was coping with the change. Although they'd done everything together growing up, there had always been a certain distinction made between them because one of them was going to be Queen eventually, and one of them wasn't. Perhaps this life would be easier for Isabella to get used to when she didn't have the same pressure as their father's successor to the throne.

'What did you do before coming to the palace?' she asked, once they were away from the crowds and she had some personal space again.

'I was in the army.' Giovanni kept walking, facing straight ahead, giving nothing away.

She'd always been curious about him. The man behind the suit. But she'd always been careful to keep that emotional distance between them when they both had roles to fulfil, duties to carry out. Tonight had changed everything. At least for her. She'd had to let those defences down, put herself in his hands, and let him see her vulnerabilities. It seemed only fair she should know a little about him in return.

'Hmm, I could picture that.' Too well. Now she had an image of him in khaki, smeared with dirt and sweat...

'Not as glamorous as you probably imagine.'

Francesca blushed, even though he couldn't see her. 'How come you ended up at the palace, then?'

'We were on a peacekeeping mission and my unit was caught up in a clash with locals protesting an election. A lot of men got hurt and I left shortly after that.'

He was very abrupt, giving little away, but Francesca was determined to get to know something about him.

'Were you medically discharged, then?' She wondered what hidden injuries he'd sustained when he looked like the fittest man she'd ever met.

'Not me, but I decided I'd had enough. Shouldn't you try Isabella again?' It was obvious he was trying to change the subject as he kept walking, with Francesca tottering on her heels trying to keep up with his fast pace.

'If you weren't injured, why did you leave?' Francesca typed out another text message to her sister as she talked.

Giovanni stopped so abruptly she nearly ran into the back of him. His shoulders sagged as he heaved out a sigh.

'Because it was my fault. I was the captain, making decisions and responsible for operations. I hadn't realised the depth of political unrest. Riot gear and barbed wire obviously were no match for the incendiary devices that had been planted at the buildings we were defending. My failure to plan, and keep my team safe, changed people's lives for ever.'

'But you didn't plant any bombs. You didn't go out with the intention of hurting your friends.' It seemed clear-cut to her. Even though she knew what guilt felt like, warranted or not.

When Benigno had called off the wedding, she'd hated the scandal it had caused her family. Regardless that it hadn't been her doing. Although her parents hadn't been physically wounded, like Giovanni's army mates, they'd been hurt by the shame the broken engagement had brought to their door. And nothing anyone said or did could ever lessen the guilt she carried over that. Something she apparently had in common with her bodyguard.

Giovanni, however, didn't have her parents' disapproval hanging over every action and decision. Francesca had learned from an early age that she had to truly earn her parents' approval, and that meant failure wasn't an option in any area of her life. A difficult concept for a young child to accept, but she'd realised quickly that her parents' love came with conditions.

Never stepping out of line, never talking back, getting dirty, or making any kind of mistake in public. It seemed she wasn't worthy of love unless she was perfect.

Isabella had a different relationship with them. Although she had her own challenges, they seemed to make more allowances where she was concerned. Probably because she wasn't scrutinised just as much as the future Queen. Their mother and father had been sympathetic to them after their respective break-ups. To a point. Francesca couldn't help but feel as though she'd failed them in some way when Benigno had called off their engagement. She'd been more gutted about that than the end of her relationship. It felt to her as though it represented a flaw in her character. Something her parents wouldn't have appreciated. She desperately didn't want to disappoint them again.

'I let it happen. That's as good as detonating the bomb in my book.' All traces of soft Giovanni disappeared, leaving behind the steely voiced, fast-walking version.

'Can you slow down? I'm in heels, and they're killing me.' They were only meant for show. It was very rare she had to walk very far in this kind of garb, and exactly the reason she and Isabella carried their 'emergency shoes'. Little ballet-slipper flats, which fitted into their bags. Isabella's bag tonight, as it happened.

Giovanni suddenly did a one-hundred-and-eighty-degree turn and dropped down to her feet. He lifted one shoe off the ground and pulled it off her foot. Francesca had to lean on him so she didn't fall over. Giovanni moved to her other foot, leaving her standing barefoot on the pavement.

He took both shoes, walked over to the small wall lining the footpath, and banged both shoes hard until the heels snapped off. Francesca could only watch openmouthed.

'There,' he said, handing back her mutilated stilettos. 'Flats. You're welcome.'

'Have you any idea how much those shoes are worth?' Her voice was at a pitch capable of shattering nearby windows.

'Have you?'

Touché.

Francesca let that one go, knowing he was just trying to rile her because she'd elicited some personal information from him.

'It's not healthy to hold onto that guilt, you know. Especially when you did nothing wrong.' She should know.

She felt bad, not only about what her parents had gone through, but also because Benigno had been right. She had been closed off from him. Such was the way she'd been brought up as the future Queen—not to show her emotions, and to put all her energy into maintaining her public persona. Though that part hadn't worked out so well.

It wasn't only her parents she didn't want to hurt again. She had no intention of marrying anyone who didn't know the score from the outset. A marriage at this stage was going to have to be something arranged by two families. More of a business transaction between two parties, then her future husband wouldn't be expecting something she couldn't give him. Love. Apparently she reserved that only for her country, and her responsibility to her position in the royal family.

'It's my fault people I loved got hurt, and not for the first time.' He muttered the last bit as he stomped away, but Francesca had caught it and it left her wondering what else he was holding back.

As they rounded the corner, they almost walked straight into the crowd standing outside the club.

'Wait.' Giovanni shot out a hand and stopped her from going any further. 'There are photographers waiting.'

'Of course there are. Why didn't I think of that?' This was a celebrity party. Wherever there was a collection of famous people, there would inevitably be press waiting, ready to capture unflattering pictures. What on earth would her parents think if they saw her stumbling into a club in her ripped outfit?

'You stay here. I'll go and make sure your name is on that list for admittance.'

'What if they see me here?'

'They're waiting for limos. The last thing they'll expect is a princess on foot.' He gave a pointed look at her ruined shoes. 'Just stay back. Let me handle this.'

Francesca had no other choice.

***

Giovanni rolled down his sleeves, put his tie and jacket on, and did his best to look like the professional he was supposed to be. Somewhere along the way tonight he'd forgotten that, sharing details of his personal life, and getting way too close to Francesca physically and emotionally.

At least when he was back in his proper role in public he might be able to put some of that professional distance between them again. All he had to do was slip Francesca discreetly into the club, where they'd hopefully find Isabella. Having two princesses to look after again was infinitely better than one, when it would take his mind off every touch he'd shared with Francesca tonight in pursuit of her wayward sister.

He'd had plenty of experience getting his clients into venues discreetly, and no one challenged him as he strode through the throng of people and straight to the security detail at the club door.

He explained he had a royal princess requesting admittance, and after some conflab over walkie-talkies, Francesca's name was added to the party list. Leanne was apparently thrilled to have her in attendance. Now all he had to do was get Francesca inside without any photographic evidence that could end up in tomorrow's gossip columns.

He walked back up to where he'd left her.

'Well?' she asked, taking a short break from biting her French-manicured nails.

'They couldn't tell me if Isabella's in there, it's possible she's under a fake name, but they have agreed to letting you in. They had to contact Leanne for permission so I'm afraid we can't just walk in, take a look and leave. You'll probably have to say hello at least.'

'Okay, but how am I going to get in there without being seen?'

'You're probably not going to like it…' Giovanni stripped off his jacket and held it above her head.

'No, but I trust you.'

He knew that was a big deal for Francesca. In her position there weren't a lot of people she could trust. It meant a lot to him too, even though it was a huge responsibility to keep her safe. Especially in these circumstances.

'Keep into the shadows until we get near, jacket over your head, and pressed close to me so no one can see your face.'

She nodded, though he could see the apprehension on her face. More pressure on him to get this right.

With the feel of Francesca's hands pressed tight through his shirt, branding his skin, he pushed his way inside the club. Determined to protect her at all costs.

It didn't matter the life-or-death situations he'd been in countless times before, or that this was just about dodging the press, his heart was still pounding, sweat breaking on his skin, knowing he had to keep her safe. She trusted him. Just as his parents had. Just as his army unit had.

Once inside, Francesca let go, and handed him his jacket back. Her eyes were shining, her smile wide, almost as though she'd enjoyed the exhilaration of the moment. 'We did it.'

'Let's hope so,' he muttered, hoping none of this would come back to bite them on the backside. Isabella had a lot to answer for.

This place was definitely not his scene. There was a seventies disco floor, which lit up as people walked on it and was nearly as bright as the strobe lights flashing all around. Then there were the life-size leopards posed between potted palms along the edge of the room. The word tacky came to mind, but it probably cost more to decorate this area than he earned in a year. It was true that money couldn't buy taste. Or perhaps he too was becoming used to the finer things in life at the palace, where everything was tasteful and elegant. The contrast between the two worlds never more evident than when the hostess of the party came to greet them.

Leanne, a petite, pink-haired teen, dressed in some kind of silver-foil bikini and fishnet tights, was the opposite to the demure appearance of Princess Francesca, whom he'd had to customise just to blend in with this crowd. Though he knew which look he preferred...

'Your Highness. I can't believe you're actually here.'

Leanne attempted a curtsey but was quickly discouraged by Francesca.

'There's no need for formalities. Just call me Francesca.'

'You have to meet everyone.' Social etiquette now out of the window, she grabbed Francesca and rushed her through to the party hub.

With leopard-print-clad drag queens wandering amongst the partygoers with trays of smoking cocktails, and half-naked men wearing crowns, handing out plastic tiaras, Giovanni thought he'd walked into someone's fever dream.

'I don't want the press to know I'm here. I'm supposed to be at an official function.' Francesca had to yell over the music to be heard, which mocked any idea of secrecy.

'It's fine. I've banned phones. You're safe.' Keen to show off her new best friend, Leanne dragged Francesca onto the middle of the dance floor.

So much for keeping a low profile. As the girls danced, Giovanni stood on sentry duty, scouting the room, not only for potential threats, but also for cameras.

'I hope you don't mind us crashing your party.' Francesca cosied up to their gracious host.

'Not at all. I'm thrilled to have an actual royal in attendance.'

Giovanni did wonder if Leanne knew Francesca wasn't a member of the British royal family...

'It's so much more fun than the one we were supposed to be attending. I was wondering if you'd seen my sister, Isabella?' Francesca was doing all the right things, flattering her host, and not making a big deal about her sister's disappearance.

'Does your bodyguard have to stand so close? He's kind of killing the vibe.' Leanne glared at him like a petulant child who always got what she wanted. Which didn't include a sensible adult.

'It's my job,' he told her, folding his arms and planting his feet firmly on the sticky floor.

Leanne grabbed one of the sparkly silver tiaras from a nearby drag queen and perched it on his head. 'There, that's better.'

Francesca was smirking. 'It does kind of suit you.'

'I think it would look much better on you, Princess.' He took it off and carefully placed it on her head, making her look like the princess she was in a room full of pretenders.

She smiled at him. 'Maybe you could take a step back, Giovanni. I think I'm safe enough here.'

'Yeah, Gio, go chill with the other stiffs.' Leanne nodded towards the edge of the floor where there was a bank of similar-looking imposing male figures. No doubt security for the other rich and famous attendees who thought looking good on the dance floor was more important than staying safe.

The one thing that irked him more than being dismissed by this precocious pop princess was her using the nickname only real royalty got to use. He looked at Francesca to see what she wanted him to do. She nodded, giving him a look of apology, and he knew she was only doing this to get closer to Leanne.

Reluctantly, he took to the sidelines as he heard Francesca ask again about her sister.

He and the other security gave each other a nod of acknowledgement, but when he spotted a familiar face he couldn't help but let that cool exterior slip.

'Dan?' Despite the smooth, polished exterior, slicked-back hair and shades, he saw the face of the man who'd once worn military fatigues alongside him.

'Giovanni?' His old mate grabbed him into a bear hug and slapped him heartily on the back.

'What on earth are you doing here?'

'Bodyguard for the spoiled teenager.' Dan grinned, letting Giovanni know exactly who his charge was.

'How did you get this gig?' Giovanni was curious for more than one reason.

'Same as you, probably. Did some work in security

and earned myself a good reputation. Are you with Leanne's dance partner?'

'Yeah. Princess Francesca, but we need to keep it on the down low.' He was sure Dan would understand the need for discretion given they were in the same profession.

'No problem. Can't believe I'm seeing you here of all places.'

'I know. The last place I saw you—'

'Was in the hospital.' The smile on Dan's face died, and no wonder. It wasn't a happy time for either of them.

'You look well.' From the outside no one would ever have known he'd been involved in such a traumatic event, which had left him with life-changing injuries.

'I suppose you're wondering how I'm even standing.'

'No, I…yes.' There was no point in trying to be polite. The matter had been on his mind since the moment he'd spotted Dan.

Dan bent down and rapped on his lower right leg. 'Prosthetic. It took a while to get used to, but no one would even guess I had my leg blown off now.'

The casual mention of the explosion made Giovanni wince. The deafening roar, the ringing in his ears, and the dust and dirt raining down on him were all memories that were still raw for him. Not to mention the screams of his fellow squaddies. Now here he was, face to face with one of the men whose life had been changed for ever because of Giovanni's negligence.

'And it doesn't stop you from doing your job now?' Giovanni kept his eyes on the dancers, making sure that Francesca didn't suffer because of his incompetence too.

'No. It's easy. I've still got hands to shove any too

eager fans or potential stalkers out of the way. You know as well as I do that this job is more about planning than physicality.'

'Don't I know it?' Giovanni grumbled, thinking about the mess he was currently in. Francesca was certainly taking her time finding out about her sister, and he hadn't seen any sign of Isabella in here so far.

'Have you seen any of the other guys from the unit?'

'No. I don't socialise much.' The truth was he'd been too ashamed of himself to stay in contact with the others when he'd walked away with just a few cuts and bruises. He didn't have the right to feel sorry for himself, yet his life had changed that day for ever too.

'Married?'

'No.'

'Most of us are now. Rossi and Dino both have kids, and I've got one on the way.'

Giovanni didn't know why that information surprised him. Probably because he'd kept himself shut off from the idea of sharing his life with anyone, and expected the others had done the same.

'Congratulations, Dan. I'm pleased for all of you.' He'd spent the better part of two decades imagining his old army friends miserable, all because of him, and it was difficult to process otherwise. It was the reason he'd shut himself off emotionally from those around him. Believing he didn't deserve a happy life when he'd stolen one from everyone else. Now it seemed as though he was running out of excuses to keep people at a distance.

'You know, it wasn't your fault, Giovanni.' As if reading his thoughts, Dan did his best to relieve him of that guilt once more.

'I should've been more aware of what was going on. It was my job to keep everyone safe.'

'You didn't mean for anyone to get hurt. You didn't plant the bomb. Stop blaming yourself for something that was beyond your control, bud.' Another slap on the back.

'A friend of mine said something similar.' He thought of Francesca trying to convince him of the same thing, and not wanting to accept it. Now it seemed as though he had no choice. Though neither Francesca, nor Dan, could convince him that his parents' crash wasn't his fault. He had form when it came to letting himself, and others, down. Even now he was abandoning his post to try and make amends for his old mistakes.

'Then maybe you should listen to her.' Dan followed Giovanni's gaze towards Francesca. If he was trying to insinuate there was something more going on than a job, he'd got it completely wrong. Even if Giovanni had inadvertently referred to her as a friend.

'It was good catching up with you, but I think it's time I got the Princess out of here before she's spotted.' He shook hands with Dan and headed back to the dance floor.

'Take care, Giovanni. And remember, none of it was your fault,' Dan called after him and the words rang in Giovanni's head even as he walked closer to the source of the deafening music.

'I think this is my cue to leave,' Francesca told Leanne, glad to see Giovanni arrive, as all her attempts to leave so far had been thwarted by a pouting pop star.

'Are you sure you can't stay?' Leanne was clinging to her hand.

'Sorry. I've got to find my sister, and if she's not here—' It had taken a while to establish that fact. Leanne had been sketchy about whether or not Isabella had been here, or even been in contact. Francesca suspected she just wanted a royal at her party, whoever that might be, and at whatever cost. In the end, frustrated, she'd had to ask directly. A sulky Leanne had reluctantly told her that she hadn't heard from Isabella since the wedding had been called off. So there was absolutely no reason for Francesca to stay. In fact, the longer she hung around, the greater the risk of her being snapped by someone.

'It's time to go.' Giovanni clearly heard the end of the conversation as he came back to join them, saving her once again.

'Thank you so much for a lovely time. Hopefully we'll meet again some time.' Francesca air-kissed Leanne on both cheeks before making a hasty exit from the club.

Thankfully, a well-known socialite was arriving just as Francesca and Giovanni were leaving. Someone only too happy to court the paparazzi, allowing the two reluctant partygoers to slip away virtually unnoticed.

They ran up the street, Giovanni's jacket covering their heads, laughing as they got one over on the press.

The moment of euphoria didn't last, however, when she remembered they'd hit another dead end.

'Now where do we go?' It was Giovanni who questioned their next move and it was unnerving to find he didn't know where they were going next either, when she'd become used to him taking the lead.

'Oh, Leanne said something about a street party going on at South Bank. Maybe she went there?' In a city this size it was impossible to guess where one person might be, but she couldn't just sit in a hotel room doing nothing to try and find her sister.

Francesca had a duty to her family, and she always did her best to never let them down.

CHAPTER THREE

THEY MADE THEIR way over towards the South Bank. Against Giovanni's better judgement. At this stage he thought they'd be better off going back to the hotel to wait for Isabella to show up. This was like trying to find a needle in a haystack, and every moment Francesca was in public put her in potential danger. As well as giving the press plenty of photo opportunities if she was spotted. The only thing in her favour was that perhaps she wasn't as much of a well-known face in London as she was back home. If they stayed away from any more celebrity-filled parties, they might have a chance of keeping a low profile.

Even if he hadn't been her bodyguard, Giovanni would have felt protective over Francesca. He knew being out in the real world was a new experience for her and, despite her years, she was naïve. It came from a world of privilege where the family was protected from everything beyond the palace walls. She apparently hadn't known the dangers of simply walking around a city at night until she'd actually experienced it. Clutching on to him as though her life depended on it. No wonder she was so worried about her sister too.

Francesca's eyes were wide as she took in her surroundings. The throng of people, and the sights and smells of London at night. Any time they were in a crowded area, she moved a little closer to him. The bustling metropolis was alien to anyone who'd grown up on their small island, but Giovanni had plenty of experience, having travelled all over the world with the army. Perhaps this adventure would help Francesca broaden her horizons the way the army had for him. Then she'd realise that her position in the royal family wasn't the be-all and end-all for her. Even though it must feel like it at times.

They stopped along the side of the Thames so he could get his bearings, and the rumble of Francesca's stomach took them both by surprise.

'I'm so sorry.' Her cheeks pinked at the indelicate sound, but it was a reminder that she was human and needed sustenance like everyone else. It was easy for Giovanni to forget to eat on the job, and he grabbed food when he could, but someone like Francesca was used to scheduled, regular mealtimes, and her body wasn't going to let her forget.

'It's okay. You haven't had anything to eat since lunch. We can grab something here if you like?' He was aware that those fancy meals they served at official functions didn't equate to a proper meal anyway. A smear of sauce and a pretentiously placed asparagus tip on a blob of celeriac mash was not his idea of a good feed.

'Umm…' Francesca glanced apprehensively at the few log-cabin-style stalls dotted around selling street food. It dawned on him that she'd probably never eaten anything that wasn't presented by attentive silver service waiting staff.

Hers was a different world from the one he'd grown up in. Though he'd lost his parents when he was a teen, life before that had been relatively happy. They hadn't had a lot of money, and both his mother and father had worked hard to put dinner on the table. It meant he'd been at home alone a lot of the time, but he'd known he was loved. Sometimes he wondered if Francesca had that. Yes, she had everything money could buy, but he could tell she was lonely at times. He recognised it, having spent the best part of two decades keeping people at a distance. Francesca didn't seem to have a lot of people in her life that weren't required to be there because of her position. No real friends as far as he could see. No one to love her just for who she was.

'I'll order for us,' he said in the end, much to her apparent relief, and he opted for the 'dirty fries' option to satiate their hunger for now.

'What on earth is that?' Francesca prodded the congealed carbs in the cardboard box with her plastic fork. This was certainly a new experience for her.

'French fries loaded with cheese, fried onions and crispy bacon. I got you a beer too.'

They sat down at one of the bistro tables set out for customers and Giovanni watched her with fascination, waiting for a thumbs up, or down. She nibbled at first, and, once she worked up the courage, ventured to taste the liberal toppings. After the deliberation akin to a restaurant reviewer, she eventually went on to eat a second mouthful.

'It's not bad,' was the verdict. Though her face contorted when she took a slug of beer from the bottle, which apparently wasn't to her taste.

'I suppose you're more used to champagne.' Giovanni regretted teasing her when he saw her flinch.

'It's not my fault.'

'I know. I was only joking.'

'You have no idea what it's like. It might seem like everybody's idea of heaven, but it's not like in the fairy tales. The wealth comes at a price you don't know about. Every move I make, everything I do, say, or wear, is calculated, because it's going to be picked apart. Whether it's by my parents, my peers, the press, or the general public, I'm always being scrutinised, and it's exhausting.'

'I understand there's a lot of pressure on you, Francesca, but you cope amazingly well.'

She flashed him a weak smile. 'That's what I want everyone to believe, because I'm a people pleaser. I have to be. I can't afford for anyone not to like me, can I? I'm going to be Queen one day. A position that depends very much on the country believing in me to do the job I was born for. Talk about pressure.'

Francesca knocked back the beer. Giovanni knew what it was like to want to drown those worries and fears in alcohol. He'd done his fair share of that over the years mourning for his parents, and after the bomb went off. It didn't achieve anything and he certainly wasn't going to offer to buy her another one.

'Everyone knows you can do it. I've never had a doubt.' Although she was a fish out of water here, she could certainly hold a room full of nobles and dignitaries. Francesca had a strong spirit. One he was sure was bursting to be free. Even for one night.

She raised an eyebrow. 'No? Not even tonight when I had no idea how to take a train, or had never eaten fast food?'

He shook his head. 'Different worlds, Princess. I'm sure I wouldn't know where to start addressing the nation, or what cutlery to use for eating peacock fritters.'

It took her a moment to realise he was making fun of her, but this time a grin spread across her lips. She lifted one of her fries and threw it at him, making him chuckle. 'Think of all the horror stories I'll have to tell my friends. That I actually ate food in the street, and had to use public bathrooms.'

Hands to her face, she gave him a mock scream, showing she was as game for a laugh as the next person. It was nice to see her this way, carefree, and like any other young woman her age. At least for the moment they were both able to forget she had the weight of a country's hopes and dreams on her shoulders. For the moment.

They smiled at one another, perhaps a fraction too long, something passing between them that went beyond their usual banter. If she weren't a princess, and Giovanni her bodyguard, he might've believed they were having the sort of moment most people longed for on a first date. The spark. That lingering eye contact denoting an interest in one another. The promise of spending more quality time together. Yet, in the circumstances, it could never be a possibility for them.

'We should probably get moving.' Unfortunately, they still had a mission to complete as quickly and discreetly as possible. He had to put all thoughts of Francesca, other than keeping her safe, out of his mind.

Giovanni grabbed their abandoned meals and bottles, throwing their rubbish into the relevant bins. 'The party's across the bridge. A quick look around and then we should probably call it a night.'

Francesca followed him over to the bridge, trying Isabella as she did so. 'Still no answer.'

'She might just be somewhere without a great reception. I'm sure she'll be in touch as soon as she can.' He was trying to convince them both of the best possible outcome.

'Isn't it beautiful?' Francesca marvelled as they joined the crowds streaming across the bridge.

It was lit up with blue neon, the city lights blazing around them. Apart from a few tourists taking pictures to post online, very few people seemed to notice the view, too focused on getting to their destination. That was something Giovanni had always admired about Francesca. Well, one of the many qualities in her he liked. She always took time to appreciate her surroundings, thanking her hosts, interacting with the public who came out to see her, accepting handmade cards and gifts as though they were the most precious things in the world to her.

Impromptu walkabouts in the crowds were a security nightmare but Francesca always took that time out from a busy schedule to acknowledge her surroundings, and the people who'd perhaps made a special trip to see her. It was no wonder she was popular with her subjects. Beautiful, smart, and caring—it was everything needed in a great monarch. The only blot on her otherwise perfect appearance was her disastrous love life.

He'd never thought Benigno worthy of her love. He'd never seen any real evidence of it from Francesca either. It had frustrated him knowing she'd promised her life and future to a man who was no real match for her. Giovanni knew Francesca well enough to understand she needed someone with the same strength that she possessed. Someone who could support her when she became Queen and had to make difficult decisions.

That wasn't Benigno. He'd seemed a nice enough guy, but he was weak. As proved when he broke off the engagement. Although he was sorry for the scandal and heartbreak it had caused Francesca and her family at the time, it had been a relief to Giovanni. She deserved someone better. Someone she truly loved, because she was going to need them by her side when she had her struggles too.

Tonight was a good example. If she'd been doing this with Benigno goodness knew where she would've ended up, or what would've happened. At least Giovanni had her best interests at heart. Not just his own, or his family's prospects, the way Benigno had.

'We should take a picture to remember this moment,' Francesca told him as she leaned over the metal rails, breathing in the night air.

He produced his phone so he'd be the one to have a record of it. With one arm around her, he held the camera up to capture the moment. Francesca placed a hand on his chest and kissed his cheek just as he snapped, the look of surprised joy on his face captured for ever. He quickly snapped another shot, this time making sure his usually impenetrable expression was on his face so he could show Francesca the photograph without fear of exposing his growing feelings towards her. The close call reminding him that the minute he let emotions get in the way of his job was the very moment she could end up getting hurt.

'Right. Let's get moving.' One thing was sure, standing here wasn't going to achieve anything.

When they reached the end of the bridge, they were transported into an altogether different atmosphere. Where the party in the club had been intense, there was much more of a carnival vibe with all the rides usually seen at a funfair, and stalls selling candyfloss and hot dogs.

'I wasn't expecting this.' Francesca clearly didn't know where to look first when there was so much going on.

'It's certainly not like any street party I've seen before.' He'd been very young when Francesca's father had come to the throne and they'd had a street party too. Except all he remembered was sitting at large trestle tables with jugs of orange squash and plates and plates of food and sweets. The only thing it had in common with this one was the bunting depicting the national flag of the respective countries, along with images of their new King. He'd even seen a few people wearing cardboard cut-out masks of the King. Which was disturbing to say the least.

'Isabella would love this. If she's going to be anywhere, it would be here.' Francesca's childlike wonder made him smile.

'I don't suppose you've been to anything like this

before. My parents used to take me once a year to the fair at the harbour back home. I always remember those dark nights in October. The air smelled of bonfires and candyfloss. It was always cold, but I didn't care. I just wanted to have fun. The waltzers were my favourite.'

A smile played on his face at the memories he'd long forgotten. His parents waiting patiently as he jumped on ride after ride, never thinking about how much it cost, but knowing now they'd likely spent money they couldn't afford so that he could enjoy himself. It made his heart ache a little more for the family he'd once been a part of and had destroyed in one night of madness.

'We went once to a theme park, but they closed it to the public so that we wouldn't be bothered by anyone. It wasn't quite the same as this. I'd love to be a part of it all. Why don't we go on the waltzers now?' Francesca took his hand and walked him over to where a queue of people were standing waiting patiently for the previous riders to disembark.

'I'm not sure I'll enjoy it as much these days,' Giovanni protested too late as an excited Francesca pulled him into one of the cars and pulled the safety bar down.

Francesca was squeezing his hand, the adrenaline clearly pumping through her body. Once upon a time a fairground ride would have done the same for him, but he'd been in more adrenaline situations than this since. Why, then, did his pulse race every time she touched him?

'Here we go.' Francesca grabbed his arm and cuddled closer as they began to move. It was only natural to put his arm around her, to stop her from sliding up and down the seat as their car spun around. Her obvious joy doing more to his senses than the spinning around, music blaring, and lights flashing.

They got faster and faster, her shrieks coming louder in his ear. Then she let go of him, shot both arms in the air, closed her eyes, and gave herself over to the moment. As though she were completely free. It was a powerful moment to witness; to be part of. And his heart ached for her.

At least he'd had a taste of normality during his childhood. Francesca's had been a round of private tutors, etiquette lessons, and public engagements. With no more room to just be herself then, than as an adult. The least he could give her was a few hours to simply enjoy herself. Exactly the reason she and Isabella had sneaked out of their engagement in the first place.

When the ride stopped, after what had seemed like an eternity since the attendant had seen fit to give their car an extra swing every time he'd walked by, Giovanni helped Francesca out and back down to earth.

'Wow. I think my head's still spinning, and my legs are like jelly.' She laughed, clinging onto Giovanni for support.

'Yeah. I don't know why I ever thought that was fun.' Perhaps as he'd grown older his centre of gravity had changed, but he'd got more enjoyment out of watching Francesca's reaction than the actual ride itself.

'What are we going on next?' She spun around to face him, obviously addicted to the adrenaline rush already. He'd created a monster.

'Can we give it a few minutes? Er, we should probably have a look around for Isabella.' He didn't want her to think he needed time to recover before the next vomit-inducing whirligig.

'Yes. Of course.' The disappointment and shame were there in her expressive eyes. She looked torn between wanting to have fun and knowing she should be looking for her sister.

If there was one thing Giovanni knew about Francesca, it was that she always did the right thing. Especially where her family were concerned. Why else would she have got engaged to a man her family had deemed a suitable match, knowing she didn't love him?

'We can keep an eye out for her and take a wander around the stalls,' he suggested, doing his best to cover all bases and keep her happy.

It seemed to do the trick as she was soon smiling again.

'Ooh. I've seen these in the movies. I'd love to win one of those cuddly toys.' She spotted the hook-a-duck stall festooned with cheap plastic toys and impossible-to-win huge teddy bears. Still, he wouldn't deny her the chance to try. It might be the only time in her life she could.

Giovanni paid the man behind the lazy river of ducks floating by, and he handed Francesca a long pole with a hook on the end.

'I'll pay you back for all of this,' she promised. Both of them knowing it wasn't true. He doubted Francesca ever had any cash of her own. She'd never needed it since everyone around her took care of that sort of thing.

'It doesn't matter. Now, just catch one of the hooks on the ducks' heads on the way past.' Giovanni held the end of the pole to steady it, and let Francesca pick her duck. She deftly hooked it and lifted it up in triumph, as though she'd just caught a prize salmon.

'Got one!'

Her jubilation was short-lived as the attendant unhooked it and showed her the 'You Lose' scribbled on the bottom in black marker.

'Don't worry. We can try somewhere else.' Seeing her disappointment, Giovanni went against his better judgement and moved to a target shoot a few stalls along.

All he had to do was shoot a ball bearing into a winning playing card. A piece of cake for the ex-soldier. Except he'd forgotten these places were always rigged to dupe the unsuspecting public.

'The sights are off,' he growled to the teen manning the booth.

The boy shrugged. 'I just work here, mate.'

Francesca grew restless beside him, and he knew he had to prove himself. Male bravado took over, and he took aim again with a new determination. He made adjustments this time for the wonky sights and fired the shot bang in the centre of the target.

Francesca squealed and fuelled him on to make the same shot two more times.

'Take your pick,' the unimpressed attendant told him, pointing to the cuddly toys hung around the booth.

'You heard him, take your pick.' Giovanni was pumped with pride, like a teenager on a date showing off for his girl.

'I guess you never lose it, huh?' She nudged him with her hip before taking her time selecting her prize.

'Something like that.' It wasn't quite the same as being on the shooting range, or providing cover fire for an army colleague, but he'd still got a buzz out of displaying his prowess.

'Can I have that one, please?' Francesca selected a huge pink teddy bear wearing a tiara.

'Very apt.'

'Thank you so much. This is like a dream come true. Except, you know, without the missing-sister and trying-to-dodge-the-press parts.' Then she did something completely unexpected by standing up on her tiptoes and kissing him on the cheek.

Such a public display of affection not only completely against her usual protocol, but also showing him that perhaps he had become more to her than a constant shadow reminding her that she was never alone.

A wake-up call for him to keep his thoughts on the job.

Francesca was practically floating on air. This night had become more than she could ever have dreamed. The only dark spot being the spectre of Isabella's disappearance. She felt guilty about enjoying herself but had to console herself with the thought that her sister was probably out there having a whale of a time with someone too. If she didn't believe that she'd never manage to keep it together.

Strolling around the fair with her giant teddy bear under one arm, and Giovanni's hand in hers, she'd never been so content. Relaxed. Free. He was being so accommodating, and, though he was always attentive to her security needs, tonight he seemed to be paying her personal attention. Something had bonded them tonight and she didn't know if it was the mutual feeling of jeopardy as they'd gone in search of Isabella or opening up to one another a little about their lives that had done it. She just knew their relationship was never going to be the same again.

The kiss on the cheek had been spontaneous, but had felt natural in the circumstances. It wasn't as though she'd snogged his face off, but the effect on her had been just the same. She couldn't get it out of her mind. The feel of his stubble rasping against her lips, the smell of his so familiar aftershave, and the look on his face were all things she'd never forget. Especially when he hadn't seemed to mind. There had been no stern scowl, or admonishment, but a fleeting expression of…interest?

She couldn't help but let her imagination run away and wonder what it would feel like to kiss him. A thought she'd had many times before. It was impossible not to when he was so handsome, and a constant presence in her life. But now she had some reality to add to the fantasy. What if he'd enjoyed it too? What if he'd kissed her back with the passion she was sure lingered there behind the cool exterior? Especially when she'd had glimpses of the real Giovanni tonight, and the very real emotions, which weren't as far beneath his surface as he liked to portray.

Not that she could do anything about it anyway. Even if they both liked each other, there was no way her parents would approve of the match. She would have to be with someone of noble birth to gain their approval and she couldn't risk losing their support simply because she fancied her bodyguard. Any desire she felt towards him, that longing for a normal relationship, would have to remain a fantasy for ever. If she let herself go, she was worried this poised princess would completely unravel, and never get back to who she was supposed to be.

'How do you feel about heights?' he asked, out of the blue.

'I have no problem. Why?' She'd spent a lifetime flying in helicopters and jets, and had had no option but to become accustomed to it. The royal family would never usually be allowed to take public transport. It was too great a security risk if nothing else.

He turned his gaze to the Ferris wheel looming over the whole fairground. 'It means we can sit down for a while, but will also give us a good view in case Isabella is nearby.'

'Good thinking.' If nothing else she could take her shoes off for a while.

As had happened so often on this night out, Francesca could only stand and watch as Giovanni paid their fare. It was such a little, but necessary, thing to carry cash or a credit card, which hadn't occurred to her or Isabella at all. An important reminder, not only of how much they took for granted, but also of how removed they were from the rest of the world. It was a lesson she was going to take back with her. When she did eventually become Queen, she knew the memories she was making tonight were going to help her relate better to the people she would rule over.

They waited on the short platform for their car to come around and quickly stepped in, practically falling onto the long seat as they swung back and forth. Her big teddy bear had ended up wedged between them and part of her was missing that closeness she'd enjoyed with Giovanni most of the night.

'You can see for miles.' As they were lifted up into the air, the people below them grew smaller and smaller, but there was still no sign of Isabella. She had hoped that her sister's blazing-red dress might've been easy to spot from this position, but perhaps she hadn't come here at all.

'We can try somewhere else.' Giovanni seemed to know exactly what to say every time her heart sank.

Francesca sat back in her seat, realising she'd been leaning out a tad too far for her liking, in her attempt to locate Isabella.

'I wish she would just let me know that she's okay so I could stop worrying. Typical Isabella. As the youngest she thinks she can do whatever she pleases without fear of reprisals. I suppose she's right.'

Giovanni laughed. 'I thought you were twins.'

'We are, but that whole five minutes between us makes all the difference. We might have done everything together growing up, been taught the same values, and shown how we were supposed to act. In the end, though, there's only one of us who'll have to give up her life to rule the country.'

She knew she sounded bitter, but it was cathartic to get that off her chest. There was no one else she could voice that frustration to. The injustice of that five minutes controlling her whole existence was something she'd held inside her for too long. There was nothing Giovanni, or anyone else, could do about it, but for once she'd felt able to say exactly what she thought. Even if it had left her trembling.

'Is that why you were going to marry Benigno? Because it was expected of you?'

She was stunned by his insight, but she supposed he'd been with her long enough to have realised she hadn't been with her ex because it was a love match. 'He was deemed acceptable to marry a future queen. Who was I to argue?'

She'd liked Benigno, tried to make the relationship work, and thought she'd been the perfect fiancée, attentive and supportive—she'd done everything she could to please him. In the end it hadn't been sufficient to keep them together. Just like her relationship with her parents, simply being her wasn't enough.

Perhaps it had been lacking an emotional commitment on her part. Something that was going to mar any partnership when she'd been taught to lock that part of herself away. Devoting everything to her position, and her future, instead of giving her heart any say in what happened to her. A sign of weakness. In future she was going to have to consider a marriage of convenience to someone who was more interested in status than love. Preferably to a man who understood the pressures on her, and that her loyalty was to the crown and country, not her personal life. The perfect royal, if not the perfect wife.

She was the one who should be scowling at the thought of her fate, not Giovanni.

'It's your life, Francesca. You should get a say in it. Especially when it comes to marriage. When you are Queen, you're going to need someone who can support you, who you can turn to, who you love. Sorry, it's not my place to say anything on such matters.'

Giovanni's passionate expression of his feelings on the matter only made her shiver more. She hadn't realised he even had an opinion, never mind that he cared what happened to her when it came to marriage. He wasn't just a big wall of stone after all.

Giovanni moved her bear out of the way and took his jacket off to put it around her again. 'Here, you're freezing.'

Francesca didn't tell him it wasn't the cold making her quiver, but the chance to finally vent. 'I'm so sorry I didn't have the forethought to wear an outer layer. We can share. It's going to get colder the further up we go.'

'I suppose you're just used to temperature-controlled venues. Not too hot, not too cold, just like Goldilocks.' Giovanni didn't protest as she rearranged his jacket to sit around both of their shoulders, drawing them closer together.

If this had been a date, it would've been perfect. It made her wonder if they weren't who they were to her family, and the rest of the world, would he have taken her out and treated her like this? She wanted the answer to be yes, but at the same time it made her sad that she'd never get to experience this again. Certainly not with a bodyguard who took his job extremely seriously. This was simply a very nice anomaly she should savour for what it was.

'I know, I know. I've been spoiled. I do realise there are people working very hard behind the scenes to make things happen around me and it's not down to little woodland creatures catering to my every whim.' If it hadn't been for Giovanni tonight she would've been completely lost. And she and Isabella had thought they could just run around London… Francesca liked to think she wasn't as naïve as she had been a couple of hours ago.

'I think you're one of the few people who does show her appreciation. I've been around my share of supermodels and movie stars—'

'Oh?' Francesca couldn't stop the wave of jealousy welling up and spilling out of her mouth.

'Work related. I did have a life before you, you know. Anyway, I've seen truly spoiled and it's not you. Privileged, yes, but I don't believe you take people for granted and that's the main thing. It's what will make you an excellent queen.' Giovanni's sincerity, along with the nice things he was saying, made her well up.

Perhaps she wasn't as awful as she sometimes thought, when nothing she did seemed to make her parents happy. They were always correcting her, telling her how she should have done things, so she never knew if she was doing a good job or not. It wasn't as though members of the royal family got an 'employee of the month' award so they knew they were on the right track. Perhaps that was something she could look to implement in the future. With extra stars awarded to anyone who managed to stay out of the gossip columns on a regular basis. Something that would be a miracle if she and Isabella managed to achieve it.

First picture on the wall would be Giovanni's for guiding her through this mess. And saying nice things she really needed to hear.

'Thank you.' As they reached the top of the ride, it slowed down to let people off. Up here, the noise of the fairground seemed far away. The city lights spread before them like a carpet of brightly coloured stars.

Francesca leaned her head on Giovanni's shoulder with a sigh, knowing this moment of peace wouldn't last for ever. He didn't move away from her, instead pulled her closer so that she could share his body heat and enjoy the safe reassurance of his solid body beneath her.

When the wheel began to move again her mood changed to one of despair. She knew the closer they got to the ground, the sooner she would have to face reality.

Eventually she had no choice but to grab her teddy bear and jump off onto the platform. Francesca checked her phone again. Tried calling Isabella, and left another message.

'What do you want to do now?' Giovanni stood beside her waiting for instruction, apparently having run out of ideas too.

Francesca checked her watch. 'It's getting late. Places will be closing soon.'

'Not the clubs. They'll be open to all hours. It's not like back home. You can party all night in London.' Giovanni was so much more a man of the world, but even he didn't have sister-seeking superpowers to help them find Isabella.

'I'm all out of ideas. We're just on a wild goose chase. And as much as I've enjoyed having these new experiences with you, I'm worried about being spotted. If Isabella comes back like nothing happened, and I'm the one who makes the papers, it'll be me our parents will be mad at. Or, worse, they'll tell me how disappointed in me they are.'

She couldn't win. In the end she'd be the one to bear the brunt of blame if any of this came out. For not keeping Isabella in line, for running loose around London, and for bringing the family name into disrepute. As future Queen, she was the one who should've known better. Even if she didn't regret the time she'd got to spend with Giovanni away from the social restraints they usually had to abide by.

'It's a lot of responsibility on your shoulders. I know how difficult it is to live with that burden, but I also know you've done your best. Always. We need to keep you safe too, Francesca. However, I do think I need to alert the rest of the security team that Isabella is missing. I wouldn't be doing my job otherwise.'

He gently broached the subject she'd been trying to avoid, because once the news was out there that Isabella was missing in London, it was going to become a worldwide story. One that no one was going to thank her for. Including her sister if she had gone off on her own accord.

'Can we check back at the hotel first to see if she's there? If not, I promise we'll make things official.' Francesca had to concede defeat. They'd tried their best to track Isabella down, but it was clear she didn't want to be found. Either that or she was enjoying herself so much she hadn't given a thought to anyone who might be missing her.

Francesca prayed for the latter, though it didn't mean she wouldn't read her sister the Riot Act when they did eventually locate her.

'Okay, but if we don't see or hear from her then I'm going to have to call it in.' Though Giovanni wasn't happy, Francesca was glad he was willing to give her more time to track down Isabella.

She understood that this situation was a nightmare for him too because he hadn't stopped them from going off in the first place. They'd appreciated his discretion at the time, but she realised now the price it had cost him. If anything happened to Isabella, Giovanni would feel to blame every bit as much as she would. Another casualty of their selfish decision-making. They hadn't taken anyone else's feelings into account tonight in pursuit of their own good time. In future she would do everything Giovanni advised when he knew best.

Straight after she enjoyed her last moments of freedom.

'There's just one stop I'd like to make on the way back, if that's okay?'

CHAPTER FOUR

AGAINST HIS BETTER JUDGEMENT—which had happened a lot tonight—Giovanni agreed to make one last pitstop before he got Francesca safely back to the hotel. He had hoped that once she was asleep he might be able to track down Isabella himself, with instruction to hotel security not to let the Princess leave her room under any circumstances. It was touch and go whether they'd still get out of this mess unscathed.

By letting her have her way now he thought he might have a chance at getting her to comply for the rest of the evening.

It was the choice of venue that had him scratching his head.

'Why Westminster Abbey?' He would've thought it was the last place she'd want to be. It was where they'd spent the better part of the day waiting and watching the King's coronation. The symbol of everything she seemed to be dreading.

'Just humour me.' She stood across from the building, staring at the Gothic architecture of the abbey, lit up in the darkness. As though picturing her own coronation day.

'It's not going to do you any good fretting over things

you have no control over.' He did his best to get her to leave instead of torturing herself even more when she already had Isabella's disappearance to worry about.

'Uh-huh? Like you blaming yourself for a bomb that someone else planted?' Arms folded, chin tilted up in defiance, she fired his own issues back at him.

Giovanni exhaled slowly. 'We've been over this. It was my fault we were there. My fault I didn't realise the danger ahead.'

'Do you think that they blame you? That they want you to spend the rest of your life feeling sorry for yourself?' This was the Francesca he knew. The fiery one he got to see beyond the cool façade, who wasn't afraid to call anyone out on their nonsense. A true version he'd like to see take the throne, free from the constraints her parents put on her.

Though in this case, someone else had already made him face this particular demon head-on.

'No.' Finally admitting it was like taking a deep, cleansing breath. Regardless that he still had another black spectre haunting his soul.

Nothing could change the fact that he'd lost the only family he'd had. The only family he was likely to ever have. No matter how much he yearned to have that cosy domestic scene in his life again, he couldn't risk a partner, or a child, getting hurt on account of him. So he'd lived a solitary existence. Kept relationships brief and non-committal. Regardless of how lonely he was at times. He couldn't run the risk of causing more loved ones pain. Nor could he face losing anyone else.

Moving on from his guilt didn't mean he was free to gamble with people's lives, or his own heart.

Francesca blinked those big whisky-coloured eyes at him. She clearly hadn't expected him to agree so readily. It seemed only fair to explain his change of heart. Then perhaps she might start to see that holding onto that kind of baggage was detrimental.

'I ran into one of them back at the club. Dan. He's doing security for that Leanne person now.'

'But I thought they'd all been seriously injured?'

'They were. He was. He lost part of his leg, but he's wearing a prosthetic. Apparently, they're all doing well. Happy. Adjusted. Settled.' It was everything he could've hoped for for his old army buddies, but he couldn't help but envy them too. All things he would never be.

'So now you can let go? It's time you got on with your life.'

'It's not that easy, Francesca.'

'Why not? They've moved on. They're still alive—'

'But my parents *aren't*.' He hadn't meant to be sharp with her, but the guilt and pain were never far from the surface.

The questioning look from Francesca was understandable since she knew nothing about his background, and why should she when he was supposed to just be the hired help?

'Anyway, that's my problem. You wanted to come here so we should probably go and let you have a last look at the abbey.' He made a move to walk over but Francesca remained steadfast.

'I thought we were way beyond keeping a professional distance, Giovanni. You know more about me than anyone. Including my own family. Please let me in.' The plea went straight to his heart. The very place he didn't want to unlock. For Francesca's sake as much as his own.

He shook his head. 'Everyone that gets close to me ends up hurt. I can't risk being with anyone. My job is my life.'

She gave a bitter laugh. 'Same.' Then she cocked her head. 'Though for different reasons, I suspect. Apparently, I'm cold and unemotional. All the things I've been brought up to be, so I stay in line.'

'Francesca, I know you are neither of those things.' Tonight was just one example. If she didn't love her sister so much she wouldn't have gone ahead with tonight, never mind being out of her head with worry now about Isabella's safety. He'd been to enough functions and public appearances to know that the way she interacted with and cared for people went against any idea of her being cold and emotionally distant. If that had come from Benigno, there was a good reason for that. Because she'd never loved him, and she'd admitted as much herself.

'I didn't mean to hurt Benigno. I thought he knew about the arrangement between our families and what he was getting himself into. I tried to make it work but I guess I wasn't enough. I probably never will be for any man, when I can't give anyone the attention they apparently need. My duty will always have to come first.'

'I suspect it wasn't so much naïvety on his part, but a damaged ego that you didn't turn into a simpering fool for him. He's probably used to being top dog, and he could never hope to compete with the standing of a future queen. A real man wouldn't need to.' If someone truly loved Francesca and had her best interests at heart he'd never ask, or expect, her to prioritise him over her country.

'It doesn't matter now, does it?' She shrugged. 'Anyway, stop changing the subject. Tell me about your parents since you seem determined to let whatever happened steal a life away from the palace from you.'

Since they were going to be together for some time yet tonight, he knew she wasn't going to let the matter drop. It was of no consequence when nothing she said could possibly change what happened, or how he felt about it.

'I was eighteen. Used to doing what I wanted because my parents were always out working. I got drunk one night, made a nuisance of myself around town and got picked up by the police. It wasn't anything serious and they knew my parents, so they called home and asked my dad to come and pick me up.' It still hurt to think about, knowing he'd got them both out of bed, and they'd still been wearing their pyjamas when their bodies had been recovered.

'Okay…doesn't sound too terrible. Lots of people do stupid things when it comes to alcohol.' Despite her attempt to placate him, Giovanni knew Francesca had never had the luxury of misbehaving in such a manner. As far as he was aware she'd never put a foot out of line. Until tonight.

'They were hit by a truck. It was never clear who was in the wrong. It's possible my dad was still half asleep at that time of the morning. They were both killed on impact.' Not that hearing that had ever been any consolation. If it hadn't been for him, they'd have still been in their beds sleeping soundly.

'I'm so sorry, Giovanni. That must've been so awful for you. You've been through so much.' The pity in her eyes for him was too much to look at. He didn't deserve it.

'More like I've been the cause of it. Now you know. I'm cursed. So are those closest to me.'

'And so you've lived a lonely life, to spare anyone else being hurt… I understand the logic. Sort of. But it's the workings of a grief-stricken teenager's mind. You know you weren't to blame for that truck hitting your parents, any more than you were for the bomb that was planted. Besides which, your army mates want you to move on and I'm sure your parents would want you to do so too. It's not fair on you to keep holding onto this guilt. You're not going to gain anything from it, other than being a martyr to yourself.'

Francesca was the first person he'd ever opened up to about the guilt he felt over his parents' deaths. He didn't even know why he was doing so after all this time of knowing her. Likely because tonight had been all about firsts and breaking the rules.

He knew she wasn't the sort of person to just tell him to pull himself together and get over it, even if 'your parents wouldn't want this' amounted to the same thing. Francesca wanted him to think about the sacrifice he'd made, giving up a life of his own as atonement for his loved ones being hurt. Yet nothing was ever going to bring them back. All he was doing was denying himself a chance to be happy. Seeing Dan, hearing about the lives he and the others had made for themselves had made him see that. He just wasn't sure if his fear of cursing those close to him would prevent him from moving on completely.

Loving someone meant the possibility of losing them and getting hurt all over again. Giovanni had already lost too much to go through that again. Even if the curse wasn't real, the devastation of people leaving him was, and that wasn't something he could easily forget. Even Francesca was going to get married some day and move on, and who knew if he would still be a part of her life at all?

'And what about you, Princess? Aren't you being a martyr by giving up any idea of love to please your parents?' If they were going to have a therapy session, it was about time someone tried to make Francesca see sense too. She deserved to have love in her life.

Her lips were a thin line of disapproval as he clawed back a point in their game of do as I say, not as I do. 'It's different for me. I have a duty to the whole country.'

'As a future queen, yes. As a woman, you're still entitled to have a personal life. Something just for you.'

'I wish it was as easy as that. I'm afraid tonight is all I have. You know I can't have a normal life. That's what this whole escapade was about. Giving me one night of freedom. Pretending I don't have the weight of an entire country depending on me. There's no room for anyone else.'

'I don't believe that. I think you're just afraid of being vulnerable if you let yourself be open to the idea of loving someone. Risking that rejection and loss you felt from Benigno when things didn't work out.' It was easy to see the flaws in her logic, because deep down they were his too. Seeing them reflected in someone he cared about was beginning to make him see how self-destructive those wrongful, long-held beliefs could be.

* * *

Francesca opened and closed her mouth, a witty comeback not forthcoming, because she knew he was right. She'd spent her whole life making sure she lived up to people's expectations. She couldn't bear to let anyone down. Not her parents, her sister, her subjects, or a future husband. At least with an arranged marriage she wouldn't be so emotionally invested in making it work. The thought of loving someone, of letting down those barriers she'd built around her heart, terrified her. It had been drilled into her to be stoic at all times. Never show weakness. To her, that was exactly what loving someone represented. Why else would her parents have kept her at an emotional distance for her entire life?

'Do you know why I wanted to come back here, Giovanni? To remind me of the role model I'm supposed to be. One day I'm going to be the one who wears the crown. I've been in danger of forgetting that sometimes tonight.' She gave him a rueful smile. That wasn't entirely a bad thing. It was exactly why Isabella had suggested this in the first place.

Though that freedom had also made her forget why she shouldn't allow herself to be tempted by Giovanni. At times it had been easy to get caught up in the fantasy of being with him for real. Letting her feelings towards him run unchecked so she could imagine he was her partner, not her bodyguard. Unfortunately, he wasn't.

However, the longer she was away from her parents' influence, and her responsibilities, the weaker her defences were becoming. Until she almost felt normal. A dangerous position for someone of her status to find herself in. As if anything was possible. Now here was

Giovanni trying to convince her of the same. That even love could be within her reach.

'I don't think the monarchy is going to crumble because you had a night off being Princess. Though you're always a princess to me.' Giovanni reached into his jacket pocket and pulled out the plastic tiara they'd been given at the club. He placed it on top of her head and arranged her hair around it.

She held her breath as he touched her, watching him carefully until he caught her staring. He held her gaze, and if this had been a movie, it would have been the moment he leant in for a kiss, unable to resist her. Unfortunately, he managed to control himself, and Francesca was forced to get a hold on her own feelings too.

'I think it looked better on you,' she teased, recalling the unamused look on his face at the time, with joy. Doing her best to put the moment behind them and forget the hungry way he'd looked at her.

She resisted placing the tiara back on his head to replay the moment in the club, fearful that if she touched him she would forget herself entirely. This feeling of wanting something forbidden scared her. Never having been so tempted to step out of her 'good girl' shoes. The very reason she needed to avoid any more lingering touches and longing glances.

There were many memories of tonight she would keep with her for ever. Even if she never got to do anything like this again, nothing could take away this time she'd had with Giovanni. Getting to know him, really talking about things that mattered to her, and actually having fun. All in public and, hopefully, without her true identity being uncovered.

'I do wonder when my big day will happen. How I will feel. If my father will be alive to see it.' Given his health, he might not make it and the thought terrified her, of losing not only a parent, but a mentor. No one could coach her through life as a monarch as her father could. She knew there was talk of him abdicating. His cancer diagnosis and the ensuing complications had made him think about his own mortality. He wasn't an old man by any means and in order to prolong his life both of her parents thought he should slow down. Perhaps step back altogether. Though that would be a preferable scenario to him dying, Francesca didn't know if she was ready to take his place.

'All things which you have no control over,' he reminded her.

'It doesn't stop my mind constantly thinking about it all. Replaying today, only with me as the star of the show. Feeling the weight of that crown, heavy on my very soul.'

'You sound as though you don't really want the position.'

Francesca realised she'd said too much, but she trusted Giovanni. In fact, she was beginning to think he was the only person she could really talk to. 'It's not as though I have a choice.'

'It mightn't seem like it, but you could refuse to take the crown. The question is, do you really want to be Queen?'

It was a question no one had ever asked her before. As though she didn't have any say in the matter at all. Only Giovanni seemed to realise she was a real person who might have thoughts and needs of her own. It was something she had to think about. Being a normal person was tempting, but she couldn't shake off her responsibilities, even theoretically. Her parents would never forgive her. Perhaps some sort of concession might make the position more enjoyable, but she'd have to be strong enough to ask for it.

'Yes. It's the role I've been prepping for my whole life. It's just that it comes with great expectations and responsibilities, and that's a lot of pressure. There's no room for error.'

'You're only human, Francesca.'

'Tell that to my parents,' she said, unguarded. Though it wouldn't come as a surprise to Giovanni to know the demands they put upon her when he was a constant by her side.

'Maybe you should.' Giovanni didn't look as if he was joking. In fact, by the set of his jaw he was deadly serious.

'Pardon?'

'Tell them how you feel. It's going to be a difficult enough job without trying to win their approval at the same time.'

Francesca felt seen, really seen, for the first time. As though he'd looked deep into her soul and plucked out her innermost fear. Disappointing her parents.

'It's not as easy as that…' she mumbled, caught off guard by his insight.

'Why not? When you're Queen you can do as you please. I'd say asking to have more control in your life is one of the smaller decisions you'll have to make.' He gave her a half-smile that contrasted with the huge grenade he'd just tossed in her direction.

As unbelievable as it seemed, she'd never imagined simply asking her parents to back off and give her more say in her own life, knowing it would upset them if she challenged them at all.

Perhaps if she actually did that, stood up and took control, her parents would be more inclined to trust her judgement on the big decisions she knew were coming.

'You should look into becoming a royal advisor instead of a royal protection officer.' If she'd had this conversation with him a long time ago, had Giovanni's support, she might've found the courage to forge her own path sooner.

Giovanni's deep laugh warmed her insides. 'I think I'll stick to the day job, thanks.'

'Yes, royal matters are not for the faint-hearted,' Francesca said with a sigh, realising with Giovanni's help, and despite feeling otherwise at times, she was made of strong stuff. She'd simply let herself be cowed by her parents, and, desperate to win their approval, had let their voices drown out her own. Something she would need to get a grip of before she did become Queen, when she wanted to be the strongest royal she could be. For her sake as well as that of the country.

'Yet this is the place you wanted to visit.' Giovanni gestured towards Westminster Abbey, which had been full of pomp and ceremony only hours ago. Everything she'd just told him she was worried about being a part of. 'Again, the word martyr comes to mind.'

Francesca stuck out her tongue. 'That's not why I wanted to come. I thought I needed some grounding after our time at the fair. It's the most fun I've ever had in my life.'

'Now that is a sad story,' Giovanni teased.

She nudged him in the ribs with her elbow. 'You know what I mean. Sitting at the top of that wheel was the freest I've ever been. It's tempting to never go back and live here in anonymity.'

It had also been one of her happiest memories. Just sitting with Giovanni, pressed close to his warmth, the world a million miles below them. In her dreams she'd be going home with him tonight, staying here for ever, having a normal life.

'You could never live in the shadows, Francesca. You will always shine.' The way Giovanni was looking at her made her heart leap. As though they were simply a man and a woman, with no gulf between them. Never more so than when he leaned into her and she felt the soft touch of his lips on hers.

Kissing Giovanni was something she'd daydreamed about, and the reality was more than she could ever have imagined.

If he expected her to push him away in disgust, stunned into silence by his audacity, he was very much mistaken. Whatever the reason for the kiss, she wasn't going to be the one to end it. Instead, she wrapped her arms around his neck and sought his tongue with hers, deepening the connection. She was sure she felt the reverberation of a growl against her lips, as he pulled her closer, his hands at her waist. If she could have this on tap, ready to go every time she worried about something, she'd be a very happy woman.

His lips were soft, yet demanding, and he tasted of beer and all things forbidden. He was addictive and she couldn't get enough. The teddy bear abandoned in the heat of their passion. A connection that was surprising, but, oh, so enjoyable. They'd always been close, even if they'd butted heads at times, but even in her fevered dreams she'd never imagined he would kiss her with such hunger. As though he'd been waiting for this moment as long as she had.

Unfortunately, Giovanni finally made the decision to end it. He pulled away, and took a step back.

'I'm sorry, Your Highness. I had no right to do that.'

'What if I wanted you to?' Francesca tried to close the distance between them, reaching for him, but he backed away.

'It doesn't matter. I shouldn't have done it. I overstepped. Please forgive me.'

'There's nothing to forgive you for, Giovanni.' She didn't know how else to make him realise she wanted to kiss him. Again, if possible.

'I just wanted to stop you from worrying, and now I've given us both an extra problem to deal with.'

'It doesn't have to be a problem if we don't make it one. A kiss can just be a kiss.' A million kisses could just be a million kisses and send her to bed with a smile on her face.

'Don't, Francesca. We both know I've messed up.'

'I'm not going to let you take the blame for this as well, Giovanni. Yes, you kissed me, but, let's face it, I was a willing partner.' She didn't want him to add to his burden of guilt when that kiss had been something she'd fantasised about for a lifetime. His guilt and regret would only tarnish the memory she was going to hold close to her heart for some time to come.

'Just…just check in on your sister again. I need to clear

my head.' Giovanni turned away from her and began pacing, his hands on his head as though he'd just committed the crime of the century and didn't know how to handle it. Instead of this simply being two people drawn to one another because of their emotional wounds, and it having nothing to do with him being paid to be there.

She walked over to the abbey, determined to walk those steps the King had walked this morning. Facing his subjects, and a life devoted to them. Knowing his future was mapped out for ever, with no escape from his duty. She just hoped she showed as much courage as he had today when the time came.

'It looks as though someone had a little party here of their own after hours.' Giovanni walked over swinging a pair of red heels on the end of his finger.

Francesca took a cursory glance, her attention caught up in her own thoughts. Then she took a second look and snatched the shoes from Giovanni.

'These are Isabella's. Where did you find them? What exact position did you find them in?' All thoughts disappeared but those concerning the safety of her sister.

'They were just lying on the steps like she'd kicked them off. Maybe her feet were sore, like yours. She didn't have a bodyguard in shiny loafers to customise them for her.' Giovanni was attempting to lift the mood, but all that was coursing through Francesca's veins was pure panic. All the time she was living it up, fantasising she was on a date with her hot bodyguard, her sister could've been in real trouble. Exactly why frivolous emotions like desire were to be avoided. She couldn't afford to be so easily distracted from the important stuff going on around her.

'Or maybe they fell off when she was abducted. If someone grabbed her from behind she might have lost them in the struggle. She might even have left them here for me as a clue.' Francesca knew she was spiralling but guilt was overwhelming her that she hadn't taken Isabella's disappearance more seriously.

Giovanni cupped her face in his hands, making her look at him, just as he had in the club. 'We don't know that. She might have just gone barefoot. We both know your sister's a bohemian at heart.'

Francesca wanted to believe his smile and words of reassurance, but her in-built anxiety wouldn't let her. 'I should have let you call the police. If anything happens to her it'll be my fault—'

Francesca didn't know what to do other than give into the urge to cry, so she followed his instruction to try and check in with her sister again. Taking her phone from her bag with shaking hands, she saw that she had missed a voice message, and her racing pulse seemed to come to an abrupt halt.

'Giovanni? Isabella has left me a message. How could I have missed it?' Her one chance to speak to her sister, to find out where she'd gone, or if she was okay, and Francesca had been too busy snogging her bodyguard to notice.

'It probably came through when we were on the Tube. You don't get great reception down there.' Giovanni came back in a couple of strides, keen to hear the message for himself.

He stood close to her so they could both hear it when she pressed play.

'I'm so sorry, but I'm okay. I'll be back soon.' That was it. That was the message.

Francesca could feel her blood starting to boil. 'It's nearly midnight. We've spent most of the night chasing after her, not knowing if she's alive or dead, and that's all she could give me. "I'm okay. I'll be back soon."' She clicked her tongue against her teeth, really wanting to throw something, or scream. Preferably at her inconsiderate sister.

'Well, at least you know she's alive. And safe.' Giovanni had dropped his tortured soul act and gone back to being her jovial travelling companion.

As though nothing had happened. Francesca didn't know who was aggravating her more. In the end she unleashed her frustration on the expensive shoes in her line of sight. Picking them up and lobbing them one by one into the dark with a yell.

'Do you feel better for that?'

'Yes.' No.

'I'm sure the unsuspecting late-night passer-by you probably hit on the head with a flying stiletto is glad.'

'There's no one else around.' She wasn't going to let him guilt-trip her about finally letting go of some of her frustration. There was more than enough of that to go around.

'Would you like me to go and look for your sister's shoes?' He couldn't keep the amusement from his voice, but if he thought this was going to distract her from what had just happened between them, he was mistaken.

'No. She has plenty of shoes. Including the emergency ones she keeps in her bag, which I'd forgotten about. All she had to do was tell me where she was,

Giovanni. Then we could have gone and got her. Crisis over. She couldn't even give me that.' Francesca was exhausted. Her emotions had been on a ride of their own tonight, between everything she felt for Giovanni and the worry over her sister. Isabella must've known she was going out of her mind with worry, but still she couldn't put her sister's feelings above her own for once.

'She's not your responsibility, Francesca. She's mine.' He went and retrieved the shoes.

'You don't get it, do you?' she shouted after him. 'Everyone…everything…it's all my responsibility. Sooner or later I'm going to be Queen, and whatever Isabella gets up to will come back on me.'

'You have to let her make her own decisions. Her own mistakes. You have to trust her.'

'And what do I do in the meantime? Just wait, biting my nails until she decides to show up?'

'Yes. Well, apart from the nails thing. I'm sure that manicure was expensive.' He was on fire with the jokes tonight, in between the heart-to-hearts and the kissing. She supposed it was to deflect the emotional vulnerability he'd shown tonight.

'Why do I have to be the sensible one? Always doing the right thing. Five minutes is all that stands between us, and yet it's a world of difference. Well, maybe I'm sick of it. Maybe I want to do whatever I want for one night too. Answerable to no one. Just acting on pure impulse.'

The fire inside her was burning bright, the injustice of her position getting the better of her for once. Usually, she was able to temper it down, but tonight had been about being honest, and emotionally available.

That was the problem, and why she didn't usually even entertain the idea. But it was too late tonight. That door had been left open and she couldn't stuff her feelings back inside just yet.

So she did what she'd wanted to do for a very long time, and kissed Giovanni.

Giovanni knew he should resist, and he did at first, but he was only human. And the fact that Francesca was taking such a risk to kiss him in public said that she hadn't been able to fight this chemistry either. He'd made a mistake in kissing her, telling himself it was the only way to stop her freaking out. When in fact it was all he'd been able to think about doing for most of the night.

For a little while he'd been able to forget his responsibilities and simply enjoy being with her. He'd almost been able to convince himself they were on a kind of date, getting to know one another and having fun. It had been a long time since he'd done that with anyone. He'd forgotten how it felt to spend time free from worry. Though Isabella had always been at the back of his mind. Now he knew she was okay, it seemed that last thread of sanity had snapped. For once he wanted just to act on impulse instead of overanalysing and planning every move. And when Francesca had her body wound around his there was only one thing he could think of.

Their lips still locked together, he backed her into an alcove, out of sight of passers-by. He wanted one moment to enjoy his freedom along with her. His admiration for her had grown over the years, but he'd seen a different side to her tonight. A Francesca free from the restraints of her duty, who allowed herself to show some emotion. The real woman beneath the tiara. It was enough for him to drop his tough exterior and admit how he felt about her. How she made him feel. Like a man who deserved a life of his own.

Everything that had happened tonight had made him reassess his choices. If those affected hadn't held a grudge against him for what had happened, why should he keep holding onto that guilt? All he was doing was punishing himself and no one was benefitting from it. Even though he might not be able to commit to a serious relationship just yet, he could enjoy being with Francesca for a little while longer. It wouldn't be long before they both came to their senses anyway and remembered the positions they held back home. Besides, he knew they could never be together long term anyway. She would marry some day, but she was his in this moment. His heart was safe when they both knew this wasn't going to last.

Francesca definitely wasn't kissing him like a princess. The desire he felt in her every touch making him forget everything about being professional. That ship had sailed the moment he'd planted his lips on hers.

'We're taking a hell of a risk here, Francesca,' he managed to get out through the butterfly kisses with which she was punctuating his every word.

'Why don't we go back to the hotel? We'll have some privacy there.' That fiery passion was there in Francesca's eyes as she made the next move.

Giovanni didn't need asking twice and took her hand to make the way back to the underground station. As buoyed up as he was by the idea of spending the night with her, he was also hoping the time it took them to get back to the hotel would wake them out of this lustful daze. Then at least one of them might find the strength to change their mind and put a stop to this before they got in too deep.

He knew sleeping with Francesca would change everything between them, but he couldn't seem to convince himself that this wasn't a good idea. They both wanted this and this was their only chance to be together with no one else around. With no emotional risks involved, because a relationship of any kind beyond this evening of madness was impossible. He could finally let someone close without any fear of commitment and the inevitable loss that surely followed.

Tonight, they were just doing something for themselves, guilt free. Like normal people.

CHAPTER FIVE

BY SUGGESTING THEY take things back to the hotel room, Francesca intimated that she was ready to move on from making out with Giovanni to something more. The only thing that had shocked her more than her own bravado was his willingness to accept the invitation. Clearly their chemistry had taken over from common sense completely, but she wasn't complaining. If this was her only night to be irresponsible and do something crazy, sleeping with her bodyguard was the perfect way to end it.

The station was busy with late-night revellers trying to get home, and when they got on the train there were few seats to be had. She spotted one on the end of the row and pushed Giovanni into it. Not giving him time to protest as she hopped onto his lap, still clutching her teddy bear.

He arched an eyebrow at her. 'What are you doing?'

'Making sure we both have somewhere comfortable to sit.' She leaned in and kissed him full on the mouth.

'Francesca...if you keep doing that it's not going to be comfortable for either of us for very long.' His warning only spurred her on. The sense of power she felt in the knowledge that she could affect the usually cool Giovanni an aphrodisiac in itself.

For once she felt like the one in control in this relationship and intended to take full advantage. She nibbled on his earlobe and he squirmed in his seat, confident he wasn't going to make a scene and draw attention. Though no one seemed to notice anything amiss anyway. The other commuters seemed to have come from a party or festival, all wearing garish outfits and glitter and rhinestones on their faces. Most appeared inebriated or horny, with no interest in Francesca and Giovanni, as they sang and flirted further down the carriage.

Emboldened by her position, and the reversal in their roles, she slipped a hand between their bodies. With her fairground prize hiding her antics from view, she wriggled provocatively in his lap. He jolted beneath her.

'Francesca...' His growled warning made her quiver almost as much as the thick bulge she could feel beneath her.

She gave him a wry smile, watching him fight for control as his jaw tightened.

'We're getting off soon.'

'Already?' She smirked, knowing she was playing with fire. As soon as they were out of sight he'd pay her back.

She was looking forward to it.

Unwilling to embarrass him any further, Francesca managed to keep her hands off him for the duration of their journey and sit still. Though he made sure they were both at the door ready to step off the train well before they reached their final stop. As he marched her through the station, her heart was hammering. She was fuelled by adrenaline and anticipation, knowing he was only just about managing to keep a lid on that simmering passion she'd already had a taste of.

'Are you in a hurry?' she called after him as he blasted his way through the station and out into the dark night.

'Yes.' He pushed her up against the side of the building, taking her breath away as he kissed her hard. If it was meant to be a punishment, her little moan of satisfaction would have told him otherwise.

He hung his head. 'What are you doing to me, Francesca?'

'I would've thought that was obvious.' There was something about this night, being with Giovanni, that made her want to be reckless for once.

'What if we got caught?'

'We won't.'

'I could lose my job.'

'You won't.'

Giovanni let out a long, heavy sigh. 'You don't want this, Francesca. This isn't you.'

It was exactly the thing to say to make her angry. 'You don't know what I want, and you certainly don't know who I am.'

She was fed up with people telling her who she should be instead of letting her just be herself. For one night she'd been able to drop that perfect princess façade, and as far as she was concerned the night wasn't over yet.

'No? So you're not a woman who has spent her whole life pleasing everyone else, and, as much as she thinks she wants to be "normal", would never give up her responsibility as future Queen?' He sounded so smug and self-righteous it should have irked her more than it did. But it seemed he knew her better than anyone.

'Okay, but that doesn't mean I can't have one night off. I'm in a different country, having new experiences. That's not a crime. I just want to have tonight to do what I want, and tomorrow I'll go back to being the model heiress to the throne.'

'Are you suggesting what I think you are?'

Francesca swallowed hard, working up the bravado she would need to pull this off. She wanted Giovanni to think that this was no big deal to her. That he would just be her bit of rough for the night.

'One night together. Free from everything that weighs us both down. Just being us. In the morning we'll go home, and back to the roles we're forced to play.'

If this was her only night to do all the things she had ever wanted, but was too afraid to break any rules, then that included being with Giovanni.

Giovanni hadn't verbally agreed to what Francesca had intimated, but when she'd kissed him again, his body had engaged before his brain had. He wanted her.

And now they were rushing back to the hotel, hand in hand, Francesca still clutching that ridiculous teddy bear, wearing a plastic tiara on her head. Apparently the sight not any more interesting than regular partygoers as no one batted an eyelid at them. He'd broken all of the rules in the security handbook tonight, but he'd never seen Francesca so happy. Never felt so alive. If one night together was all they could have, he was going to make each second count.

It took every ounce of strength he had waiting for

the elevator doors to close, shutting them off from the world, before he kissed her.

'Giovanni…' Francesca dropped her cuddly toy to wrap her arms around him instead and he pulled her flush to his body so he could feel her soft curves against him.

He didn't know if it was because they'd dropped all defences in pursuit of this undeniable passion, or if it was because they both knew this was a one-time deal. But there was a hunger now in their kisses, in their hands exploring one another, that spoke of their urgency to be together.

It was a wrench to break away from her when they arrived at her suite and the door opened.

'Once we do this, there's no going back.' He was giving her one last chance to change her mind, because he no longer had the strength to deny his feelings for her.

One night would probably never be enough for him. If anything, it would only make it worse for Giovanni, wanting her, knowing he couldn't have her. And yet there was something between them that he'd tried hard to ignore for years. All the times they'd clashed he suspected were out of sheer frustration, denying this attraction between them. Spending time together tonight without outside interference had let it flare to life. It wasn't likely to disappear after sleeping together, but at least they could have one night where they didn't have to pretend those feelings didn't exist. In the end he was going to lose her—to her role as Queen, and to another man—but for tonight she was his.

'Then why are we wasting time talking?' Francesca closed the door behind them and, with one hand on his chest, pushed him back towards the bed.

He liked this side of her. It was honest, real. The confident woman who didn't need anyone to tell her what to do and was quite capable of making her own decisions. He wasn't going to question them again tonight.

He took the plastic tiara from her head and placed it on the dressing table. 'Not tonight, Princess. I want to be with Francesca.'

That made her smile. 'Good, because I'm tired of being a perfect princess. Tonight I just want to be your lover.'

Francesca tilted her chin up as she always did when she was trying to portray confidence. Biting her lip was the giveaway that she was a little nervous, but then, so was he. He didn't get emotionally involved in the short-lived dalliances he had with the opposite sex. This was different. Francesca and he already had a bond, and he'd shared more with her about his life tonight than he ever had with anyone else. It was going to be difficult to separate the personal and professional side to his relationship with her from now on, but at least they both knew where they stood. After tonight they had to go back to their respective sides on the class divide between royalty and the hired help.

'I like the sound of that.' At least if they went into this with that mindset, that they were just two adults embarking on a night of passion, without any emotional baggage or outside problems, they could enjoy themselves. And each other.

He captured that bottom lip she kept nibbling with his mouth, kissing her softly, letting her know they would take this at her pace. If they only had one night together, he wanted it to be special.

***

Francesca didn't think she'd ever been this nervous. Not at any royal engagements, or even when she had lost her virginity. She felt more vulnerable because she was doing this with Giovanni as Francesca, not a Princess of Monterossa. Even though she didn't have the eyes of the world on her, she still felt under pressure. To please Giovanni as much as herself. He only had to touch her for her body to go into raptures, and she wanted to do the same for him.

However, she had limited experience, and hadn't had the same emotional connection with Benigno that she had with Giovanni. She'd tried, but obviously she hadn't been able to fake that bond, which came so easily with her protector. At times she'd wondered if she was even capable of feeling so strongly about someone that she could lose all sense like this. Apparently she'd just been with the wrong man.

In hindsight, Benigno had been too much like her. Cosseted his whole life, living in his ivory tower looking down on the world too, he knew nothing of real life either. Could never have given her half of the experiences Giovanni had given her tonight. Because her feelings for her ex-fiancé had never been as strong as they were for her bodyguard, and Benigno had realised before even she had. He'd resented Giovanni's constant presence in her life, but Francesca had always defended the need to have him there. Even though they'd clashed at times, he was the one steadying presence in her life who never expected anything from her in return.

Perhaps it was just as well that he was out of bounds, when it would be too tempting to lean on him as she had tonight. Then, when he decided, like her parents and Benigno, that she wasn't enough and rejected her too, she'd be devastated. Despite the pain of not being able to be with Giovanni long term, at least she wouldn't have to experience that level of vulnerability unsuitable for a future queen.

Now, she wanted to show him exactly how much he meant to her. As well as fulfilling one of her most erotic fantasies…

Even a kiss from Giovanni was more erotically charged than a night in her ex's bed. She never knew what to expect as he veered between tender and loving, to feverishly passionate. Everything he did causing new sensations to wreak havoc inside her until she was incapable of a coherent thought or staying upright.

Rather than let him think she'd been reduced to a pathetic puddle of need, she backed him towards the bed. Straddling him once he was lying atop the mattress. He seemed content to let her take the lead. For now, at least. It made it easier for Francesca to feel more in control of what she was doing. Even though it was completely out of character for her. Or, perhaps this *was* the real her, and she'd simply never had an opportunity to be herself until now. It had taken Giovanni, a night in London, and finally opening up about how she truly felt for her to truly be herself.

She began to unbutton his shirt, but her trembling fingers weren't co-operating with her seduction plan.

'Let me,' Giovanni said softly, deftly undoing his shirt.

'Sorry.' This wasn't helping her convince him that she would be the kind of woman who could sleep with a man and walk away without giving it a second thought. Probably because it wasn't true.

'Hey, you don't have to prove anything to me.' He reached up and brushed her hair away from her face. Then he kissed her again and she melted into him. Barely noticing, or caring, when he rolled her over so they were lying side by side.

Francesca was more interested in exploring that muscular chest she'd often fantasised about. The smooth taut reality under her fingertips was warm to the touch, reminding her that this was real and no longer merely a dream. She let her hands drift down his torso to the waistband of his trousers, but Giovanni stopped her.

'It's your turn,' he said, lifting her hand to kiss it, putting an end to her exploration for now.

'I might need some help.' Only hours ago Isabella had helped her into this dress, and Francesca had never expected Giovanni would be the one helping her out of it.

She swung her legs over the edge of the bed and sat up so he could reach the zip at the back. He brushed her hair out of the way over her shoulder, and slowly unzipped her, every rasp of the zip, every touch of his fingers on her bare skin, sending her nerve endings haywire. When he finished, he unclasped her bra in one slick movement and pushed her underwear and dress over her shoulders. The cold air on her exposed skin was incredibly arousing. As was the touch of his lips across her back, over her shoulders, and along her neck.

She turned into him, meeting his mouth with hers, as she discarded the rest of her clothes. He cupped her breasts from behind, kneading and squeezing her nipples, flooding her body with arousal.

When Francesca joined him back on the bed he'd stripped off his trousers and was lying there in just his boxer briefs.

'What?' he asked when he saw her wry smile.

'That's just how I pictured you in your underwear.' Black fabric clinging to his sizeable asset and looking sexy as hell.

'Oh? So you've thought about me a lot, then?'

'No.' She was quick with the denial, but could feel the heat in her cheeks giving away the truth. 'Yes.'

Giovanni grinned but gave little away himself. She knew it would eat her up if she didn't ask. 'Did you ever think about me like this?'

She hated to sound needy, and knew she would be despondent if it turned out he hadn't felt the same way up until now, but needed to know the attraction hadn't been one-sided.

He rolled onto his side and fixed her with those intense, deep brown eyes. 'I was afraid to think about this because I knew it would drive me crazy being with you every day. That doesn't mean I didn't admire your courage and strength, or think about how incredibly beautiful you are. I never thought that this, being here with you, was possible.'

He saved himself with the sincerity of his compliments.

'And now?' With the confidence boost, Francesca brazenly pressed her naked body against his.

He palmed her breast possessively. 'Now, you're mine.'

The throbbing need for him inside her began even before he claimed her nipple with his mouth, leaving her gasping. She'd never felt such longing, an actual ache she knew only Giovanni could relieve. But he wasn't ready to pacify her so easily. Instead, he only prolonged the exquisite agony of her wait, attending to that tight bud of sensitive flesh with his tongue. Flicking the tip, teasing it with the graze of his teeth and the rasp of his beard, until she was clutching his hair in her hands, begging him for release.

Though she didn't want him to stop what he was doing either. Her whole body was in turmoil, wanting, enjoying, needing only Giovanni.

She slid her hand back down his body and gripped his erection through the thin fabric of his boxers, enjoying the sharp gasp in response. A taste of his own medicine. Undeterred, she slipped her hand inside and took hold of his thick shaft, though it distracted him momentarily from his own task at hand.

Just as she thought she was getting some relief from the sweet torture, he pulled her flush against him. Pressing the hard evidence of his arousal between her inner thighs.

'Giovanni…' It was a desperate plea. She had waited so long for this moment, for him to give her the release she needed so badly.

'Hold that thought.' When he left her to retrieve a condom from his jacket pocket she thought she was going to pass out from the intensity of that pressure inside her. And he'd barely touched her yet.

She waited not so patiently for him to come back to her, watching his magnificent naked form, and marvelling that he was hers for tonight. Although she tried to relax, it had been a while since she'd shared her body with anyone, and she was tense when he thrust into her.

'Are you okay?' The restraint was there in his quivering voice as he checked on her before going any further.

Francesca bit her lip as she nodded, willing her body not to betray her. To let him know this was more than physical. Her mind fighting against those primal urges, telling her this wasn't a good idea. That one night of passion with Giovanni wasn't something she'd get over easily. More likely it would completely ruin her future prospects for a husband when no other man could hope to compare. Yet he was the one man she couldn't have. At least, not past tonight.

Giovanni took his time kissing her, waiting until she relaxed before he moved inside her again. She felt so full of him that when he withdrew, the loss was immense. Every time he returned to her, relief and pleasure hit all at once.

Sex with Benigno had been perfunctory at best. Something she'd thought she needed to do. It was expected of her, like everything else in her life. She'd wanted to keep her fiancé happy, the relationship important to their families and their country.

This was different. It wasn't just a step-by-step routine to fulfil a need. Or a promise. This was raw passion. Desire. Lust. All things she hadn't thought she would ever get to enjoy. At least not without a scandal. Though she supposed there was still time for that…

Giovanni thrust again with a groan, sending fireworks off in Francesca's head. A celebration of her sensuality and freedom she could feel in every erogenous zone. She was getting close to a feeling she'd never had before, though she'd often professed otherwise with a smile to keep Benigno happy. At the time she'd thought it was her fault, that there was something wrong with her because she couldn't fully give herself to the moment.

It turned out she'd simply been with the wrong man. If she married someone else like Benigno, for all the wrong reasons, she would likely never feel this way again. The most she could hope for in the future was to find someone who respected her half as much as Giovanni. After feeling this way tonight she didn't want to settle for anything less. She hadn't realised how important a satisfying sex life would be to her either. Perhaps this was one area she shouldn't compromise. Something she should have a real say in. After all, it was her body, her heart, that would live with the consequences if she chose the wrong man to spend the rest of her life with again.

If only she could combine Benigno's public standing with everything Giovanni was, she'd have the perfect husband. As it was, she knew she was going to have to hold onto every second, every emotion and physical experience tonight to remember how it felt to simply be herself when free will was taken from her again.

A hungry kiss, a flex of hips, and Giovanni brought her back into the moment with him so she stopped thinking and just enjoyed feeling.

She let Giovanni take her higher and higher, until the world seemed to explode around her and her body shuddered with release. He followed, crying out with a primal roar she suspected he'd needed to let go of for some time. Francesca had a feeling this night had been cathartic for both of them.

Regardless that the future was likely to be more complicated than ever.

Giovanni was no stranger to good sex, but this had been on a different level. Perhaps it was due to years of pent-up feelings, about both Francesca and himself. Tonight had been a journey of discovery for them both. About each other, and themselves.

Nothing was going to change their lives outside this room, but he hoped being honest tonight would help him move on. Especially when it seemed he had the blessing of his old army buddies.

He didn't know what that meant in terms of his future, but for now he was content. Happy. What he did know was that he didn't want this night to ever end.

'Was everything...was I all right?' Francesca was watching him, worrying that sexy bottom lip with her teeth again.

She could obviously tell he had things on his mind, and immediately thought she'd done something wrong. Most likely because that was how she'd been brought up. Always being criticised and told how to do things the 'right way'. Well, he certainly had no complaints about their time together.

'Amazing. Sorry, I'm just thinking about what happens when we go home.'

Francesca screwed up her pretty face. 'Please don't. It'll spoil what little time we have left together.'

He didn't want that either, but there was a concern he'd get carried away by what this meant. It was going to be difficult going back to work, being with her every day, and pretending this hadn't happened. Worse if he did have to watch her meet and fall in love with someone else when he'd just discovered he had feelings for her that obviously went beyond that need to protect her for a pay cheque. It had been bad enough seeing her with Benigno, but now that they'd shared a bed, and so much more, the prospect of seeing her start a life with someone else was going to be hard to stomach.

He'd been trying to keep a lid on the feelings he had for Francesca but tonight had thrown them together closer than ever, and forced him to face how much he liked her. Unfortunately, admitting his feelings didn't guarantee that happy ever after. At least, not for him. He was going to lose her the second they stepped back onto Monterossan soil.

'No regrets?' he asked. He didn't have any at this precise moment, but he had an inkling he might curse himself further down the line for giving into temptation. The memory of sharing this bed haunting him for ever.

How could he go back to nameless, meaningless encounters when he knew what he could really have? A real connection, with emotions involved he didn't think he'd ever share again. Unfortunately, all with the one woman he knew he couldn't have. She was the future Queen of his country, for goodness' sake. The woman he was paid to protect, not sleep with.

'Stop thinking.' She slapped his chest. 'No regrets. Why, have you got any?'

'Definitely not.' That was one thing at least he didn't have to overthink. He wouldn't change anything that had happened tonight for the world.

She let out a long sigh. 'Why can't I just have a normal life?'

'Because you were born for greater things.' He rolled over and kissed her. At least when he was touching her, he didn't have to think about anything else. There wasn't any room for anything else in his head but the taste of her, and how much he wanted her.

He wondered how long he could survive on a diet of sex and Francesca. Actually, on second thought, he didn't care. He'd die a happy man however long it took.

'I can't think of anything better than this,' she murmured contentedly against his lips.

'Nor me. Do you think we can just order room service and live here for ever?' He knew these sweet nothings were simply born of their post-coital bliss, but this room was their safe space. The one place they'd been free to express themselves, and that would all end once they stepped back out of those doors.

'It would be nice, wouldn't it? Do you want some room service? I've worked up quite a thirst.'

Although he could do with something to drink, Giovanni was reluctant to make the call. 'I don't want to burst our bubble here. Getting room service would require me getting out of your bed and putting on some clothes.'

'You're right. I don't want that either.' Francesca smoothed her hand over his backside before giving it a firm tap. He liked it when she showed a possessive appreciation for his body. Often his looks were the only thing women were interested in, but he knew it was different with Francesca. It had taken a real connection between them to finally act on that physical attraction, and it meant so much more.

The fact that she couldn't keep her hands off him was an extra bonus.

'We do, however, have a fully stocked mini bar, and all the fruit we can possibly eat. I suppose there are some perks to being royalty.' She pulled the sheet off the bed and wrapped it around her, leaving Giovanni lying naked on the bed as she wandered out of the bedroom.

After a moment without her, he decided to go after her and pulled his boxers on to preserve some of his modesty.

'What have you found?'

He found her with her head stuck in the fridge, the light showing the flushed glow on her cheeks after their bedroom workout. She looked the most carefree and happy he'd ever seen her. He couldn't help but wonder if he'd ever get to see her like this again. The only thing worse than thinking it wasn't possible was the thought of someone else making her this happy.

She stood up with her arms full, the sheet tucked carefully toga-style to leave her hands free. Hair mussed, lipstick smudged, she was as far as she could possibly get from the tabloid image of the Princess of Monterossa. This was his Francesca. Even if it was just for tonight.

'We've got wine, crisps, nuts, chocolate…all the things I'm not supposed to eat if I want to keep my figure.' She rolled her eyes and he guessed that was a statement she'd heard many times from her 'advisors'. He'd certainly been privy to some conversations that had made him want to step in when stylists and the like had treated her like a clothes horse rather than a human being.

'I thought we'd established that none of the usual rules apply tonight.' He wrapped his arms around her and nibbled the skin at her neck.

'In that case I'm going to be really wicked.'

Before he got his hopes up for an extra round in the bedroom, she deposited her goodies on the glass table in the luxurious lounge area. It never failed to amuse him that in his line of work he got to see how the other half really lived. Private pools and presidential suites were a far cry from the stark army barracks that he'd lived in after his parents' deaths.

Even now, when he was old enough and could afford his own place, it was a modest apartment close to the palace so he was always on call for duty. He didn't spend much time there so there had never been a need to splash the cash on expensive furnishings like those Francesca and her family were used to. The gilded mirrors and sparkling crystal chandeliers were another reminder that he and Francesca were worlds apart.

'I need a drink.' Alcohol preferably, to make him forget that he'd put his job and everything else on the line by being with her like this. Though, it was worth it.

Francesca poured two glasses of wine and beckoned him over to sit with her in front of the full-length windows, the city at night providing the view for their late-night picnic. Rather than sit in any of the well-upholstered wing-back chairs, she'd chosen to sit cross-legged on the floor. Another moment of rebellion, he supposed. It occurred to him in that moment that perhaps that was all he'd been, too. Francesca sticking her two fingers up at her social standing by sleeping with the hired help. Something that didn't sit well with him when he knew he'd had altogether different reasons for bedding her.

Francesca had added the overflowing fruit bowl to their supplies and was currently enjoying the strawberries along with her wine. 'I hope wherever Isabella is, she's having as much of a good time as I am.'

'Do you? Really?' Giovanni raised his eyebrows, sure that if Isabella had been up to half of what they'd done tonight Francesca would've had a conniption.

She thought about it for a moment. 'Within reason. As long as nobody gets hurt, and nobody finds out.'

He knew that went for them too. They hadn't exactly been discreet, despite their concerns at the start of the evening. It had been easy to get complacent as the barriers between them had fallen. Though at this moment he didn't think either of them particularly cared. That was a worry for tomorrow. Or, as he checked his watch, later today. It was tempting to stay up all night and eke out every last second of this time with Francesca.

Giovanni helped himself to some very fine chocolate and broke a piece off for Francesca, who took it directly from his fingers with her mouth. An intimate act that aroused more than a passing interest. Especially since she took her time, slowly and deliberately prolonging the exchange, her eyes not leaving his. A hunger blazing there for more than all the chocolate and strawberries in the world.

He stopped pretending he wanted anything other than her to eat, pushing everything aside, not caring what spilled, as he pulled her towards him. Francesca's eyes blazed with an already familiar passion, encouraging him more. He wrenched the sheet away, exposing her body, and, with a predator-like crawl, covered her body with his until she was lying flat on the floor. Her naked breasts rose and fell with her every shallow breath as she waited for his next move.

Giovanni took one of the strawberries from the fruit bowl between his teeth and began tracing it along all the soft, sensitive parts of her body. He started between her legs, up along her inner thigh, dipping into that most intimate part of her to make her gasp. On he went, the sensation causing her to contract her stomach muscles and he remembered she was ticklish there. He carried on, leaving a trail of strawberry juice over her breast, and around her nipples. Enjoying her squirm and make little meowing noises beneath him. When he finally brought it to her lips she bit down, the juices running down her chin and neck as they consumed the fruit between them.

He licked the tart but sweet trail, travelling back down her body.

'I'm all sticky.' She giggled as he swirled his tongue around her nipples.

'Just how I like you.'

Down he travelled until his head was buried between her legs and he lapped her sweet juices, enjoying her moans of ecstasy. He felt her body convulse around him as he brought her to the edge of orgasm on the tip of his tongue. And when she spilled over, Giovanni was almost ready to go with her.

He waited until she'd come back down to earth and was able to breathe again before he attempted conversation.

'Are you okay?'

Her grin told him all he needed to know. 'More than okay.'

'In that case, can we take this back to the bedroom? I don't want to be lying here in full view of the great British public when the sun comes up.' Though he didn't want to say it, he wanted their last few hours together to be spent in bed, where he could have her in his arms in comfort.

CHAPTER SIX

FRANCESCA STRETCHED AND smiled before she even opened her eyes. The night had been the best of her life and she didn't want to admit it was over.

She was even more bereft than anticipated when she did finally look around, only to find the other side of the bed empty. The dream was definitely over. She grabbed the pillow, which still smelled of Giovanni, and placed it over her head, trying to stay firmly in denial. If he was gone already, their time together was at an end and once she got out of this bed it was business as usual. A difficult thing to come to terms with after spending the night pretty much doing what she wanted.

'I've ordered some room service for you, but I'm heading out to pick up Isabella. She's staying at another hotel nearby.' The sound of Giovanni's voice coaxed her out from her pillow cocoon.

He was already showered and dressed and back to his polished, professional self. As handsome as he was, Francesca preferred him a little more unbuttoned.

'Have you heard from her? Who is she with?' She couldn't help but think if her sister had chosen to stay at a different hotel, it meant she'd spent the night with someone. Likely a man. And goodness knew if he was going to be discreet about whatever had taken place between them. All she could do was trust Isabella hadn't picked someone entirely unsuitable to entertain her romantic fantasies.

She wasn't a hypocrite. Hooking up with Giovanni likely hadn't been the best idea for her either, but at least he could be trusted to keep the details to himself. All they needed was someone keen to make a name for themselves, or looking to make a few pounds from the tabloids, and their cover was well and truly blown. Not to mention Isabella's reputation.

'I just got the message to go and pick her up. You two should probably talk if you want the details. It's not my place.' His face was set in steel, giving nothing away about their tryst only hours ago in this bed, and on the lounge floor.

'Giovanni, we need to talk about what happened between us.' She had hoped they'd have some time together before they had to go home, where they really wouldn't have any privacy to dissect the events of the previous night. Although they wouldn't have a chance to explore any kind of relationship, she would've liked to at least talk about where they went from here. He was still going to be in her life and it was going to be difficult pretending nothing had happened. Although he seemed to be doing a pretty good job of it so far.

He dropped his head, letting the façade of the cool and collected bodyguard slip a little. 'I know, but not now. I need to go and get your sister and exert some damage control if necessary. I promise we'll have a chat, but I still have a job to do, Francesca.'

'I know.' More was the pity. She could have quite happily spent the rest of her days in this hotel room with him and forgotten about the rest of the world.

He crossed the room in a couple of strides and came to her side of the bed. 'Last night meant a lot to me, Francesca.'

He dropped a kiss on her forehead, and she had a feeling he wanted to say more. Something she probably didn't want to hear right now, but which they both knew was inevitable. All she could do was let him go, and pray their escapades in London weren't going to come back and bite them all on the backside.

Francesca tried to keep herself busy until Giovanni and Isabella returned. Although she was hungry, her churning stomach wouldn't let her eat more than a few bites of toast and some orange juice. Regardless that Giovanni appeared to have ordered enough food to feed a small army. She used the time to try and make herself presentable, transforming herself from the wanton she'd been last night to the picture-perfect princess for any waiting press.

After her shower, she changed into a stylish pale blue coat dress with contrasting white buttons, and a sash belt tied at her waist. An outfit that had been chosen before she'd even left Monterossa and probably cost a fortune. Though as far as she was concerned, the outfit she'd returned to the hotel in last night was worth a lot more. She stroked her hand over the torn dress she lifted from the floor, caught sight of the shoes customised courtesy of Giovanni. They represented the spontaneous nature of their adventures perfectly, and to her they were priceless. When her things were packed for the journey home, they would be the first to go in her case.

Before Isabella, or anyone else, came into the lounge area, she made sure to clear away all evidence of her and Giovanni's carpet picnic at the window. In the light of day she could see what a chance they'd taken of being seen. Even though they were twenty storeys up, the entire city centre was visible below them. Who knew if anyone could actually see into the room? Now she was back into her royal role, her paranoia had flared back into life. It had been nice to take a risk or two, but now she had to fall into line.

It didn't matter about the passion he'd awakened inside her, or what her heart wanted. Once they left this hotel room she had to resume her 'perfect princess' role and that did not include causing a scandal by getting caught in a compromising position with her bodyguard. Her public profile had to take priority over her desires or she would lose support on a grand scale. It was necessary to leave last night behind her if she was ever going to move on and marry as expected.

She threw the rubbish and leftover snacks in the bin, set the glasses to the side, and lifted the sheet she'd discarded on the floor to take back into the bedroom. The sight of it brought back some heat-inducing memories. What Giovanni had done to her, what they'd done together, had been beyond her imagination, and she wished that it didn't have to end here and now.

Francesca had spent so much of her life doing the right thing by everyone, and seeing how different her life could've been was as much of a curse as a good time. Now she knew how it felt to be with Giovanni, to have a more than satisfying sex life, and to be able to express herself without censorship, it was tough to leave all of that behind.

How could she walk into an arranged marriage when she clearly had feelings for someone else? Someone who was still going to be in her life every day. Worse, how was she going to share a bed with anyone else when her heart, along with every other part of her body, belonged to Giovanni? It seemed marriage was going to be even more of a prison than life at the palace. One with added torture.

Before she could get too maudlin, mourning a life she could never have with the man who'd opened her eyes to so much last night, Giovanni returned with Isabella in tow and her relief at seeing her sister overtook everything. Right before the anger kicked in.

'Where have you been? Where on earth were you? Are you safe?' Francesca had her by the shoulders, desperately searching to see if she'd suffered any physical injuries.

'Yes, yes, I'm safe. I was…a few places.'

Eventually Isabella admitted she'd spent the night with Rowan James. The ex who'd called off the wedding, leaving Isabella broken hearted.

Francesca couldn't believe she'd been so reckless. Though she supposed if Isabella had been here last night, she wouldn't have been able to do half the things she'd done with Giovanni. Still, as the older sister it was her right to be annoyed at her little sister going AWOL in the middle of the night.

Flashes of London last night came to mind. Being on the underground, eating fast food in the street, having fun at the fairground—all with Giovanni, under the guise of looking for her sister. She was angry, not only at Isabella for putting them all in danger, but at herself for forgetting about Isabella at times when she had been so caught up in Giovanni's attention. Mostly, she was angry that they had to be sneaky to have a night doing what everyone else in the world took for granted.

Isabella apologised for leaving her shoes behind and making her worry she'd been kidnapped. For not staying in contact. For making her go to Twilight in the first place. For everything.

And then she burst into tears.

'It's all right.' Francesca folded her sister into her arms. 'We're both to blame. I guess we needed to let off some steam last night.' She glanced at Giovanni, who made brief eye contact before looking away again. A silent, neutral sentry. Nothing like the man she'd shared a bed with just this morning.

'You don't understand… I hadn't planned any of it. Believe it or not, I was trying to stay out of trouble.' Through her sobs, it was clear Isabella had a lot to tell her.

It seemed wrong to hear her confession in front of the man Francesca had sinned with herself. She felt enough of a hypocrite without having Giovanni witness it.

'Okay. Why don't you tell me about it whilst we go and get you freshened up?' Francesca led a clearly distraught Isabella to the bathroom. Whatever had occurred between her and her ex mustn't have ended well given her current state. Francesca's upset at having her time with Giovanni curtailed paled into comparison next to her sister's distress. She'd had an actual relationship with Rowan; nearly married him. There was no way she would've spent the night with him unless something significant had happened between them. Yet, there was no sign of him now. The fact that he wasn't here to see them off back home, or to try and persuade Isabella to stay with him, spoke volumes. She'd had more heartbreak.

Francesca taking out her frustrations on her too wasn't going to help her current mood or get her to open up. For everyone's sake she was going to have to find out what happened and figure out a way for everyone to leave London with their reputations intact. Even if their hearts were more than a little bruised by everything they had to leave behind.

She was going home with a lot more than a tacky snow globe with a London landmark inside that tourists usually brought home as a souvenir. Thanks to her night off from being a princess, she was taking back deeper feelings for her bodyguard than a simple crush, and an existential crisis about her future as Queen.

Giovanni was trying not to listen to Francesca and Isabella's heart-to-heart on the plane, though it wasn't easy in the close confines of the cabin. He was supposed to stay close, and objective, at all times after all. Needless to say, it involved a lot of tears from Isabella, who'd apparently spent the night with her ex. The one who'd hurt the family with the scandal before the wedding that never was. Or one of the weddings that had been called off. The Princesses really deserved better, and appeared to have appalling taste in men. He included himself in that category when he was probably the last person on earth Francesca should've bedded.

Though he couldn't bring himself to regret anything that had happened when they'd been so good together.

It just made things all that more complicated when they got home.

He had to admit, though, he was beginning to have some empathy with Isabella's ex. It wasn't easy being involved with the family. Impossible to have the sort of normal relationship he longed for in his post-sex delirium when anything seemed within his reach. Even happiness. Only news of Isabella's whereabouts first thing had jolted him back to reality, reminding him he had a job to do. And, if he wasn't more careful, Francesca was going to end up another casualty of the curse. By getting close to him she'd put herself at serious risk, which, although not physically dangerous, left her open to hurt in other ways. In reputation and her relationship with her family.

They had agreed that last night had to be put firmly in the past so they could carry on with their lives as they were. Yet, the way she kept stealing glances at him gave him the impression they weren't done just yet. He supposed she had said she wanted to at least discuss what had happened. Goodness knew what that was supposed to achieve other than make them both yearn for a repeat of last night.

The mere memory of her touch, her taste, and sleeping with her in his arms was enough to make him forget his position. Leaving her this morning was one of the hardest things he'd ever had to do, but he'd had to put his duty above his heart. Giving him some idea of what Francesca had to go through. It was torturous.

He held his tongue until Isabella seemed to have cried

herself to sleep, and Francesca got up from her seat to go to the bathroom.

'Francesca—'

He stopped her in the small alcove at the back of the plane, away from prying eyes and listening ears, before she went back to her seat.

When she looked up at him, that amber gaze so full of yearning, he couldn't help but reach out and touch her. She closed her eyes as he brushed his knuckles against her cheek, and Giovanni was tempted to cart her back into the bathroom for one last hurrah before they reached home. Unfortunately joining the mile high club wasn't going to make any of this easier for either of them.

He cleared his throat and did his best to rid himself of thoughts unbecoming to a personal protection officer assigned to the princess he was fantasising about.

And failed.

Instead, he unfurled his fingers and cupped her face. 'I miss you already.'

When she did venture to look at him again, it was easy to see she felt the same. How they were going to conceal their secret from her parents, he didn't know.

'Me too, but we can't go back no matter how much we might want to.'

There was no 'might' about it. If he could relive last night ad infinitum he'd be a happy man. But she was right, they couldn't possibly pick up from where they'd left off last night. Even if they'd been denied time together this morning.

Still, they weren't back on home soil just yet.

'No, but I don't think we got to say one last goodbye, did we? How can we possibly have closure without that?' He brushed his thumb over her full lips, mesmerised by the memory of how soft and pliant they were against his.

'Indeed.'

If he'd been expecting Francesca would be the one to see sense and bat away his advances, he was mistaken. In fact, she was moving closer, closing the slight distance between them. Until all that was keeping their lips apart was his thumb. A matter he took care of quickly.

One soft kiss. A goodbye, and a return to their normal status quo. That had been his intention. However, the second their lips met it seemed as though they'd once again set events in motion that even they had no control over. Their mouths clashed together with an urgency that hadn't been present last night. They didn't have the luxury of time or privacy here on the plane to indulge this chemistry that had finally been allowed to be unleashed after years of being suppressed. Now it seemed it was going to be impossible to put the lid back on it.

Though he was aware that the rest of the Princesses' entourage was sitting at the back of the plane, and he didn't want to compromise her any more than she already might be, he backed them both into the bathroom, locking the door behind them. Their lips not parting from one another.

'Do you have any contraception?' It was Francesca who finally broke away.

He nodded and produced a condom from his wallet. 'Are you sure you want to do this? Here?'

'Why not? We may as well end things with a bang.' She had a wicked smile when she was being un-princess-like. Giovanni liked this wild side of Francesca that no one else got to see and reap the benefits from.

He grabbed her backside and lifted her onto the dressing table. Thankfully the bathroom on a royal jet was more spacious than the standard commercial airline, so they were afforded a little luxury.

As much as he wanted to rip her dress open, buttons scattered to the floor in his haste, he was aware Francesca's appearance on arrival would be scrutinised as always. So he carefully unbuttoned her all the way down the front, watching her chest rise and fall as he slowly undid her belt, and let her dress fall open.

He took in the sight of the lacy white underwear against her tanned skin in case it was the last time he got to see her like this. Wanting, needing, only him.

He kissed her hard, Francesca already unzipping his fly and urging him on. Following her lead, he quickly divested her of her panties, before sheathing himself. It was a struggle to contain himself when he entered her in one quick thrust. The overwhelming natural response to cry out his instant satisfaction only quelled by the thought of everyone else outside the door.

Francesca, on the other hand, seemed unable to suppress her delight, her little moans of appreciation, which he'd so enjoyed last night, now in danger of giving them away.

'Shh. Someone's going to hear you.' He tried to quiet her, but every tilt of his hips against her, bringing their bodies together, seemed to make her more vocal.

In the end he resorted to putting a hand over her mouth to quiet her. A move that served to make her eyes sparkle with mischief as she licked and nibbled at his palm. That touch of her tongue on his skin heightened his arousal, increasing his pace in search of that final release.

Francesca wrapped her legs around his waist, tightened her hold inwardly too, until he was consumed by his need to let go completely. Then she pulled his hand away from her mouth, leaned in and sucked on the skin at the base of his neck. That pleasurable pain and further display of her wild side sufficient for him to lose the last of his control. He had to bury his head in the crook of Francesca's neck so he didn't roar the place down, and when she climaxed too, he had to cover her mouth again.

His exertions left him gasping for breath and he all but collapsed on top of her, his jelly-like legs struggling to keep him upright. Francesca had a devastating impact on him both physically and emotionally, but he'd never felt so alive.

It was a shame this was their goodbye.

CHAPTER SEVEN

'FRANCESCA? IS EVERYTHING all right?' Isabella knocked on the bathroom door and sent Francesca and Giovanni into a tizzy of trying to rearrange their clothes and not get caught out.

'I—I'm not feeling very well. Could you ask someone to get me a glass of water, please?' Still struggling to get her breathing under control, and panicking that her sister was about to figure out what she'd been doing in the bathroom with their security detail, Francesca tried desperately to buy them some time.

The reflection of her flushed face in the mirror, along with her partially naked body, would definitely give the game away. At least Giovanni had managed to make himself look respectable in double-quick time, despite ravishing her so thoroughly. She was afraid her vocal satisfaction had drawn some attention after getting carried away in the moment.

'I'll go and get it myself. It's probably all the stress I've caused, making you unwell.' Isabella's contriteness made her grimace in the face of her fib. Lying to her sister wasn't something she did easily, but in this instance it would save them all from further embarrassment, as well as keep Giovanni in his job.

'Thank you,' she said, meekly. 'I'll be out in a moment.'

Once the sound of Isabella's footsteps receded down the aisle, Francesca opened the door slightly to check the coast was clear. 'You should go now before anyone sees.'

'We still haven't had the chance to talk,' Giovanni reminded her with a grin.

'Later. Go.' She ushered him out, and just when she thought they were safe, he ducked his head back in through the door and kissed her thoroughly. Leaving her dazed and wanting more.

'Later.' He gave her a wink and disappeared to the rear of the craft, leaving the coast clear.

Francesca took a moment to compose herself. Fixing her hair back in place, and splashing some cold water on her face, to take away the look of impropriety. Though she couldn't resist a sly smile at her reflection. This certainly had been an interesting, if unexpected, turn of events making an otherwise tiring flight into something exhilarating.

It seemed they couldn't be alone without giving into that passion that flared so easily to life between them. A matter that was going to make life tricky at the palace. Though they'd agreed that their escapades should end once they were back on home ground, their 'eventful' use of alone time meant they would have to raise the subject of their night in London at a later stage. Carrying it over the border into real life in Monterossa. And now they had another indiscretion to add to the list of topics they needed to discuss.

She ran into Isabella as she exited the bathroom.

'Come and sit down. Would you like me to inform the pilot? He can radio ahead for medical assistance, or divert us to a closer airport.' Isabella's concern was touching, but only made Francesca feel more wretched about her ruse.

This was partly why she and Giovanni couldn't carry on their 'arrangement' at home. It was one thing being anonymous and alone in London, where no one else was concerned about what they got up to. But it would take a certain level of subterfuge to keep seeing each other, involving lots more lying to her family, as well as increased personal risk involving his job and her reputation. She wouldn't be such a good match for a well-heeled gentleman if she was involved in yet another romance scandal. Sleeping with the hired help would seem tawdry for a woman of her standing, even in this day and age.

Giovanni wasn't promising her for ever, and having a relationship meant risking her entire future as well as her position in the family. He would probably tire of her like everyone else and where would that leave her? As much as she wanted to be with him, she had to be logical. Practical. Being Queen was the only future she could count on. She needed someone who could present that perfect façade with her, and who wouldn't distract her. Take a piece of her heart when she needed to give it entirely to her country.

'That's really not necessary. I'll be all right once I sit down and have some water.' Guilt wouldn't let Francesca accept her sister's fussing, not to mention inconveniencing everyone else just to cover up her dalliance with Giovanni.

She took a seat in the luxurious, spacious area reserved for the family and their security. Thankfully Giovanni had made himself scarce for now so she could try and think clearly without images of him, head buried in her shoulder as he climaxed, dominating her thoughts.

Isabella threw herself down into a neighbouring chair with a sigh. Clearly, there was something other than her sister's well-being on her mind.

'What's bothering you, Bella?'

Isabella stared at the hands resting in her lap for some time before answering. 'Last night wasn't just about meeting up with Rowan. There was a photographer—'

Francesca's heart plummeted into her stomach. Those feel-good endorphins Giovanni had whipped up inside her fast becoming a distant memory. 'Who? What? Where?'

More importantly, what exactly had they captured? She was sure between them she and Isabella had provided plenty of salacious photo ops. There were some innocent moments with Giovanni, which could probably be explained away, but there was also the matter of them naked in full view of the city last night in the hotel room. Now she was beginning to feel genuinely ill.

Tears, it seemed, were never too far from Isabella's eyes since they'd left London. 'It was a photograph of Rowan and I in a…compromising position. We spent most of the night chasing down the owner of the paper to beg him not to publish it.'

'And?' Francesca wished she'd asked for something stronger than water. Though glad it wasn't incriminating evidence of her rash behaviour with Giovanni, she didn't wish her sister's name to be sullied further either.

Isabella screwed up her face, and Francesca's stomach almost made a leap for freedom too.

'We had to come to an arrangement in exchange for them not publishing the photograph.'

'What kind of "arrangement"?' She had a feeling she wasn't going to like it even though it had to be preferable to Isabella being on the front page.

'Rowan and I have agreed to give an exclusive interview.'

'Why would they want to interview a couple who've already broken up?'

'Because they want the juicy details. Because they want the credit for breaking the story, and now, perhaps, they think they're going to get an exclusive that we're back together.'

'And are you?' Certainly, spending the night together would have suggested that, but Francesca didn't think her sister's tears had come from simply saying goodbye to Rowan until their next meet.

Isabella shook her head, dislodging some of those leftover tears. 'No. We made a mistake last night. One that's not going to be repeated.'

Francesca felt for her in that moment. Knew exactly what it was to have that one night of surety, only to realise in the cold light of day that being with someone from such a different background simply wasn't feasible.

She moved over onto Isabella's seat and wrapped her arms around her sister. 'It's not easy, is it?'

'What?'

'Falling for someone you can't be with.' Francesca sighed as Giovanni strode into the cabin on his way to the cockpit to check in with the pilot.

Isabella followed her gaze. 'Oh, my goodness! You and Giovanni?'

'What? No. What makes you say that?' Francesca spluttered, knowing she'd stuffed up. She'd been too blasé about the whole thing, and Isabella had sussed what was going on between them within a matter of hours. How the hell was she going to keep it secret from her parents and everyone else when they were going to be together every day? Especially when they didn't appear able to keep their hands off one another.

'Er, the way you're mooning after him. I was too caught up in my own complicated feelings about Rowan to notice before, but there is definitely a vibe between you both. Now I come to think of it, he seemed grumpier than usual this morning. I assumed it was because I'd caused him a security nightmare, but now I'm wondering if it was because I got him out of your bed this morning.'

Francesca neither confirmed nor denied the accusation.

Isabella's eyes went wide as saucers. 'I'm right, aren't I? I want *all* the details.'

Apparently Francesca's face had done all the talking, and now she was sure she was scarlet at being found out. The whole reasoning behind her and Giovanni giving in to temptation was because no one would know. It was supposed to be a secret just between the two of them. How long that was going to last there was no way of telling.

'We both acted out of character last night, Bella. Let's just leave it at that.'

'No way. Here I am pouring my heart out to you, blaming myself for causing everyone so much stress, and all the time you were otherwise engaged. With your bodyguard.' She shook her head, and Francesca knew she was disappointed in her behaviour.

Once they were back home, Isabella wasn't going to be the only one.

'It was a one-off. Never going to happen again. Not worth mentioning.' More lies. It had already happened a second, now a third, time and it was definitely worth shouting from the rooftops if it wouldn't put her entire future as Queen in jeopardy.

Isabella continued to stare at her, and Francesca did her best not to react. Even as Giovanni passed back through the cabin.

'So what's going to happen once you get home?' Isabella whispered.

'Nothing. I told you. It's over and done with. Back to normal as soon as we land. Now, enough about my mistakes, what are you going to do about Rowan?' It was playing dirty perhaps to put the ball back in her sister's court, but Francesca didn't want to examine everything that had happened with Giovanni with her. Mostly because she was afraid she was already in too deep, and didn't know how she was going to move past it.

Isabella shrugged. 'There's not much I can do. We have to give this interview, then I guess it's back to normal.'

Francesca recognised the pain and uncertainty in her sister's eyes because she was feeling the same way as Monterossa came into view below them. Their plans to have one night of being 'normal' had completely backfired, leaving them more conflicted than usual about their lives at the palace. And the relationships they'd left behind in London.

Though Francesca had returned home to freshen up first, Isabella had gone on ahead to the hospital to speak to their parents about Rowan and the upcoming interview. She'd decided to be upfront about what had happened in London. To a point. Francesca suspected her sister left some of the more lurid details out. As would she.

Thanks to Isabella's confession that they had ditched the party and had a night in the city, she was sure she'd be in for a grilling from her parents. Not to mention a stern ticking-off. But there were some things they were better off not knowing. It wouldn't achieve anything by letting them know she'd spent the night with her bodyguard, except a lot of disappointment, worry, and Giovanni likely losing his job.

They'd gone to a lot of trouble to cover their tracks, but she understood her sister's need to confess. Guilt was a terrible burden. Giovanni was proof enough of how it could destroy a person's life, and she didn't wish that on her sister. Secrets had a way of eventually coming to the surface anyway. It had barely been twenty-four hours since she and Giovanni had shared one and it had already been uncovered by Isabella.

Of course, Giovanni had escorted her to the hospital, but they hadn't yet had a moment alone. Even now he was outside her father's room conversing with the other security detail. No doubt making plans for when the King was discharged home. She realised now how much planning went into their every move, and why they needed it. Without Giovanni's guidance in London, things could've turned out very badly for her. Naïve, alone, and without the foresight to even carry any cash, that had been her first risk. Sleeping with Giovanni had been her second. Not because it put her in harm's way, but because she'd endangered her heart.

'It's so good to see you.' Francesca kissed her parents on the cheek. Her stomach rolling at the prospect of this conversation. As ridiculous as it was to be afraid of her parents' wrath at this age, it had been uppermost in her mind since London. Especially when she knew Isabella had already told them of her failings.

No doubt they would blame her for the events that had unfolded because she should have known better. She was the one who had most to lose by running wild in public. Being at the coronation should have reminded her of her duty. Unfortunately, it had only reminded her of the lack of control she had over her own life.

If she was honest, she still held some resentment. Mostly about not being able to be with Giovanni. Someone from a normal family wouldn't have any trouble pursuing a relationship with someone she had an incredible bond with. But she didn't have the luxury of exploring anything with Giovanni publicly.

She couldn't bring herself to say it was good to be home because that meant saying goodbye to the freedom she'd so enjoyed with Giovanni.

'I hear you had fun in London.' Her father gave her a pointed look and she hung her head like a scolded child.

'I'm sorry. I should've known better. It won't happen again.' She didn't know what else she could say, knowing she'd let the family down with her wayward behaviour.

'We're very disappointed in you, Francesca.' Her mother's sharp tone made her wince.

She knew she'd let them down, but hearing it come from them struck her deep in the heart.

'I know.' Nothing she could say would ever make up for what she had done. Even if she could find the words to express her remorse for letting them down.

'You're going to be Queen some day. You can't afford to be seen falling out of clubs, or acting irresponsibly. The whole country needs to believe you're capable of being a leader. That you're not just a privileged princess taking her position for granted. You need public support and you're not going to have that if you embarrass us all abroad. Now, more than ever, your reputation needs to be pristine. You represent Monterossa, Francesca.' Her father's face was sterner than she'd ever seen, and she was devastated that she'd caused them this much anguish.

She'd spent a lifetime trying to gain their approval and she'd stuffed everything up with one stupid mistake. There had been small misdemeanours in the past when she'd forgotten certain protocols in public when her parents had admonished her, reminded her of correct etiquette. This was on a different level. And she hated the look of disappointment she saw reflected in their eyes.

'I'm sorry. I'll do better.' Her voice was small, though she was determined to prove herself worthy of her place in the family now more than ever.

She'd made one slip-up, which they'd hopefully look

past as long as she did her best to live up to their expectations. With no more room for mistakes.

The King beckoned her over to his bedside and took her hand. 'I understand the pressure you are under as the next in line to the throne, daughter. I was there myself once too. I remember that urge to run and hide from my duty, but it is not a luxury either of us can afford to indulge. I trust now that you've got that out of your system, we can expect you to return to being the loyal Princess of Monterossa who we know and love?'

He raised an eyebrow at her to let her know exactly what was expected of her. She wanted to replace the frowns and scowls on their faces with beaming smiles. Pride.

'Of course. Thank you for being so understanding, Father.' She had to accept her fate was to eventually rule the country, and with the privileges she so enjoyed came the responsibility she was born into. There was no getting around that. There was no room for anyone, or anything, else. Including Giovanni.

At least she'd had London.

'With your father getting out of hospital soon, we've decided to go away for a few days so he can recuperate,' her mother interjected.

'Good idea. I wouldn't recommend London for a relaxing break though. In my experience, it can get a bit hectic.' Some day she knew she'd look back on it and think it was probably the best time of her life. Once the worry about Isabella and Rowan dissipated, and her own dalliance with Giovanni was likely a distant memory, she'd remember how free she'd felt. Uninhibited. Normal. Everything she'd wanted to experience, and more. The most exciting night she knew she'd never forget.

'No, we're planning on doing a little less…socialising.' Though her mother's carefully chosen words were probably referencing her sister's time with Rowan, Francesca couldn't help but think about Giovanni and what her parents would think if they knew what had happened between them.

Their parents had been very accommodating at the time of Isabella's engagement, given Rowan's very different background. Likely because the King had married a commoner too. An actress no less! The fact that their mother, Gloria, had been a Hollywood star had probably given them more kudos. However, Francesca was the future Queen. Even if her parents did accept him as a suitable match, there wouldn't be room for a husband, or anything, other than her duty to her country. She had feelings for Giovanni, but he needed someone who was going to be there for him. He needed a wife, not a queen. Not that either of them was even thinking about marriage…

'We want you to take the reins for a little while in my place. Hopefully it won't be a permanent arrangement, but we thought perhaps now was the time for you to step forward and assume more royal duties. I'm not physically able at the minute, and I think it will help your credibility to be more visible in my absence.' As usual, her father was very matter-of-fact, and she didn't have to try very hard to read between the lines.

He wanted her to prove herself. Understandable, given the circumstances, along with her recent behaviour. Not only did he have his own health struggles, but she'd dropped the ball when he was most likely hoping she was ready to take over when the time came.

So was she. Francesca knew she was capable, but she would admit that recently she'd questioned if it was a role she really wanted. Being Queen meant giving up any thoughts of ever having a life of her own. Being with Giovanni in London had given her a glimpse of that parallel universe where she had no responsibilities, and was free to do whatever, be with whoever she wanted. It was akin to having cold feet before your wedding day. Except the repercussions for Francesca would be so much more than a distraught groom if she decided not to go through with her big day. She'd already let her family down, and she felt awful. Without their faith and support, she had nothing. And she would only have that as long as she proved she was still their perfect princess.

'Of course. I will liaise with everyone to take over your royal duties for now so you can recover. We need you fit and well.' Hopefully to return to the throne where he belonged. Francesca wasn't ready to lose him, or to follow in his footsteps just yet.

'Thank you, Francesca. We know we can rely on you.' Her mother put her hand on her arm and gave her a squeeze.

Francesca swallowed the sudden ball of fear in her throat and forced a smile.

She supposed in the circumstances she and Isabella had got off lightly. For two people who'd always been so strict about how their children should act in public, her parents were surprisingly calm about their daughters going rogue in another country. Especially when there apparently was photographic evidence of at least one of them.

At least they were giving her a second chance. To prove her worth as Queen. To do the right thing. To put everything that had happened in London behind her. Including sleeping with Giovanni. He was a temptation she couldn't afford to give into again.

CHAPTER EIGHT

'I DON'T SEE why I have to go.' Giovanni understood why Francesca had distanced herself from him since their return. Even why she'd been colder towards him after speaking to her parents. However, he didn't understand why she felt the need to punish him.

Thankfully, she apparently hadn't told her parents everything that had happened in London as he still held his position at the palace. Something that was now under threat with this particular senior royal.

'It's not that I'm firing you, Giovanni. You're just moving to another team. I think there's too much baggage between us now to carry on. My parents have given me an opportunity to show the country I'm a natural successor to their King, and I can't have anything jeopardising that. And, please, I think it's better that you address me by my proper title from now on. I think being too familiar is exactly why I should appoint someone else as my personal protection officer. How can you be subjective in your job when we have a...history?' As she stumbled over the last word, it betrayed the cool, calm demeanour she'd displayed since calling him into the study to talk to him in private.

With her parents gone, and taking on more royal duties, she needed him more than ever, but she was trying to tell him otherwise.

'You know I'm good at my job, *Your Highness*. I would never let anything get in the way of your safety. I can assure you of that.' He was trying to keep the anger out of his voice, but it wasn't easy when she was threatening to replace him. Especially when it wasn't his capability in question.

He had wondered how they were going to work together after everything that had happened, but he hadn't anticipated the prospect of losing her altogether. Now she was apparently expecting him to move away and leave her safety in someone else's hands. Not an easy thing for him to do when looking after her had been his sole purpose for so long. This wasn't just a job to him. Certainly now that they'd forged such a bond. And he couldn't trust anyone else to keep her safe the way he had. No one could possibly care for her more than he did.

'I don't think either of us were particularly professional in London, and I can't afford any more mistakes.'

That one hurt. Almost as much as when he'd heard her telling Isabella that their time together meant nothing. The fact that she didn't want him in charge of her personal safety suggested it might be more.

Of course she might have had regrets, but then they'd indulged their carnal urges on the plane as well. Now he wondered if she was simply afraid of them continuing to work together in case it happened again.

Since she had referenced their personal relationship, he thought it safe to talk about it. Regardless that they'd avoided it for the few days since they'd been back in the country. They'd had plenty of opportunity to address what had happened, with the rest of the family caught up in their own dramas, but Francesca had kept her distance. He hadn't thought it his place to chase her down and discuss how things had changed between them, but that didn't mean she hadn't been on his mind constantly.

If things had been different, if she weren't royalty, and he a member of staff, they might've had a chance of exploring some sort of relationship. Meeting Dan, talking to him, and to Francesca, had made him realise that the unnecessary guilt he'd been carrying was preventing him from having a life of his own. Without the worry of hurting those closest to him, he might have thought about settling down, maybe even having a family. But that was never going to be with Francesca. She'd made that abundantly clear, even if there weren't that huge class divide between them.

'I understand that, but we both agreed that when we got home we'd put London behind us. Sacking me, or restructuring, or whatever you want to call it, doesn't sound like we're doing that. Do you honestly think I'm not capable of doing my job, Francesca?'

'No, I—'

He saw her bottom lip quiver and knew there was a chink in her steely defences. 'I am the one who has been planning every detail of these engagements for you. You know I'll keep you safe. I would give my life for you.'

That much was true. Francesca had come to mean so much more to him than a job, even though nothing could come of these growing feelings he had towards her.

He thought he saw her soften, the tension ease in her shoulders, but just as quickly she recovered herself.

Standing up straighter, tilting her chin into the air in that way that she did when issuing a challenge.

'Fine. You can remain in your position, but my father is counting on me to make a good impression; counting on us to be professional.' The meaning was clear. Francesca was letting him know that there was no room for any more mistakes. Unfortunately, that meant taking their relationship back to the one they'd had before London.

Something that wasn't going to be straightforward when the memories of her touch, and the taste of her, were imprinted on him, body and soul, for ever.

Francesca had tried to put some distance between her and Giovanni by moving him to another security team. In her wisdom, she'd thought it the only way to stop thinking about him so she could focus on her royal duties. She hadn't thought about how that decision would impact on him. He had no family, no partner, no life away from the palace. His job was his life, and she couldn't take it away from him just because her resolve was weak where he was concerned. Because she was worried she wouldn't be able to keep her feelings for him under control.

It had taken a plea from him to make her realise she was being selfish, as well as foolish. Giovanni was the best at what he did. He could read her every move, knew when she was uncomfortable in a situation and needed to get away, or when to back off and take his cue from her. More than all of that, he took her safety extremely seriously. To change the security he provided at the last moment was an unnecessary risk to take. Although the family was popular, there was always a chance of someone launching an attack of some sort, or even just the crowds getting a little too raucous for comfort.

As the limo pulled up outside the school she was visiting today, her stomach was aflutter like the time when she accompanied her parents on her first public engagement. She'd never gone to an event on her own and she was glad now that she at least had Giovanni for support.

'Relax. Your father only wishes you to smile and wave. He's not asking you to get involved in diplomatic matters. Yet.' Giovanni, it seemed, still wasn't above teasing her, and Francesca resisted scolding him for his familiarity again. After all, this had been the nature of their relationship before they'd succumbed to temptation.

'I know. I'm just feeling the pressure of being here alone.' She fidgeted her hands in her lap.

Giovanni reached across the back seat and stilled them with his own. 'You're never alone. I'm always by your side.'

Francesca made the mistake of looking into his eyes, seeing those dark pools express so clearly how much he cared for her. As if realising he'd given away too much, he sat back, and withdrew his touch.

'You know the signal if you want to leave at any time, Your Highness.'

'Yes. I shall take my handkerchief out of my pocket to let you know.' She missed the slightly sarcastic way he used to call her 'Princess'. Even more, the way he used to say her name. Lovingly, in the heat of passion. Exactly why she'd had to put a stop to it.

'Ready?' he asked, before getting out of the car.

'Ready.' She took a deep breath, knowing the circus would begin the moment she stepped out.

Giovanni used to tease her that she didn't know how it felt to walk on solid ground since there was always a red carpet rolled out for her arrival. Now she did, having spent a night running around London in mutilated shoes, thanks to him. This was her first public duty since then, a reminder of her status. And she was worried London had changed who she was for ever. That it would affect her in how she fulfilled her role as future Queen. Today was going to be a test of her mettle, as well as her capabilities in her new role.

Giovanni exited the car first, liaising with the rest of the security team, before opening the car door. Francesca steeled herself and took her time getting out, as demure as possible, so as not to give any waiting photographers a flash of anything she shouldn't.

The cheers of the waiting crowd as she smiled and waved were overwhelming at first, but the touch of Giovanni's hand at her back was as reassuring as the words he whispered in her ear.

'You got this.'

The rest of the security fell into formation around her as she did a walkabout around the playground, where pupils and teachers were lined up behind barriers waiting to see her. She was directed towards a tall, conservatively dressed middle-aged woman hovering nearby, who she was informed was Mrs Bruno, the school principal.

'We're so honoured to have you here, Your Highness.' The woman curtseyed, though appeared a little off balance.

Francesca was used to people being a little nervous, though none would realise she was often just as anxious that the event went well. Especially today, when she felt particularly under scrutiny in light of her father's absence. There would be those waiting to criticise, deeming her unsuitable to follow in her father's footsteps. Too young, too single, too modern, and likely too female for some dinosaurs. So she didn't want to give them any ammunition against her.

'It's my pleasure. I've heard such wonderful things about your school, but I'm keen to learn more. Perhaps I should just say hello to some of the families first.' It was the cue, not only to the security team, but also her host, about her itinerary.

She knew they didn't like it when she did a walkabout with the crowd, from a safety point of view, but she thought it necessary. When people made such an effort to come and see her, it would be arrogant and amiss of her not to acknowledge that.

'Oh, yes, they'll love that. The children have prepared a little something for you too.' Mrs Bruno looked delighted that Francesca was willing to do more than a quick stop. No doubt it would earn her some brownie points with the children and parents too.

'How lovely. Why don't you introduce me to some of the parents and children?' She invited the principal to walk alongside her as they approached the expectant crowd.

Giovanni made sure he was between her and the public, ready to step in if necessary if things got a little out of hand. Not that there was any cause for concern. As Mrs Bruno made introductions to the parents and families, they were very respectful. Most wanting to shake her hand and say hello. There were a few wanting to take selfies, but, as instructed by Giovanni, she wasn't to lean into the person taking them. According to him, this new trend was a security nightmare. She understood that such close contact with strangers was risky, but she doubted anyone here had reason to want to hurt her.

As they were coming to the end of their mini tour, a little girl in her mother's arms handed her a posy of wildflowers.

'Chiara picked those herself,' the mother told her.

Francesca was touched by the gesture, even though Giovanni probably wouldn't recommend taking gifts from strangers. He saw danger everywhere, where she saw only a little girl who wanted to give her a present. Francesca certainly wasn't going to upset her by refusing it. 'Well, Chiara, thank you very much. They're beautiful.'

'Just like you. I like your pink dress and your pretty princess hair,' Chiara said shyly, her head partially buried in her mother's shoulder.

'Thank you.' Francesca reached up and pulled out one of the crystal pins decorating her French chignon. She tucked it into the little girl's blonde ponytail. 'Now you've got pretty princess hair too.'

'When I grow up, I want to be just like you,' Chiara told her.

What should have been taken as a compliment managed to chill Francesca's blood. She thought of this beautiful little girl and the future that lay ahead for her and compared it to the life Francesca had mapped out for her. Whilst she had no control over what happened to her, she didn't want anyone else to fall into the trap of trying to live up to impossible expectations. She wasn't going to perpetuate that myth that a child could only be loved if she was perfect.

'You just be you, Chiara. That's enough.' It took a lot to stop her voice from cracking. Wishing someone had told her the same at that age and saved her a lot of heartache.

'Thank you for everything. It's very brave and kind of you to take the time with everyone.' Chiara's mother shook her hand and Francesca managed a shaky smile before walking away.

Brave. It wasn't a title she thought she deserved. She'd never fought for anything in her life. Not even herself. Letting fear and other people's expectations rule over her. It wasn't something she'd want for any of the children here. Yet, she'd accepted it for herself. Just once she wanted to do something deserving of that description. If only for a little while.

It made her think of what she had with Giovanni. What she wanted with him. How she hadn't fought for him when being with him was the one thing she truly wanted in her life. For however long they could have together.

Although they might not have for ever, she would never forgive herself if she didn't try. She needed to be brave enough to be with him in any capacity she could.

If he still wanted her.

The entourage carried on into the school where she met staff and was invited to sit as guest of honour as the choir sang the national anthem. Something that brought a tear to her eye for many reasons. Including the knowledge that one day she would be the monarch the children were singing about.

She listened as the little ones sang their hearts out, watched the parents beaming with pride, and felt a pang for that simple life. One in which she would have a loving husband by her side, watching their child perform, where nothing in the world was more important than her family's happiness. A dream beyond possibility because she'd been born into royalty. The only time she'd felt normal, that this kind of life was available to her, had been in London. With Giovanni.

She wanted to capture that feeling all over again.

When Francesca got back into the car, she was positively buzzing with adrenaline. The smile on her face as she waved goodbye to the children a genuine display of happiness, as opposed to the one she'd worn when she'd first set foot in the playground. Giovanni was simply relieved she was still in one piece.

'You took some risks there today.' Perhaps he was speaking out of turn, but he wouldn't be doing his job properly if he didn't warn her about the dangers of getting too close to the general public.

And, okay, he worried more about her these days. Not just because she was undertaking more royal duties in place of her father.

'Shush. They're just children. Were you worried that little girl was going to stab me to death with my hairpin?' She was mocking his concern, but that wasn't what was bothering him. In future she was going to be in more of these situations than ever, and she had to take some accountability. Otherwise, the consequences would likely kill him too.

As she reached up to adjust her hair, he shot a hand out to grab hers. 'I'm serious, Francesca. I don't want you to get hurt on my watch.'

'Do you care about me that much?' Her eyes blazed with a fire that had been missing since their night in London.

'You know I do.' They were both aware he wasn't talking about his loyalty to her in a professional way, the blacked-out back seat of the car now filled with a tension he hadn't felt since their time alone in the city.

'So what are you going to do about it?' There was the chin tilt: the challenge for him to act on those feelings he'd been trying to keep at bay for days, for her sake as much as his own.

In the end, he was only human.

'This.' He lunged forward, wound his fingers in her hair and pulled her into a hard kiss. If he'd expected it to shock her into backing away before they repeated past mistakes, he'd underestimated the strength of her need for this too.

That spark reignited, passion soon flared dangerously into an inferno, Giovanni's need for her overriding all common sense once more. Their bodies clung together like long-distance lovers finally reunited after years apart, rather than two people who'd tried to avoid each other for mere days out of self-preservation.

It was only when the car came to a stop that they were thrown back into reality.

'We're back at the palace.' Giovanni had only just said the words when the staff were at the door, readying themselves for the Princess's arrival.

He looked at Francesca, for some clarification of what she wanted, what she expected from him. Braced himself for another 'We made a mistake, this won't happen again' speech.

She leaned her hands on his knees, bent forward so he had a clear view down the front of her dress, and whispered, 'My parents are away, Isabella is busy with Rowan, and I can send the staff away.'

The implication was very clear. Enough that she didn't even wait for a response, getting out of the car and walking into the palace with her head held high.

Giovanni smiled. Despite all the complications that would surely follow, they both knew he was going to follow her in there. She had his heart, and hopefully soon other parts of him, in the palm of her hand.

By the time he'd reached her bedroom, Francesca had already dismissed the rest of the security team and her personal assistant. She was waiting in the doorway for him, unpinning her hair so it fell in dark waves around her shoulders. As he stood in the hallway he knew this was the last chance for him to walk away. Once he crossed that threshold, they couldn't use the same excuse they'd used in London. This wasn't a one-night fling, something that they could claim was simply exploring the freedom of her anonymity. It was a conscious decision to be together, and at some point they were going to have to acknowledge what that meant. For the future, for his position at the palace, and for them.

However, right now, he simply couldn't seem to stop himself from walking into that danger. Drawn to her like a moth to a flame; unable to resist the beauty, but knowing he'd get burned.

'Francesca—'

She put a finger to his lips, stopping him from uttering another word. 'Before you do the whole "Are you sure? Isn't this a bad idea?" speech, the answer is yes to both. But I don't want to think about anything right now. I've done too much of that these past days. Thinking, worrying, planning…it all gets a bit much. When I'm with you I just want to feel good. And if there's one thing I'm sure of, it's that you know how to do that.'

It wasn't a glowing indictment of how she felt about him, more about what he could do for her, but in that moment he didn't care. He wanted her, and perhaps it was better if at least one of them was only interested in the physical side of things. It might just keep her safer than everyone else who'd got close to him.

As per instruction, he didn't open his mouth to speak, but put it to better use. Lips on Francesca's, he backed her into the room and closed the door behind them. From the moment she'd shown her nerves in the car, he'd wanted to kiss her, hold her. Despite the numerous breaches of security protocol on the visit, it had only made her more attractive in his eyes. Her kindness and patience with the children, and everyone else, showed what a great queen she was going to make. As well as a fabulous mother.

His heart ached that she was going to go on to have a family with someone else. A man who might fit socially, but would never know her the way he did. Having a family wasn't anything he'd even dreamed he could have, but being around Francesca, seeing her with the children, made him want it all. With her. For now, though, he'd have to simply settle for being with her.

This time they didn't need a seduction scene, both knowing what they wanted. As their mouths mashed together, they made their way over to the large four-poster bed in the middle of the room. Stripping off their clothes as they went. Giovanni only stopping briefly to find a condom and put it on before joining Francesca, who was lying naked waiting for him. The sight of her alone strengthening his already flourishing arousal.

Francesca, apparently in as much of a hurry as he was to get carnally reacquainted, pulling him on top of her. Giovanni entered her quickly, and easily. Both of their bodies primed for this moment from the first time they'd given in to temptation.

'I've thought of this every minute since we landed back on Monterossa.' Francesca gasped as he drove himself inside her. The admission spurring his pace in that race to find mutual satisfaction.

'How did we manage to wait so long?' The time they'd spent apart seemed a waste. Regardless that they'd both been trying to do the right thing. Putting aside their desires to prioritise their roles at the palace.

'Sheer stubbornness,' she suggested, arching her back and offering up her nipples for his attention.

Giovanni obliged, sucking hard on the sweet pink tips as their bodies rocked violently together. Francesca's breath was already becoming increasingly ragged, her moans of satisfaction getting higher, and louder. Watching her come to climax at his behest was a privilege he was getting too used to. Knowing he could make her feel this way, that she enjoyed him as much as he did her, urging him on to reach that pinnacle with her. Until their cries of ecstasy rang out around the room. Thank goodness she'd dismissed the staff, or they would've been the talk of the palace, and likely beyond. It seemed playing with fire was their particular kink.

CHAPTER NINE

'I MISSED THIS.' Francesca threaded her fingers through Giovanni's, lifting their hands up so she could see them. Proof that this was real and not just another one of her erotic dreams.

'Me too.' Giovanni rolled over on the bed and kissed her cheek.

'I've been thinking…' She turned to stare into those beautiful dark eyes, which she apparently couldn't resist, along with the rest of him.

'Hmm…' His sleepy response stirred that ache inside her all over again, despite her body being sated only moments ago.

He had that effect on her. Bringing her body alive at the mere sound and sight of him. Ruining her for any other man who could never hope to do the same. The idea of marriage even more of a prison to her now when she knew she could never feel this way about her future husband.

The reason why she was about to suggest something very un-queen-like. 'Clearly, we can't stay away from one another.'

'Clearly.' To prove the point, Giovanni was back, nibbling at the skin on her neck, his hand roaming her naked body again.

'I thought perhaps we could continue to see each other, in private.' Now she had his attention.

Giovanni sat bolt upright. 'How would that work?'

She'd been thinking about it a lot in that ride back in the car, trying to find some way of keeping him in her life in more than a professional way, without causing a drama. In the end, she'd come up with the idea of a casual arrangement.

'Sleeping together in private, yet outwardly maintaining that professional façade, seems like having the best of both worlds to me. Though of course it will mean having to keep our hands off each other in the car, and anywhere else we could be seen. Any physical contact will have to be kept behind a closed bedroom door.'

'Is that really what you want?' He held her gaze, as though willing her to say what was really in her heart.

There was no point when they couldn't be together properly. No one at the palace would be happy about the match, and she didn't want to start her reign on a bad note when the time came. She and Giovanni would burn themselves out eventually and it would cause a lot of unnecessary worry and scandal to go public. This passion between them couldn't last for ever. One day she would have to marry someone suitable, and she'd have her duties to occupy her every waking moment.

Besides, he'd made it clear he wasn't in the market for a serious relationship anyway. At least this way they'd be able to reap the benefits of a no-strings arrangement without anyone getting hurt. And she'd have some very pleasant memories and experiences to cling to when she did finally marry someone suitable as a husband to a queen. Someone who could never make her feel the way Giovanni did.

'Yes,' she lied. He might not agree if he thought she had any feelings for him other than the ones he stirred in the bedroom.

'And how long will this arrangement last?' He cocked an eyebrow at her as though he didn't believe she was actually proposing this. Francesca supposed it was out of character for someone who always played by the rules, but once London had unleashed that wild side of her character it was difficult to keep it hidden. Since Giovanni had been the only one to see that version of her, the real Francesca, it seemed apt that he should be the one to reap the benefits of her too.

'Until any future engagement. Or before, if either of us decide we're no longer content with the arrangement.' Francesca didn't imagine she'd get bored of having Giovanni in her bed, but there might come a time when it got too risky, or one of them met someone else they were better suited to. The idea of him hooking up with another woman who could give him a normal life, the one thing she couldn't, was already hurting her heart. If she was going to really enjoy this, she had to get any feelings for him out of the game and focus on the physical aspect of their relationship.

Francesca was surprised when he hesitated. Here she was, offering him sex on a plate, with no complications. Well, as long as they didn't get caught, in which case they'd have some serious explaining to do.

'And you think we can do that? Sex without getting involved or affecting our lives here?' He was wearing his serious face now. The one she usually saw when he was talking about her personal security. She supposed in a way he was talking about that, even if he didn't know it. It was inevitable that she'd get hurt at some point when it all ended, but that was going to happen now regardless of how or when things ended between them. She was already emotionally invested. He just didn't need to know that.

'I don't see why not. If we're careful.' She swallowed down the lie. If this was going to work she was going to have to smother her feelings. At least she'd had years of practice in that area.

'Okay.' He nodded.

'Okay?' She was a little deflated by his reaction. It wasn't exactly in keeping with the nature of an illicit affair when he didn't seem that bothered to be part of it.

Just as she was about to backtrack, pretend it wasn't a big deal if he didn't want to be a part of this, Giovanni rolled over.

'Okay. I'll be your dirty little secret. For now.' He kissed her, adding to the frisson of excitement already bringing her out in goosebumps at the thought of continuing this fling for the foreseeable future.

He was more than her dirty little secret, he was where she could be herself, do what she wanted. Be free. She was expected to marry, to produce heirs, and be a good little queen, but perhaps that freedom had awakened something in her. That need to control her own life, or at least have a say in it. A strong queen would be able to make her own decisions. Perhaps she'd never marry at all…

'Your father wants to see you in his study.' Francesca's mother approached her in the palace gardens where she'd gone for a stroll to clear her head.

It had been a couple of weeks since she and Giovanni had embarked on their casual fling, and her parents had now returned from their trip. Keeping their relationship secret was becoming trickier. Although that also made the time they did spend together all the more exciting. Which was part of the problem. She was enjoying being with Giovanni a little too much, and perhaps her parents had noticed.

'Why?' Her mother hadn't given anything away, and Francesca would prefer to be prepared if she was about to get a grilling about her love life.

'You'd better speak to him.'

'Okay.' Dread pitted in her stomach. If she and Giovanni had been caught out, there was going to be hell to pay. Not only had they been indiscreet, but her parents would be disappointed, and disapproving, in her choice of partner.

They liked Giovanni well enough, but, as a commoner, he wouldn't be deemed suitable as the husband of the future Queen. She'd known all of this going into the relationship, but somehow her libido had taken over from that usual need to do the right thing. It had felt good at the time, but now she was sure she was about to pay a heavy cost. There was no way Giovanni would remain employed at the palace after this.

She took her time walking back into the palace, her steps echoing around the hallway and marking every move closer to the possible end of her relationship with Giovanni. It was tempting to turn and run. To grab him on the way out and go and hide away somewhere where no one knew them. Maybe even London. Just so she could keep him in her life. She'd already been thinking about how close they'd grown over these past weeks and how she was ever going to move back into her public role without him to bolster her confidence, physically and mentally. This was too soon.

'You wanted to see me, Father?' She put on that calm demeanour expected of her during all of her other royal duties, regardless of her stomach doing the fandango.

'Yes, Francesca. Sit.' He gestured at the chair on the other side of his desk whilst he carried on with the paperwork at hand.

'If this is a bad time I can come back later.' Sitting here listening to the loud tick of the grandfather clock in the corner wasn't helping her nerves.

'No. I just have to sign a few of these letters. That's the thing about taking time off. It's all still waiting for you when you come back.' Another of his little nuggets of advice about running a country he liked to drop into conversation every now and then. It seemed there was no area of her life she could enjoy without the heavy weight of responsibility hanging around her neck.

No wonder she liked time away from it all with Giovanni. He was an escape from everything for her. Though she'd come to realise he meant more to her than that. He was the man she wanted by her side no matter where she ended up in life, regardless that it was impossible. Giovanni believed in her more than anyone, probably even more than she did. He brought out the best in her. The woman she wished she could be in public, as well as in private with him.

A few minutes of her father scratching his fountain pen on a mountain of papers, then he sat up and gave her his full attention. 'Right. We need to talk about your actions whilst I and your mother were out of the country.'

Francesca was regretting the chicken pesto pasta she'd had for lunch. 'Oh?'

She batted her eyes innocently, all the while images of everything she and Giovanni had done in her bedroom these past weeks playing an erotic movie in her head.

'Yes, your mother and I have had a chance to speak to the aides and security who've accompanied you on your engagements, and we've seen some of the footage filmed on your visits.'

Oh, please don't let anyone have taken any snaps of me and Giovanni snogging in the back of the car like two horny teens at a drive-in!

'You shouldn't believe everything you hear, or see.' She was trying to decide whether to brazen it out or just come clean. Neither option holding any appeal at the moment.

'Well, we thought you were the happiest we'd seen you look in a long time. I know everyone has felt the strain with my health problems, and uncertainty about the future. No one more than you, I expect. But you've obviously found a coping strategy.'

Apparently her parents were more open-minded than she'd ever realised. Giovanni was many things to her, but she'd never thought of him as a coping strategy. She supposed he was in a way. Was her father actually suggesting that they keep on their illicit bedroom antics if it kept her happy in her work?

'And—and you and Mother are happy for me to continue?'

'Most definitely. It will make life easier for us too.'

That lead weight began to lift, making her feel lighter

than she had since her mother had come to fetch her. 'I'm so glad. I didn't know how to bring this up with you. It will of course bring us some challenges with the general public, but I hope when they see I'm still capable of doing the job, I'll win them over.'

This was more than she could ever have hoped. If her parents were accepting of her relationship with Giovanni, perhaps they could really try and make a go of it. It wasn't going to be easy, and she still had to find out the strength of his feelings, and if they went beyond the bedroom door. But she thought they made a good team. With her father's blessing, she was sure the country would soon get behind them as a couple too.

'Exactly what we think too. Your mother wasn't sure if you were ready to take on more responsibilities just yet, but I think you've more than proven yourself capable.' Her father was smiling as though a great weight had been lifted from his shoulders too, but Francesca had a niggling feeling that they weren't on the same page.

'Capable of what?' Although her last relationship had ended badly, she wasn't sure even the royal family needed to be vetted publicly before getting involved with someone else.

The King frowned. 'Taking on more royal duties on a more permanent basis. I'm not planning on abdicating, but I do think that for the sake of my health I should scale down the number of public engagements I undertake. As next in line, you would be expected to take on most of the ones I can no longer do. Of course, your sister will attend some of the low-key events, but you might have to attend some of the more…diplomatic meetings if I'm unable to be there.'

That brief moment of happiness quickly evaporated. Instead of having her relationship with Giovanni out in the open, she found herself agreeing to burying herself further under the burden of royal life. Something that would surely leave less time and privacy for her to be with him.

Not that she could tell her father any of this now. He was still recovering from his illness, and he needed the reassurance that she would be there to take up the slack. Neither of her parents needed the added stress of her telling them that she was beginning to doubt she even wanted to be Queen. Or that she was sleeping with her bodyguard.

Especially not on the back of Isabella's revelations. They were lucky that their mother and father had held their tempers upon hearing about their escape into the city, and Isabella and Rowan's brush with the press. Telling them any more bad news would be testing their limits, and goodness knew she didn't want the added responsibility of making her father even more ill with stress.

So she did what was expected of her, and smiled and nodded. 'I will do whatever you need from me, Father.'

After all, she was always the dutiful daughter.

Giovanni had been looking forward to spending some alone time with Francesca all day. They had to be careful when they were out and about, and when they were around other staff. More so, now her parents were back in residence. It wasn't easy getting privacy when there was so much more security on site for the King and Queen. He'd had to resort to sneaking about the hallways at night, ducking behind pillars when he heard someone coming, waiting for the all-clear from Francesca to bundle into her room. One night he'd even had to hide out on the balcony stark naked when Isabella had unexpectedly come to her room, with Francesca hurriedly kicking his clothes under her bed.

Their passionate, exciting love affair had become more of a bawdy sex comedy.

They couldn't carry on like this long term. As much as he wanted to carry on seeing her, the more they engaged in this behaviour, the sooner they'd get caught out. With the likely outcome that he'd get fired, and never see her again. One of those things he knew he couldn't bear. He could always get another job, but he'd come to realise there would never be another Francesca for him. If her father found out from someone else that they'd been seeing each other, the fallout was going to be huge. Giovanni didn't want this becoming a self-fulfilling prophecy, with Francesca getting hurt, if it could be avoided.

He knew he wasn't good enough for her, but that didn't mean he didn't have feelings for her. Before he could decide what he wanted to do, he needed to know if this was nothing more to her than the casual hook-up they'd intended it to be. If so, there was a chance they could go back to the lives they'd had before London, before they'd let their defences down and got to know each other outside the palace walls. Although, if she did have feelings for him in return, he didn't know where that left them. If they came clean to her parents, would they, or the rest of the country, accept him as a partner to the future Queen? Would Francesca even want that, when she'd been so eager to please everyone she'd almost married someone she didn't love?

Tonight, they might have to do more talking than kissing.

The one good thing about a carefully regimented royal household was that he knew the schedule. When security took their breaks, when the next shift arrived, so he could slip through to Francesca's room virtually unseen except for those unplanned trips the family took to the bathroom or kitchen when there was a risk he'd be spotted. Thankfully, tonight was one of the occasions where everything went to plan. He hoped it was a sign of things to come.

As had become their custom, he knocked lightly three times on her door to let her know he was there. Within seconds, she'd opened it and practically dragged him inside.

'You're just what I need right now,' she said, pushing him up against the closed door and kissing him as though she hadn't seen him in years.

Normally, he wouldn't have an issue with her taking control. He was all about equal opportunities, especially in the bedroom. Tonight, however, he'd hoped they could have something more meaningful. He wanted them to talk about the future, and if they had one together.

Not that she was making it easy for him to think, never mind talk, when she was already stripping off his jacket and undoing his tie.

'I heard your father called you in for a private chat today.' There wasn't much that happened here that he didn't know about. It was his job to plan for all eventualities concerning the Princess's safety. A conflict of interests, of course, given their current relationship, but useful for him to know small details about these things, which might involve him to some degree.

The moment he said anything about it, he regretted it. Francesca's good mood immediately faltering. 'Can we not talk about it?'

It went against all his instincts to pause their nightly passionate tryst when it was the highlight of his day, but her reluctance told him something important had happened in that private meeting.

'You can tell me.' He stroked her hair and kissed her softly on the lips. If there was a chance of them having more of a relationship, then they needed to open up to one another for support.

Francesca heaved out a sigh that seemed to have come all the way up from the soles of her bare feet. 'He wants me to take on some more of his official duties on a permanent basis.'

Giovanni could see why that would be vexing for her, but didn't explain her reluctance to talk about it. 'Surely that was to be expected, given his health issues, and your increased workload lately.'

Seduction set aside for now, Francesca paced the room. Eventually collapsing onto the edge of the bed. 'I just… I thought, by the way that he was talking, that he and my mother knew about us. That they were happy for us.'

'I don't understand. How? Why?' It didn't make any sense to him why she would've assumed that the King knew about them, or why she would have preferred that conversation to one about her work. He would've thought that if their relationship had come to light then all hell would have broken loose. With him getting the roasting.

Francesca threw herself back dramatically onto the bed. 'He said I was the happiest I'd looked in ages and he was glad. That I should keep doing more of what I was doing. I assumed he was giving his blessing for us to be together.'

'Okay. And that's a good thing because...?' He closed the distance between them and sat down beside her. If she was saying what he thought she was, he was going to need to be sitting down to deal with this.

'Because I thought that meant we could keep on seeing each other, minus the sneaking about. Like a normal couple.'

'You know we could never be that.' He smiled and threaded his fingers through hers. The one act of solidarity they dared to do in the daytime when they were sure no one was watching. Their 'thing'.

She wasn't declaring her undying love for him, but at least she was letting him know he meant more to her than merely a sex buddy. That was all that he wanted, wasn't it? To know his feelings for her were reciprocated?

Yet it meant by having a deeper connection it was going to be that much more painful when they were forced to part. Their feelings could never change their circumstances, and he was going to have to face that fact. He couldn't be any more than a fling or it would cost her her crown. That would devastate her, and was exactly the reason he'd fought his feelings for her for so long. He never wanted her to get hurt.

Another sigh. 'I know. It doesn't matter now. I'm not going to upset everyone by saying how I really feel.' She was smiling, but he knew her well enough to know that it did matter. The more she acted the perfect princess, the more she'd grow to resent it.

'You know you can talk to me.' She'd opened up in London about her troubles, and though they weren't supposed to get emotions involved these days, he knew they were beyond that now.

He'd wanted to know that she felt something for him beyond the physical, but now it was real, he had to face the fact that there would be consequences for her if they acted on it. He cared too much for her to let that happen.

'I don't want to talk, Giovanni.' Francesca grabbed the front of his shirt and pulled him into a long, sensual kiss. As though she was trying to express how she felt without actually saying the words. Probably for the best in the circumstances. Then he could pretend that there weren't going to be repercussions if they gave into temptation again.

She set about unbuttoning him, undoing his belt, and he realised he didn't want to do any talking either after all. That meant a conversation he wasn't ready to have just yet. A realisation that this was probably coming to an end. They couldn't be together in the real world because of all the reasons he'd told her about. She was bound to get hurt. Along with her parents, her sister, and everyone else.

'You know what? Neither do I.' They could have one last night together. Before someone got hurt. Unbridled passion. A goodbye that they could remember for ever. Then it was back to real life.

On opposite sides of the palace walls.

CHAPTER TEN

'I SHOULD GO before anyone else gets up.' Giovanni gave her a quick peck on the cheek and made a move to get out of the bed, but Francesca pulled him back down beside her.

'Not yet. Stay and cuddle with me for a while.' She wanted to luxuriate in this land of make believe for a little while longer.

'I've already stayed later than I usually do.' It was a feeble protest as he was already wrapping his arms around her and letting her snuggle into his bare chest.

She didn't want to let him go. Her talk with her father had reminded her of just how far she'd come out of her shell with Giovanni. It was a challenge to go back to that dutiful daughter so eager to please, rather than the woman she was with Giovanni, who did as she pleased for a change. Her time with him was making her want change in her life more than ever, but he'd been right when he'd said they could never be a normal couple. Her future as Queen was something that could never change that fact.

'Wouldn't it be nice to do this every morning? A lie-in, breakfast in bed, and making love without the worry of being found out.'

'Of course, but we'll both get into trouble if we get too complacent. I know how important it is to you to be with someone your parents approve of. As much as they might like me, they'll never approve of me as a suitable match.'

Their little love bubble had burst. Giovanni had given nothing away about his feelings to her, when she'd risked her reputation just to be with him. The scandal of that could have jeopardised her future as part of the royal family and she wouldn't have done that for just anyone.

'I wish I had a normal life, Giovanni.'

There was a soft knock on her door, interrupting Francesca before she was able to tell Giovanni how she felt about him.

'Francesca? Are you awake?' Isabella called through the door.

'Just give me a moment,' she shouted back, then whispering to Giovanni, 'Put your clothes on.'

Francesca pulled on her dressing gown and belted it to preserve her modesty, whilst he was hopping about on the floor now, trying to get his trousers up.

'I want your opinion on this outfit…' Isabella walked on in and caught them both in a state of undress. 'Giovanni?'

'I should go.' He didn't stick around to plead for Isabella's discretion. Apparently, that was down to Francesca. Instead, he put on his shirt and walked out of the bedroom with the rest of his clothes in his arms. At this point she didn't know where things stood between them.

Isabella blinked at her. 'Did that just happen?'

'It depends what you think happened.' Francesca tried

to bring some levity to the moment, knowing there was no way of bluffing her way out of this. It was exactly what it looked like.

'Um, that you and your bodyguard have been having some sort of torrid love affair.'

'Pretty much. Although, given the conversation you interrupted, I'm not sure there's any love involved.' At least not on his part anyway.

Isabella flopped down onto her bed, settling in for story time. 'I thought it was a one-time thing?'

Francesca grimaced. 'Apparently not.'

'After all the grief you gave me about being with Rowan, you and Giovanni have been risking a scandal right here under everyone's noses?' Isabella had every right to be annoyed at her. She hadn't been a very good sister, or daughter, or princess. It had been selfish of her to ignore everyone else's feelings, but it had also been nice to think of herself for a change. Everything about this thing with Giovanni had been confusing. Conflicting what her head was telling her with what her heart wanted.

'I know. I'm sorry. In my defence, that night we spent looking for you brought us closer together. We haven't been able to stay away from one another since.'

'What are you going to do?'

'That's the million-dollar question, isn't it? We've been seeing each other in secret, but I realise I want more than that.'

'What's stopping you?' It was all so much easier for Isabella. She'd wanted to be with Rowan and just gone for it.

This was it. This was the moment everything was

going to hit the fan and she had to decide what road she wanted to take. The one as part of the royal family with all the responsibilities she'd been primed for her whole life, or the one that would see her jeopardise it all to be with Giovanni, who might not love her anyway.

Francesca made a 'pfft' sound. 'I'm not you, Isabella. I can't do as I please and sod the consequences.'

Although she'd been doing more of that lately.

'Nice, Frannie.' Isabella gritted her teeth, her hand clenching the rumpled bed covers.

'You know what I mean. What you do has no real impact on anyone. Whereas I have to be the dutiful daughter, or else the whole monarchy would fall.' A tad overdramatic perhaps, but the royal family needed to be popular. They needed people to look up to them and respect them to have any sort of power. If she messed up, she'd lose that respect and that would be devastating for a future queen. She'd rather disappear into obscurity than deal with the impact a scandalous relationship with her bodyguard would have around her.

'Yes, I'm of no significance at all. Merely a spare princess. A second thought. Someone who has no need to be kept in the loop about any serious matters.' Obviously, Isabella had a bee in her bonnet about her position in the family too.

It had never been her intention to annoy her sister. Simply bad wording and timing on her part.

'You know that's not true, Bella. Trust me, it's not all puppy dogs and fluffy bunnies being the oldest either.'

'At least you get some respect. I'm just expected to stay in the background and not bother anyone. Not that I've been doing a great job of that either lately.' Isabella picked at the hem of her silk nightie, clearly with things on her mind too.

'But it all worked out for you in the end,' Francesca reminded her, hoping she would forget about Giovanni being half naked in her sister's bedroom, and whatever other grievances had arisen from this chat.

Isabella was undeterred. 'What are you going to do about Giovanni? Is it serious?'

'Not yet. I'd like it to be, but you know it's not possible.'

'Why not? He's a nice guy. The strong, silent type. Unless he's telling us off for going against protocol.'

That made her smile. They'd had their fair share of lectures from him over the years when they'd gone off script. Though they both knew it came from a good place. He cared about them.

'He's a commoner. Not a suitable match for a queen-to-be.' It wasn't a nice thing to say, but she was scrabbling for an explanation other than her unrequited feelings.

'So? This isn't the eighteen hundreds, Francesca. Our mother was an actress, in case you've forgotten.'

'No, I haven't forgotten. She was a Hollywood actress. A well-known name, and the marriage brought them some challenges, don't forget.'

'As all marriages do.'

'Apart from anything else, I'm going to be Queen some day, Isabella. I'll have a responsibility to the throne, not a partner. Giovanni deserves more than being second best.'

Isabella took her by the shoulders. 'Listen, sis. I know you've been under pressure your whole life to be perfect, with focus on the day of your coronation. But you're entitled to have a life too. Otherwise it's going to be a very lonely place up on that throne.'

'That's why I think I'm entertaining the idea of a marriage of convenience. That way we both know where we stand and I won't disappoint anyone else if I prove not to be a good enough wife.'

'Oh, Frannie. You both deserve better than that. You don't have to be perfect. Don't you see? You just have to be yourself for people to love, and I'm pretty sure Giovanni's smitten otherwise he wouldn't be risking his job to be with you.'

It was refreshing to hear a family member say something positive to her when compliments were hard come by lately. This was also the first time she'd been told she didn't have to be perfect. That she was enough. She wondered if it was true. Certainly, Giovanni had seemed to think so in London when she'd been free to drop her public persona. Still, it didn't guarantee that they'd get their fairy-tale ending.

'And if things don't work out? Then I've caused a scandal by hooking up with my bodyguard, and jeopardised my future for nothing.'

'Don't use that as an excuse to not even try. People will get over it. If you want to be with Giovanni, be with him. These things have a way of working themselves out.' Isabella made it all seem so easy. Possible.

'I hope you're right, sis.' Without all the what ifs, and other people's expectations, at the end of the day, she just wanted to be with Giovanni. If only she could be sure he felt the same perhaps they could have dealt with anything that challenged their want to be together.

Isabella hugged her before leaving her alone to process the conversation they'd just had. Along with the revelation that for once she might actually have a chance at love herself. That spark of hope enough to bring tears to her eyes that if she was brave enough, there was a chance she could have it all.

Giovanni made himself presentable in one of the guest bathrooms, wishing he had gone home last night and avoided this scene. Something that hadn't been easy to do when Francesca was lying naked next to him, not having to try too hard to persuade him to stay in bed with her. Which unfortunately had come to bite them both in the backside. He was likely going to have to face a firing squad for his grave offence of debasing the future Queen.

Since the sisters were close, he hoped no one else in the palace would have to find out about the discovery.

Even thinking about the way Isabella had walked in on them made him cringe. Trying to get his clothes on and scarper out of Francesca's room was not becoming of a personal protection officer, nor a man who had any sort of future with her.

This morning had been a wake-up call. This wasn't just about having a relationship that her parents frowned upon and would get over down the line. There was much more at stake than their disapproval. Though that alone would be enough to hurt her. She might claim otherwise, but she was someone who'd spent her life trying to please her parents. And everyone else. There was no way she could live with herself if she upset them.

Since their night in London, all she'd talked about

was her freedom, and being normal. But it was a pipe dream. The importance of her status in Monterossa wasn't something she could pretend didn't matter. They'd been fooling themselves with this casual arrangement that a different world was available to them, but in reality it never could be. Even now she was probably taking a verbal battering from her sister, and that was more pain than he'd ever intended to cause her.

Once he felt less exposed, he was about to make his way back to Francesca's room to face the fallout. Only to catch sight of her heading out into the gardens. He followed her past the manicured lawns, resisting the urge to call after her and draw attention from the security detail stationed outside. Instead, he waited until she'd gone past the fountain and taken a seat in the wooden arbour. Where the pink-rose-trimmed trellis sides would afford them some privacy.

'Francesca?' Giovanni spoke quietly so as not to spook her.

'Hey,' she said, turning her tear-stained face towards him.

Seeing Francesca so visibly shaken after the encounter with her sister was a punch to Giovanni's gut, knowing he was the cause.

'Are you okay?'

'I'm fine.' She gave him a wobbly little smile that broke his heart. He knew she was trying to project a strength that she obviously wasn't feeling, just to protect him. To prevent him from shouldering more guilt.

Too late.

'You are not fine,' he gritted out, taking a seat beside her.

'I'm sorry if it seemed as though I was running out on you this morning. I thought you and Isabella needed some time and space to talk alone. Perhaps I should have stayed.' He grimaced, knowing it was entirely down to him for putting her in such a compromising position.

Another sad smile as she shook her head. 'There was no need. Isabella pretty much called me a hypocrite, and she has every right to. I gave her a lot of grief over London, when I've been acting just as inappropriately.'

'We all took risks that night.' He wasn't going to let Francesca take all the blame. They'd all messed up, but by continuing to see her in secret, he'd jeopardised her reputation and her relationship with her family. Not to mention her future as Queen. It was too great a risk to let her take any more.

'I guess.'

'It's something we can't afford to do any more.'

Francesca frowned at him. 'What do you mean?'

'Be realistic, Francesca. It was never going to work between us.' He'd been holding on for too long to the pipe dream that they could be together. It had taken a dose of reality for him to see exactly what was at stake for Francesca, and that wasn't just her reputation. This was a warning, and they were lucky it was only her sister who'd caught them.

It was the reminder he had needed that Francesca was risking her reputation, her relationship with her family, and her future as Queen. All for someone who should have known better than to get close to her. He'd known she'd get hurt. The best he could do now was some damage control before she lost everything because of him.

'This was nothing more than a romantic fantasy that

should have stayed in London. Or never happened in the first place.' It broke his heart to say that, when being with Francesca was the best thing that had ever happened to him, but he needed her to think it meant nothing if they were going to sever ties completely.

He wanted to fight for her, but that fear of hurting her overrode everything else. There was no point in delaying the inevitable pain when he'd already caused a row between her and her sister. He would never forgive himself if he caused problems for her with her parents too. Nor would they, or the rest of the country.

At least by accepting the end of the relationship he could prevent the same thing happening to Francesca as had happened to everyone else in his life.

'Well, if that's how you really feel, then I guess there's nothing more to say.'

It wasn't. If he was honest, he knew he'd fallen hard for her, but admitting that wasn't going to help either of them come out of this unscathed. He simply had to push through this pain now, and go and lick his wounds later in private. Then hopefully he'd go back to the life he'd had, with this serving as the perfect reminder as to why he shouldn't get involved with anyone.

'I'm sorry, Francesca. For everything.' Giovanni didn't wait around to hash out everything they'd been through, or what they could have together. He knew exactly what he was walking away from.

Francesca couldn't believe what he was saying to her. He didn't even wait for a response. Simply walked away without looking back. As though she didn't mean anything to him. When she'd just realised how much she wanted him in her life. When she'd dared to hope that she could have that love match she thought was out of reach.

It seemed she'd been right to be wary. She couldn't have everything after all.

Once Giovanni was out of sight, Francesca stood up and walked with her head held high into the palace. She smiled at the members of staff who passed her.

'Francesca? If you're free, we'd like to discuss your upcoming schedule.' Her mother caught her in the corridor.

Francesca's smile faltered a little, as did her voice. 'I just have something to do first. I'll be with you as soon as I can.'

She didn't even stop to make her excuses, her jelly legs threatening to give way soon. They just about held her up until she got to her bedroom door. At which point every part of her stopped pretending she was strong enough to bear the loss of Giovanni, their time together, and the future she'd hoped she'd have with him.

Her body folded onto her bed. The one she'd spent so many nights and mornings in with Giovanni. Where they'd made love, where she'd fallen asleep contentedly in his arms, where she'd realised she'd fallen for him and wanted him in her life long term. And now, the memory she had left here was crying her heart out knowing it hadn't meant anything to him.

Giovanni was gone, and he'd taken a huge chunk of her heart with him.

Deep down she supposed she'd been hoping he'd fight for her. That he'd break down and tell her how much he loved her, proving that she was more important to him than anything.

Now Francesca had to figure out where she went from here. If he wasn't her future, the only thing she had left in her life was her family, and the position she held in it. Perhaps if she put all her focus back where it used to be she wouldn't spend the rest of her days mourning the love she'd lost.

One day she might even get over him.

CHAPTER ELEVEN

'ALESSANDRO, WE NEED to know your plans in advance. You can't just say you're waiting for a call from your friends at eleven o'clock on a Friday night and expect us to keep you safe.' Giovanni didn't like having to give the responsible adult speeches, but sometimes it was necessary. If futile.

'Chill, Gio. It's your job, so just do it.' The minor royal he'd been assigned to since leaving the palace flicked his floppy hair out of his eyes and went back to his phone.

Giovanni gritted his teeth, as he'd been doing these past few weeks for the Princesses' cousin on their father's side. The spoiled teen who attracted a lot of attention because of his online antics, and obvious disdain for protocol, was not as endearing as his past charge. He didn't appreciate him adopting Francesca's nickname for him either.

'That would be easier to do if I knew where you were going.' And if he didn't simultaneously post his location on social media and cause a scrum of screaming girls that they had to push their way through.

Unlike Francesca, Alessandro adored the attention. Most likely because he didn't have any other purpose in life, yet was still afforded a life of luxury due to his family connections. Francesca didn't have the ego of this self-entitled prat, regardless that she was going to be Queen some day.

Ignoring Giovanni's concern, Alessandro answered an incoming call. 'Yo. Sure. See you there, bro.'

The only thing Giovanni hated more than the teen's ego was his insistence on affecting an accent that related in no way to his privileged background. If he really wanted to be 'one of the people', he could easily give up his wealth and status. Alessandro never would though. It was all an act. Unlike Francesca, who took her royal role seriously.

It still hurt not being with her. Although his new job had taken him away from her, it hadn't managed to stop him thinking about her. Still being part of the royal protection team also meant that he got to hear what was happening at the palace. It appeared his sacrifice hadn't been entirely in vain. Francesca had stayed where she was supposed to be, and by all accounts was taking on more duties as her parents had planned. It had all worked out as it was supposed to. Yet, he was still desperately unhappy. He supposed he always would be when he couldn't be with her but was still in her orbit.

'Let's roll, Gio.' Alessandro grabbed his jacket, still leaving Giovanni in the dark about where they were supposed to be heading.

He'd give anything to be back with Francesca in any capacity, but he knew that just wasn't possible. One thing he did know was that he couldn't stay here. He needed a new start. Somewhere away from the entire royal family. Away from Monterossa altogether.

Preferably where there wasn't an incredibly beautiful princess who'd captured his heart.

'He's going where?' Francesca tried not to freak out in front of her parents, who'd just casually mentioned Giovanni was leaving the country.

Her father dismissed her interest with a wave of his hand. 'I don't know… England, I think. Now, can we tell Mattia you'll be attending the charity ball? He's keen to see you again.'

'I've more important things to think about. I've told you, marriage is not uppermost on my mind at present. I'd rather put my energy into actually helping charities than dressing up to impress people I don't know. That's why I've agreed to be patron of a local women's group that raises money to put less fortunate girls through university, who otherwise couldn't afford to attend.' Since resuming her role as a senior royal, rather than her bodyguard's secret lover, she'd been more assertive in what she wanted to do. Or not do.

She knew it was being with Giovanni, being herself and being honest when she was with him that had prompted her to do the same with her parents. So far, there had been no resistance. It seemed she'd just needed to break out of that mould she'd cast herself in as dutiful daughter and have some confidence in herself to speak up. Things had been better. Except for the huge gap in her life where Giovanni used to be.

She'd thought that once he was gone she'd get back to being her. Now she realised how fundamentally she'd changed just by being with him. And he was leaving the country. She might never see him again. It was a thought that wouldn't go away no matter how much she pretended it didn't matter to her. At least when he'd transferred elsewhere, there had still been a chance she might see him. The fact that he was going back to England without her was like rubbing salt in the very raw wound.

Her parents were still trying to set her up, but no man could hold a candle to Giovanni, no matter how much money or status they had. Suddenly, the thought of him being in London, on the underground, in clubs, or hotel rooms, without her, was unbearable. Being confronted with the possibility of losing him for ever made her want to be that brave princess she knew was inside her. For someone who'd vowed to fight for what she wanted, she'd let him go too easily. She hadn't told him how she felt about him, given him a reason to stay and believe it was worth taking a risk on them.

Francesca only hoped it wasn't too late to stand up for what she wanted. Even if there was a chance of being rejected again.

Giovanni stacked the last of the boxes in the lounge. Not that there were a lot. It was sad that he didn't have much in the way of personal possessions, but he supposed it would make it easier to ship his belongings over to England. This apartment had never really felt like home. The palace had been more of a home to him. Probably because Francesca had been there. Anywhere with her had felt like home.

He shook his head. It was about time he stopped thinking of her. Especially when he was leaving the country to distance himself from everything associated with her. His old army pal, Dan, had got him a security assignment with a famous young British actor who'd suddenly found himself flavour of the year since starring in a Hollywood blockbuster. Another new start. Though in a city that still held many good memories of her.

He was a lost cause.

The doorbell rang and he climbed over the packaging materials strewn around, and the bags of clothes he was going to donate to charity before he left.

He pulled his wallet out to pay the delivery driver for the Indian meal he'd ordered for his dinner. The last person he'd expected to see when he opened the door was the Princess of Monterossa.

'Francesca? What are you doing here? And where is your security?'

She pulled down the hood of her coat. 'I gave them the slip. I'm surprisingly good at that. Can I come in before someone sees me?'

'Yes. Of course.' Stunned by her arrival, he stood back to let her in. 'Ignore the mess. I'm packing.'

'I heard you were moving. That's why I'm here.'

'Oh?' Since she obviously wasn't here in an official royal capacity, he doubted it was to award him a medal for his service to his country. He had to admit he was intrigued by her appearance when she'd gone to so much trouble to see him. And he wasn't going to deny himself one last chance to see her.

Francesca sat down on the lone hardwood dining chair that was left after he'd got rid of most of his furniture. A symbol of the key difference between them when she was used to nothing less than silks and designer fabrics to rest her backside on.

She cleared her throat, seeming uncharacteristically nervous.

'I can't believe you're going back to London without me.'

Her attempt at a joke would've been funny if it weren't so painful.

'I've been offered a good job. I thought it would do us both good to get some distance between us.' Giovanni didn't need to tell her it was going to take a move to another country to help him forget about her.

'Are you sorry we ever got involved?' Her voice was a whisper, and he could see the sorrow in those big eyes.

But it didn't change anything. He couldn't afford for her to get hurt because of him again.

'No. I'm not sorry about anything we did, but I have to go. It's too painful to be so close to you and not be able to touch you.' Especially now when they were in the same room, and she looked more beautiful than ever.

Her hair was loose around her shoulders, and she'd opted for casual jeans and an off-the-shoulder cream wool jumper. She didn't need personal hairdressers, or expensive couture, or even titles, to be the prettiest princess in the kingdom.

He didn't miss the knitted brow when he admitted his feelings. It was difficult to tell if it was disgust or regret. In the end, he supposed it didn't matter. He was leaving. End of story. There was no happy ever after. Not for him, anyway. Francesca would still be Queen of Monterossa some day, would probably marry and have children, and live the fairy tale at the palace. She deserved it. He just didn't want to be around to witness it.

Francesca got up from her chair. Giovanni held his

breath as she approached him and touched his arm. 'Don't go. Or if you must, at least take me with you.'

Now his head was in as much turmoil as the rest of him. He'd made peace with the fact that he wasn't going to see her again. That he was going to have to start his life over again and try to forget about her. He hadn't accounted for her coming last minute to throw all his plans out of the window.

'What are you asking of me, Francesca?' He didn't know what she wanted from him, unless she was simply trying to mess with his head one last time as some sort of revenge for ending things.

'To be with me. I'm done living my life for other people. I want you, Giovanni. I'm finally taking control of my own life and I want you to be part of it whatever happens.'

'I told you from the start you'd only end up getting hurt. I saw how devastated you were when Isabella caught us together. We both know that it would make things impossible for you if we were a couple. It's for the best if I go.' Whilst a huge part of him was thrilled that she felt so strongly for him, and that she was standing up for herself, in the end it didn't matter how they felt about one another. It wouldn't change their circumstances.

She grabbed his other arm now too, trapping him, forcing him to look at her. Not playing fair with her continual touch reminding him of every time they'd been intimate together. 'Isabella already knew about us in London. When you saw me in the garden I was just coming to terms with the fact I'd fallen for you and I was hoping you felt the same. I don't want to be a queen, princess, or anything else, if it means we can't be together. I'll give it all up for you, Giovanni. I'm finally standing up for what I want, and that's you.'

His heart was beating so fast he was dizzy, afraid that this was all a dream when she was saying everything that he wanted to hear. 'Really? This isn't simply a guilty conscience speaking now that you know I have to leave the country before I can even think about getting over you?'

'No. I love you, Giovanni. I was afraid to admit it to myself because I know things aren't going to be easy, but, trust me, I'll do anything if it means we can be together.'

'It's not going to be that easy to simply give everything up that you've ever known. Do you honestly think you can just disappear from public life and the press will lose interest? That's never going to happen. They're still going to want that perfect snapshot of you doing something mundane, comparing it to the life you should be living. I don't want that for you, and I'm sure, deep down, you don't either.'

Whilst he was thrilled that he hadn't been wrong about their chemistry, and he was looking forward to having that future together he'd dreamed of, he knew how much of a sacrifice she'd be making. It would cause her immeasurable pain to leave her family, and her position. It wouldn't be fair to ask that of her.

'I want to be with you, Francesca, but we both know you'll get hurt. I would never do that to you.'

She smiled. 'What about all that stuff about me standing up for myself, and not just going along with what everyone else wants? This is me making my own decisions. I just need to know that you love me.'

Giovanni took her in his arms. 'You know I do.'

Francesca shook her head. 'That's not enough. I need you to say the words.'

'You've become very demanding, Princess.' He threaded his fingers through hers, renewing that bond he'd thought gone for ever.

'Someone told me I need to be brave and say what I want. It's supposed to make life easier for me, apparently.' She shrugged and gave him a bright smile as though the world had been lifted from her shoulders. Not as though she'd just added more to her burden.

'I hope so. I don't want to make your life any more difficult than it already is, Francesca, because I love you very, very much.' He leaned in and kissed her as he'd been longing to do these past weeks.

Though he still had no idea how they were going to make this work.

'Even if I'll no longer be a princess, or even have a job?'

'Always. I'll be here as long as you need me to love and protect you, Francesca.' If she was willing to give up everything so they could be together, he had to let go of everything that had been holding him back too.

He loved Francesca, she loved him, and he knew that was enough for both of them.

EPILOGUE

Two months later

'How are you feeling?' Francesca turned to Giovanni in the back of the car. This was his first official appearance alongside her, though they'd been spotted out and about over the past weeks.

Thankfully, the public had been won over by the match, with most saying it showed she was a princess of the people, marrying for love, rather than status. Others called it a family tradition. Her parents, too, were happy for them. It seemed they were content just to know she'd found someone who loved her, and they'd always been fond of Giovanni. All that worry she'd harboured over his suitability had been unnecessary. Though these days she didn't care as much about what others thought, not when she was so happy simply being with Giovanni.

He was a loving, supportive presence in her life, and she knew when the time came for her to step up, he'd be right there with her.

'Inadequate,' he said with a laugh.

It was true, her outfit tonight was a tad OTT for a film premiere, but she wanted to look good next to him. He didn't need a diamanté-encrusted silver sheath dress and bling to make an impact. She was aware their appearance together tonight was going to generate a lot of publicity and she simply wanted to be photo ready. It didn't hurt that Giovanni hadn't been able to keep his hands off her either. That was one part of their lives that hadn't slowed down yet. If anything, they were more passionate than ever, and she hoped that sizzle would last between them for ever.

'You look amazing. As always.' She fixed his black dicky bow and couldn't resist trailing her hands down his fitted shirt, feeling every taut muscle under her hands.

He caught her before she went any further. 'Careful. I don't want to be making headlines for all the wrong reasons in tomorrow's papers.'

He was right, of course, but he looked so good in a tux.

'Mmm, we haven't done it in a car yet. We might have to add that one to the list.' Since the aeroplane incident, they'd confessed to a number of locations where they'd like to engage that risky side of their nature. Careful, naturally, that they wouldn't be seen or compromised in living out any of their fantasies. With Giovanni's helpful knowledge in avoiding detection, so far they'd managed to make love out in the palace gardens and in the pool, without being spotted.

'Not right now, though. I'm desperate for some popcorn.' He was teasing—Giovanni probably didn't even know what film they were going to see—but he was always ready and willing to accompany her wherever she needed to be. He'd even expressed an interest in helping charities too. By becoming a member of the royal family he'd have to give up his security work, but he'd discussed wanting to be involved with ex-military personnel who were dealing with PTSD.

Although both of them were content for now to concentrate on the present, and being together, Francesca hoped one day he would be able to put the past behind him once and for all. Perhaps even make some sort of commitment so she knew exactly the depth of his feelings for her.

Not that she was going to rush him and jeopardise the happiness she'd found with him.

'I suppose we should go in. Remember, smile, and wave. I know it's a new concept for you, but we're here to win people over, not push them away.' She grinned, only half teasing him.

As she reached for the door handle, Giovanni reached out and grabbed her hand.

'Wait,' he said, looking more nervous than she'd ever seen. As a man who'd served in hostile environments with the military, and whose security job meant dealing with danger every day, he was looking pale and uncertain for the first time since she'd known him.

'It'll be okay, Gio. I promise. A couple of minutes on the red carpet, we'll meet the cast, and we can disappear out a side door if you want.' If he was really so ill at the thought of this, she wasn't going to push him. She would never force him to be in a situation that made him uncomfortable.

'No. It's not that.' He fumbled in the inside pocket of his jacket and pulled out a small velvet box.

Francesca swallowed hard, trying not to let her heart persuade her this was what she thought it was.

Giovanni knelt on the floor and opened the box to reveal the most beautiful diamond engagement ring, so big it was dazzling. It must have cost him a fortune, yet she would have been happy with anything as long as the sentiment was the same behind it.

'Princess Francesca, will you do me the very great honour of becoming my wife?' The sweat was breaking on his forehead, his nerves clearly showing, and she appreciated the gesture even more.

'Yes. Yes, I will.' She let him slip the ring perfectly on her finger before he joined her back on the seat and kissed her.

'I love you, Francesca,' he said, which were more important to Francesca than any other four words in the world.

* * * * *

*If you missed the previous story in the
Princesses' Night Out duet
then check out*

How to Win Back a Royal *by Justine Lewis*

*And if you enjoyed this story,
check out these other great reads
from Karin Baine*

Cinderella's Festive Fake Date
Highland Fling with Her Boss
Pregnant Princess at the Altar

All available now!

MILLS & BOON®

Coming next month

INVITATION TO HIS BILLION-DOLLAR BALL
Cara Colter

Layne was silent for so long, he wondered if his history had given her pause about tangling with him, which he thought maybe it should have.

'I like that it's all part of you,' she said. 'I like it that you talk about your family without blame and without bitterness. I like it that it's kept you humble and made you strong. I like who you are, Jesse Kade. I like all of you.'

It was a gift, like walking out of a snowstorm into warmth. One he was too aware he did not deserve, at all.

And that he could lose that look that filled her eyes in an instant.

When the other secret came out.

Selfishly, he could not walk away from what he saw in her eyes, not just yet.

And yet, he was aware he was holding back.

'Hey,' he said, suddenly feeling way more naked than his lack of clothing had ever made him feel, as if he had already said way, way too much, 'let's go try out the shower in this creaky old castle.'

She gave him a searching look. But then she returned his smile. 'Okay. And after that, would you like to make a girl's dreams come true?'

He pretended to sulk. 'I thought I already had.'

'I want to dance with you. In the ballroom.'

Her voice was so shy and so hopeful—as if he'd been entrusted with a secret dream—that he could not refuse her.

Continue reading

INVITATION TO HIS BILLION-DOLLAR BALL
Cara Colter

Available next month
millsandboon.co.uk

Copyright © 2025 Cara Colter

COMING SOON!

We really hope you enjoyed reading this book.
If you're looking for more romance
be sure to head to the shops when
new books are available on

Thursday 22nd May

To see which titles are coming soon, please visit
millsandboon.co.uk/nextmonth

MILLS & BOON

FOUR BRAND NEW BOOKS FROM
MILLS & BOON MODERN

The same great stories you love, a stylish new look!

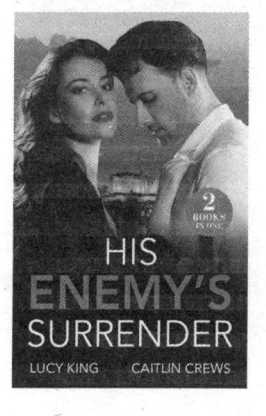

OUT NOW

Eight Modern stories published every month, find them all at:
millsandboon.co.uk

afterglow BOOKS

Afterglow Books is a trend-led, trope-filled list of books with diverse, authentic and relatable characters, a wide array of voices and representations, plus real world trials and tribulations. Featuring all the tropes you could possibly want (think small-town settings, fake relationships, grumpy vs sunshine, enemies to lovers) and all with a generous dose of spice in every story.

♪ @millsandboonuk
◉ @millsandboonuk
afterglowbooks.co.uk
#AfterglowBooks

For all the latest book news, exclusive content and giveaways scan the QR code below to sign up to the Afterglow newsletter:

SCAN ME

afterglow BOOKS

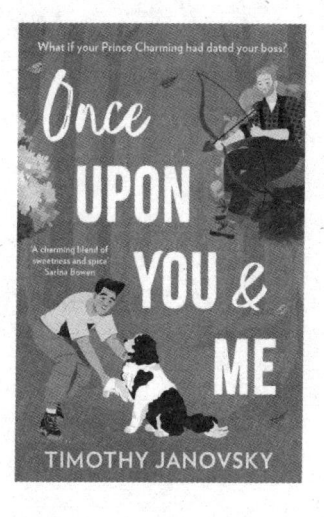

Ms. V's Hot Girl Summer
THE TEMPERATURE'S RISING...
A.H. CUNNINGHAM

Once Upon You & Me
What if your Prince Charming had dated your boss?
A charming blend of sweetness and spice — Sarina Bower
TIMOTHY JANOVSKY

- ✈ International
- ☯ Opposites attract
- 🌶 Spicy

- 💻 Workplace romance
- 🚫 Forbidden love
- 🌶 Spicy

OUT NOW

Two stories published every month. Discover more at:
Afterglowbooks.co.uk

LET'S TALK
Romance

For exclusive extracts, competitions and special offers, find us online:

- **f** MillsandBoon
- **X** @MillsandBoon
- **◉** @MillsandBoonUK
- **♪** @MillsandBoonUK

Get in touch on 01413 063 232

For all the latest titles coming soon, visit
millsandboon.co.uk/nextmonth

OUT NOW!

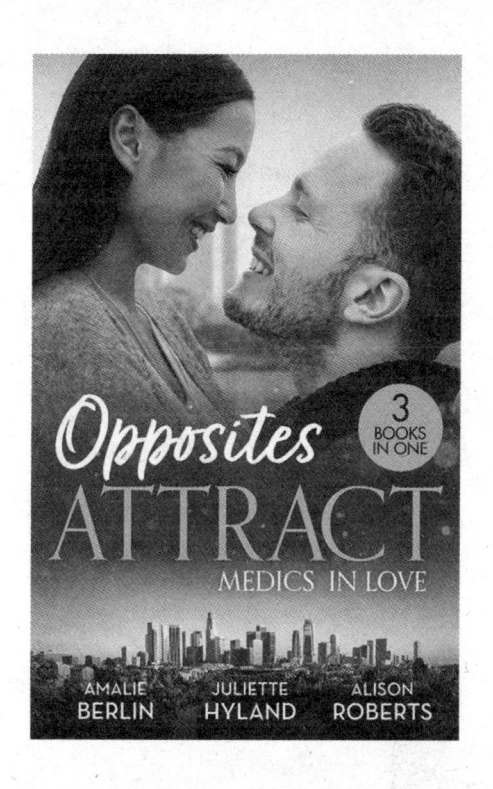

Opposites Attract
MEDICS IN LOVE

3 BOOKS IN ONE

AMALIE BERLIN JULIETTE HYLAND ALISON ROBERTS

Available at
millsandboon.co.uk

MILLS & BOON

OUT NOW!

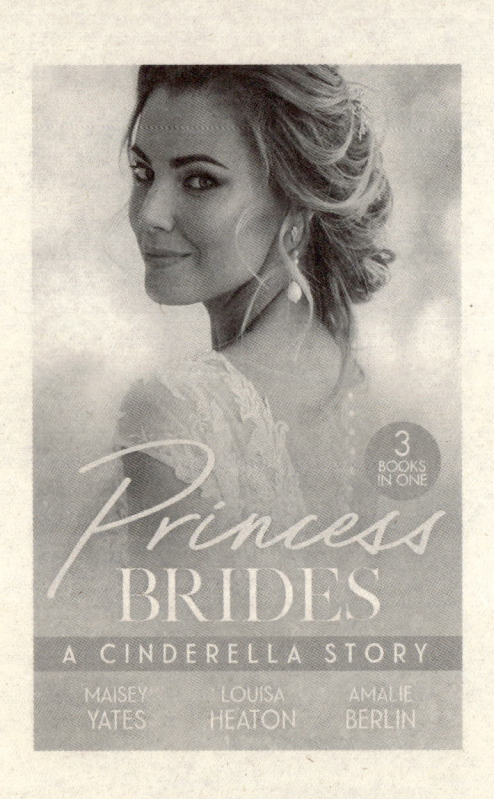

Princess BRIDES
A CINDERELLA STORY

3 BOOKS IN ONE

MAISEY YATES · LOUISA HEATON · AMALIE BERLIN

Available at
millsandboon.co.uk

MILLS & BOON